THE END
VOLUME 1

This story is purely fiction and is based on a dream. It is in no way intended to add to or to detract from the Word of God.

Revelation 22:18-21 (ESV), "I warn everyone who hears the words of the prophecy of this book: if anyone adds to them, God will add to him the plagues described in this book, and if anyone takes away from the words of the book of this prophecy, God will take away his share in the tree of life and in the holy city, which are described in this book. He who testifies to these things says, 'Surely I am coming soon.' Amen. Come, Lord Jesus! The grace of the Lord Jesus be with all. Amen."

NEW BOOKS

ISBN-13: 978-0692264171

Acknowledgements

To the Lord my God
And to my loving wife, for putting up with me.

CHAPTER 1 – CONFUSION

Psalm 55: 1-8 (NIV), "Listen to my prayer, O God, do not ignore my plea; hear me and answer me. My thoughts trouble me and I am distraught because of what my enemy is saying; because of the threats of the wicked; for they bring down suffering on me and assail me in their anger. My heart is in anguish within me; the terrors of death have fallen on me. Fear and trembling have beset me; horror has overwhelmed me. I said, 'Oh, that I had the wings of a dove! I would fly away and be at rest. I would flee far away and stay in the desert; I would hurry to my place of shelter, far from the tempest and storm."

Psalm 55: 16-17 (NIV), "As for me, I call to God, and the Lord saves me. Evening, morning, and noon I cry out in distress, and he hears my voice."

I wake up. Something is wrong. As I come to my senses, I lift up my head and look down at my body. Everything appears to be in order as I study my limbs in the dimly lit room, but I am wearing a strange white robe. Nothing appears to be hurting as I begin to sit up on the hard concrete floor on which I am lying, but I have that groggy feeling that you sometimes get when you first wake up. No bed this time, just a hard concrete floor.

A few small windows at the top half of the square-shaped room allow enough daylight for me to see that I am not alone. Not comforting though, as there are hundreds of bodies lying on the floor all around me, all wearing white robes. Wall to wall bodies. What is going on here? Where am I? Why am I here?

I hope everyone is just asleep like I was and will wake up soon. This is a nightmare. Maybe that's what it is. It gets worse as I begin to study the bodies right next to me. Josh, my oldest son! Julia, my wife! Nate and Dave, my twin sons! My in-laws, Ted and Mindy! All lying motionless, wearing white robes.

I am not sure how much time passes from this discovery to when I am able to discern that all are breathing, sleeping so peacefully, but it feels like forever. The next step is to try to wake one of them up, if I can. They all are in my immediate vicinity; I pick Julia first. Gently rubbing her back I try to coax her awake. I whisper into her ear, and I try to move her limbs. After a while she begins to come to. I immediately move to Josh. Slowly, I begin to coax each one out of this most unnatural slumber. Julia is now awake, resting on her forearms looking at me with a terrifyingly puzzled and dazed look, much like I must have had that eternity ago when I woke up on my own. She is squinting, trying to piece together the new world in which we exist. I have made it to my in-laws at this point, gently waking them into this terrible place. At least everyone is alive; hopefully the same goes for the others in the room.

Julia and I are whispering now. For a short time she is mad at me that I can't answer her questions about where we are, but she is not as mad as I usually get when she wakes me up from a dead sleep. Then it hits her – something is very, very wrong. The kids are coming to; my goal is to keep them quiet. Ted and Mindy are the most stubborn of the bunch to wake up, but they should be mostly together in a few minutes. I whisper to each kid to be very quiet, dutifully telling each one the same thing while looking them in their dazed and confused eyes. I can safely say that nothing like this has ever happened to us before, and I really want to know why it suddenly has.

It's not like I have amnesia or anything; I am Matt Hall from Cincinnati, OH. I remember, of course, my family, both those who are in the room with me, as well as the others who do not appear to be with us. The room is way too large to tell for sure unless I venture around the room to see who the other guests are. We had to have been placed in the room while unconscious, because there is just enough room between each person for someone to walk. Everyone is lying, fully extended, on their back or side except for the seven of us who are now awake. I need to think; what is the last thing that I remember? Were we at home, were we out, and how could we have arrived at such a place without knowing how we got here? This is a tough one; I am having trouble remembering the last thing we did. I remember what our house looks like inside and out with intricate detail, but I cannot remember if we should be there instead of here. Suddenly an image of my in-laws cabin flashes in my mind, the one they have on a quiet lake in northern Kentucky. Just as suddenly as the memory comes to me, it leaves me when I hear my mother-in-law call out, in a relatively loud voice, "Where in the hell are we?" I think she hit the nail on the head. Or maybe, somehow, we're dead and in a waiting room to go to heaven. It must be a good sign that we have these nice white robes on.

After we all shush Mindy, we huddle together to come up with a plan. We need to find a way to get out of this room. There are at least two doors at opposite ends of the room, but we need to quietly work our way through all of the other sleeping bodies and test to see if one of the doors is unlocked. And then what? Before any plans come to fruition, however, Ted gives us all another shush. Voices, male voices, are coming from outside the door to our far left. What do we do? I tell everyone to quickly lie down and make like the rest of the crew in the room. The doorknob clicks. The door opens.

■■■

When I lie on the floor, I position myself facing the door where the men are coming in. They seem to be having a pleasant conversation; the one man has a voice similar to Ted's. They do not seem at all phased by the fact that they are walking into a room with hundreds of sleeping people dressed in white robes. One good thing I had noticed previously is that our regular clothes are on underneath the robes. For me that means jeans and a t-shirt. As the men talk, one of them flips on the lights. The lights are very bright; I shut my eyes for a few seconds and then ease them back open; not only to get them used to the lights, but also to make sure the men aren't looking in my direction. They are facing the

3

wall by the door, fooling with something, but my attention quickly shifts to Nate, who is lying directly in front of me. His breathing is growing very heavy, like he is starting a panic attack or something. I slowly reach my hand along the floor and touch his back to try to calm him. After a few breaths it seems to work, and after a few more breaths I slowly inch my hand back to where it was before. As the two men continue their work and their conversation, I hear the other door behind me click and then open. This time I hear two female voices, both speaking rapidly and in teenage vernacular. After a few seconds the men turn toward the direction of the voices. I quickly shut my eyes and hope they didn't see me awake. "All right ladies," one of the men says, "wake 'em up!"

Over the next fifteen minutes or so, I open my eyes as often as I can to survey the situation. The two men leave the room after a few minutes. I can't see what the women / girls are doing for the first several minutes, but I assume they are carrying out their orders. Are they going to go to each person and gently persuade them to wake up as I had done to my group? I don't hear them talking to anyone. Once they come into my line of sight, after several minutes, I can see what they are doing. Each has two baskets, one hanging from each arm allowing their hands to be free. The one basket is full of syringes, filled with something that evidently is going to wake us all up. The other basket is to hold the empty syringes after use. The teenage girls had started their work by going around the perimeter of the room, giving their "patients" the necessary medication, and are working their way in toward the middle where we are stationed. They are quite efficient at the task at hand – rolling up the patient's sleeve, dispensing the contents of the syringe, placing the empty into the other basket and reaching for another full one as they go to the next person. It doesn't take long for me to realize that in another few minutes it will be our turn to get juiced up even though we are already awake. I am not a fan of having something injected into my bloodstream, especially if it is not necessary.

Should I sit up and ask for help, or pretend to be waking up on my own? Could this all be just a big misunderstanding and everything would be OK if I just spoke up? Something inside of me is telling me that such a plan would be a bad idea. I continue to lie on the floor, trying to remain motionless except for a slow, steady breath. I have to come up with a way for us to avoid being injected with whatever is in the syringes. The girls continue in a somewhat circular fashion, going in and out of my view periodically. As I focus on the edges of the room, I notice that the folks on the perimeter have begun stirring. One or two sit up, looking very groggy as I'm sure I did when I first awoke. But why did it take a shot to wake them up when I woke up on my own and was able to wake up the others without medication? The girls continue to work and are getting very close now. One girl runs out of syringes in her basket, and heads for the door behind me to get more syringes. Her friend says, "Don't worry about it; I have enough to finish the rest." She is standing almost directly in front of me, looking back at her coworker. Just then I realize that I should be shutting my eyes because the girl could quickly return her eyes to her work, and she is almost to us. Too late! I've been discovered. There's no use closing my eyes now. She returns the stare for a few seconds, barely cracking a smile, and then she looks away and acts as if nothing unusual happened and continues with her work. As soon as she starts working on the next person on the floor, who happens to be one person away from Nate, the door in front of me opens and the two men come back in. "We need your help. Are you two finished?" one of the men asks. The girl who caught me awake responds, "Close enough. If we missed any, we'll get them later." With that, the two girls take their baskets and head out the front door with the two men. The door makes a clicking sound after it is shut, and I make a mental note that I had never heard a click from the door behind me after the girls first came into the room. We have been saved from the mystery medication just in time.

CHAPTER 2 – THE ABOMINATION

Proverbs 24: 11-12 (ESV), "Rescue those who are being taken away to death; hold back those who are stumbling to the slaughter. If you say, 'Behold, we did not know this,' does not he who weighs the heart perceive it? Does not he who keeps watch over your soul know it, and will he not repay man according to his work?"

Many more people around the perimeter of the room and into the interior portions of the room are stirring, and some are resting on their elbows. Now that the coast is clear, I sit back up and everyone else in our crew follows suit. We all discuss how we lucked out avoiding the mystery shots and try to guess what is going on. Soon the people next to us begin to stir. Each one of us picks a person in our immediate vicinity to help awaken, as we decide that we could possibly get some clues about what is happening from those around us. It is tough for me to work through the grogginess of my patient, an older woman. No one else seems to be having much luck, either. Looking toward the people at the perimeter of the room, no one is standing, and no one is talking. Dazed and confused stares pervade throughout the nearly silent room. After a few more minutes, none of us are having any luck with our individual patients. I try to speak to my patient, hoping to coax something out of her. She simply stares back, not able to return to full conciseness. Ted jokes, "There must have been some good stuff in those shots." We continue to make attempts to converse with our patients. The most I can get out of mine is a very quiet mumble. I can't even begin to understand what she is saying.

Frustrated, I tell the group, "We need to get out of this room." Julia responds with, "Where do you want us to go?" I say, "I don't know, but we need to not be in here." After several more minutes of conversing, Ted points to the door behind us and says, "That door might be unlocked; let's see what happens when we try to open it." He evidently heard the same thing I did. Since I was the one who first proposed the escape I feel obligated to lead the charge to the door behind us. Ted follows, but Mindy and Julia stay with the kids on the floor in the center of the room.

We reach the door, and then we freeze to listen intently to determine if anyone is outside of the room. No one is making noise inside the room, so we feel pretty confident that the silence outside means that the coast is clear. But do they have a guard stationed quietly outside the door? Do they need guards where we are? Ted and I look at each other, as if to say, "Here goes." I turn the door handle, and just that easily, the door opens into the room. If this is supposed to be a secure area, then those in charge aren't doing a good job. I slowly open the door. Suddenly Julia, Mindy, and the kids are right behind us. I peer out the door and see no one. Ted sticks his head out the door next to me and gives a silent "all clear" to the group by motioning with his hand. None of us are talking now that the door is open. Ted and I lead the way, taking in our surroundings. We seem to have come from a room that is above ground level, and there is a gray, painted concrete walkway with metal railing that appears to wrap around the building. I look back making sure no one appears behind us. We decide to turn left out of the room, even though we could just as easily have turned right. As several of us gaze over the edge of the railing, we see that we are about one story above the ground. The vegetation surrounding the building is very thick and appears tropical. We aren't anywhere near Ohio anymore, or so it seems. It reminds me of some of the rural areas of Florida that my family and I drove past when I was a kid, visiting Grandma and Grandpa Holson once they had moved to Arcadia. It is very hot and humid, but not unlike a hot and humid Ohio summer.

We get to the corner of the building and everyone freezes. Ted carefully peers around the corner. This time he whispers, "All clear." The group proceeds around the corner. I have moved to the back of the group now, allowing Mindy, Julia, and the kids to pass me. I look down to the end of the next stretch of walkway and whisper, "Stairs!" I have evidently stated the obvious as everyone looks back at me with less than excited looks on their faces. Perhaps our escape from the building was just made easier. Perhaps not, if the guards I keep thinking about are actually at the bottom of the stairway. We get to the stairs. We start to hear faint rustling. Ted starts down the stairs and peers over the railing. The stairway turns around every ten stairs or so, and Ted is looking down to the ground through the middle of the stairwell. He stops, and the rest of us catch up to look below. People are coming up the stairs. A seemingly large group of people, all in white robes, is moving toward us from below. Since I am at the back, I rush back up the few stairs to the walkway. When I get to the top I can hear voices on the other side of the building past the stairway. We are in a jam.

Everyone else has followed me back up, but I motion with one hand to keep their mouths closed, and with the other hand I let them know that people are soon coming around the corner opposite from where we came. We all freeze, for what seems like way too long, as we argue through archaic sign language about what to do next. Our options are to either go back the way we came, or to go up the stairs. Our decision is quickly made for us, as the two men who first met us in the large room come around the other corner of the building from where we just came. By now the group of robed persons is upon us, so we fall in line leading the charge up the stairs. The two men quickly lose their initially puzzled looks as we proceed up the stairs with the group, and any other wandering thoughts they may have had are erased when another group of two men come around the corner by the stairs and begin speaking with them. "Just found out the other group is about ready; would you mind helping us keep an eye on them?" one of the men from the new group asks the other two we had seen before. "That's where we were headed!" says the one who sounds like Ted. "I didn't expect them to be ready so soon, but the cooks asked us to move them along quickly. Everything is out of whack today. They didn't even send this group up the normal route, and it got split up for a while." We continue to listen to the conversation as we slowly walk up the stairs. Other than the rustling noise made by the group going up the stairs, not much else is distorting the sound of their conversation. "Yeah, we had to rush the girls out of the waiting room so they could get to the cafeteria. A few of the people were coming out of their stupor quicker than expected. I think we let the last group sit too long before we sent them up the Stairway to Heaven." Well, I guess that answers my question. Somehow we must be dead and in limbo on our way to the pearly gates. I didn't realize the trip to Heaven would be so hot and muggy...

■■■

The men's voices begin to grow faint as we continue up the stairs. We are leading the group as slowly as we can without getting pushed by the expressionless, silent people behind us. I am getting kind of worried given the additional piece of information that we are on a path referred to as the "Stairway to Heaven." I can still hear the men talking below, and I return my focus to them. I hear the one of the men say, "At least this little bit of commotion made today the most exciting one in a while. Some people in the middle of this group almost made a wrong turn up the stairs as we came around the corner. I thought for a split second that we were going to have our first runners. Not sure what it is about today, other than maybe the effects are starting to wear off due to the first group sitting too long." He must have been referring to whatever was in the shots we missed receiving. "It almost makes me think we need to get back to the level of security that we stuck to for the first six months. Things got so boring, though, as everything worked down to a science every time. The drug is so effective at keeping everyone sedated, but conscious to the point of following orders and being able to walk." Another clue. We reach a stopping point, even though we are not at the top of the stairs. Ahead of us is an additional group of robed clientele that is waiting mid-way up the current portion of stairs. As we stop, additional noise is made by the group below us as we stop. A few grunts and a few other sighs. I miss a sentence or two from the attendants below. I vaguely hear one say, "Let's wait here a few more minutes to make sure no one falls down the stairs, and then we should be good to go. Will you guys give us a hand with the next group in the waiting room? They should be good and hungry by now."

He went and did it. The man mentioned the "H" word. It is usually my weakness around 10 AM when I am at work. When I start thinking about food it's all over. Most of the time I pull out my lunch and get a head start well before anyone else is thinking about lunch. Of course, I get up earlier than most so I should be hungry by 10 AM. After my short musing I return to the situation at hand. For the first time, I realize that I am really, really hungry. Almost to the point of feeling sick, I ask the Lord for strength. The Lord! What is wrong with me? How have I gone all of this time without even thinking about Jesus? If anyone can help us now, it's him. I quickly forget my hunger and begin a prayer to ask for the Lord's help. I thank him for helping us to avoid the shots, and I ask him to rescue us from whatever is going on. And then my prayer is interrupted by an extremely loud noise. BOOM! The noise startles all of us in our family group. Julia and Mindy let out screams. The stairwell gently rocks back and forth. Josh and his brothers are very perturbed by the noise, as am I. I turn to Ted, and he says, "I don't like that noise." I respond with, "Neither do I." Dave whispers loudly, "I am totally freaking out! Did you notice how nobody else even flinched at that noise?" I look up and I begin to notice that the stairway does seem to end after this flight of stairs. I also notice that the people standing on the walkway at the top of the stairs begin to shuffle to the left. It takes a minute or two for the movement to reach our position in line. We begin to lead our group the rest of the way up the stairs. But what are we leading them to? Perhaps the Spaceship to Heaven that takes off in one loud sonic blast?

It seems like a long time before we get to the top. Our group's arguing and questioning from earlier has gone away. Even though we are all still fully engaged in the situation, we are beginning to conform to the slow, quiet progression into the unknown that is displayed by the rest of the group. We finally arrive at the top walkway. We survived the "Stairway to Heaven." But what comes next will change our lives forever. We still can't see very well where the front of the group is headed. We are pretty high up, with only the standard three-foot tall railing keeping us from the ground far, far below. We are way too high to make a jump for it, and there does not look to be anything for us to use to climb down. I didn't pay attention to it at the time, but I now remember that there was a sort of thick netting that surrounded the exterior of the stairway we just left. If there was some way to get back to the outer edge of the stairway, perhaps we could climb down the netting and escape into the tropical woods.

I now see why we couldn't get a view of the end of the line from our initial positions on the walkway. The walkway extends about twenty feet ahead of us and then steps down four or five steps to another, shorter walkway, and then onto a platform. The platform connects to or holds up a metal structure, much like a railcar or like a shipping container that you would see on a large ocean ship that transports goods to other countries. At one end of the rectangular container is a metal contraption that looks, well, like a contraption. It has a large metal pipe of some sort sticking out of the middle, with motors, gears, wires, and control panels either connected to it or off to the side at the front of the container. It works out well for us to gain a better view of the contraption, and of all our surroundings, as the line has stopped again just prior to us going down the short flight of stairs. "Spaceship to Heaven," I mutter. I again receive some agitated stares from my group. I actually get a dazed smile from someone outside our group standing directly in front of us on the first stair. Success! I finally got through to someone.

As I continue to look around, I look back and notice that we are level with the top of the strange building in which we awoke. There are several large air conditioning (chiller) units on top of the roof, as well as many large and small vent pipes. Steam is coming out of just one of the smaller pipes, and once I look at the chiller units I can also hear that at least one is running. As I turn my head back toward the strange metal container on the platform, I can see that the line stops at what looks like a door. The door is shut and there are two men, not in white robes, standing nearby. One is standing next to the door and the other next to the conglomeration of control panels. The door is positioned a little more than half-way down the container. The one man standing closest to the line turns and grabs the handle on the door to the container. He gives it a firm pull with one hand, with his other hand raised in the air. The door does not budge when he pulls. His other hand lowers to his side as if giving a signal. The second man then addresses the control panel in front of him. He pushes a button. "KABOOM!"

As if the noise wasn't bad enough, I realize with absolute horror what it means. We are being led into the container where the door will be shut behind us. Once inside, the operator will initiate the contraption, which we now can see is a very powerful pusher arm that smashes the living daylights out of those in the container. I can tell from our angle that the pusher arm makes it most of the way into the container before stopping. It remains engaged for a short time, and then slowly slides back into its place ready for the next mass murder. The question of why is quickly replaced with looking at each other with horrible expressions that could not even begin to show what we are feeling. Panic quickly overtakes Josh and he takes off in the opposite direction. We all chase him, not because we want to stop him, but because we aren't going to stick around any longer, either. I frankly do not care if the men are still guarding the stairs below, because I'm not going down without a fight.

It is tough at times to push through the rest of the crowd, none of them having any idea what we are trying to do, and none of them coherent enough to try to get them to follow us. We make it back to the stairway. Before I can test my theory of somehow climbing down the netting that surrounds the stairs, Josh and Nate have already made it around the first turn on the stairs. I have to catch them in case the guards are still midway down the stairs. I had fallen in line between Dave (ahead) and Julia (behind), with Ted and Mindy behind her. I try to grab Julia's hand at first, but it proves too hard to get through the crowd. I catch Dave and say, "Stay behind me!" Down a few more stairs

I see that the line of people is ended. I yell-whisper to Josh and Nate, "Stop!" as they have just passed the end of the line. After a few more steps they stop, breathing somewhat heavily. I catch up to them and survey where we are on the stairs. I am not sure for a second where we are since each floor looks the same. The others quickly catch up to us. I peer down the rest of the stairwell and can see someone with the same color shirt as one of the men from earlier holding onto the rail at the bottom of the stairs. We again are faced with the same dilemma as earlier. Follow them and go down the stairs, or try to go back to the waiting room.

I feel somewhat safer than I did perched on the walkway with the grand view of the murderous contraption, but I know we cannot remain here for long. We whisper quietly and agree to head down the stairs and hope the men are gone by the time we get there. We start down the stairs slowly, but then we naturally speed up given that we want to get out of this place. We reach the bottom of the stairs. No one is there. A single gray door meets us at the bottom. It looks like it opens out toward us, but it has no handle to grab. No way out of the stairwell, netting on all sides. A door with no handle means it was likely installed that way on purpose, and is likely locked. What do we do?

I make an effort to grab the slightly ajar edge of the door with my fingertips. Success! I am able to pull the door open. I am not enthused about going back into the building, but it has to be better than heading back up the Stairway to Heaven.

We all go through the door. As Ted gently guides the door shut behind us, we find ourselves in a rather dim hallway about forty or fifty feet long. Nothing is on the walls except for one door on the left about a quarter of the way down. Nothing is on the floor, either, not even litter. Near the end of the stretch of hallway is a light, perhaps emergency lighting at best. As we pass the door on the left, I meekly try the knob to see if it is unlocked. Locked. We continue down the hallway toward the light. I am in the lead, Josh is right next to me, Nate and Dave are with Julia right behind us, and Ted and Mindy are at the back. We are making every effort to be as silent as possible, not knowing what will come next. As we get to the end of the hallway, I can tell that the hallway meets up with another hallway that goes to the right and to the left. I motion for everyone to stop just before we get to the turn. I move toward the wall on the left and peer around the corner. Ted then moves toward the wall on the right and is doing the same thing. The hallway to the right is much brighter and longer than the one we are in, and it has a door to the outside at the end of it. The hallway to the left has minimal lighting and ends about twenty feet away. Neither hallway has any sort of decoration. The longer hallway to the right has doors on both sides all the way down. The shorter hallway to the left has one open doorway on the left at the dead end. There is a closed door almost straight ahead of me on the far wall of the adjoining hallway.

The rest of the group takes turns peering around the corners to also see that the coast is clear. Ted and I huddle up to decide which direction to turn. We are speaking quietly, but we feel a little more confident to make some noise seeing that the hallways are empty. Soon the others join the conversation with their opinions. Ted and I agree that we need to stay behind the scenes as much as possible until we get a better understanding of where we are. We elect to go to the left. Josh, calmer now than he was when we were made aware of our pending doom, begs us to go to the right toward the door to the outside. He changes his mind quickly, though, as we peer down the hallway toward the exit door and see advancing people through the rectangular window on the door. We quickly take the hallway to the left and go through the doorway at the end. It looks like we have walked into a supply closet, with open doorways at each end. Ted gingerly peers back through the open doorway we just walked through. As quickly as he pokes his head out, he returns it. Evidently the people came through the door. Hopefully they are not heading this way. There is nowhere to really hide in the roughly eight foot by eight foot room.

Many aprons hang on hooks attached to the wall directly in front of us, and some kitchen supplies are on shelves on the wall behind us, and to our left. The other doorway, larger than the one we walked through, opens to a large kitchen area that appears to be empty but well lit. I peer into the kitchen area. There is no one in sight. Then I have an idea. We need to get these robes off and try to pose as short order cooks. If it doesn't work, then at least we tried. We will be better off getting out of these robes than keeping them on. I hear voices coming toward us from the hallway. The people who came through the door at the other end of the hall, I presume. I grab some aprons off of the shelf and turn to hand them to everyone. I drop my apron on the floor and start to take off my robe. Everyone else follows suit. I realize how much cooler the room feels once the robe is off. With the robes off, we apply our aprons quickly as the voices continue to get louder. I pick up all of the robes off of the floor and look around for a good place to dispose of them as I move toward the kitchen. The voices don't seem to be getting closer any more as the people continue talking. Perhaps they made a turn down the first hallway where we entered, or perhaps they went into one of the other doors. The pressure is off, momentarily at least, and I notice a plastic trash can with a lid that will be able to hold the pile of robes I am carrying. Before I get to the trash can to dispose of the evidence, a rather large older woman walks into the room from another doorway I hadn't yet noticed to my right. "What are you doing?" she asks. Busted.

Chapter 3 – A Helper

Psalm 116: 1-9 (NIV), "I love the Lord, for he heard my voice; he heard my cry for mercy. Because he turned his ear to me, I will call on him as long as I live. The cords of death entangled me, the anguish of the grave came over me; I was overcome by distress and sorrow. Then I called on the name of the Lord, 'Lord, save me!' The Lord is gracious and righteous; our God is full of compassion. The Lord protects the unwary; when I was brought low, he saved me. Return to your rest, my soul, for the Lord has been good to you. For you, Lord, have delivered me from death, my eyes from tears, my feet from stumbling, that I may walk before the Lord in the land of the living."

The woman looks normal enough, just like all of the other workers we've seen so far. When I look into her eyes, though, I notice a detached, almost wild look in them. I try not to look her in the eyes. Instead, I focus on the apron she is wearing. It has a few gray stains on it, likely faded from several washes. Whatever goulash she has been preparing in the kitchen doesn't appear too appetizing based on the stains on her apron. The whole group is right behind me, and we are exposed for the first time after all of the close calls we have experienced in this terrible place. I muster an, "I'm sorry…," trying to buy some time to think of a good excuse. But I am at a loss. No one else in the group offers anything witty to get us out of the predicament we are in. I look back up at her face, but it is a mistake as her eyes really freak me out. What makes it worse is that she has very large, thick glasses that magnify her eyes to larger-than-normal size. Maybe that is what is making them look funny to me.

The woman begins to speak. "You shouldn't be in here. You are sinners, and we need to purify you of your sins. All of the Saints need to be purified before they can enter Heaven, and you must eat the meal of purification before you can continue your journey." If I had thought I was going to figure out something to say before, I really won't be able to think of anything now. She continues, "You must be exceedingly sinful given that you haven't remained with your group. I will need you to come with me so that you can rejoin the group." I say to her, "This is all a big mistake. We're here to help..." She cuts me off before I can continue. She starts her spiel again, almost as if it is on a script. "You shouldn't be in here. You are sinners, and we need to purify you of your sins." I have to admit, even with the absolute severity of the situation that we are in, I quickly lose my focus on what she is saying and start to think of a plan to get out of the room. Seven of us versus one of her. It seems like good odds, but we would have to incapacitate her so that she wouldn't yell for help. I would really have a tough time knocking out a woman that looks kind of like my Grandmother, but things are getting pretty dire for us. We cannot get sent back with the group of Saints that were sufficiently "purified" to be smashed to bits.

Before we have to do anything drastic, another voice comes from the left. "Mom!" the voice says sharply. In the next instant a young man comes through a doorway to the left. "These people are with me. They're the new help that we requested. I've been assigned to get them trained." Mom turns and answers, "Thomas, I didn't hear of any new workers arriving today. How did you find out before me?" she asks. "I don't know, mother," Thomas answers, "Mike saw me in the hall and asked me to do him a favor. He told me the new workers arrived early and needed to begin training before the next set of groups arrives in a couple of days. It's going to get very busy again, so they need to start their training now. He told me to meet up with them in the kitchen and get started right away. They can shadow us when the next group comes in." Mom seems to be placated. "Leave it to Mike to forget to tell me something I should know as the kitchen supervisor," she says. Mom adds, "Thomas, I am so impressed at your change of attitude all of a sudden. I can hardly get you to help *me*, but as soon as Mike asks you for help you are eager to impress. Good job, son, even though I really don't like Mike or care to speak to him any more than I have to." Thomas responds, "Mike also told me that one of the groups has some V.I.S.'s in it, so you know what that means." Mom answers,

"Yes, I had heard that the Leader is coming. He always seems to line up some V.I.S's for his visit." If I had to guess, V.I.S. means Very Important Saints, based on Mom's sermon to us earlier.

Thomas then looks at us. "Hi," he says, "I'm Thomas Fields. This is my mom, Beth Fields." Thomas moves forward and offers his hand to me for a handshake. "We've been volunteers at Camp Happy since it opened about a year ago," Thomas says. "Thomas!" Beth shouts, evidently not caring for the Camp Happy reference. I shake my new-found friend's hand and am about to introduce myself, but he quickly moves to Ted and shakes his hand. He follows suit with each member of our group, quickly reintroducing himself with each handshake. Beth joins in the official introductions, but she doesn't offer a handshake. Beth asks, "What's your name?" as she approaches me first. Before I can even think of answering, Thomas responds for me. "You must be Tim." Looking at Julia, he says, "And you must be his wife Mary." We shake our heads eagerly as if our new names are critical to preserving our lives. Josh is now TJ (Tim Jr.), Nate is now Scott, and Dave is now Billy. Ted and Mindy are now Mike and Kathy. After the introductions, Beth begins to walk out of the room. As she walks around us she says, "I'm leaving you in good hands. Good luck and welcome. We really need the help." I respond with an obligatory, "Thank you, we're glad to be here." Suddenly Beth stops. "I do have one question, though. Tim, why did you have that pile of robes that you threw into the trash can as I was walking in?" It takes me a second to realize she was talking to me. Out of thin air I come up with, "Someone handed them to me on the way in and asked me to take care of them. I didn't know what he was talking about, but he walked away before I could ask what to do with them. I figured they were dirty and needed to be thrown out." I hope the excuse flies. Beth answers, "Rookie mistake. The robes only get one use, but if they're clean they can be put back in the good pile. Thomas will explain everything to you over the next few days. Right Thomas?" Thomas answers, "Sure Mom!" And with that, Beth leaves the room via the supply closet exit.

Our new best friend Thomas doesn't waste any time starting his training once Beth leaves the room. He proceeds to one of the counters that runs almost the full length of the kitchen and motions us to follow. Two equally-sized counters are positioned in the room, starting about eight feet from where we entered the room (through the supply closet) and extending down to the other end of the room. The counters have about six feet of space between them, with about six feet of space between the counters and the walls in the rectangular-shaped room. Thomas motions us over and begins to open some cabinet doors under the stainless steel counter. Now that I have time to think about it, the kitchen appears to run alongside the first hallway that we walked through when we came back into the building. I do not see the other side of the door that I remembered being on the left side of the hallway, the one that I tried to open that was locked. I then realize that there must be another hallway or set of rooms in between the kitchen and the hallway, because that is what Thomas would have had to walk through to enter the kitchen through the other doorway. The more I think about it, the more it seems perhaps that the kitchen is instead perpendicular to the first hallway. The next question I ask myself is where the eating area is, but I quickly surmise that it must be through the set of double doors about halfway across the room past the second counter on our right. Shelves line the walls, and pots and pans hang down over the counters at arms' reach. The only curious thing is that I do not see any cook-tops, griddles, or ovens in the room. I only see what look like refrigerators or freezers with sliding glass doors that fit in between the shelves on the wall to the left. There are also some refrigerators, not set in the wall but flush with the shelves, on the right side of the room on either side of the double doors.

Everything is so clean, and the stainless steel shines brightly in the light of the room. Beth runs a tight ship. Even though it took a matter of seconds for me to make my observations, I have already missed a few sentences of Thomas's instruction. I decide to start listening and hear Thomas say, "All of the utensils you will need will be in the three sets of drawers at your station. The busboys will set out the empty bowls at your station before the kitchen opens. You'll have to get the porridge out of the fridges along the wall when you first get here. On a day the kitchen is open you will need to be here at least thirty minutes before the first group. You are responsible to have at least twenty-four bowls filled and ready on trays, eight to a tray, before the porridge gets distributed to the Saints." Thomas points to open shelving under the counters, where several stacks of large trays sit from just above the spotless, white tiled floor to under the utensil drawers.

Thomas continues, "The porridge will be in five gallon buckets, which are really heavy. If anyone can't lift the pails, all of the busboys are able and will help. You'll find that some of the workers don't speak English, but just motion to the refrigerators and they will understand. Keep in mind that things get pretty crazy as we transition between groups, and it usually hits us the worst between the second and third groups of the day. We asked a long time ago to have a limit of three groups in an eight hour period, because it gets way too crazy to try to cram in a fourth group. The four group scenario has only happened once since Mom, err, Beth, made the request, and we had some problems that got the higher-ups attention as a result. Once they saw it for themselves, they made our request part of the standard procedure." Ted speaks up. "May I ask what is in the porridge?" Without hesitation, Thomas says, "No, not yet." He immediately returns to his instruction. "Make sure you eat plenty of food before your shift starts, because you won't have time for any breaks. This may be one of the hardest jobs you've ever had." I respond with, "It's better than the alternative." Thomas looks at me like I shouldn't have said that. There is evidently more to his game, so I nod as if to say I will go along with the ruse that we are actually the kitchen workers that this Mike fellow was expecting. I hope the real kitchen workers don't arrive anytime soon, because that could make things dicey.

Thomas goes on to say, "You'll have a chance to see how the operation works starting in about a half hour. Today we only have two groups, which is unusual, so there is time for a short lunch today. The kitchen crew is on break waiting for the next group to wake up. They should start filing in soon." My stomach realizes that Thomas has mentioned lunch. "May we get something to eat before the next round starts, and could we possibly use the restroom?" I ask. "Sure," Thomas says, "That's a great idea. I'm hungry, too, and I can continue with your orientation while we quickly eat some food." Thomas leads us through the doorway that he used to come into the room. We walk through that doorway into a small room that butts up to the other side of some of the refrigerator units that we saw in the kitchen. "Porridge room," Thomas says. I'll show you how that works later." I look to my left and see a rather strange-looking contraption. It does not look nearly as shiny as the stainless steel in the kitchen, but it is made of some type of steel. It has several round bowl-like chambers with steel pipes running between them. Several gauges protrude from the machine, and a rather foul odor is coming from it. One of the chambers is open, and a worker is standing there running water through the machine with a green garden hose. The worker doesn't seem too interested in us as we walk by. "That's the strangest looking moonshine machine I've ever seen," Ted says. Thomas turns and smiles, and then continues forward out of the room. We walk through a hallway about twenty feet long that dead-ends into stairs. At the top of the stairs, a large window lets in natural light. I can see tropical foliage through the window. Halfway up the stairs, a landing turns us 90 degrees to the other half of the stairs. At the top, we enter a large room with many people sitting at tables eating food. It is a rather normal-looking full service cafeteria, and the food smells really, really good. I wonder to myself, "How long has it been since I last ate?" But I really have no idea. Everyone else in the group looks equally hungry, and Thomas doesn't waste any time bringing us to the beginning of the line. He motions to a doorway nearby. "The restrooms are right out there," he says. Oh no. This is a really tough decision. I am so hungry, but I also realize for the first time that it must have been a really long time since I last went to the

21

bathroom. Very quickly the bathroom becomes the best choice for all of us.

We return several minutes later refreshed, but still starving. As we pick up our trays and start down the line, Thomas recommends the chicken and rice dish, along with a fresh salad. That sounds really good to me, so I choose to pick up one of the steaming bowls of chicken and rice from under the heat lamps and then a smaller bowl of salad at the next station. Everyone but Josh picks the chicken and rice; he has his eye on something else. He finds the pepperoni pizza station, and proceeds to pick up three slices before he asks Thomas, "Is this OK?" Thomas nods approvingly, and sets a fourth piece on Josh's tray. Nate and Dave pick up a few pieces as they pass by, evidently to serve as appetizers before their main course. We get our drinks, silverware, napkins, and straws, and sit down at a nearby open table. Everyone, even Thomas, is very quiet as we wolf down our food. I am a notoriously slow eater as I prefer to enjoy my food; however, I empty my large bowl within minutes and ask for another. Thomas says, "Don't be shy; I never am!"

When I get back, several others are already enjoying their seconds. Ted is the last one to return, this time with a piece of pizza. This round we eat at a more normal pace, and Thomas defers his seconds to be able to continue our orientation. "I call it Camp Happy, but it really doesn't have a name that I know of. All of the people you see around you are volunteer workers. I call everyone 'Camp Counselors,' but the title hasn't caught on very well. Their job is to get the Saints ready for Heaven." I ask, "Where do the Saints come from, and how do they get here?" Thomas responds, "We'll talk more about that later." We don't have anybody sitting close enough to us, in my opinion, that could overhear us with all of the chatter noise in the room, but I have evidently asked a question with a similar sensitivity level to Ted's earlier question about the porridge. Thomas continues, "Mom and I helped open the place up a little over one year ago. We were due for a vacation last month, but Mom deferred the R&R to someone else. She says we'll go in a few more months. I'm beginning to wonder if I am ever going to leave this place." Mindy asks, "Where was home before you moved to Camp Happy?" Thomas answers, "Grand Rapids, Michigan. It's a toss-up which place is worse." I'll second that, being from Ohio and having visited Grand Rapids several times. "And what made you guys want to move here?" Mindy asks. Thomas gets a serious look and says, "It's always been just Mom and me since Dad died, and she's been looking for something to believe in ever since. She got started with this group in Grand Rapids, and," Thomas pauses momentarily to look around and then leans in toward the middle of the table, "she drank the Kool-Aid pretty fast. Then we just *had* to go on this mission trip. Mom sold the house and the car, and put the money into the group's community fund. I warned her that she was getting scammed, but she doesn't usually listen to me." At this point I am almost finished with my second bowl of food. Everyone else in our group is almost done as well. I look around, and the room has emptied considerably since we came in. Thomas notices me looking around and says, "Yep, it's almost time to get back to work." We take our last sips of our drinks, all waters, collect our dishes and trash, and proceed to the garbage cans near the stairs where we came in. I suddenly reflect on the doom we were facing less than an hour ago, and how our fortunes changed so quickly, all thanks to our new friend, Thomas. In my mind, I say, "Thank you, Lord!" I look over at Thomas, who is emptying his trash in the can right next to me, and I say, "Thank you. You are a life-saver." Thomas replies, "There you go again Matt; I mean Tim." Thomas knows my name.

Chapter 4 – Keeping it Real

Matthew 22:36-40(NIV), "'Teacher, which is the greatest commandment in the Law?' Jesus replied: 'Love the Lord your God with all your heart and with all your soul and with all your mind. This is the first and greatest commandment. And the second is like it: Love your neighbor as yourself. All the Law and the Prophets hang on these two commandments.'"

We walk back downstairs toward the kitchen. As we pass the porridge machine the one worker is still in the room running water through the machine with the garden hose. Once we get to the kitchen we are immediately in the way of several people trying to do their jobs. There are roughly fifteen people in the room now, banging and clanking dishes together while quietly talking in several different languages. I can hear noise coming through the double doors that most likely lead into the eating area. I hear someone, probably Beth, speaking very methodically and melodically in a loud voice. I assume the group that we woke up with is in the eating area. I can't make out the words she is saying unless a worker hurries through the doors with trays of porridge. Once the doors close her words are again too muffled to understand. Thomas leads us to an empty station, the same one as before. He asks us to observe the workers directly to the right of our station, as we are on the end. The workers are tipping the pails filled with porridge, a little bit at a time, into bowls placed onto several trays. Once eight bowls are filled on a tray, then spoons are taken from piles on the counter and placed in the bowls. Each station has stacks and stacks of empty bowls toward the middle of the counter. The bowls are stacked to a height just under the pots and pans hanging from the hooks above the middle of the counter. Workers routinely come by looking for a tray ready to serve. When a tray is removed, then the worker in charge of pouring the porridge grabs a new tray from under the counter and sets eight empty bowls on the tray. Some workers have room for as many as three trays at their stations, and some have room for only two or one depending on how their bowls and spoons are spread out over their station.

The worker that we are observing has her act together. She is able to lift the pail of porridge without trouble, and she has perfected her pouring technique without even a drip outside of the bowls. As I look around, I can see other workers with wet towels having to wipe drips off of the trays or off of the sides of the bowls. All of the workers are wearing clear latex gloves and are in long sleeves. None are wearing hair nets, though. I feel like we are crowding the worker that we are observing with most of us leaning in toward the middle of the counter to peer down to see her. Ted and Mindy are close to being right behind her, and are causing the workers serving as waiters to have to alter their usual course to keep from hitting them with the trays. Our worker sets down her now empty pail of porridge right in front of Josh. She lifts another one off the floor that is tucked right beside her legs and continues her work. One small drip falls onto the counter from the lip of the empty pail. Josh reaches out to wipe it up with his finger, presumably to then wipe it on his apron. "Stop!" Thomas says sharply. "Let me get you some gloves." Everyone in the room except us is too busy to give more than a fleeting glance at Thomas's loud warning. He finds a box of gloves and makes each one of us put on a pair. "Sorry," he says, "I should have had you put these on when we first come in. The most important rule in the kitchen is that you cannot get the porridge on your skin, and you can never eat it." I shouldn't be surprised at what he just said, but I am. Why aren't the workers allowed to touch the *food*, especially if it is supposed to purify the Saints before their trip to Heaven? I assume this is another one of those questions for later.

We spend the next half hour or so observing the process. After about twenty minutes trays with empty bowls begin coming back into the kitchen. I notice a series of large sinks and dishwashers lined up against the far wall of the room. The groups at the ends of the two counters quickly shut down, clean up their porridge pouring operations, and move to the dishwashing area. As time progresses, and as pails empty, more crews shift to clean-up mode. The waiters continue to bring in more and more trays of empty bowls back into the kitchen. I can see that the workers are cleaning up their workstations in preparation for trays of empty bowls to be placed on the counters until the dishwashing station can catch up on rinsing and loading dishes. A few people are going around to the stations looking for any partial pails of porridge. They combine partials, return the full pails to one of the refrigerators, take lids from a stack next to the refrigerator (presumably clean, but maybe not) and affix them to the tops of the full pails. The empties are stacked and set on the floor next to the dishwashing area. These folks have it down to a science, which makes sense if the operation has been in existence for at least one year. After about forty minutes from the start, Beth enters the kitchen. Her eyes lock on us as she walks through the double doors and she gives us a proud smile. Then she moves on. She looks at another lady who is walking toward one of the refrigerators on the other side of the two counters. The woman returns the look and Beth nods. The woman picks up a phone that is hanging on the wall between two refrigerators, and presses one button on the phone. After about ten seconds, the woman says, "The last group is ready." After a short pause, she says, "Thank you," and returns the phone to its station and goes back to cleaning up.

Then it hits me. The next group is going to die. I begin to tear up, thinking about what happened to the group we joined on the stairwell and to all of the groups before who were led to their death over the last year. I have to find a way to stop this from happening. But how? I need more time to come up with a plan, but I can't stand by while this group is led to their death. I feel guilty that I couldn't figure out a way to stop the rest of the group we had joined on the stairs from dying a short time ago. I just ran scared, away from the death machine. I need to get us alone with Thomas so that we can speak freely to him and figure out what to do, and I need to do it quickly.

"What's wrong, Dad?" Nate says to me. As soon as Thomas hears Nate ask me the question, he turns and looks at me. Thomas quickly says, "The rest of the time here is spent cleaning up and washing dishes, so as long as you all know how to do that, we can move on to the next part of your orientation." I quietly ask, while choking back the tears, "Is it to a quiet place?" Thomas nods affirmatively and quickly ushers us through the supply closet and out of the kitchen. I look at Julia and she has a tear streaming down her cheek. Either she has thought of the same terrible end for the well-fed group as I have, or she just has compassion for me. The kids look troubled, and Mindy looks like she's choking back tears as well. Thomas leads us out of the supply kitchen and down the long hallway with the door at the end, the one with a window to the outside. "Let's see here, at least one of these should have a vacant sign. Yes, here it is." He opens one of the doors on the left side of the hallway, about halfway down the hall. Thomas takes down a piece of paper taped to the door with the word "Open" written on it in ink pen. We follow close behind and into the room. Thomas says, "Your group is large enough that you get a whole room to yourselves."

As he shuts the door, his expression changes as he looks back at us. Now all of us are fighting hard to choke back tears, and we are all failing miserably. We have all been in "pretend and survive" mode for long enough. Now the emotions are coming out. "Help us understand what's going on!" I exclaim as pointedly as I can in a quiet voice. "Why do these people have to die? I can't sit idly by while another group is led to die in that machine. I need to go save them right now, or die trying. Will you help me?" Nate and Dave grab each of my arms, as if to hold me back from leaving the room. Thomas replies, with a troubled look on his face, "It's too late for them, Matt. They will be dead within a couple of hours whether they go into the Saint Smasher or not." I ask, "But why?" Thomas retorts, "It's the porridge. It softens up their inner organs so they smash easier." Now Thomas is crying. "They'll either die a painful death during hours one to two after they eat it or they'll avoid the misery by being smashed to bits. I've seen it a few times where the end of the line doesn't go through fast enough, and it is horrible to

27

watch the pain and suffering that overtakes the drug they're given to wake them up." Mindy asks, angrily, "Why do these people have to die? And why do you keep calling them Saints? Are they all Christians, is that what it is?" Thomas answers, "Yes, they are, you are all Christians who have been kidnapped and brought here to die. It's been happening for over a year now. Groups of our 'missionaries' travel, mostly to third world countries until recently, to search and find Christians and follow a procedure to 'harvest the Saints' and bring them here without detection. You and your crew are among the highest-profile group that has ever been brought to the death-camp, and a lot of pre-planning was done to ensure your disappearance will be a mystery. I can't see how several hundred, soon to be several thousand Americans gone missing won't raise some serious eyebrows. But the people here are very powerful, otherworldly powerful, and they have been building up to this for some time. You weren't supposed to get here for a few more days, but I changed some things around to get you here sooner. I risked my own life to do it, but please don't ask me how."

As he finishes his sentence, I ask, "How and why did you switch us around? Why didn't you get us out of this mess if you could?" Thomas moves to one of the beds directly behind me and sits down, putting his face in his hands. As I turn, I notice for the first time how big the room is, about thirty feet by thirty feet, dressers and beds scattered evenly throughout the room. Windows at the back wall of the room are allowing bright sunlight to shine in, with tropical foliage in full view. A decent-sized lawn stretches to the tree line, but it is hard to gauge a distance. I look down at Thomas. I remember what he has already done for us. "Thank you," I say, "for rescuing us earlier and for saving us from certain death. We are all overwhelmed right now, understandably, but we should not be taking it out on you." Thomas looks up and says, "Thanks Matt." After a pause, he collects himself and says, "To answer your question, I switched things around because I knew you guys could help me. I have watched too many people die, and the only way I can live with myself is to put a stop to it." I am not sure why Thomas thinks we can help. "What makes us so special that you specifically picked us to help you? Even though I am having trouble remembering where we were right before we were abducted, I have a pretty good idea that we are no more special than anybody else," I say. Thomas answers, "I can shed some light on that. When the abductions occur, the victims are usually gassed in their house or dwelling to render them unconscious. Then they are injected with drugs to keep them sedated until they get here. During long trips, they may wake up but are in a strange state. They are given water to keep them alive until they get here, but they can get multiple doses of the drug. When they arrive, they are dosed with a different version of the drug that keeps them spaced out until their death. Either version causes memory problems. We had one counselor accidentally stick herself with one of the needles. It took her several months to regain her full memory. She got it back in stages, but certain memory strings remained unaffected. I am impressed how alert all of you are; you must have missed out on some of the doses. They got you down here pretty quick, though." Ted then asks, "Where is here?" Thomas answers, "I haven't found out exactly where we are, but we are somewhere near Central or South America. They didn't blindfold us or anything on the way down, but it's always been a secret. A lot of things are secretive around here, understandably, and there are only a few people 'in-the-know' in this place. It's only been a few months since I've started snooping in places where I shouldn't be. I hit the gold mine last month and have learned a lot about how things work. I learned enough to switch your paperwork with another group about the same size to get you here a few days ahead of schedule. You are the VIS's that Mom and I were talking about, but she doesn't know it. You are the Very Important Saints."

This is too much. I can't even remember what would make me important, but I am pretty sure I am no more special than any other Saint. In fact, there are lots of people that should have been picked ahead of me on a list of importance. I know I am no pastor or missionary, unless that's blocked by my short term memory loss. At least I wasn't one as recent as I can remember. I have a very boring life with no even remote claim to fame. Only Jesus could make me something special anyways, and even then he would have his work cut out for him because I let my selfishness get in the way too much. There I go again, assuming that I would make the group special. Maybe one of the kids or Julia, Ted, or Mindy has done something special recently that got somebody's attention.

At least we are getting some answers now, and at least Thomas is on our side. I then ask, "Are you the only one here who wants to stop this, besides us, or are there others?" Thomas doesn't answer because his cell phone rings. He pulls it out of his pocket and answers, "Yea Mom?" After a few seconds he stands up and begins to walk toward the door. "I'll be right there," he says and hangs up. Before he opens the door, he turns and looks at us. He says, "Stay right here. There are fresh sets of camp counselor clothes in the drawers you can change into. You may want to change because you probably peed in your pants several times on the way here. There are at least two restrooms in here where you can shower. I will be back in about an hour. They need my help to get this last group up the Stairway to Heaven." With that, Thomas leaves. We are alone, together, but at least we have hope. And I know that God is with us.

Chapter 5 – The Lord our Strength

Psalm 28:7 (NIV), "The Lord is my strength and my shield; my heart trusts in him, and he helps me. My heart leaps for joy, and with my song I praise him."

Everyone else, short of Ted, is still crying, but I actually feel better now. God is with us, and will continue to be until the end and beyond. He will accomplish what he needs to accomplish through us, and if we die in the process he will give us new life with him forever. "Guys," I say, "everyone come here and let's say a prayer." No one objects. I take a knee on the hard concrete floor, and everyone else either gets down on the floor or sits on the nearest bed. We join hands and bow our heads. I close my eyes as tightly as I can, as if to ensure that my complete focus is on God. "Dear Jesus," I begin, "we love you and thank you for being with us during this terrible situation. You spared us from death, and you have given us a pretty clear mission: to try to stop the death that is occurring in this place. Thank you that we are here together. Please help us to comfort each other and to strengthen each other. Please help us to remind each other that you love us, and that we are yours forever, Lord. Please also help us to continue to learn the things that we need to learn to somehow destroy this place, or to reveal to the world what is going on here so that it can be stopped. Thank you for Thomas, Lord, and for putting him here to help us, and for putting us here to help him. Please help him to find you if he has not already, and please use us to teach him about you and your love for him. Please seek him out Lord, and any others who can help us have victory over this place."

"You are the God of the universe, the One who delivered Moses and the Israelites from the Egyptians. You are the One who stopped the sun for Joshua and the Israelites so they could defeat their enemies. You are the One who delivered King Hezekiah and the city of Jerusalem from the Assyrians, and you are the One who loves us enough that you sent your

Son to die for us and to gain victory over the evil and death that are in this place. Give us the faith to trust in you, to believe that you brought us here to rescue many from death. We love you Jesus; help us now. In your name we pray, Amen."

We all rise, as if to go somewhere, but for a minute we just stand, looking at each other. Everyone has stopped crying now, so maybe my prayer helped. "So what do we do now?" Ted asks. I respond, "I'm going to go to the bathroom, take a shower, and put on some clean clothes. After that, I'm not sure yet." Josh likes my plan, and soon everyone is determining the order in which we go into the two bathrooms to get cleaned up. I remember Thomas's earlier comment about us soiling ourselves during the trip down here, but my clothes show no signs of trouble, at least on the outside. No one else's do, either, which is a good sign. The kids get assigned to take turns in one bathroom, and the adults take the other. I start pulling clean "Camp Counselor" uniforms out of one of the drawers and we check sizes. All large pants and shirts are in the top drawer. The drawer below has mediums and smalls, so we should have everyone covered. I can find only long-sleeved shirts in any of the sizes. Thomas happens to be wearing a short-sleeved variety of the shirt that I cannot find in the drawer. The bottom drawer is full of socks and men's boxers. In another dresser across the room Julia and Mindy find women's apparel. The uniforms are nothing more than fake-looking scrubs. Ted and I defer to Mindy and Julia so they can use the facilities first, and Ted and I converse about the craziness of the situation. The kids head over to the other bathroom and discuss who will be first. "I never in a million years would think that we would end up in a place like this," Ted says. I agree with him wholeheartedly. "How could anyone pull off an operation like this for over a year without getting caught?" I ask. As we continue to converse, I lean against the dresser. It reminds me of my dresser at home. I instinctively think that I need to empty my pockets if I am going to change clothes soon, so I reach into my left pocket. Nothing there, as usually my keys and comb go in that pocket. I reach into my back pocket to pull out my wallet. Not there. I guess these people rob you before they kill you. I reach into my right front pocket expecting that I was also robbed of my cell phone, but it is there. My cell phone!

"Does it work?" Ted asks. "I don't know yet," I respond. I don't know if the phone is off because the battery is dead or if it was turned off. I press the on button, and after a few tries the start-up screen appears. "It's working!" Ted says as the password prompt comes up on the screen. The kids run over to take a look, and Julia comes out of the sink area in the bathroom to see what is going on. Mindy is already in the shower. I enter my password. I am not expecting much in the way of a signal, but it is too early to tell. The battery is almost dead, and the message immediately appears that less than 20% of the battery life is remaining. I dismiss it, but I still do not have any bars. No network symbol comes up on the phone, either, as I expect. As the hope starts to fall in everyone's mind after about thirty seconds, I start to wonder if there are any wireless networks in the building that do not have a secure connection. It is not very likely, but worth investigating further when Thomas gets back. I go to the wireless network screen in the settings, but the waiting dial turns with no success in finding a nearby network. After about two more minutes of waiting for a signal or a network to appear, I decide to turn the phone off to try to save the last sliver of battery. It will be worth asking Thomas if there is a compatible charger lying around anywhere that he could let us borrow. Since he is allowed to carry and use a cell phone, he should be able to find something.

"Why did you turn it off, Dad?" Nate asks. I respond, "So I can save the battery for when Thomas gets back. He might be able to help us somehow connect to someone on the outside." Nate answers, "Like who; 911?" I say, "Not very likely, but we will figure something out. For right now, let's get back to getting cleaned up and into our costumes." A few of them give me a confused look until they figure out that I mean the scrubs, and then they return with the rest of the group to the task at hand.

It takes about an hour for all of us to get showered and changed. Ted and I converse more about next steps until it is one of our turns to use the facilities. We both agree that we need to find a way to mess up the porridge machine and the smashing machine, but we will need Thomas to get us more information about both. When Julia comes out of the bathroom, I defer to Ted to go first. Julia is changed and heads over to the other bathroom to check on the kids. The feelings of terror and dread have almost left me for now, but as soon as I think about starting to feel better they return. How are we going to do this? "Faith, Matt," I tell myself. Mindy comes over and asks, "Does my hair look crazy enough to pass for a camp counselor?" She exclaims, "I couldn't do anything with it in this humidity!" I respond, "Unless you can mimic the crazy eyes, I don't think you'll fit in exactly." Mindy says, "I know, Beth's eyes were driving me crazy! I'm glad I wasn't the only one who noticed." I say, "I wish we could find out where we are. I can't believe that Thomas hasn't been able to figure out where this place is located." Mindy says, "It's got to be somewhere near the equator. Did you feel how hot it was when we were at the top of the stairs?" I tell her I hadn't noticed at the time, and I look over and see Julia coming back across the room. She walks over and gives me a hug and says, "I'm scared." I respond, "Me too." It's probably not the uplifting answer that she was looking for, but it is the best I can do. "You smell," she says. "Thanks," I respond.

After a few more minutes, Ted is showered and changed. I quickly shower and change. When I emerge from the bathroom, I realize that the costumes don't include shoes, so I will need to put my old ones back on. Nothing like sliding clean socks into shoes you have likely worn for at least forty-eight straight hours. Maybe Thomas can direct us to some camp-issued shoes when he gets back. When I look up at the group as I come out of the bathroom, everyone is crowded around the bed directly in front of me with their backs facing me. As I get closer, I can see that Thomas is back, sitting on the bed. He seems pleased with everyone's disguise, as he is smiling at the group. "Hi Matt," he says. "Hello again," I respond. Now it's time to make a plan.

Thomas explains, "Sorry, I had to help with the last group. This one was the toughest for me so far. A few of the women at the back of the line were starting to feel the effects of the porridge. I felt so bad for them. It's almost a blessing for them to quickly be put out of their misery when they step into the machine." I say, "Hopefully this is the last group that ever goes through that machine. Thomas, what we need your help with is to come up with a plan to cause the machine to stop working permanently, and a way to mess up the porridge-maker so that the porridge has no ill effects. Is this possible?" Thomas answers, "I'm not sure, but anything's possible. If someone left the active ingredient out of the porridge, which comes in little packets and is added to one of the chambers while it's being made, I guess the porridge would be just mostly ground rice and water. And as for the smasher, I know where the blueprints are. I don't know much about machines, but if someone else does I'm sure there's a way to make it explode or something." I look at Ted, who has been rebuilding cars and other machines most of his life. Ted says, "No, we probably don't want to make it explode, because that would draw attention to us or kill us in the process. Will the machine be used between now and when the next groups arrive?" Thomas answers, "No, but the two guys you saw up there operating it do regular maintenance, mostly at night, and they will definitely be out there the night before the Leader arrives to make sure it is running in tip-top shape."

I ask, "How long do we have to make all this happen?" Before I finish my sentence, Julia asks, "Wait, you weren't with us when we were about to go into the smashing machine. How did you know that we were up there?" Thomas smiles and says, "I have my hiding places. I saw you from the roof across from the machine. I can't believe you were able to escape without Tom and Barry noticing you, or anyone else at the bottom of the stairs. Nate snickers at the names Tom and Barry. Dave gives him a smirk, but the rest of us remain serious. "When you guys took off running, I thought you were goners right there. It goes to show that someone is looking out for you. To answer your question, Matt, the Leader will get here on Wednesday afternoon, ahead of the three groups of Saints. He'll hold a staff meeting, go on a facility tour, and then he'll do his all-hands address over the PA system on Thursday morning. Only a select few of the in-the-know people ever see the Leader. They're the really bad guys you have to be careful of. Tom and Barry are two of the five bad guys, and they will go nuts if they catch us anywhere near their machine." No smiles this time. "They should wrap up their late-night maintenance around eleven PM Tuesday night, and their rooms are on the other side of the building so they won't be able to see us messing with the machine from their windows or anything." I ask, "So what is today?" Thomas answers, "It is Monday afternoon, so we have some time to figure this out. The first step is to get you guys trained on operation of the porridge machine and the filling of the pails. Those activities need to start tonight and finish tomorrow to get enough made for Thursday. Luckily for you guys, nobody ever wants porridge duty since it smells so bad while it's being made. The new recruits always get stuck with porridge duty. I will train you on how the process works tonight and then we'll run the first batch. Once Mom lets us alone we will finalize plans on how to keep the poison out of the mixture and not affect the consistency. Somehow the poison smell goes away when it is mixed into the porridge, so as long as it looks right, we should be OK." I ask, "So tonight and tomorrow morning, porridge-making, and then tomorrow night, late, smashing machine. Anything else we need to do to stop this operation in its tracks?" Thomas answers, "There is one more thing." He pauses for several seconds. He begins to look troubled again. He says, "We need to stop the release." Julia quickly asks, "What release?" Thomas looks like he's going to cry again. "From the reservoir," he says. Before I can stop myself I ask, "What's in the reservoir?" expecting the answer to be water. Thomas surprises me by saying, "The blood." I don't like the sound of this.

Mindy gasps and says, "What blood?" Thomas responds, now crying again, "The blood of the Saints! What do you think happens when everyone gets smashed in the machine? The blood has to go somewhere, and so do the guts. After a group is smashed, the liquid portion doesn't take long to get removed from the solids. That's the purpose of the porridge. After about ten seconds the pusher arm slowly moves back to its starting position. The liquid drains into an outlet pipe that runs to the reservoir on the edge of the property. The solids get dumped down a chute into a dumpster under the machine that gets hauled away as soon as it is filled up. Several such runs happen on a day when the machine is running. The machine actually tips to the right to move the solids to the one end, and then a trap door opens in that side of the floor to help the solids go down the chute. Then the machine is returned to level and the rest of the blood drains out." I have to stop him. "Thomas, this is the most disgusting thing I have ever seen or heard in my life! Why would the 'Leader' be doing this? What is the point?" I really don't want to know the answer to my question, but at least it may get us off of this extremely gross topic that is making my stomach turn in knots. Thomas answers, "The Leader is crazy, but he is smart and powerful crazy so he can do whatever he wants. I didn't learn the real reason for the reservoir until recently when I spied on his super-secret meeting the last time he was here. All along I thought it was an in-equals-out kind of thing. The solids had to go somewhere and so did the liquids, but it didn't make sense why the liquids had to remain until the Leader got here each time." Julia asks, "How often does he come?" Thomas says, "About once every month or two, depending on his schedule. He's very busy, you know." Julia asks another question that she set up with the first one. "Doesn't the blood really start to smell after a few days, let alone a month or two?" Thomas responds, "We don't go near the reservoir, so I don't really know how bad it is up close. After a few weeks, if the wind is blowing toward the building from that direction, you can detect an unpleasant smell. I've learned that there's something in the porridge that works to preserve it, though, and to reduce the smell."

I butt in. "Now back to my question. What does the Leader do with the blood? Does it power his super-secret space-ship so that he can travel the galaxy at warp speed using the blood of the Saints?" Thomas, who has collected himself by now, gives a minor smirk at my theory. "No," he answers, "he sees it as a sacrifice, a pleasing aroma. He comes just so he can see the blood of the Saints flowing like a river. The reservoir empties into a river and then out to sea. He has a perch where he can sit and watch it flow to the sea. I haven't seen the perch, but he talked about it at the last meeting. He told the guys what changes they had to make for the releasing operation to be better this time. Evidently, the release of the reservoir has never gone right according to the Leader. He told the guys in the last meeting that if it didn't go right this time heads were going to roll."

It goes without saying that if the Leader says heads are going to roll he means it. Ted jumps in, returning us to the task at hand. "What do we need to do to stop the release?" Thomas responds, "The Leader has a button that he pushes from the perch that opens up the drain from the reservoir to the river. It's another stretch of piping down a hill to the river. I have never ventured down there to see it in person, but the blueprints for the whole series of pipes and valves are in the same drawer as the blueprints for the smashing machine." I ask, "Would it be easier just to disconnect the button at the perch than to try to override valves and controls down at the reservoir?" I selfishly ask this because I don't want to go anywhere near it. "No," Thomas answers, "because I don't know where the perch is. I can at least get us to the reservoir and we can find the valves on the west side of it, closest to the edge of the property. I heard the Leader say at the meeting that he likes to watch it as the sun is starting to set, because it makes the blood almost glow as it heads down the river." Josh exclaims, "This dude is messed up!" As if my heart could sink any further, I realize how terrible it is that my kids have to hear and experience all of this. They have remained so protected, so sheltered all their lives, just as I have been, that I can't even begin to imagine how this is affecting their young minds. I have to ask one more question, even though I really don't want the answer to it, either. "To whom is the Leader making this sacrifice?" Thomas answers, "I didn't hear him or anyone else say it at the meeting, but whoever or whatever it is can't be good."

"Do you think we have a chance?" I ask Thomas. "To do all of this," he says, "sure we do. But we can't waste much more time. I have to get you trained on how to make porridge." Josh says, "Then let's go, times a wasting!" Mindy interrupts. "Let's say we make the porridge without the poison, and let's say we somehow destroy the machine and it doesn't work right, and let's say we plug the drain to the reservoir so that it can't drain. Then what? If they find out what we've done, then we can't stick around waiting for them to catch us. How do we get out of here, and then where are we going to go if we do?" I answer, "We can't worry about whether or not we are going to live through this. We may need to give our lives to save many others." Mindy then adds, "But everyone in the groups will still be drugged and won't be able to escape or fight or anything. The Leader will find another way to kill them, and he'll kill us, too."

Thomas interjects, "I do know how we can get out. I thought of running away from this place several times, and I concocted a plan a few months ago where I would escape through a broken area of fence on the front side of the property opposite of the reservoir, on the other side of the building. It is covered by dense brush, and evidently no one else knows about it but me because it hasn't been fixed. Once outside of the fence, my plan was to hitch a ride on one of the solid waste trucks that leave here when the smashing machine is in operation. At that point, even though it's been a year, I think I remember enough to eventually make my way by the makeshift roads to get to the landing strip where the cargo planes bring in new recruits and new groups of Saints. If we could find a way to sneak on board one of the planes undetected, we could get off of this island and get out of here. I know it's a long shot, but it's our only hope. Beyond that, it's like Matt said. We may have to die trying to destroy this place."

I add, "And don't forget that we called on the name of the Lord a little bit ago. We can be very certain that he is not happy with what is going on here, and I believe very strongly that he has sent us here to stop it. Why else would things have worked out like they have so far? I am going to put my trust in Jesus that he is stronger than this situation, and he will help us to accomplish whatever he needs us to do, even if we end up getting killed. Besides, as soon as we die we will be with Jesus in Heaven forever anyways."

I continue. "Thomas, I had another idea a little bit ago. I found my cell phone in my one pocket, and I noticed that you had one, too. Is there any way that we can contact the outside world from here?" Thomas answers, "Not that I know of. I mean, I'm sure there is, but they have it set up so that these cell phones are for internal use only. They are very restricted in what can be done with them, and they only function on the secured wireless network. We get a signal on the phones inside the building, but it drops quickly as you walk away from the building. It's amazing that you still have it; it's standard protocol for the missionaries to confiscate all personal belongings from the Saints and to leave them wherever they are abducted." Another sign that God is with us, I think to myself. "Can I check your phone's charging port to see if mine is compatible?" I ask. Thomas says, "Sure," and pulls out his phone. We have a match. "I'll let you borrow my charger tonight and we can see if your phone can do anything in the morning." I say, "Thanks. I did turn it on earlier and tried to see if we had any signal or if I could connect to a wireless network, but no luck. It is very low on battery, so charging it up will give us more time to see what we can do tomorrow."

"Can we go already?" Josh asks. "We are wasting too much time talking. I want to get this over with, however it is going to turn out." Thomas answers, "Sure, let's get going. We can talk more later on this evening after we make porridge and get some dinner. If we make the porridge without the poison, it won't smell that bad and we should still have an appetite afterwards." I ask, "Will anyone get suspicious if it doesn't smell right while we are making it?" I can tell Josh is upset that I am dragging this out more. Thomas says, "We can open a few packets of poison right near the two exits to the room so that the unpleasant smell wafts out of the room. There are fans in the room that we can use to blow the smell away from us and out into the hallways." Julia says,

"You have all the answers, Thomas! I'm glad you are on our side!" We all add a, "Me, too," and that makes Thomas smile for a second. Then his expression turns serious. He looks at me and says, "But I feel kind of weird. You all seem very connected to God and Jesus and whatever, but I really don't feel like that. Since my Mom joined this group, I had a bad view of God based on what I heard. Once I got here and learned some things, I realized that this group doesn't have anything to do with God. But I don't know much about God, and I never read the Bible. I've only recently read some things about Him, but it just didn't make sense to me until now. I'm really scared that I've been associated with this place and stood by while so many bad things have happened to God's people. I'm afraid that he's mad at me and I will get sent to hell forever for what I've done, even if I didn't want to do it." Now Thomas is crying. I move closer to him and put my hand on his shoulder. Thomas continues, "How can I prove to Him that I'm sorry? If we die, I want to go wherever you guys are going, but I'm so afraid I won't." Thomas puts his face into his hands and begins to sob.

CHAPTER 6 – THOMAS'S CONVERSION

Romans 10: 9-15 (NIV), "If you declare with your mouth, 'Jesus is Lord,' and believe in your heart that God raised him from the dead, you will be saved. For it is with your heart that you believe and are justified, and it is with your mouth that you profess your faith and are saved. As Scripture says, 'Anyone who believes in him will never be put to shame.' For there is no difference between Jew and Gentile – the same Lord is Lord of all and richly blesses all who call on him, for, 'Everyone who calls on the name of the Lord will be saved."

"How then, can they call on the one they have not believed in? And how can they believe in the one of whom they have not heard? And how can they hear without someone preaching to them? And how can anyone preach unless they are sent? As it is written: 'How beautiful are the feet of those who bring good news!'"

It doesn't look like Josh is going to get his wish to get out of the room and make some porridge quite yet. In my mind I pray for God's help for us to say the right words to Thomas. Mindy sits on the bed next to Thomas and says, "Thomas, God knows you don't want to be here. You have been forced into a bad situation, just like we have, but you've had to endure it a lot longer than anyone else. I am amazed that you have been able to survive this place, and God knows that your heart is in the right place. All you need to do is trust him now, and you will be OK." I add, "Once you trust him with your life, he will hold you in His loving arms forever. He sent his Son, Jesus, to earth a long time ago to die in place of the rest of us for all of the bad things that we do. Our God got what we deserved so that we could enjoy life forever with him. I know you don't understand much about God, but the good news is you don't have to. All you have to do is trust in Jesus and ask him to be a part of your life, to come into your heart, and he will take care of the rest. You have the rest of forever to get to know him better, and he will give you the gift of his Holy Spirit to guide you and teach you for the rest of your life and beyond."

"That's what I want," Thomas says, "to be on Jesus' side." I answer, "All you have to do is ask." Thomas asks, "Will you help me? I don't know how to ask." I respond, "Yes, let's all bow our heads and close our eyes." I kneel down next to Thomas, who is still sitting on the bed, and pray, "Jesus, we pray to you today for Thomas. He is tired of this world, and of this place. He is tired of everything he's seen and endured for so long, and he needs your help. Save him now, by your power, and lift him up out of this place. Come into his heart; be a friend to him forever. Help him to realize that you have been with him all along, and the times that he has felt the loneliest, the most scared, are the times you have actually been the closest to him." I pause for a second. "Thomas, if this is what you want, pray these words with me, even if it's not out loud. Jesus, come into my heart. Forgive me for everything bad I've ever done. Never leave me or forsake me, and I will never leave you or forsake you. All that I have, and all that I am, I give to you. In your name I pray, Jesus. Amen."

I open my eyes and look up at Thomas. He continues to bow his head and to keep his eyes closed. After a few seconds he looks up. Thomas's expression now is one like the weight of the world being lifted from his shoulders. Fear has been replaced with peace, perfect peace. "Did you do it?" Josh asks Thomas, his impatience now replaced by genuine concern. "Yes," Thomas says. "I asked Jesus into my heart. I'm not sure exactly what it means yet, but I know it's what I want." I stand up, realizing that my knees are sore from the concrete floor, but I don't really care. What started as the absolute worst day of my life has become one of the best. A soul has been saved, rescued by Jesus, and I had something to do with it! What a miracle! Thank you, Jesus!

■■■

Now back to reality. Ted asks Thomas, "Thomas, are you fit for duty to train us how to make our special brand of porridge?" Thomas smiles and answers, "Yes, let's do this." We all proceed toward the door. The kids start in front of everyone else, but they quickly move out of the way for Thomas to take the lead. Out the door we go, and back down the hallway toward the kitchen. I begin to get that sick feeling again as we walk down the hall and past the first hallway that we entered from the outside. We reenter the kitchen through the supply closet, and now that I know the full breadth of the treachery that's gone on here for a long time, I am none too happy to even breathe the air in the room. We pass the place where Beth discovered us and proceed into the smaller side room where the porridge machine sits. The worker who was washing it out is no longer there, but Beth is there bent down behind the machine as we walk in. She stands up, with a clipboard in her hand. I notice that the clipboard has a piece of paper with a checklist typed on it. The paper has several blue checkmarks in boxes that run down the left side of the checklist. The corner of the paper is flapping in the breeze being generated by several fans blowing air in the room.

As Beth begins to speak, I look up at her face and make eye contact. I remember what a mistake that is, and quickly divert my focus to her mouth. "Hello everyone!" she says rather loudly to speak over the fan noise. We all return with our hellos, as enthusiastically as we can muster. "Thomas, I was just about to call you. We need to train your new team on how to make the purification food." Beth drops her pen, and she bends down to pick it up. I notice Thomas start to wave his arm. We all look over at him, and he quickly shakes his head in the "no" direction and mouths the word "porridge." Beth must not appreciate it being called porridge. She quickly picks up her pen and continues. "Thomas, when was the last time you trained a new group on the procedure for making the meal?" Thomas answers, "Last month." Beth responds, "Good, just let me go over a few things with you while they go into the kitchen and get some gloves, sleeves, and aprons." Beth turns to us. Hopefully we don't all appear to pull back as her crazy eyes lock onto us. She says, "The aprons are in the supply closet, and the gloves and sleeves are in any of the kitchen drawers. Is anyone allergic to latex?" We all shake our heads no. "Good," she responds. Thomas says, "Tim, will you get me a pair of gloves too, please?" It takes me a second to remember that Tim is my alias. "Sure," I say. Beth asks, "Tim, would you please get him some sleeves, too?" I respond, "Sure thing," and head into the main kitchen with the others. I hear Beth say, "I know you hate wearing the sleeves, but you need to wear them. This stuff cannot touch your skin." That's some motherly love right there, I think to myself.

We all proceed to the first set of drawers under the counter closest to us. Mindy gets there first, and starts pulling pairs of gloves out of the box that she finds. These are mediums, she says, and hands to all requiring the size. She does the same with a box of large gloves. She pulls the drawer out further, and finds the protective sleeves at the back of the drawer. She hands out pairs of sleeves to everyone, and then gets an extra pair for Thomas. She puts the unused sleeves back in the drawer, shuts it, and then picks up a pair of gloves she had set out for Thomas on the counter. We all don't waste any time heading back into the room. My hope is that Beth is gone when we get back, but I find that is not the case. She is pulling out a box from under one of the counters against the side wall of the room, near where we have walked back into the room. She opens the box, and we have to walk past her to fit everyone in the room. Thomas is standing next to her, looking in the box. His eyes still look like he has cried recently, so hopefully Beth doesn't notice. I get a front row view of the box, so I look inside. The box is full of fairly flat plastic packets of reddish-purple liquid, about four inches square. The packets have what looks like a spout at the top, and I see a dashed black line printed onto the top of the spout, evidently a cutting line.

"What's this?" Ted asks, playing dumb. Thomas keeps silent, so Beth then responds, "This is the special ingredient. You want to make sure you don't get it on your skin, but once it blends with the rice and soy ingredients, it creates a perfectly edible food to purify the Saints for Heaven." Catching her in the lie makes me feel more than a little angry inside. How can a grown woman, a mother, be responsible for feeding thousands of people poison that will soon kill them if they aren't first murdered in another way? Another question comes to mind based on earlier comments Thomas made about his mom. Is she in the know, or was she fed some bogus information about the porridge and doesn't know the real story? Before I can think of any more questions, Beth opens a drawer under the section of counter by which we are standing. She pulls out a pair of scissors, and cuts the top off of the poison packet. We all instinctively take a step back. Beth says, "Don't be afraid, just be aware that you can't get it on your skin in this form. Very potent stuff." I notice that she is wearing gloves, and she already has on long sleeves, so at least she is practicing what she is preaching.

"At this point," Beth says, "you pour four packets into the first chamber that I have open here." She walks over to the porridge machine, and I see where she had previously opened the chamber on the left side of the machine as it is facing us. Thomas's eyes get big all of a sudden, and he walks toward his mother. "Mom!" he calls out, "Let me do it. You have plenty of other things that you need to be doing to get ready for the Leader's visit. I've done this hundreds of times; I can take it from here. Besides, shouldn't we load the bottom chamber with the rice / soy mix and start pressurizing it before we add the packets? Remember the time it backfired?" Beth stops, looks at Thomas, and smiles. "You're right, Thomas. You have it more together than I do right now. It must be the stress of getting ready for the big visit. You take it from here, but I want to watch the first cycle to make sure your pupils get the instruction they need." My heart sinks to the floor. We need to get Beth out of here to un-spike the porridge.

Just then, as she hands the poison packet to Thomas, a young teenage-looking girl walks into the room. I immediately recognize her as the girl who caught me with my eyes open while she was giving shots to everyone in the waiting room. This time she has her reddish hair up in a ponytail. I turn away so that she can't see my face. Nate does the same thing; evidently he was caught with his eyes open, too. He is standing next to me, so we give each other a worried look. "Ms. Fields," she asks, "I need some help in the upstairs kitchen. Would you have some time?" Beth responds, "What do you need, Katie? I'm kind of busy right now." Katie answers, "The upstairs oven is out of control again, and I can't remember how to fix it without having to unplug it and mess it up again." I hear Beth grimace, but I can't see her face. I hope her eyes don't get crazier when she is upset. "Katie," she says, "I showed you how to fix it last week." Katie answers, "I know, I'm sorry. I just know how much reprogramming you had to do when I unplugged it last time, and I don't want to do anything to mess it up without watching you one more time." Beth says, "OK Katie, I'm coming. Thomas, you are on your own. Please make sure you get out the recipe book and follow it to a tee." Thomas replies, "Yes mother." I turn to look and see Beth walking out of the room with Katie through the doorway opposite of where we came in, both of their backs facing us.

Once they are out of the room, I look at Nate again. "I hope she didn't recognize us!" Nate says. "I don't think she did," I say. I turn and look at Thomas as he says, "You hope who didn't recognize you, Katie? When did *she* see you?" I answer, "Thomas, she was one of the first people we saw when we woke up. She was in the room giving everyone the shots to wake us up. When she almost got to our group, she caught me with my eyes open looking at her as I was lying on the floor. I thought I was busted, but she just smiled at me and didn't say anything." Nate interrupts, "I thought she was smiling at me, because she caught me, too!" I continue. "The two men who were also in the room asked her and the other girl to leave before they had given the shots to us and to several others in the room, and they both agreed and left the room with the men." Thomas asks, "You had already woken up before getting the shots? I haven't heard of that happening before, but I guess it's possible." I answer, "Yes, I had woken up ten or fifteen minutes before the two men came into the room and turned on the lights. Talk about being freaked out. And then to see everyone else

lying beside me; at first I didn't know if they were dead or alive."
Thomas says, "That worries me a little bit, that Katie saw you awake and
didn't make anything out of it. She used to be my friend, but they got to
her and I can't trust her anymore." Julia asks the question on the tip of
everyone's tongue. "What do you mean they got to her?" Thomas
answers, "The youth Leader here, Jared Evrel. It's one of his many roles.
He is one of the in-the-know guys, and he is downright bad. He puts on
an amazing front of being the nicest guy on earth, and all of the teens
here love being part of his youth group. He's brainwashed all of them
but me. Katie held out until a few months ago, but he kept working on
her and working on her until she broke. I think she finally gave up from
the pressure from her friends more than anything. Matt, we have to
make sure she never sees you or Nate, or we could have a big problem."
I ask, "Does she work in the kitchen down here also, or just in the
kitchen upstairs?" Thomas answers, "Like most of us, she works both
and does a lot of other jobs as well. Most of us can work from one end
of this place to the other in a given week. They work us pretty hard, but
at least they feed us well. There's no telling where you are going to run
into her over the next few days, but just be ready to duck and cover
whenever you see her. I still can't believe how lucky you guys have
been." I say, "I can believe it because God is with us. That is the only
way that we are still alive right now."

Thomas looks down and remembers the open packet of poison in his
hand. "Can someone get me two empty bowls from the counter over
there? Julia is the closest to where the bowls are, and proceeds to pick
up two bowls from one of the stacks. She moves over to Thomas and
un-nests the bowls. Thomas takes the packet and empties the contents
into one of the bowls. Julia is the first one to make a face at the smell.
It takes no time for the smell to hit the rest of us. It is very unpleasant,
and it reminds me of a smell similar to cooked kale, but much worse if
one could possibly imagine. Thomas sets the bowl near the edge of the
counter, nearest to the doorway, and then he climbs up on the counter.
"Be careful!" Mindy says, half gagging, as Thomas walks on the counter
to the fan attached to the wall with a swivel bracket. He aims the fan as

best as he can to waft the poison smell out of the room. He climbs down and grabs a second packet out of the box. He grabs the scissors that Beth left sitting on the counter, and cuts open a second packet. The smell is starting to dissipate from the first packet, so the fan placement must be good. Whoever walks by the room will definitely want to steer clear of the area. Thomas picks up the second bowl and walks over to the other doorway. He sets the bowl on the edge of the counter and pours out the poison. He immediately moves to the back corner of the room where a second fan is sitting on top of the counter. He aims it at the bowl, which will hopefully have the same effect to push the terrible smell out of the room.

Thomas looks at us and says, "Let's make some porridge!" My stomach is not sharing in his excitement, whether it's real or sarcastic. Ted asks, "How many of these pails do we have to fill?" I look behind us, against the wall between the two doorways, and see lots of nested empty pails stacked on the floor. "All of these?" I ask. Thomas says, "Between tonight and tomorrow." Dave asks, "How is this little machine going to fill all of those pails?" Thomas answers, "Let's get to work and I'll show you."

CHAPTER 7 – MAKING PORRIDGE

John 6: 1-13 (NIV), "Some time after this, Jesus crossed to the far shore of the Sea of Galilee (that is, the Sea of Tiberias), and a great crowd of people followed him because they saw the signs he had performed by healing the sick. Then Jesus went up on a mountainside and sat down with his disciples. The Jewish Passover Festival was near."

"When Jesus looked up and saw a great crowd coming toward him, he said to Philip, 'Where shall we buy bread for these people to eat?' He asked this only to test him, for he already had in mind what he was going to do."

"Philip answered him, 'It would take more than half a year's wages to buy enough bread for each one to have a bite!'"

"Another of his disciples, Andrew, Simon Peter's brother, spoke up, 'Here is a boy with five small barley loaves and two small fish, but how far will they go among so many?'"

"Jesus said, 'Have the people sit down.' There was plenty of grass in that place, and they sat down (about five thousand men were there). Jesus then took the loaves, gave thanks, and distributed to those who were seated as much as they wanted. He did the same with the fish."

"When they had all had enough to eat, he said to his disciples, 'Gather the pieces that are left over. Let nothing be wasted.' So they gathered them and filled twelve baskets with the pieces of the five barley loaves left over by those who had eaten.'"

The porridge room, though now well ventilated, is fairly loud with the fans running. If I hope to talk freely to Thomas during this process that will most likely take several hours, I will need to stay close to him to avoid talking too loudly to be heard by a passerby. If the camp counselors are smart, though, they will know to stay away from the smell coming from the room. I move close to Thomas and ask, "Will we get many visitors during the porridge process, or will they steer clear of the smell?" Thomas answers, "You're right; nobody is going to bother us tonight. Mom may stop back in to check on us, but she is usually tied up for a couple of hours with the oven problem. You see the upstairs kitchen, along with making everyone's food, also has the stoves and ovens to make the slurry for the porridge. The slurry we need for tonight is already made and in the kitchen down here." Thomas looks over at Josh, Nate, and Dave. "I need you guys to start bringing in the filled pails that are around the corner and most of the way down in the kitchen, over by the sinks. They are really heavy, as the slurry is thick stuff, so don't take more than one at a time. We can't have you guys getting hurt, so take breaks in between trips. Mindy and Julia, if you can check the drawers or the supply closet for a couple of black plastic spatulas, about two feet long; we'll need those to make sure we can scoop out the slurry stuck to the sides of the vat."

I ask, "Do we need the machine if we aren't going to add the poison to the mixture?" Thomas answers, "Yes, we do, as we always add quite a bit of water to thin it down as it processes through the machine. We also need to add some food coloring or something to darken the slurry. The dark red in the poison changes the slurry color from a light tan to a darker gray. I'm hoping we can find some food coloring in the supply closet down here and not have to go upstairs raising suspicion." Thomas looks over at Ted. "I'm on it!" Ted says. "I think I saw some on the shelf when we were in there the first time. Do you think I should grab blue and red so we can experiment?" Thomas answers, "Go ahead and grab all of the colors in the pack, and we'll trial and error it in a bowl first to get it right and then scale it up."

The kids each return with their first full pail of slurry. The room isn't that big, so I am pretty sure that we won't be able to fit a large amount of full pails into the room at one time. "Where do we set them?" Josh asks. Thomas answers, "Find some open space on the counter and fill it up. Then stack a row of pails about two high in front of the back counter until the space is filled up. That should be enough to get us going." Mindy and Julia return with the large spatulas. Soon after, Ted walks in with two boxes full of food coloring. Thomas looks at Ted and says, "I hope this will be enough." Ted says, "This was all I could find, but that's not to say there isn't more." I momentarily remember the story of Jesus feeding the five thousand. It would certainly be applied in a new and different way here.

Thomas opens one of the pails of slurry. He then asks for an empty bowl and Mindy gets one from a stack on the counter. She hands it to Julia who hands it to Thomas. He also takes a spatula from Julia and begins to scoop some slurry into the bowl. "Now let's try the food coloring," he says. Ted opens up one of the boxes and takes out the red and the blue. He takes off the lid to the red vial after setting the box on the counter. Ted asks, "How many drops?" Thomas answers, "Let's start slow." Ted drips a few drops into the slurry, and Thomas stirs it up with the spatula. He is choked up most of the way on the spatula given its size. The spatula makes quick work of the mixing and the slurry turns surprisingly pinkish-red. "Let's try a few drops of blue," Thomas says. Ted unscrews the lid off of the blue, and three drops go into the slurry. Now it's a purplish-gray. "Close," I say. Ted picks up the box again and looks inside. "Oh," he says, and pulls out a black. "This might help." He takes off the lid and hands it to Thomas. Thomas puts one drop in. "Perfect!" he exclaims, as he stirs it in. He stirs several more times and it remains a dark gray. Now we have the recipe: two drops of red, three drops of blue, and one drop of black per cup of slurry. Then I remember about the water addition. "Thomas," I ask. "How much water is added per pail that gets dumped into the machine?" I assume that a pail of slurry is a standard unit of measure for the operation. Thomas responds, "You fill the pail about two-thirds with water once you empty the slurry into the first chamber of the machine. Then you pour most of the water through the pipe into the second chamber. You'll save a little water in the bucket to rinse the first chamber after the slurry has drained into the second chamber. There should be a funnel around here somewhere to put over the pipe opening. After the water addition you are supposed to empty the poison packet through the funnel into the pipe. After that you open the valve from the first chamber, where the slurry is poured, and let it all mix together under pressure and agitation in the second chamber. You set the timer for three minutes, and when it dings you open the valve to let the porridge go into the third chamber where it is then emptied back into the original pail through the valve at the bottom. The problem is that the water addition makes it take at least one and a half pails, so that's why we have all those empty pails behind us. After every five batches or so, we need to open the third chamber and clean it out with the spatulas. We've found that if we don't clean it out periodically, the machine gets clogged up."

I now have a pretty good understanding of how the process is going to go. I just don't have a good feel for how we are going to get it all done in a few hours. I smell the poison in the bowls from time to time, which makes my stomach turn each time. I would be happy to have a skunk in the room right now to help displace the smell. "Thomas," I say, "I think I'm ready to make some porridge." The kids are already back with their second load of pails. Josh is carrying two pails, even though Thomas recommended against it. Thomas says, "Great, let's get started. The tricky part will be to determine how much food coloring to add to the second chamber in place of the poison." Ted interjects, "I think we need to add the food coloring to the water before adding it to the chamber. Can we estimate how many bowls full of slurry are in each pail?" Before Thomas can answer I add, "And then we need to determine how much the water addition will lighten the gray color, since our test bowl didn't have water added to it." Thomas responds, "Yes, that's a good idea to add the food coloring to the water, and I already factored in the lightening of the color with the water. The color in the bowl is somewhat darker than what you saw earlier today." I remember that he is right. It seems like we almost have our act together. Now it's time to make some new and improved porridge.

The first batch begins. Thomas pours the rest of the opened pail of slurry into the sphere-shaped first chamber. The lid is basically the upper hemisphere, which flips open via hinges on the left side. Once the slurry is poured into the first chamber, Thomas closes the lid. There are several clamps that Thomas locks down to seal the chamber. He then presses a button and the machine seems to power up. "The slurry is heated to one hundred degrees in the chamber while the machine builds pressure. It takes about two minutes." I see a temperature gauge directly under the hinges on the far left of the first chamber (the left-most point on the machine). In the meantime, Thomas takes the empty pail and begins filling it with water from the same hose that the worker was using earlier to clean out the machine. I didn't notice it was on the floor coming out from under the counter. It had been hidden by the box full of poison packets. By the time he fills the pail most of the way and returns the hose to the floor, the temperature reading is already in the mid-nineties. Ted and I are observing most closely; Julia and Mindy are talking quietly behind us, and the kids periodically return with pails. They take the longer way around the machine and set the pails on the counter behind the machine. Once the temperature reaches one hundred degrees, Thomas turns the valve handle on the pipe that comes out of the bottom of the first chamber and into the middle of the second, larger chamber.

He brings the pail of water around to our side of the machine, and I notice he has already added the food coloring to the water. It looks dark purple in the pail. "I added about twenty drops of red; about thirty drops of blue, and about ten drops of black. Let's see if it works." He looks around for a few seconds and says, "Oops, where's the funnel?" None of us know where the funnel is, but Ted leaves the room momentarily. He returns in about twenty seconds with a large, orange funnel. "Good work," Thomas says. Ted says, "I remembered seeing it in the closet on the shelf." Thomas places the funnel into the pipe, which is on the back side of the machine (from where we are standing.) He then lifts the pail and slowly pours in the colored water. After he empties the pail, he sets a dial near the bottom of the second chamber to three minutes. He then closes the hand valve that allowed the slurry to enter from the first chamber. I can see another gauge showing pressure in some unit of measure I have long since forgotten.

"Now we let it mix and pressurize," Thomas says. "Does it really only take three minutes?" I ask. Thomas nods affirmatively, and then starts looking around. On the counter he spots the spatula that he used to mix the test porridge in the small bowl. He grabs it and walks over to the hose on the floor, behind the machine. He gives the spatula a quick rinse, aiming for a drain in the floor underneath the machine. He then walks over to the far end of the machine, where the third chamber sits. One minute left on the dial. Mindy then asks, "Do we need to worry about any leftover poison in the machine from last time?" Thomas thinks for a second, and then responds, "No, I think we'll be OK. Each chamber is washed with hot water for quite a while, and the checklist can't be completed until clear water runs from one end of the machine to the other."

We all wait a little bit longer, until the timer runs to zero. I was expecting the typical "ding" noise of an egg timer, but instead the only sound made is an actuated valve opening. The hissing noise from the valve lasts about ten seconds, and I can see the pressure dial slowly returning to its starting position. The third chamber, sitting somewhat lower than the second chamber, is likely accepting the finished porridge from the slightly angled pipe between the two. The kids return to the room with another load of slurry pails. I look at the counter and realize that the kids have been busy filling it with pails while I have been observing the machine. Thomas says, "Guys, take a break for a minute. Just set those pails right next to that end of the machine." All three set their pail near the first chamber. I notice Josh only carried in one pail this time. Thomas then says, "We need to give the porridge about one more minute to drain, and then we'll open the bleeder valve to release any remaining pressure before opening the main valve at the bottom of the third chamber to drain the slurry back into the pails. The machine wasn't designed very well, so we have to tip the pail a little bit to get it under the valve opening. In the meantime, Ted or Matt, if you want to do the honors and dump another pail into the first chamber, we can keep the process moving." I grab one of the filled pails, and Ted gets to work releasing the clamps to open the lid to the first chamber. I pick up the pail, which is really heavy, and try to control how fast I pour the slurry into the chamber. While I'm doing the pouring, I hear the actuated valve closing via the hissing noise. I finish pouring in the slurry, and bring the empty pail around to the other end of the machine. Thomas says, "Don't forget we need to fill up that pail with water to put into the second chamber." I respond, "Oh yeah, sorry about that." Thomas says, "That's OK. We probably need to do a color check on this first batch before we add the food coloring. Thomas is opening the valve at the bottom of the third chamber, and porridge soon starts to come out into the pail. It looks somewhat gray, but not as dark as the test porridge in the bowl. As I walk around the back of the machine toward the hose I ask, "Is the color right?" Thomas answers, "It's actually still a little dark, but no one is going to notice on this one. Let's cut back the food coloring to ten drops of red, twenty drops of blue, and five drops of black and see how it turns out." I start to fill the pail with water and say, "Got it. About two-thirds of the pail, right?" Thomas answers, "Right." Then he asks, "Ted, did you hit start on the first chamber?" Ted answers, "Sure thing!" from right behind me. I didn't notice that he had walked over with the food coloring.

I finish filling the pail, and Ted adds the food coloring per the revised recipe. I remember that once the temperature of the first chamber hits one hundred degrees, the hand valve needs to be opened to move the heated slurry into the second chamber. I walk around Ted and over to the first chamber. Julia says, "You're at one hundred." I am still on the back side of the machine, but I reach around and open the hand valve. I then head back over to Ted and the pail. It still looks dark purple, but slightly less so than last time. He stands up, lifts the pail, and I gesture to take the pail. He says, "I got it," and gives a loud grunt as he hoists the pail up to pour the colored water into the funnel. He does so, saving a little back for me to chase the rest of the slurry through the

56

pipe from the first chamber. After the quick rinse I close the hand valve. Julia then reaches for the timer and sets it. I look over at Thomas, and he has put the lid back onto the pail of finished porridge. He has a rubber mallet in his hand and is gently pounding on the lid. He tells the kids, "The filled pails go into the refrigerators. If I were you, I would start with the farthest refrigerator and work your way closer to this room. It will make tomorrow all the easier." Even though there is only one pail, Nate and Dave follow Josh out of the room as he carries the pail. Thomas says to me, "You can go ahead and dump another pail into the first pot, now that the valve is closed." Mindy reaches for a pail, but I quickly come around to help her. She scoots it in my general direction, and I remember how heavy the pails are as I pick it up. I dump the pail into the first chamber, which is open from when I rinsed it. At this point I feel we are well on our way to completing phase one of our mission.

■■

We spend the next hour or so, rather quietly, making porridge. Ted modifies the food coloring one more time to use less red and blue, and more black, but less food coloring overall in the hopes of preserving the two vials of each color that we have. I am way too busy to spend much time talking to Thomas. About thirty minutes into the operation, the kids have brought all of the slurry pails into the room. The back half of the room is pretty well packed with slurry pails, but at least I can see an end to today's quota. Not that I want to even think about eating right now given the smell, but whenever we finish it will be way past our normal supper time. Hopefully we can get done in time to look at the blueprints for the smashing machine. I want Ted to have a good look at them before we hopefully get our hands on the machine tomorrow night. As I start the next cycle at the first chamber, I notice Dave standing behind me observing the process. I teach Dave how to work the front side of the machine, as he shows the most interest. Josh pairs up with Thomas, who shows him how to quickly open the third chamber and clean out the porridge that builds up from several batches. Each batch yields about a pail and a half, and the cleanout after every five batches yields another half pail. Nate is the odd man out and gets to carry the full pails out to the refrigerator. Josh helps with carrying the pails each time the half pail from the previous batch gets filled and there are two pails to carry. Julia, Mindy, and Ted are keeping chamber two going. Hopefully if I can get Dave going on chamber one, I can talk more with Thomas. I figure the more information I can get from him the better off we will be over the next several days. I want to find out more about the reservoir, and how and when we can sneak down there and break the valves to keep them closed. I really want to stick it to the Leader and make sure nothing goes right on his "special" day.

Given the memory thing, I'm not sure if I should know the Leader or not, but probably and hopefully not. Then something strange happens. I suddenly see myself standing in the family room of our house in Ohio. The TV is on, and it looks like the evening news is airing. That in itself is strange, because I don't like watching the evening news. It's usually too depressing to want to watch. I've gone through phases in my life where I've tried to watch it every night to keep connected with the world, but more often than not I'd rather not. On the TV, a news story is showing a younger-looking man in a suit walking into a room, followed by a large crowd of other men in suits. Media personnel are around him with microphones and cameras. The broadcast is in HD, but it looks like the HD that you would see in live feeds from across the ocean where you can see trails of motion behind the people as they move. Julia is sitting on our dark brown sectional couch in front of where I am standing, and she is not paying attention to the news as she is reading a book. I then hear myself say in a rather loud and nervous voice, "Antichrist, Antichrist!" Julia puts down her book and turns around, startled. I say it again. She says, "What are you saying?" I say it again, like I can't control myself. She yells, "Stop that." I say, "I can't!" and then I say it again. "Why are you saying that?" she asks. I say, "It's him, on TV. He's the Antichrist!" She turns and looks at the TV, and likely catches a brief glimpse of him before the video feed ends and the news anchor appears. I grab onto the couch, feeling strangely weakened by the whole event. She glares at me, thoroughly disgusted, which I can fully understand. Why did I say that? Who was that guy? Did that really just happen?"

Dave pulls me back into reality. "Dad!" he says. Not sure how many times he said my name before I came to. "I need you to open the lid so I can dump in this pail." Dave has the pail about waist-high, so I hurry over, release the clamps, and flip the lid open. Dave pours in the pail, and I help him to take some of the weight off. That flashback or whatever it was felt really strange. If it was a memory, perhaps it's all part of the effects of the drug starting to wear off. But who was that man on TV? Whoever he is, I don't like him.

I notice that I am working so hard that I am starting to sweat through my uniform shirt. I am starting to notice how humid it is in the building. Dave is sweating profusely as well. I think we are all motivated to finish as fast as we can to avoid any kind of detection of our covert operation. The machine can't function fast enough, but there is enough busy work in between the different cycles to keep us moving.

We spend the next two or three hours slowly working down the pile of slurry pails. Little by little, the pile is reduced to below half, and then to a quarter of what is was. We cross train on the different parts of the operation. Mindy floats between Julia and Ted. Nate stays near Josh the whole time. Dave rotates amongst all the groups, as do I. It makes for smooth transitions to always have one person at the station who has been there before. Thomas, as young as he is, is a very good supervisor and a very patient teacher. I get teamed up with him after about two hours. He and I are working on the easiest of the jobs; filling the empty slurry pails with water, adding the food coloring, which doesn't look like it's going to last much longer, and pouring the colored water into the second chamber. Now is my chance to have a good conversation with Thomas. I can't remember half of the questions I want to ask him.

"Thomas," I ask, "how are you feeling about our progress? Are we making up some ground to be able to get everything done before the big day?" Thomas smiles and answers, "Yes, you are definitely the most capable and efficient team we've ever had on porridge duty. We are still on track, as much as I can guess." I say, "Thanks for the compliment; I think we have some extra motivation and help compared to any of the previous groups." Thomas replies, "Another thing that I think is really helping us is to not have to constantly open the poison packets and take in that smell every few minutes. I still catch the smell from the bowls every little bit, but it is not nearly as bad as usual. I usually rotate people much quicker so that they don't get completely sick from constantly smelling the concentrated poison when the smell is in the air."

I look up to check on the rest of the group, and everyone is still working away. No one is showing any signs of slowing down. "Thomas," I say, "I want to talk to you more about what happened earlier when you asked Jesus into your heart. You may not fully understand what it means to 'have Jesus in your heart,' and I really don't understand the 'how,' of it, either. I accept it by faith because Jesus talked about coming into our hearts when he came to earth as a person several thousand years ago. It's all about a relationship with the God who made you, a personal relationship where you learn to love him because he forever loves you with infinite and unending amounts of his love. He proved his love for us when he sent his Son Jesus to die on the cross to take the punishment for all of the bad things we have done. When you start that relationship, he sends his Holy Spirit to live inside of you, along with your spirit, to guide you and to help you through the rest of your life. It doesn't mean that life is going to be perfect after you choose to start your relationship with Jesus; in fact, it often gets harder before it gets easier. Even Jesus had to die the painful death on a cross to make the universe right again after all the bad things that mankind has done, is doing now, and will do in the future. But don't worry. I asked Jesus into my heart when I was a little kid, and nobody is ever going to tell me that he is not there and that he is not Almighty God. One of my favorite

Bible verses was written by a follower of Jesus named Paul. In his letter to the Romans, he said, 'For I am persuaded, that neither death nor life, neither angels nor demons, neither the present nor the future, nor any powers, neither height nor depth, nor anything else in all creation, will be able to separate us from the love of God that is in Christ Jesus our Lord.' The reason why I love that passage and have committed it to memory is because it reminds me that Jesus will always be in my heart. Once you make the decision to fall freely into his loving arms, there is no one anywhere, not even you, who can take you away from Jesus. He will always be there, he will always love you, and he will take you to be with him forever after this life. Whatever anyone says to you or tries to teach you, never forget this truth. You are his; he is yours, forever."

"Thanks Matt," Thomas says. "I know I have a lot to learn about Jesus, but I've never felt such a feeling of peace as when I said yes to him earlier. I wish I could tell somebody else about it, especially my mom, but that would pretty much be a death sentence around here." I respond, "You'll get your chance to tell everyone when the time is right here in the next few days. Until then, we'll be happy to share in your joy and will be happy to answer any questions that you have."

"Dad!" Josh yells, "You guys are slowing down the operation! Quit yapping and keep moving! " Thomas smiles and responds, "Sorry Josh!" and pours the water into the chamber. We then go right back to talking, but this time making sure we continue to work. "Thomas," I ask, "how do you see the rest of the night going after, or if, we ever finish this first batch?" Thomas answers, "We are down to about an hour now to finish the rest of the pails. We won't do much cleanup tonight; the machine can sit until the morning. One thing I just thought of is we need to get rid of the bowls of poison on the counter, and we need to remove some of the poison packets and stash them somewhere else in case mom stops by after we are done." I then ask, "What if she stops by before we are done? Should I find an empty box and transfer some of the packets to it and hide it in the supply closet for now? And should I set some things in front of the bowls to hide them if she walks in unexpectedly?" Thomas answers, "Mom usually acts interested when you start, but she really hates the smell of the poison. I don't expect to see her until after we go upstairs to get a late supper. Once she knows it's cleaned up for the night, then she'll come down and take a look. Just in case, though, go see if you can find an empty box in the closet and we will fill it up and hide it really good."

I immediately head toward the supply closet. I squeeze past Ted, who is pouring slurry into the first chamber. I go into the somewhat dark supply closet, and I get the chilling feeling that I had when we were in the room for the first time while running for our lives. I shake it off and look for any kind of empty box. I don't see any on the floor, but I see a smaller-sized box on one of the shelves. The top flaps are open, and I pull it down to see what is inside. The box has a few containers of disinfectant wipes, so I pull them out and set them on the shelf. I don't know if the box will be big enough to hold enough of the poison packets, but I will give it a try.

I head back into the room, and Ted asks, "What are you doing?" I answer, "To get a box to hide some of the poison packets to make it look like we used them." Ted says, "Oh, good idea." I pull out the box with the poison packets and starting scooping as many as I can into the smaller box. Thomas says, "Fill that box up and it should be good enough. One of the full boxes of poison packets can last through four or five rounds of porridge making." I fill the box up, close the flaps, and then head back to the supply closet. Ted follows me in. He has the same idea as me while I look for a good hiding place. He pulls out several boxes in one of the corners under the shelves, each one with other supplies on top. I set the box of poison packets in the very back of the corner, and then Ted and I shove the other boxes and supplies back into the corner to hide it.

We head back into the room. I grab a couple of empty pails from the dwindling stacks and set them in front of the nearest bowl of poison. I catch a nasty whiff as I pass near the bowl. Ted goes back to his station, where Josh was filling in while he was gone. I grab two more empty pails and set them in front of the bowl on the other side of the room. Good enough. Now as long as Beth doesn't have some special test she runs on the porridge as part of her post-production checklist, we should be successful in our first phase of operation "Save the Saints." And hopefully that includes us and Thomas, too.

The last quarter of the first batch seems to take longer than the first three quarters. My hands are getting very tired of wearing these gloves. I realize that since we weren't dealing with the poison that we probably didn't need to be wearing the gloves all this time. I spend more time talking with Thomas, and most of the crew overhears the conversation as they sweat with us through the last of the slurry pails. I learn that Tom, Barry, Mike, Tim, and Jared are the five bad guys that are on the Leader's "Executive Team." Tom and Barry, as we already learned, run the smashing machine, and are the engineers / mechanics for the facility. Thomas calls them "The Mecaniacs," because of how he has seen them behave at times. Mike is the operations manager, Tim is his sidekick, and Jared is the youth leader who brainwashes the teenagers brought along by their parents. Beth supervises the kitchens, where the majority of the workers do their work. There are general workers, among the volunteers, who perform general cleaning and grounds maintenance duties. Mike and Tim oversee all of the deliveries into and shipments from the compound, as well as manage the drivers. They also keep in touch with a small crew stationed at the takeoff and landing strip at the nearby harbor.

This place was built over many years, as Thomas learned when he first rifled through the file cabinets in the Leader's office. Evidently he recently found a way to crawl through a shared air intake vent and into the Leader's office from an adjoining supply closet. Previous to that he had lain down on the floor of the small supply closet and listened to the Executive Team's most recent meeting that was held in the Leader's office during his last visit. Thomas plans to take me and Ted through the supply closet ductwork and into the Leader's office after we retire to our room tonight. Everyone else will stay back in the room, and will hopefully pray for us as we sneak in and review the blueprints of the smashing machine and of the reservoir piping and valve system. Evidently our room is surprisingly close to the Leader's office, which doesn't make me feel good.

Finally, the last pail is dumped into the first chamber by Julia. She wants to do the honors since everyone else but her and Mindy have had a turn lifting the very heavy pails. Over the next several minutes, we see the last bit of porridge pass through to completion. I help Josh carry the last pails to the refrigerator after Thomas does a final scoop-out of the built up porridge in the third chamber into my pail. I am curious to see just how full the refrigerators are so far. Josh leads me to the refrigerator that has room for a few more pails. The refrigerators are about a third of the way full. The kids did a good job loading the pails starting with the farthest refrigerator first. Josh sets his pail in the refrigerator, and then I follow with mine. Josh closes the refrigerator door, and then turns to me and asks, "Dad, are we going to make it?" I look him in the eyes and pause before I respond. His eyes start to glaze over with tears. Mine probably do, too. "I don't know buddy," I say. "But I do know one thing; that if we don't make it out alive, Jesus will take us right home to be with him forever. It will turn out OK, whatever happens. And just remember, that I always love you, and I am so proud of you for being strong during this whole thing. We've never had to deal with anything like this in our lives. During our whole lives we have never been in danger, and we have lived nothing but blessed and comfortable lives the whole time. The same God who blessed us with a lifetime of peace and security will see us through this situation, and, whatever happens, we will be OK. OK?"

Josh smiles, choking back the tears, and gives me a hug. I hug him back, hoping and praying that God will deliver us so that we can live to tell about it. I keep saying to myself, "Not my will, but yours Lord. Not my will, but yours." Josh and I head back to the porridge room and find that everyone is waiting on us. I start toward the counter where the first bowl of poison was sitting with the intent to clean it up. I quickly see that it has been cleaned up along with the other bowl. Thomas asks, "Who's ready for supper?" in a tongue-in-cheek sort of way. "I'm ready for bed!" Ted exclaims. "Ready for bed?" Thomas says. "You probably slept for at least thirty-six straight drug induced hours, and you're ready for bed already?" Ted answers, "Yes, yes I am." We all get a chuckle. Dave says, "Well I'm hungry." Dave's been hungry since the day he was born, much like me and his brothers. Not even the poison smell could turn his stomach. "Let's go," Thomas says, and leads us out of the far exit of the room toward the upstairs kitchen. As we walk toward the exit, I see Ted pull out several mostly empty food coloring vials from his pocket. He slides open the drawer under the counter nearest to the exit and places the vials into the drawer. He shuts the drawer, and he and I are the last ones out of the room. Part one of phase one of the plan is complete.

CHAPTER 8 – THE LION'S DEN

Daniel 6: 16-23 (NIV), "So the king gave the order, and they brought Daniel and threw him into the lions' den. The king said to Daniel, 'May your God, whom you serve continually, rescue you!'"

"A stone was brought and placed over the mouth of the den, and the king sealed it with his own signet ring and with the rings of his nobles, so that Daniel's situation might not be changed. Then the king returned to his palace and spent the night without eating and without any entertainment being brought to him. And he could not sleep."

"At the first light of dawn, the king got up and hurried to the lions' den. When he came near the den, he called to Daniel in an anguished voice, 'Daniel, servant of the living God, has your God, whom you serve continually, been able to rescue you from the lions?'"

"Daniel answered, 'May the king live forever! My God sent his angel, and he shut the mouths of the lions. They have not hurt me, because I was found innocent in his sight. Nor have I ever done any wrong before you, Your Majesty.'"

"The king was overjoyed and gave orders to lift Daniel out of the den. And when Daniel was lifted from the den, no wound was found on him, because he had trusted in his God.'"

I remove my latex gloves and throw them in a trash can as we enter the cafeteria. That feels really good to let my hands free from their sweaty prisons. The eating area is not nearly as busy as it was earlier in the day, but there are still a few people eating or talking at various tables. There are at least ten workers tending to the food on display and working in the upstairs kitchen, which is open to viewing to those in the eating area. We all grab our trays, as before, and proceed through the line. I realize that I am thirstier than I am hungry, but I have to pick up my food before going to the drink station. They have all sorts of soft drinks, milk, coffee, tea, and juices. My body is telling me that I really need water.

I take two large slabs of roast beef. I take several scoops of vegetable medley, and find a large wicker basket at the end of the line with fresh apples and bananas. I take one of each. Not sure where my mind was at lunch, forgetting my fruits or vegetables. Maybe it was the near death experience combined with the mind-altering drugs that caused me to forget. At least my mind feels like it is coming back together, but I still can't remember for the life of me what we were doing before we got here.

At last, I make it to the drink station and fill up my cup with water. No ice, for the first cup, and I drink the whole thing and then refill my cup with ice and water the second time. Dave is next to me, and his plate is piled high with unhealthy food. He fills his cup with water. I ask, "Why all the unhealthy stuff? Shouldn't you at least get an apple or a banana to get some nutrition?" I already know what his answer will be. Dave says, quietly, "What does it matter? We aren't going to get out of here anyways." I sense a teaching/preaching moment coming on, but he leaves for the table too quickly. Maybe it's for the best, because I feel kind of the same way, too.

We all sit down at the table farthest from anyone else in the room and start to eat. I quickly realize, as I so often do, that we all started eating without saying grace. I'm about ready to say something, but then I remember where we are. Perhaps we'll get in trouble for saying grace. I decide to chow down and say a quick thank you to the Lord in my mind. We again eat very fast, but most all of us filled our trays more this time than we did our first time through the line at lunch. We don't talk very much, instead focusing on the really good food in front of us. As our gorging piles wane, we begin to slow down our eating. Nate speaks up and asks Thomas, quietly, "So what do you do for fun around here?" I half expect Thomas to offer to show Nate the game room after supper, but instead he says, "There's not much to do around here. This cult is really strict on fun, so there's no chance of finding any video games or games of any sort. It's especially rough on the teenagers here, because there is nothing else to do except spend a lot of time together. The problem with that is that it is almost always with the youth Leader, Jared. I spent time with the group for most of my prison sentence here, but I never let Jared get into my brain like he did the rest of them. Even during the special 'one-on-one' sessions that he has with each teenager pretty early on when they get here, I didn't let him brainwash me with his incessant teaching about why this cult is the only true religion. I learned to block him out pretty early, pretending to listen and agreeing with him. Recently, because I wouldn't do the things that the other kids were doing, they started ragging me pretty bad. It worked out well, though, because I convinced Mom to talk with Jared and explain that I wanted to take a break from the group because of their meanness toward me. That freed me up over the last couple of months to take up my new hobbies of snooping and reading. I have done a lot of snooping over the last two months and have learned a lot. I found some good reading very recently and have almost finished a really good book I found. The next book I want to read is the Bible, but I can't find a copy in this place."

I look around. No one is listening to us, or should be able to hear us, but we are sitting near the restrooms and the adjoining hallway where someone could possibly overhear us. I ask, "Thomas, if everyone is done should we head back to the room?" Thomas agrees, and everyone immediately stands up. We take our trash and place it in the receptacles near the stairs. We go back down the stairs and back through the porridge room, which really stinks now that we have been away from the smell for a while. I am kind of startled by Beth, who pops up from behind the machine. "Great job, guys!" she exclaims, smiling and looking at Thomas. "You guys finished really fast, and I can tell you did a great job." Thomas replies, "Thanks mom. This is a really good group. We found ourselves some real workers here." Beth says, "I guess. It's about time we get a good group who can actually help us out." She looks down at her clipboard, which I couldn't see at first behind the machine. She brings it up closer to her crazy eyes, and makes a mark on the attached sheet of paper. Then she says, "All right. I'm all done here. I think I am going straight to bed. I will probably be asleep before my head hits the pillow. They really wore me out today." She again looks at Thomas. "You won't be too late coming in later, will you?" Thomas makes a disgusted look and says, "Mom, we don't even stay in the same room anymore." He then changes his face and his tone. "But I will be really quiet when I come into my room later so I don't wake you up." Beth answers, "Thank you, Thomas." She then gives us all a good night with one last sweep of the room with her crazy eyes and walks out. Thomas holds us back for a minute to let her get to her room. I'm not sure why, but I'm not going to argue. Once he gives us the signal, we then proceed to leave the porridge room, go through the supply closet, and then down the hallway that leads to our room.

Back in our room with the door shut, we all find a place to sit or lie down on the many beds in the room. After all of the hard work and a big meal, all I want to do is lie down and sleep. I start to lean back on the bed, but I stop myself as I know I can't. "Thomas," I ask, "what's the plan?" as I sit up. Thomas answers, "I want me, you, and Ted to go to the Leader's office and look at the blueprints for the smashing machine and for the reservoir. Meanwhile, everyone else do that praying thing because we are going to need it. It is going to be tough for us to get into the supply closet and back out without anyone walking through the hall and seeing us. People bustle through the halls all through the night it seems, so sneaking around can be kind of tough. I do more snooping during the day than at night because of it. I'll come up with a story if someone sneaks up on us."

"Where is the supply closet?" I ask. It's just down the hall a little ways. There's no direct access to the Leader's office from this side of the building, but his area butts up to the porridge room and to the hallway that you would have first walked through when you came into the building." I remember now, the locked door on the left side of that first hallway we walked through. Remembering that it was locked I ask, "Do you need a key to get into it?" Thomas pulls out a set of keys from his pocket. "Mom eventually got tired of me having to use her keys all of the time, so she got permission for me to carry a spare set. It has been totally awesome for snooping purposes." He muses for another second and then asks, "Are you two ready?" I nod, sheepishly, and Ted answers, "As ready as we will be. I hope this doesn't take too long, because I could sure use a nap." I can only assume he is joking. With what is before us, I am not sure how any of us are going to sleep for the next several days. It will take God himself to get us to sleep in this place.

Julia comes up and hugs me, and then she hugs her dad. The kids come up and hug us. Josh asks, "Can we say a quick prayer?" We all answer by bowing our heads. "Dear God," Josh starts, "please help Thomas, Dad, and Grandpa to be safe and to find the information they need to break down this place. Please help no one to catch them, and please help them to get back to this room quick. In Jesus name, Amen." I say, "Thanks Josh," as we raise our heads. I continue. "Prayer is what we need to get us through this. It will help strengthen our faith. I saw how you guys were pigging out at dinner, kids, and it reminded me of something I wanted to tell you. Even though we are staring death straight in the face, we shouldn't give up the things that have gotten us to this point. Until a few days ago, our lives have been an awesome blessing. These life-long blessings have come from God. There is no reason for us to change the good things that we have always done, like taking care of ourselves through eating good foods that God has made and keeping our bodies in good condition to better serve the Lord. Especially now, we need to be in tip-top shape to accomplish our goals." I am looking mostly at Dave as I say this, and he mutters, "Sorry." I respond, "Don't be sorry about it; eat whatever food you want while you're here. I'm not talking about the food; I'm talking about the motives behind the choices that you make over the next several days. We're going through a tough situation, and we need to make sure we eat and somehow sleep. But don't eat only junk foods because you think we are going to die and so you just don't care anymore. Don't make any decision here thinking that we are going to die and it won't matter whether or not you do the right thing. Make the same choices that you would make any other day, and have faith that the God who has blessed our entire lives will continue to bless us, even here and now. Have faith that he will deliver us by his mighty hand and we will live to tell a great story to the world about how Jesus rescued us from this place."

Everyone agrees and sees me, Ted, and Thomas out the door. As we start down the hall, Thomas, says, "I will show you where the mops and mop buckets are since you'll be helping me mop the kitchen tomorrow afternoon sometime. I think that will give us our reason to be in the room if anyone notices." We reach the fork in the road where we can either continue straight and into the kitchen supply room or go left down the other hallway toward the locked supply closet. No one is coming or going either way, so we turn left and continue down the hallway. Again I remember the absolute fear that I was feeling when we first entered the building. It seems like so very long ago, even though it couldn't be much more than twelve hours after the fact.

We stop at the door. Thomas tries the handle. The door is locked as before. He pulls out the keys, finds the correct one, and inserts it into the lock. With a turn of the key the handle turns and the door pops open. The door opens in, making it tricky for the three of us to maneuver once inside the small closet. There is a faint smell of the poison in the room, and a stronger smell of cleaning chemical. I scoot back into the room to allow Ted to enter the room far enough for Thomas to shut the door. He locks it from inside. On the floor under the shelves, behind where the door opens, I notice several more boxes resembling the poison-filled box in the kitchen. Ted takes a few more steps to the shelves at the back of the closet and picks up a box. "This looks familiar," he says, and he opens it. More food coloring! Ted has that knack for finding things. It's a good thing, too, because we were likely going to need more for the second batch of porridge tomorrow morning.

"Good job!" Thomas says. Then he says, "Excuse me, please." Ted moves over toward me a little more, and I move over to where the door would sit if it were open. Thomas moves some boxes out from under the shelves on the wall opposite of me, and then he lies down on the floor. He scoots under the shelf. I squat down to look at what he is doing. I see a large vent cover against the wall under the shelf. The grate cover stands higher than the shelf, which is not completely flush with the wall. Thomas is wiggling the vent cover and scooting it back toward the shelf. It pops out and hits the shelf. He gently slides it over to the left, exposing the opening. He momentarily scoots out from under the shelf, looks at me and Ted and says, "And now, the hard part." He tucks himself back under the shelf and crawls into the hole in the wall between the two rooms. Ted says, "That's odd that they put the cold air return on the floor and not up higher." It's actually the air conditioner vent," Thomas echoes from the hole. Ted says quietly, "We'd better not talk too much so that the sound doesn't carry."

Still down in my squat, I scoot closer to Thomas to see what he is doing. I have room to crawl under the shelf and look into the hole while avoiding the lower half of his body still sticking out of the hole in the wall. He is gently tapping the vent cover on the other side of the wall with his finger. After about twenty taps, the vent cover appears to become slightly loose. Thomas reaches up with his left hand, and the tips of his fingers disappear. He then gently jiggles the vent cover for about ten seconds until it releases. He grabs the side of the vent cover with his right hand and pushes it into the room. "That was easy," he half-whispers.

Thomas crawls through the hole and into the other room. He reaches back into the hole with his hand and motions for us to come through. Since I am halfway there, I come through next. Ted follows, grunting as he comes out the other side. As I stand up, I get a bad feeling. I should be getting used to the bad feelings by now. The room is fairly dark, but there are a few lamps on in the room emitting a yellow light. The décor is very wooden, very throwback to a previous era. The Leader has some rich tastes. Very antique-looking desks, tables, chairs and other furnishings decorate the room. In front of us, by a few feet, appears to be the Leader's desk. It is surprisingly small and fits well into the back corner. The room opens up to the left, but I have not yet walked into the room far enough to see around the corner. The desk is less than five feet wide and about three feet across. It has a few drawers on each side, and one in the middle. The top of the desk is very clean, with a single book sitting in the middle of the top of the desk. A black protective cover sits between the book and the wooden top of the desk. There is a stapler, tape dispenser, a fancy pen-holder, and various other things including an antique-looking lamp that is off.

Ahead of the desk, about ten more feet into the room, is a large conference table. It is far fancier than any conference room table I have seen in my experience in the business world. The wood is very shiny and has a rich finish. The yellow light from a nearby lamp illuminates the tabletop beautifully. Thomas walks slowly around the corner to the left, and I follow. Ted follows as well. I look back, wondering what Thomas did with the vent cover. It is propped up against the back wall to the right of the opening, near to the wall that juts out several feet and is blocking my view of the rest of the room.

As I go around the corner, I see the reason for the wall that juts out a few feet away from the vent. A door is open and I can see a very elegant bathroom. I can tell that the floor is a brilliant white tile, even though the light is off in the bathroom and yellow light shines in from the main room. The conference table end lines up with left edge of the bathroom door. And then I see it. As we are walking through the room with the bathroom on our left and the conference table on our right, I look directly ahead to the far wall. Above a very retro but fancy-looking beige couch hangs a painted picture. I know who it is; at least I think I do. It's the guy I saw on TV in my vision while we were making porridge, the one where I was freaking out Julia by yelling, "Antichrist!" He looks a little different in the painting, but paintings don't usually look exactly like the real person anyways.

73

I stop walking. Thomas stops, too. I ask Thomas, "So that's the Leader, right?" Thomas's eyes widen momentarily and he responds with a "Yes." Ted, from behind, asks, "How do *you* know?" I answer, "Lucky guess." Ted chuckles from behind, but my mind starts to drift away.

■■

I return to the first vision I had in the porridge room. The news woman is talking. This time, I can hear her. "The new Prime Minister of Israel officially took office today." She begins another sentence, but I am quickly ripped away to another memory or vision. Now I am sitting at a table in a large store. Books line the shelves all around me. I quickly realize I am in a bookstore. There is a large crowd of people in front of me forming a line, and several people beside me and behind me. Julia is standing next to me on my left, smiling. A man is talking to her from the other side of the table. I have not been paying attention to what he is saying. She chuckles, and the man looks back at me. I realize that I have a pen in my left hand, and I have a book in my right hand. I give him the book, and then he moves on. Things then seem to move at a strange speed; not like a fast forward, but more like a recorded TV show where you use the button on the remote to skip ahead thirty seconds at a time. People move through the line, and I am signing books. If this vision is truly a memory, then it looks like I am a writer. I remember being a manager in the chemical industry, though, and not a writer.

At one point we are all singing the chorus to the old church hymn, Victory in Jesus, which seems strange to do in a bookstore. There is a rather flamboyantly-dressed woman standing to the left side of the line about ten feet in front of the table where I am seated. She seems to be leading the singing. As I continue to skip ahead, we have stopped singing and the woman is loudly praising Jesus and appears to be prophesying, which seems weird since I am not sure how one goes about prophesying. A very large man to my left, behind Julia, asks me if the woman needs to be removed. I respond that she is fine to stay. The skipping ahead continues, but the line in front of me never seems to have an end. Whatever I wrote in this magical vision land must be pretty good.

Suddenly the brakes get put on the skipping ahead with the ring of a bell. There is constant crowd noise, but somehow I hear the bell that rings when the door opens to the bookstore. I had heard it earlier in the vision, but this time it is accompanied by a feeling of dread. I can feel the presence as it enters the room, the moment his foot hits the floor. I can't see the front door from where I am seated, but I just know the moment he steps inside. I had this happen once before to me, but that story is for another time. I look up at Julia, whose smile is quickly replaced by a worried look that probably matches mine. The flamboyant woman who was really, really happy a minute ago now starts shouting, "He's here, he's here!" She's not talking about Jesus anymore. From around one of the shelves full of books, toward the front of the bookstore, come three men. The man in the middle of the three is, of course, the guy in the painting, the guy on TV, the Leader.

He ignores the line, like it doesn't apply to him, and walks directly over to my table. Everyone in line immediately gets quiet, with a few people murmuring back and forth to each other. Even the loud woman gets quiet. He picks up a book from one of the stacks next to me, and says, "Nice to finally meet you Mr. Holson. Everyone is telling me I need to read your book." I don't answer. He sets the book in front of me, and I am glad to look away from him and look at the inside front cover of the book as I sign it. I close the book, and when I look up, instead of looking at him I choose to look at one of the men in his entourage. I feel Julia's hand on my shoulder. It is shaking. Or maybe it's me doing the shaking. The flamboyant woman blurts out, "Don't touch him! Don't touch him!" The large man who asked me about removing her earlier is next to her, prompting to her to leave along with another very large man. They cut through the line and lead her toward the door. The man, the Leader, extends his hand, expecting me to shake it. I look back at the woman as she is being led around the corner toward the front door.

She looks back at me. She doesn't say anything, but she squeezes her face, squints her eyes, and puckers her lips as if she just watched someone get really hurt. I heed her words and her look, and instead of shaking his hand I place the book into his hand. He smirks and walks away without saying thank you. His two cohorts each give me a smirk, eyes shielded by sunglasses, and then they turn and walk out as well. As soon as the door jingles again, the feeling of dread starts to subside.

Why did I feel so weak? What just happened? I start to stand up from the table, and then I am catapulted back to reality. I quickly look around and see Thomas to my left along with Ted. "Are you going to stare at that picture all night, or are you coming?" Thomas asks. I am glad to move on past the picture. Questions that are naturally coming to mind as I walk over toward them are, "What went on in my life that led up to being here?" and, "Are these visions really things that happened in my life?" They have to be; my mind couldn't have made up a near-match image of the Leader before I saw his caricature on the wall. The pieces are starting to come together, but as Thomas said before, it can take months to get your memory back after being injected with the drugs we likely got on the trip here.

I make it over to Thomas and Ted vision-free, thank goodness. They are standing next to a file cabinet with the top drawer open. Thomas is opening a manila folder that he has pulled out. Ted is holding another manila folder in his hand. "How long was I in vision land?" I wonder. The file cabinet is wedged in the back corner between the bathroom wall and the back wall of the room. The drawer opens away from the bathroom wall. The room extends several feet further back on this side of the bathroom than it does on the other side. It makes sense to me in my mind because of the supply closet on the other side. There are windows with shades on the wall to my right, the wall that extends past the brown couch with the Leader's picture hanging on it. Past the couch is the other wall to the room, which runs parallel to the conference room table. A closed wooden door with a very elegant-looking door knob stands in the wall about five feet away from the beige couch. It splits the difference between the edge of the conference room table and the edge of the brown couch. Now I have my bearings based on our earlier trip into the building. As I turn around and look at the wall in front of Ted and Thomas, I realize that the on other side of the wall is the beginning of the hallway from where we first came into the building. The door where we first reentered the building is just on the other side of the wall. The Stairway to Heaven has its start right outside the Leader's office.

By now Thomas has unfolded the large schematic that was in the folder. He quickly decides we need to take it somewhere where we can lay it flat and study it. He and I walk toward the conference table; Ted splits off toward the couch. I hesitate momentarily, looking at Ted over by the couch, and then at Thomas who is laying out the blueprints on the conference table. I look at Ted and say, "I'm not sitting under that picture." He shrugs, and we join Thomas at the conference table. Thomas says, "That's why I wanted you guys to come with me in here. I don't come in here at night with that picture hanging there. It's freaky enough during the day. I didn't notice it at first, but once I did it freaked me out every time from then on."

The schematic diagram of the smashing machine looks like what we saw outside. Beyond that, all of the symbols and gibberish written on it don't mean much to me. It's a good thing I majored in engineering. After a few minutes of silence, Ted moves around behind us from our left to our right. He bends down closer to the paper. There is a second drawing of the pusher arm shown separately from the rest of the contraption. It also shows the control box and has some notes regarding its design and construction. After many more minutes of quiet studying, Ted says, "These pistons on each side of the pusher arm are what control its movement back and forth. If we can find a way to bend one of them without breaking it and make the pusher arm go catawampus, it will either wreck the holding bay, the pusher arm, or both." Thomas says, "Those things are really powerful. We will need to be very careful tomorrow night when we are working on them." Ted

77

answers, "Yes, but we will most likely only need to work on one of them. We want the pusher arm to extend fully, but we want it to go off course and break when it tries to pull back.

"Wait," I say. "What about all of the people who will be inside during the first run? We can't let anyone die in that thing ever again." Thomas relieves my fears when he says, "The first run of the machine on a smashing day is a test run. It's standard protocol for Mike and Barry to complete their startup checklist prior to the first group going into the smasher. That's when we need it to break." Ted then says, "I won't know for sure how much we will need to loosen or adjust the piston until we get out there. Will we have access to any tools on the platform?" Thomas answers, "Yes, they keep a toolbox up there. We should be able to find whatever we need since the tools are what they use to adjust the machine." Ted responds with a, "Good."

We all study the diagram for several more minutes. I notice that the control panel has a test button and a run button. I am not sure what the difference would be between a test cycle and a run cycle in this case, but Tom and Barry probably know. I also notice the flip switch on the panel that tips the holding bay up and back down to drain the contents after smashing. I see where the standing area near the control panel is separate from where the contraption tips, which makes sense. What I am trying to come up with is a Plan B in case Plan A doesn't work. That leads me to realize that if Plan A doesn't work, we will need to be in the immediate vicinity to enact a Plan B. But how are we going to get back up there without being noticed? "Guys," I say, "We need to be prepared if our plan doesn't work. We need to have a Plan B. If the smasher arm doesn't break, I was thinking that we need to get Tom and Barry away from the machine so that we can take control and try to break it a second time." Ted says, "I wasn't planning on being anywhere near it when it breaks, but I guess you're right. We need to be hiding somewhere nearby in case our adjustments aren't enough."

We stay silent for a few moments looking at Thomas. "There really won't be anywhere to hide up there. But you're right, Matt, we need to be up there in case something goes wrong. Or in our case if something doesn't go wrong." Thomas pauses, and then continues. "The only way we are going to get up there is if we put the robes on and head up the stairs at the front of the first group. I will need to be behind you guys so that Tom and Barry don't recognize me." Thomas looks at Ted. "If something goes wrong, Matt and I will need to try to tackle both of those guys so that you can get to the control panel." Ted adds, "We will probably need more than one person to get the machine to break if it doesn't break the first time." Thomas says, "Josh, Nate, and Dave will be there to help." I hadn't thought of that. I would rather not take the rest of the group with us back up the stairway, but, sadly, when it all goes down on that fateful day we will probably want to be together as a group.

"So Plan B is to basically take out Tom and Barry long enough to completely break the machine," I say. "Then we need to run back down the stairs and get to the reservoir. The trick will be to keep Tom or Barry from catching one of us, and to keep them from sounding any kind of alarm. I'm starting to think we just need to take those guys out. I'd never dream of killing someone, but they've done more than their fair share." Thomas nods in agreement. I continue with a question. "Thomas, once the door to the holding bay is closed can it be opened from the inside?" Thomas answers, "No. One of the guys shuts the door once the bay is full and latches it shut." That's what I was hoping for. "Good," I say. "If we can push those two into the smasher and shut the door behind them, then they can't follow us back down the stairs or alert anyone that something is awry. Whether the smasher arm breaks with Plan A or Plan B, those guys need to end up locked inside the holding bay."

Thomas begins to fold up the blueprint. He stops and asks, "Are we done with this one?" Ted answers, "Sure." I nod affirmatively. Thomas finishes folding it up and returns it to the folder still resting on top of the drawer of the file cabinet. In the meantime, Ted opens the folder he's been holding, presumably for the reservoir system. He finds another blueprint, and unfolds it onto the table. Thomas returns and I ask him, "Do we need to worry about anyone coming in here? Does the cleaning crew come in periodically to dust or run the vacuum?" Thomas answers, "No, no one is allowed into the Leader's office unless he is here and unless he invites them in. Mom was called in once. That was a big deal for her since it was the first and only time she met the Leader in person. She said he sat in the dark so she could not see his face. It also sounded to her like his voice was somehow disguised." I think of another question. "Thomas, do you think there are any security cameras in here?" Thomas again calms my fears. "No, I proved that to myself before I first came in here. There is a camera right outside the entrance into his lair, but no cameras inside. I guess he doesn't want anyone to be able to see what goes on in here, whether he's here or not. That door over there goes to a hallway that leads to his living quarters, and the camera is right outside of the main door into that hallway. I have never been in that portion of the building because I don't have access. Even if one of these keys let me in, I wouldn't want to be caught over there.

Thomas continues. "Before I first busted loose the vent covers to come in here, I snuck into the security room and made sure there was no video feed from inside this room. I also freaked out the first time I was in the security room thinking that there would be a camera recording me in the security room, but thank goodness there wasn't. I know where all of the cameras are, so I know where to avoid when I don't want to be seen on camera." I ask, "Is there someone who reviews the monitors or the tapes?" Thomas answers, "There used to be a guy when we first got here. He left about eight months ago, and no one replaced him. I'm not sure where he went. For about two weeks after the guy left the five in-the-know guys tried to rotate shifts at night to watch the monitors. The rotation quickly ended. I had overheard Mike and Tim talking about how nothing ever happened on the monitors anyways, so there was no point in continuing with the rotation." Ted ruffles the papers on the table to get our attention. "We need to finish up and get back to the room before we get caught," he says. Thomas and I shift our focus to the reservoir diagram. This diagram looks even more complicated than the one for the smashing machine.

The diagram shows the circular reservoir and various stations around it. I can see where the pipes come in from the smashing machine, and where the pipes come out that presumably feed to the river. That part seems simple, but there are all kinds of other things that are not very clear to me. Another set of pipes, labeled water and chemical feed, goes into the reservoir. There are many other notations all over the bottom half of the document that I don't want to take the time to read and attempt to understand. I focus on the portion of the drawing that shows the exit piping and the associated valves and controls. I point to this part of the drawing and ask, "Could it be just as simple as opening up the control box and ripping out the wires?" Ted answers, "Maybe, but the question is which wire or wires control the valve we want to keep closed. There will probably be lots of wires to lots of different things in the control box. It would be easier to disconnect the wires from the valve, but they may not be accessible. If we can somehow get to the wires, then we still need to be careful that we don't get zapped."

There are several blowup drawings of each set of valves on the main blueprint. The one we are looking at is toward the top of the drawing, so I scoot the blueprint closer to us. "Not that I know too much about automated valves or anything," I say, "but there should be a manual override on the valve that we can use to keep it shut. Also, most valves are programmed so that if there is some kind of failure, they fail to the off position to keep the contents of the tank, or in this case the reservoir, from being discharged. If we can just get the valve to fail, it should stay off no matter what." Ted answers, "Yes, but there is likely some programming that controls when the valve opens and closes, based on all of the information written at the bottom of the blueprint. One of the components of the program is for the button that the Leader presses to open the valve from his viewing point. I can see which wire it is supposed to be from the drawing, but until I can physically see the whole thing I am not sure how we are going to identify it and disconnect

81

it. Even then, if we are being chased after busting up the smashing machine, we won't have much time, if any, to study the valves once we get there."

We all think for a minute. After that I say, "Then maybe it goes back to my theory of just ripping out wires." Ted responds, "But that might not do anything if we can't get to the right ones, and it might get one of us killed. Besides, the control box is likely locked shut, and Tom and Barry are likely the only ones with keys to it." I make a mental note that we need to find a large screwdriver or crowbar before the big day in case we need to force open the control box. Maybe we can find one in Tom and Barry's toolbox by the smashing machine.

Ted looks at the drawing for several more minutes, and then says, "I can't go any further until I physically see the valves. Is there any chance we can get down there tomorrow night after we mess with the smashing machine?" Thomas says, "They usually keep the grounds well lit at night; I doubt we could get down there and back without being seen. We would definitely be on camera if we walked across the yard at night. If we tried to sneak through the brush around the perimeter of the property, we would probably get bitten, attacked, or eaten by some nocturnal bug or snake that we couldn't see. The fence keeps most of the animals out, but the ones that fly or can climb trees sneak in from time to time. It's fun to watch the grounds crew try to catch a group of howler monkeys that get over the fence. They usually try to herd them back to the fence so that they get zapped when they try to climb over it. It's a noisy place when the howler monkeys get in."

Ted asks, "Do we really need to prevent the valve from opening? By this time the Leader is going to know something is wrong, and he probably won't make it to his perch to be able to push the button for a while. And does it really matter whether he pushes the button or not? The people are already dead, so it's not like we're doing them any favors." Thomas answers, "Other than further ruining his day, I guess it's not the end of the world if we don't disable the valve." I ask, "Where is the reservoir in relation to the opening in the fence that we will try to escape from?" Thomas responds, "They couldn't be farther from each other. The place where the fence is raised up from the ground, just enough for us to crawl under, is close to the main gate. The thing I'm worried about is that the front of the compound will be heavily guarded when the Leader is here. My thought is that since we will be running for our lives anyways, we could take our chances running through the brush from the reservoir to the hole in the fence to minimize the chances of being detected once we get in there. It will be easier to watch out for snakes and spiders during the day, and by then we probably won't care as much anyways. The hole in the fence is about ten feet into the heavy brush at the front of the property, so the rest of the area is wide open for us to be seen and to be shot. We could potentially skip the reservoir and just make a run for the edge of the property as soon as we get down the stairs from the smashing machine."

I remember the thick rope netting that encased the stairs when we were in there. I say, "I guess we will need to bring something to cut the netting around the stairs if we want to get out at the ground level." Thomas says, "Very good point, Matt. We won't want to go back into the building once we leave it for the last time. I really hope we don't get caught, or the Leader is going to make us pay dearly. I can't imagine what he will do to us." I respond with, "The worst he can do is kill us. Then we're in heaven with Jesus and we can forget about all of the nonsense that we just went through." I continue, "I still really want to be able to break the reservoir so that the Leader can't make his unholy sacrifice. I just want him stopped at everything he's trying to do here." I make the mistake of looking at his picture on the wall. He is staring right back at me with his evil eyes.

I quickly look away, and then Ted says, "Let's make it a game time decision. If our path takes us down by the reservoir, and we have a minute to try to wreck it, then we'll give it a try. If we're running for our lives and don't have time, then that will be our answer." We all agree, and Thomas begins to fold up the second drawing. Ted retrieves the manila folder from the conference table, and Thomas puts the folded blueprints back into the folder. Ted closes the folder and hands it to Thomas who puts it away. He can't walk fast enough back to us so that we can leave this creepy office.

We crawl back through the vent. Ted and then I crawl out from under the shelf and stand up. Thomas goes last, and he crawls through backwards. His feet are the first to come through the hole, and then his legs. I bend down to see what he is doing. He has the vent cover in his hands. He lines up the cover with the screw holes and gently pulls it back until his fingers are wedged between the wall and the vent cover. He then carefully slides his fingers back through the opening. He takes a deep breath, and then uses his fingertips to grab under the slanted grating on the vent cover. Then, for the next several minutes, he gently wiggles and pulls back on the vent cover to try to get it back to its original place. It takes long enough that my knees start to ache, so I change position. He stops momentarily, keeping his grip on the vent cover. The metal flexes and it makes a popping sound. He then continues his method of wiggling and pulling for another minute or so. He pauses, as if waiting for the metal to flex again. Nothing happens, so he gently removes his fingertips from the grating.

After pausing for a few more seconds, Thomas emerges from under the shelf, stands up and says, "I've had some practice doing that." Ted says, "Good job." Thomas then remembers that he needs to return this room's vent cover to its original position. After he completes that task, all we have left is to walk about fifty feet back to our room. Then we can worry about how to fall asleep.

Chapter 9 – The Youth Movement

Matthew 7:15 (NIV), "Watch out for false prophets. They come to you in sheep's clothing, but inwardly they are ferocious wolves."

Thomas goes over his plan to sneak back to our room. "I'll come out of the supply closet first, and then I will give you the all clear to follow. If someone is in the hallway and they see me before you come out, I'll shut you in the closet and come back for you in a little bit. If we make it out of the closet, but then someone comes up on us before we get back to the room, just leave the talking to me." Ted and I have no issues with the plan. Thomas pulls out his keys from his pocket. He opens the door and steps out into the hallway. No sound. He looks back into the closet and motions us out. Ted goes first, and then I emerge. I grab the door handle as I exit and pull the door shut behind me. Thomas puts the key into the lock and turns the key to lock the door. Then we walk. We make it to the end of the hallway, where it dead ends at the hallway that leads to the kitchen to the left and to our room to the right. As we start the turn to the right, I look left toward the supply closet that leads into the kitchen. I see a man with his back to us, walking toward the kitchen supply closet. I quickly look away, even though he can't see me, and we make the turn to the right. I look over at Thomas, and I can tell that he also saw the man. He lets out a quiet sigh. Hopefully the man keeps on walking and doesn't notice us. "Thomas!" the man says. We freeze, all three of us, in the same instant. Busted again.

"Hey buddy, how you doin'?" the man says. We all turn around. Thomas says, "Oh hi Jared. How's it goin'?" It's Jared, the youth Leader, I presume. "I'm doin' great. We just finished a cool fellowship evening and sent everyone back to their rooms for the night. I was going to run up to the kitchen for a quick midnight snack before I hit the hay." Jared pauses for a minute, looking me and Ted up one side and down the other. Then he looks back at Thomas and continues. "We need to get you back in the group, dude. It's so awesome. I've worked with the guys, finding out why they were giving you a hard time and working with them to change their attitudes. I think it will be cool now." Thomas cuts in and says, "Yeah, that would be great."

Jared changes topics. "Are these some of the new recruits you've been training?" Thomas nods affirmatively. Jared says, "Yeah, your mom was telling me all about them after the fellowship meeting. It looks like we lucked out with a really good crew this time." I mutter a quiet, "Thanks," and only then remember that Thomas said to let him do the talking. Jared moves closer to me and reaches out his hand to shake mine. "Hi, what's your name?" he says. I freeze. I can't for the life of me remember the pretend name that Thomas gave me when we were first discovered by Beth. Luckily, Thomas jumps in with my alias. "This is Tim," he says, "and this is his father, Mike." Jared answers, "Oh great, another Mike. Just what we need around here." He laughs as he further extends his hand into my personal space to get me to shake his hand. I look down and connect hands. BIG MISTAKE.

If I could imagine the embodiment of all hopelessness and despair, of a lack of all goodness and love, it immediately felt like it was flowing into my hand somehow from his hand. I look up. ANOTHER BIG MISTAKE. Jared evidently has the same crazy eye problem that Beth has. I'm starting to think that what is making their eyes look crazy is just a glimpse of the evil that resides in them. The handshake has confirmed that. After a few seconds, I am able to wrestle my hand away and to look away. Based on Jared's expression for the few seconds I saw it, it's like he knew what he was doing, and rather enjoyed making me uncomfortable by his death-like grip on my hand. Hopefully my likely expression of sheer terror that I returned to him didn't give him any clues that I am not who he thinks I am. Before Jared has a chance to give Ted the same greeting, Thomas, who is standing between me and Ted, steps forward as if to block Ted behind him somewhat. Thomas asks, "I hope they have some food left upstairs. I might grab a quick bite of whatever's left after I show these guys to their rooms after a long first day of training." Jared asks, "So you guys are just now finishing training?" Thomas responds, "Yeah, I was just showing them what we'll need to do in the morning after we finish in the kitchen. That way these guys can help me keep the rest of the group moving because it's going to be busy getting ready for the big visit."

Jared seems pleased. He also seems to change topics rather often. "From what you're saying already, it looks like we have a few good candidates for supervisor here. We need some better supervision as we continue to grow." Jared changes topics again. "You guys are so blessed to have the Leader coming to visit so soon after you arrived. You must feel really special to have been selected to serve here and to have the opportunity to be in the direct presence of the Leader. Most people won't get that privilege their whole lives. You'll be changed forever once you hear his official address that he gives over the PA system on the morning after his arrival. His voice transcends the walls when he speaks and they penetrate everyone's hearts. It's really, really special."

My hand is still tingling from Jared's grip. I try to gently shake it out without him noticing, but he quickly does so I stop. He looks at me and smiles, but I try to focus on his mouth instead of his eyes. "So you have kids?" he asks me. I start to open my mouth to answer him, but Thomas jumps in. "Yeah, Tim has three kids. Their names are TJ, Scott, and Billy. TJ stands for Tim Junior." I make the mistake of looking Jared in the eyes again, but this time it's different. His eyes light up at the idea of having three more kids to add to his group and show no signs of craziness. He says, "That's great. My son is a junior, too. Everyone but his mother calls him JJ. I held out and called him Jared for a long time, but JJ is easier." Then Jared says, "I can't wait to meet your kids. I don't know if Thomas told you, but I'm the youth Leader here. They will have a great time being part of the youth group, and I will teach them the principles and beliefs that we hold dear. I think it is so cool that you guys are representing three generations of members here. You *deserve* the chance to serve at one of the Mecca's of our faith here, even if it is new. Once the Leader blessed it, it became sacred ground."

At this point I am dead set against Jared meeting the kids, let alone having them spend time with him without me in the room. I can't have them exposed to whatever evil protrudes from him. It was too much for me to handle when I shook his hand. Then I think of something to say, and, for the sake of the kids, I muster enough courage to say, "Jared, I have always had a love for helping children learn our way. I try to be involved as much as I can with the three kids in their activities. Would it be OK for me to sit in on your next meeting so that I can start to get involved, too? Then I could meet some of the other kids that will be their new friends." Jared again seems pleased. He takes it hook, line, and sinker. "Tim, that is a great idea. I could always use more help, given that Beth, uh, Thomas's mom, is the only other adult who helps me with our activities. Thomas, this might be the perfect opportunity for you to make amends with the other guys by introducing Tim's kids to the group and asking for everyone's support to make them feel welcome. Everyone's already heard or noticed how you've really taken them under your wing and will understand why you want to try to make things work again."

Thomas thinks for a second, and then says, "Yeah, it's time. For these guys' sake I'll do it. Thanks Jared." Jared nearly squeaks with excitement and says, "Thank you, Thomas!" Just then a door opens behind us. We all turn around. Beth is standing in the doorway in her night clothes. She does not look happy. She doesn't say a word, but she doesn't have to. Her eyes still look crazy even though she is squinting in the somewhat bright hallway light. Thomas and Jared both look at the floor. Thomas mumbles, "Sorry mom." Jared mumbles while smiling, "Sorry, Mrs. Fields." Jared then whispers, "Nice to meet you both. We'll talk more tomorrow." He then turns and walks away, back toward the kitchen supply closet. Beth slowly closes her door and latches it quietly. I can then hear her turning the lock.

The three of us stand in the same spot until Jared disappears. Then all three of us breathe a big sigh of relief. The door to our room is only a few feet away, and we set out on the last part of our journey. We arrive without issue, and Thomas reaches down to open the door. It's locked. Thomas knocks very gently, as if his mom is still scowling at him from through her door. The door pops open slightly, and Mindy peers out. Once she sees us, she closes the door and removes the safety chain that was preventing the door from opening any more. She reopens the door and we can't squeeze in quickly enough. I half expect at least one of the kids to have fallen asleep, but everyone is still wide awake and very happy to see us. We all embrace as a group, with Thomas standing to the side. Mindy sees this and quickly grabs Thomas and pulls him into the group hug. The hug seems to last forever, and it helps me to forget the awfulness that I felt from shaking Jared's hand. What a good way to celebrate successfully reaching another milestone in our plan to destroy this place.

"Now what do we do?" Josh asks as the group hug finally ends. After a moment of silence, I chime in, "How about we get some sleep?" Nate asks, "What time is it, anyways?" Thomas pulls his phone out of his pocket and looks at the time. "It's just after midnight, he says." Ted interjects, "I've been ready for bed for a long time now." Thomas replies, "It's a good idea for us to turn in tonight. We need to get a good night's sleep, because tomorrow is going to be busy. We need to make the second batch of porridge in the morning, and then after lunch we need to get the kitchen cleaned up for the big day on Thursday. Mom likes to have everything ready the day before the Leader arrives, because he will inspect everything on his tour of the facility when he arrives Wednesday. He usually arrives by the early afternoon, and the tour is the first thing he does. It's a really weird situation, because he doesn't want anyone to see his face except for the select few included in the in-crowd. The place is basically on lock-down until he makes his rounds, and everyone needs to stay in their assigned rooms."

"Doesn't anyone think that is kind of strange?" Mindy asks. Thomas answers, "One of the kids asked Jared a question about it at one of the youth meetings, and he gave some BS answer that the leadership team has to go through some special consecration ritual to be able to see the

Leader's face without dying. That, combined with the years of training and preparation, are the only way they are able to survive such a 'divine' experience." Ted chuckles and says, "It sounds to me like a cover-up. He doesn't want anyone to see his face so that he doesn't get recognized." I couldn't agree more. I know I've seen that face before, the one in the painting in his office. My mind still can't make a direct connection, however, between that face and any decipherable memory. It's like the visions that I saw involving the Leader are just recollections from a dream long ago, and they aren't really connected with reality.

Thomas continues. "After his tour, he'll meet with the Leadership team for several hours. Then the weird stuff starts to happen." I don't like the sound of that, especially since any hope of being calm enough to fall asleep just went away. "What do you mean?" Julia asks. Thomas answers, "It's not bad as long as you aren't in the Leader's office. Everyone else stays locked in their rooms to do their own little worship thing, and you can hear some weird stuff as you walk by their rooms. Some people sing, some people scream at the top of their lungs, and some people speak gibberish to each other. After the PA address, the Leader and his crew start some ritual in his office. I for one did not want to stick around for it when I spied on them during his last visit. The good news is, since everyone was locked in their rooms, and since no one monitors the security cameras any more, I had free roam of the place until the lockdown was over around six PM. After the lock down ends the kitchen crew heads up to the upstairs kitchen to prepare a late supper for everyone else. The hungry masses come up around seven PM, and everything seems to get back to some sort of normal until the next morning. The only thing different about a Saints day when the Leader is here versus when he is not is that everyone follows protocol to a tee when he is here. Other than that, everyone just gets to work and business goes on as usual."

Thomas looks around at everyone and evidently sees the looks of concern brought on by thinking about what is to come. He pauses momentarily and then says, "But we will worry about all that tomorrow.

Now we all need to get some shut-eye. I'll be back for the seven AM wake-up call." Ted grimaces, and then says, "The what?" He wasn't really asking a question. Thomas replies, "I'll actually knock on your door around six fifty-five so that the music doesn't startle you at seven." Mindy asks, "What music?" Thomas answers, "Oh, they pump some annoying song through the PA system that's supposed to lift everyone's spirits first thing in the morning. Most people set their alarms for around six thirty to avoid being jolted out of bed." Dave says, "Thanks for the warning." Dave likes his sleep, and doesn't like anyone or anything to wake him up before he is ready.

Thomas turns to begin walking toward the door, but then stops. He says, "Wait, Matt, your phone." I say, "Oh, yeah, thanks for remembering," and hand him my phone. Thomas takes my phone, puts it in his pocket, and says, "I'll get this thing charged so we can try it out in the morning."

Thomas gives us a "good night" and heads for the door. Mindy puts her hand on his shoulder and stops him from continuing. "Thank you," she says, and gives him one more hug. "Thank you for being here," Thomas says. After the hug he opens the door, steps into the hallway, and quietly closes the door behind him. The rest of us are left standing in a strange room, thousands of miles from home. Josh asks again, "Now what do we do?" I answer with one word and say, "Bed."

Everyone shuffles around the room, trying to figure out how to get ready for bed without any supplies. Josh heads to the bathroom on the left, and within a minute yells back, "Found toothbrushes!" A few seconds later he yells, "Found toothpaste!" Mindy and Julia find the same in the other bathroom. We all take turns in the bathroom getting ready for bed. Even though I can smell a hint of the poison smell coming from my clothes, my body suddenly feels too exhausted to change or to shower. I come out of the bathroom and find that just about everyone else has already claimed a bed. I see an open one against the wall underneath the windows. The blinds are already shut, so I don't have to worry about dealing with that. I first sit on the bed,

91

remove my shoes, and then lay back. That feels really good. "Dad," Dave calls out. I open my eyes and sit back up. "What?" I answer. "Shouldn't we say a prayer or something?" Josh says. I answer, "Good idea." After a few seconds of silence, I realize that everyone is looking at me to say the prayer. I take a deep breath in, and then I sigh. One by one, everyone else lies down in their beds. I start the prayer. "Lord God, thank you," I begin. "Thank you for sparing our lives today. Thank you for watching over us and giving us Thomas to help us pose as camp workers. Thank you for giving us the hope that is in your Son. Thank you for already giving us the victory that comes through Jesus." I pause again, praying internally for the right words. "Please give us your peace that passes all understanding, and keep our hearts and minds in you. Please grant us amazing peace so that we can sleep through the night. Thank you, and we love you. In Jesus name we pray, amen."

At that moment I lay back, close my eyes, and then I realize that no one turned off the lights. I again sit up, only to see Ted heading toward the light switch by the door to the room. He turns off the light, and the room gets very dark. I lay back down, close my eyes once more, and I start to think about whether my prayer will work for everyone else. As tired as I feel, it's working well for me.

CHAPTER 10 – THE CRY FOR HELP

Psalm 20:1 (NIV), "May the Lord answer you when you are in distress; may the name of the God of Jacob protect you."

I wake up. Something is wrong. As I come to my senses, I lift up my head and look down at my body. Everything appears to be in order as I study my limbs in the very dimly lit room, but I am lying on a twin-sized bed in a room with many other twin beds. As I look around the room, I can see other people asleep in beds in front of me. After a few seconds of studying, I realize that it's Josh, Nate, Dave, and Julia in the beds in front of me going left to right. The beds directly to my left and right are vacant. I see two others (Ted and Mindy) in beds in a row past the one in front of me, and then I remember where I am.

That was a strange sensation. It felt much the same as my experience yesterday when I woke up in the room full of bodies on the hard concrete floor. What a feeling to wake up and not know where in the world you are and not know how in the world you got there. At least this time I woke up on a soft bed. Then, suddenly, I hear a gentle knock on the door. I sit motionless for a few seconds, and then I remember Thomas and his planned six fifty-five AM wakeup call. I sit up on the bed, and I put on my shoes. I then stand up and walk over to the door. I look at the chain, but it is not latched. I turn the lock on the door and open it. Thomas is standing outside. He quietly whispers, "I'll be back in fifteen minutes. We'll get some breakfast." I whisper, "OK," and Thomas quickly walks away.

I quietly shut the door, intending not to wake anyone else in the room. As I turn, I remember the music that will soon be playing over the PA system. As I look in the bed directly in front of me, I see Ted beginning to stir. He looks up at me, eyes barely open, and gives me a quizzical look. I let him absorb his surroundings for a few more seconds, and then his confused look adjusts to a weak smile. He lays his head back onto his pillow as he closes his eyes. I bypass Mindy, deferring responsibility to Ted, and make my way to Julia's bed. I sit down on her bed where she is resting peacefully on her right side. I lay my hand on her shoulder, as her back is facing me. She wakes with a start, which was not my intention. She turns her body around to face me, and gives me the same quizzical look as her Dad. "It's morning," I say quietly, as if I'm saying something that isn't completely obvious. Julia doesn't appreciate being woken up, and lays back down in the bed with her back facing me. At least she's awake enough. I move over to Dave's bed, and gently shake him until I get some movement. I do the same for Nate and then for Josh. Josh pops up the quickest, and then takes his minute to regain his memories of yesterday's events.

I walk over to the windows and look for the cord to open the hanging slat blinds that are blocking the majority of the light from coming into the room. I see that there are three sets of blinds that cover the three large windows that run the length of the room, starting at the bathroom wall on the right side and ending at the bathroom wall on the left. I open the first set, the one in the middle. I can tell that the sun is coming up to my right. One of the kids lets out a groan at the increased amount of light coming into the room. As I move to my right to open the next set of blinds, I see Ted get up out of the bed and head over to Mindy. He must have remembered that the music will be starting any second. I open the next set of blinds, allowing much more light into the room. With that, Julia pops up out of her bed, as if reality suddenly hits her. She moves to Dave's bed, and I see Josh walking over to Nate's bed to make sure he is awake enough to not be startled by the music. I make it around the beds to get to the cord that opens the left-most set of blinds. I open them, and the room is now sufficiently filled with the warm glow of the sun. And then the music starts.

The song starts quieter than I expected. It is a peppy jazz tune that sounds like it was composed in the 1920's. Everyone looks at each other with quizzical expressions. As the song plays, the volume slowly increases. I let everyone know that Thomas will be back in about ten minutes to take us up to breakfast. Josh asks, "Do I have time to take a shower?" Ted answers, "We're going to be making more porridge right after breakfast, so I would wait until after that." Josh thinks for a second and then answers, "Right."

Everyone takes turns using the restrooms and freshening up for breakfast. We are already in our camp uniforms, so we are sufficiently dressed for breakfast. Before everyone is done, Thomas returns. Julia opens the door and lets him in. He shakes Josh's hand, as Josh was one of the first ones out of the bathroom. "Are you ready to bust out some porridge?" Thomas asks. Josh says, "Not really, but some breakfast might motivate me. I'm really hungry." Thomas responds, "Me too!" My stomach agrees with both of them.

After another five minutes everyone is ready to go to breakfast. Things seem different as we walk into the hallway with the bright morning sun shining out of our room and onto the hallway floor. This place is a lot less scary during the day, and when that day does not involve running for your life. I can already detect a very pleasant smell of breakfast food, even though we are a significant distance from the upstairs kitchen. As we make our way through the downstairs kitchen and into the porridge room, the good breakfast smell is temporarily reduced by a faint poison smell. Once we get through the porridge room the fullness of the good smell returns. I try not to think about what lies ahead of us over the next several days. I want to enjoy this good moment and the rest of breakfast with the family. I momentarily think that it could be one of the last few meals we have together, but I quickly put that thought out of my mind. I instead remind myself that each new day I need to renew my commitment to the Lord, which will in turn renew my strength and my faith. He will deliver us no matter what, and if this is one of the last breakfasts that we will have on earth, then the Lord will invite us to the best breakfast we have ever had once we get to Heaven.

We get to the top of the stairs. There is actually a line of people this time that extends into the eating area. Thomas, who is leading the convoy, turns and says, "Breakfast is the busiest meal. Most everyone

95

makes a mad rush on the place at 7 AM when it opens. The food is really good at breakfast, and it is the best when it's hot and fresh." We get in line. A few people are talking quietly in the line, but most of the ones who have not made it to the point of filling their trays with food are looking at us as we take our place at the back of the line. Thomas shakes the hand of a man who is directly in front of us in line. He has two teenagers with him – a boy and a girl. The man doesn't say anything to Thomas, and Thomas responds with equal quiet. The kids do not look at Thomas or at us. A few people in the line continue to stare at us, but most of them have returned their focus forward toward the food ahead of them.

Within a few minutes, we are within reach of the food. I look behind us, and the line has extended almost to the top of the stairs. After another minute, as we start picking up our trays, the line is at the top of the stairs. We move through the line fairly quickly. My intention, which is likely the same as the rest of the group, is to draw the least amount of attention to myself as possible by moving quickly, yet calmly, through the line. And then I see it. Crispy bacon. If I'm going to eat bacon, it has to be extra crispy. Not burnt, but crispy. If I am allowed to like one thing about this place, then I want it to be the bacon. I pile a healthy amount onto my plate, leaving enough room for the eggs I see up ahead. I see some seasoned potatoes as well, which round out my plate nicely. I then head for the drink station and fill a glass with orange juice. It does not look like my typical breakfast, but I want to enjoy this one with the family.

The group makes it through the line, Thomas first, and we all follow his lead and sit at the same table as yesterday. Before I begin to eat, I say a prayer in my mind, eyes open, thanking God for this food and this time together. I look around at each person in our family, and at Thomas, and I ask for God's blessing to be upon them and upon me. And then within ten minutes my plate is empty. Everyone else finishes near the same time as me. I am sitting with my back facing the line, so I turn to look to see if the line has been reduced since we sat down. No chance;

the line is still at least to the top of the stairs, if not further. Thomas breaks the silence, but quietly. He says, "Given that everyone on our side of the building goes through the porridge room for breakfast, we won't be able to get in there until about eight thirty. Once we start, though, we probably won't see a soul until we finish." Ted says, "So I guess we have a little time then." Thomas answers, "Yes, time for seconds, once the line dies down."

We wait about fifteen minutes to see the line start to retract from the stairs. Not long after that some of the people done with breakfast walk back down the now open stairs. After a few more minutes, the line is short enough that several people get in line for seconds. We quickly follow suit. As I get closer to the bacon tray, I see a fresh batch of deliciously crispy bacon dumped on top of the few remaining pieces. I reflect on how blessed I am to have a second plateful of fresh, crispy bacon. We get through the line and return to our seats. This time two older women are sitting at the other end of our table. I nod and smile to them, and they return the pleasantries. We sit quietly and eat our second plates. The women are quietly talking in a different language. They converse the entire time we eat. Thomas finishes first, and then the kids. Thomas quietly strikes up an innocent-sounding conversation with the kids about baseball. He wonders about how things are going, and which teams are doing well. The kids have trouble remembering what was going on in baseball before we came here, so they try to piece together the last things they remember about the Reds (their favorite team) and how some of the other teams were doing. They do a good job not letting on why they can't remember recent events, for the sake of the women within earshot, but it is strange even for me that I can't place some of the baseball names that Thomas brings up. He is a big Detroit Tigers fan, which is understandable since he is from Michigan. I recognize several of the names he brings up, but while several more sound familiar, I can't quite connect the dots. I again reflect on the absolutely absurd situation we are in, and stop short of thinking how we are ever going to get out of it.

The kids discuss several various topics while we wait for the people in the cafeteria to clear out through the porridge room. Playing sports, video games, fishing and traipsing around through the woods are topics of conversation. Thomas was evidently an avid hunter before his dad died. He tells some good stories about his hunting adventures, and before I know it, the cafeteria is almost empty. The two women next to us are among the last ones out. A few minutes after they leave, we are the last ones left other than the kitchen workers. Thomas finishes his last deer hunting story, looks around at everyone, and asks, "Is everyone ready?" Ted lets out a quiet groan. I'm not looking forward to repeating the work of last night, but the sooner we get to it the sooner we will finish.

Everyone stands up, and we clean up our mess on the table. We take our dishes and trash and place them in the appropriate receptacles. A kitchen worker is preparing to wheel the cart with the dirty dishes back into the kitchen area. She smiles and says, "Good morning," to each of us as we place our dirty dishes in the top bin of the full cart. We return the pleasantries and each make our way toward the stairs. We start down the stairs as a group, walking very deliberately and slowly. I am certain that no one is looking forward to the task ahead, especially since each thing that we start or complete brings us closer to Thursday morning.

We walk into the porridge room, and everything is exactly as we left it. I take a deep breath. We have a lot of work ahead of us. Thomas reminds us of the first step. "Everyone get your supplies ready," he says. "Do we need to wear gloves this time?" I ask, thinking that we can get away with it since we will not be handling the poison. Thomas answers, "Please do, just in case we get visitors." Mindy and Julia go into the kitchen to find more gloves and sleeves. The spatulas from last night, while rinsed, are sitting on the counter near the doorway to the kitchen. Mindy and Julia decide to find clean spatulas in the kitchen as well as the gloves and sleeves. The wall that was full of stacks of empty pails when we started yesterday now contains only a few partial stacks of empties. Josh notices the lack of empty pails and asks, "Do we get the empty pails from the kitchen, too?" Thomas answers, "They actually come from the upstairs kitchen. If you want to come with me, we can bring down a few more stacks. Nate, and Dave, if you could start bringing in the full pails of slurry and stack them on the counter like yesterday, Josh and I will come help you once we get the empty pails."

I remember our food coloring procedures from yesterday. I do a quick inventory of the three food coloring vials that Ted had hidden in the drawer nearest to the exit. Each one is almost empty. Thomas and Josh are walking past me to leave the room. "Thomas," I ask, "do we need to get into the other supply closet to get more?" as I show him the vials. From behind me Ted answers, "Not necessary, at least to start." I turn around and he pulls a small box full of food coloring vials from his pocket. Thomas smiles and heads out of the room with Josh. "How did you get that?" I ask. Ted walks up next to me and half-whispers, "I shoved two boxes in my pocket when we were in the other closet last night." That was pretty sneaky of him since I didn't notice. Then Ted says, "I'm impressed that I didn't roll over on them last night during the night and bust one open in my sleep." I retort, "You didn't take them out of your pocket when you went to bed?" Ted answers, "I forgot, I guess."

Thomas pops back into the room. "I almost forgot something," he says as he looks at me. He pulls something out of his pocket. It is my phone. He hands it to me and says, "I guess Ted and his food coloring reminded me I had something in my pocket, too." He rushes back out of the room, presumably to catch up with Josh on the stairs up to the other kitchen. I look at Ted. "Let's fire it up," I say. He gives me a quizzical look, as if I think I am going to be able to call the police or something. I press the "On" button, only to see that it is already on. The battery gauge reports back a full charge. I enter my password to access the phone. It opens to the main screen, and then Ted says, "Maybe we should move into the supply closet in case anyone unauthorized comes down the stairs." I agree, even though someone unauthorized could just as easily walk into the supply closet. We move into the closet, and Ted says, "Oh yeah, we need aprons." He walks over and grabs some aprons off of the hooks where they are hanging. After he pulls down eight aprons, he heads over to the exit into the hallway. He stands guard as I watch the signal bars. No signal. The phone doesn't seem like it is going to help me.

I take a chance and go into the settings. I open the wireless network option, remembering what Thomas said yesterday about no network connections allowed to the outside world. I ask the phone to check for available networks anyways. The phone churns for at least thirty seconds, but it seems like an eternity. I'm about to give up when I look up and see Mindy and Julia walking into the room. "What are you doing?" Julia asks me. Before I can answer, she is already next to me looking at my phone. "It's not going to work," she says. Ted walks over to where Julia, Mindy, and I are standing. Just then, Nate and Dave come into the room with the same question. No one answers, because Julia, Mindy, Ted and I see a potential network connection pop up onto the screen. "No way!" Julia scream-whispers. "But we need to be able to get the security code," Ted says quietly. Josh and Thomas then walk into the room, presumably back from carrying a load of empty pails. "What's going on?" Thomas asks. Julia and Mindy allow him to move right next to me. "No way!" he says, just like Julia did a second ago. Even though I have no experience hacking into networks, I select the network. Then an amazing thing happens. It connects without a password. "Unbelievable," Ted says. I exit out of the "Settings" menu option and then go back to the main screen. Sure enough, I have a full connection to the network. I also notice that the signal bars go from zero to half strength. "Text Grandpa Holson!" Nate says. "Why him?" Dave asks. Even though I have no idea how Dad can help in this type of situation, I open up my contacts list. I find the Holson's contact name, which is for the home number at my parent's house, and for my Dad's cell phone. I choose his cell number, and select message. The text screen comes up. I type the following message:

"Dad. We have been abducted and taken to some death camp near South America. Contact the authorities and have them trace this GPS signal. Send lots of help fast."

I take a deep breath, say a momentary prayer asking for God's help, and hit the send button. The sending bar pops up at the top of the screen. It gets about a quarter of the way, and then stops. We all stare at the screen of the phone, hoping, praying that the send button will move again. After what seems like an eternity, the bar moves slightly. Our attention shifts toward the exit into the hallway. Voices are coming from down the hallway. Ted moves toward the exit, aprons still in hand. I look back at the phone, and the bar is now at halfway. "Come on," I say, becoming impatient with the phone. "Thomas!" someone calls from the other room. It sounds like Beth. Thomas quickly walks back into the porridge room to greet her. The bar moves again, but very slowly. Ted walks back to us, and starts handing everyone aprons. He saves me until last. He hands me the apron and says, "It looks like they're coming this way." I try to slide my apron on while still watching the phone. I turn and look to my left out of the exit, and I see two men coming into view. They look at us momentarily, and then they turn the other way and open a door against the wall across the hallway. The men go in, and they shut the door behind them. Ted motions to Nate, Dave, and Josh, and leads them out of the room. The sending bar is past three quarters of the way to the end, but it is stuck again. Julia and Mindy leave with the gloves, sleeves, and spatulas. The sending bar jumps to the end of its line, but it doesn't disappear from the screen. I won't feel comfortable until the message moves to the sent status. But that won't happen, because I notice that the wireless connection goes away, along with the bars of service. In an instant, my hopes are dashed.

"Tim!" Thomas calls from the porridge room. I shove my phone into my pocket and hurry back. Beth is standing in the middle of the group. I join the group, remembering to stare at her mouth instead of her eyes. "Everyone," Beth starts, "I have an announcement to make. Our esteemed Leader will arrive tomorrow for his sacred visit. This will be your first time in his direct presence, so you will need to prepare yourselves for this special time both today and tomorrow. Thank you for putting in the time and effort to be selected to serve at our facility. You deserve it. Thomas will take you through the preparation activities for the rest of today, and then I will need everyone's help with some additional preparation tasks in the morning. Once the Leader arrives tomorrow, we will return to our rooms for some quiet preparation and meditation time. We have a very important job ahead of us on Thursday to get the chosen Saints purified to be worthy of Heaven. I wish you the best during the next few days." As soon as she finishes, Beth leaves the room. I pull out my phone just to see if somehow the message went to the sent status. My text never advances to "Sent" status, so I angrily close the text messaging screen and lock my phone before returning it to my pocket. It was a long shot anyways. I guess it's time to make some more porridge.

■■

We get right to work making porridge. Ted starts at the food coloring station, and I start at the first chamber. Nate and Josh are bringing in the slurry pails, and Thomas and Dave are stationed at the third chamber. Julia and Mindy take their place at the second chamber, on the front side of the machine. I open the lid on the first slurry pail, while Ted asks Mindy for an empty pail to make his water and food coloring mixture. Once I pry off the lid to the slurry pail, I open the first chamber of the machine. I pour the slurry into the chamber, and off we go.

Now that I have my phone, I am able to check the time periodically. I change gloves each time I look at my phone, mostly to give my hands some air. Things seem tougher today. The pails feel heavier, the machine seems to cycle longer, and everyone seems to move a little slower. My muscles are aching, as I'm sure is the case for everyone else. We aren't talking nearly as much as last night. Everyone is focused on getting the job done.

After three long, sweaty hours of hard work we are almost finished. I'm not sure if our pace is slower or faster than yesterday, but I thought it would take longer to get to this point. I am currently shuttling porridge pails from the room to the refrigerators with Dave. It is impressive to see our progress when I look around and see all of the refrigerators almost full of porridge pails. The kids brought the last slurry pail into the room about two hours ago; they were on a mission today.

"Dad, are we going to get out of this alive?" Dave asks as we make our way from the refrigerator back to the porridge room. I stop. I look around to make sure no one is in the kitchen, although I already know there isn't anyone nearby, and then I quietly respond. "Dave," I start, "I want so bad to give you a good answer, but I can't. I don't know what's going to happen. But I do know that we can't stand around and let a whole bunch of innocent people die in a few days. We may die trying to save them, but it's like I said before. If we don't make it out of here alive, we'll be in heaven with Jesus just like that. No matter how bad things get over the next few days, we have forever with the Lord to make everything better again."

I can tell Dave is choking back tears. "I don't want to die," he half-whispers. I start to tear up as well. "I don't exactly want to die, either," I say. I continue, "But if I have to, I want to die doing what God wants me to do. And I feel that the right thing for me to do is to try to stop the evil things going on here." Dave changes expression, and almost smiles, a tear streaming down his left cheek. "I want to do the right thing, too," he says.

"Good," I answer, "and you better believe that our God will be fighting with us and for us. And remember: if our God is for us, who can be against us?" Then Dave says, "We will make it. We will win. We will stop them!" I motion for him to keep his voice down, and then we start walking the rest of the way back to the porridge room. We get back into the room, and I take stock of how many slurry pails are left on the counter to go into the machine. I count twelve pails left. We are almost done.

Within an hour, we finish processing the last twelve slurry pails. I remain on porridge pail transport duty through the end. My aching muscles are telling me I'm getting too old for this. During the last trip to the refrigerator, I attempt to determine how old I actually am. How sad it is that I can't zero in on my age. I can't wait until the effects of the drugs wear off. I hope that someday soon they do. Maybe I, we, have a better chance of regaining our memories sooner since we were spared the second round of injections when we got here.

I return yet again to the porridge room. Next, we have to get the room cleaned up. I ask Thomas, "Do we need to wash out the machine?" Thomas, who is rinsing out one of the leftover buckets next to the floor drain, answers, "Yes, we will give it a pretty good rinse. Each chamber will need rinsed out separately, and then we'll heat a few batches of water in the first chamber and run them through the rest of the machine. I usually turn the temperature up to about 180 degrees to get the water good and hot." That reminds me of my experiences working in hair care product manufacturing plants with "Clean in Place" washout procedures for the filling machines. To avoid having to complete chemical sanitizations of the piping and the machines, the water had to reach 180 degrees for at least ten minutes.

Thomas continues. "Once we get the machine in pretty good shape, it will still get washed out prior to the next batch per the procedure. I recall the man we saw washing out the machine yesterday, and then I say, "I hope the machine never runs again." Thomas answers, "Me too. For as much sweat as I've poured out spending countless hours of my life working with this machine, I want nothing less than to take an axe to it and destroy it. I would, since hopefully this is the last time the machine ever runs, but it would kind of raise suspicion at some point if the machine was all smashed up."

I think for a few seconds. I then ask, "Is there a way we can sabotage the machine in a way that's not noticeable? My only worry would be if your mom has a post-operation checklist that would cause the issue to be detected." Thomas quickly answers, "No, Mom doesn't do any checks until the day the machine is going to operate. Let's get the machine washed out, and then I'll try out my idea." I ask, "What's that?" I then realize that Ted is standing right behind me. Thomas looks at us, and then says, "If I can mess with the pressure control switch on the second chamber, I think I can make it look like the machine is at a lower pressure than it actually is. If someone starts the timer on the second chamber, hopefully I can set it high enough that the chamber will come apart at one of the welds. It happened once before when the pressure switch malfunctioned, and the machine was down until Tom and Barry could fabricate a new chamber. That was a big deal about three Leader visits ago. As Tom was installing the new chamber, he explained to me what went wrong with the pressure control switch. I think I can make it happen again."

Ted pulls his hand out of his pocket and says, "That sounds complicated." He opens his hand and I look at what it is holding. Two food coloring vials, each one almost empty. He then reaches back into his pocket and pulls out a third vial, which is completely empty. "I think this was the last of them, so I'm glad we're done," he says. Thomas smiles, and then the three of us get to work washing out the machine.

The rest of the crew focuses on cleaning up the porridge room while we sanitize the machine. Within a half hour, the work is done. We all stand as a group in the middle of the room. Thomas asks me what time it is. I look at my phone. I watch it turn to one PM. "It's one o'clock," I say. "Wow," he says, "that should have taken longer. Lunch gets delayed until about two PM on porridge days to give us time to finish, but I can let the kitchen know that they can open sooner than normal. I'm not sure how that happened, since the processing time on the machine usually dictates how soon the process finishes. Usually people are braving the poison smell and starting to walk through before we have finished cleaning up the room. "Maybe the second batch of slurry ran short." It's at this point I realize that we never set out the bowls of poison this time. I also remember that I need to hide some more poison packets to make it look like we used them. Nate says, "Maybe it was divine intervention that let us finish faster." Ted suggests, "Maybe we're more efficient than any other group and we got close to the theoretical time it should take to complete the operation with no lost time due to human causes."

Thomas says, "Everyone stand around me while I mess with this pressure switch." I then say, "While everyone else does that, let me stash some more poison packets in the closet to make it look like we used some more." Thomas answers, "Good idea, Matt." I pull out the box of poison packets while Thomas starts meddling with the machine. Everyone is looking intently at him while he goes about his work. I walk out of the room and enter the supply closet. It takes me more time today to find a suitable empty box, but I eventually find one that will work. I pull out my phone, just to check one more time to see if the message was ever sent. The message is still hanging on in the sending mode, and I notice my phone battery is getting low already. It must be due to the phone trying to send the message over the last four hours.

I turn off my phone and return it to my pocket. I return to the porridge room, and I fill my empty box with poison packets after putting on what seems like the one-thousandth pair of latex gloves. Thomas is still working on the machine. I return to the supply closet, and I close the flaps to the box. I move some of the larger boxes that Ted and I placed in front of yesterday's box of poison packets. I place this box on top of the other one, and then I return the larger boxes in front of them to hide them. When I get back to the porridge room, it looks like Thomas is finished. I look at him and ask, "All finished?" He nods affirmatively. Ted asks, "Do you think it will work?" To that Thomas answers, "I hope we never find out." Everyone agrees with that answer. Thomas, with a wave of his arm, leads us out of the room toward stairs to the main kitchen. I realize that I still have on the last pair of those annoying latex gloves, and I angrily remove them and toss them into a small trash can near the door. And with that we have officially reached the first milestone of our master plan, regardless of how shaky the plan may seem.

CHAPTER 11 – NO FEAR

"Courage is not the absence of fear, but it is acting in spite of it." – Mark Twain

Thomas asks us to wait in the eating area while he goes into the kitchen to let his mom know that we finished ahead of schedule. I'm somewhat worried that her suspicion will be raised because of our early finish. Thomas is in the kitchen for several minutes. We can see him talking to his mom through an opening in the kitchen wall where the cooks slide the trays of food onto a counter for the workers to transport to the serving line with the heat lamps. Several other kitchen workers are standing around them, but we can't hear what anyone is saying. I notice that one of the kitchen workers is the red-haired girl that we have had several run-ins with since our arrival. Katie, I think, is her name. Now I understand why Thomas asked us to remain outside the kitchen.

After several more minutes of conversing, Thomas is dismissed from the kitchen and returns to us. By this time Ted, Nate, and Josh have sat down at one of the tables. When Thomas has nearly reached us, he gives us a secret thumbs up that can't be seen by anyone but us. Thomas says, "Well, I have good news, bad news, and then more good news." I answer with a nervous, "So what's the bad news?" Thomas replies, "OK Mr. Negative, the bad news is that the food isn't ready, so the kitchen probably won't open much earlier than normal." He then pauses until someone asks him what the good news is. Mindy bites and asks, "So...what's the good news?" Thomas answers, "The first good news is that everyone is really impressed with you guys and how well you work. As a result of your hard work, you will get to be the first ones in line for lunch today once it's ready." Dave then asks, "And when will that be?" Thomas responds, "That's the other good news. Mom says the first food should be ready in about ten minutes or so. That should give us time to freshen up in the restrooms and then the food is all ours until two-o'clock." The kids all give a quiet fist-pump, and off we go to the nearby restrooms to get cleaned up for lunch.

In the restroom, I decide I want to wash my face. Just touching the air that also touches the poison packets makes my skin feel grimy. I'm sure it is a mental thing, but I want to wash my face anyways. As I rinse my face at the sink, I look at myself in the mirror. I think to myself, "Boy, I look really old. I don't remember being anywhere near this old." What a strange feeling. I am not sure how old I am, or how old I should be, or even how old I think I am. One thing is for sure, however, that I shouldn't be this old. One of the kids, Nate, emerges from one of the stalls behind me. This distracts me from pondering my age while staring at myself in the mirror. I walk over and crank the paper towel dispenser until I get a large enough paper towel to dry my face. Josh emerges from another stall and washes his hands at a sink next to Nate, who is using the sink I was using. Ted is just now entering the restroom, and as he walks by Nate turns off the sink and walks toward me.

"We're doing great, right Dad?" he asks. "Yes, we really are," I answer. Nate then says, "I'm really proud of us for holding it together after everything we've been through." I immediately worry that someone not in our group could be in the restroom listening, even though I am pretty certain that we are the only ones in the room. I put my index finger to my lips, and then I quietly answer, "I am, too, buddy." Nate smiles and we walk out of the restroom together. Josh exits right behind us.

We come out of the restroom and Dave is standing next to Thomas. The two hungriest guys are chomping at the bit, ready to go. Soon thereafter the first kitchen worker emerges from the swinging doors with the first tray of food. Several other workers follow with their own trays of food. We give them time to get set up. Several more trays are set on the counter that spans the opening in the wall between the kitchen and the eating area. The workers retrieve them and set them in their places. Julia and Mindy emerge from the Ladies' Room, and Ted arrives a minute later.

Beth sticks her head out of one of the swinging doors, looks at us, and gives us an affirmative nod to get in line. She then returns to the kitchen. The food smells so good, and I can't wait to fill up my plate. Today's main course, at least the one that is ready now, is roast beef. Next to the tray of roast beef that is simmering in its own juices under the heat lamp, is a tray of steamed broccoli. It looks like chopped onions are mixed in the broccoli. The broccoli may have been cooked in beef broth, which is my favorite way to eat it. Next to that is a tray of mashed potatoes, and then a tray of beef gravy. A large, flat tray of rolls follows the gravy, and is the last of the food that is ready for us to eat.

We all eagerly pass through the line, thankful to the workers who seem delighted to serve us their delicious creations. Everything is going swimmingly until one of the workers says, "You guys are really awesome." It is a young female voice, and when I look up I immediately get a sinking feeling in my stomach. I am staring face to face with Katie, the girl who caught me with my eyes open on the floor of the holding room for all of the unconscious Saints that she was charged with waking up. Whatever comfort level I had been building up inside over the last day due to our alibi constructed by Thomas has immediately vanished.

I quickly realize that I can't return a look of dread back at her smiling face. I force myself to give the most convincing smile that I can and say, "Thank you. You guys are awesome, too. This is the best food I've had in a long time." My voice cracks slightly with the last word. For as old as I looked in the mirror a few minutes ago, that shouldn't have happened with my voice. Much to my surprise, she never gives me any indication in her facial expression that she recognizes me as someone who was in the group earmarked for death yesterday. I decide to prevent her from focusing on me any more than I have to, so I give her a courteous nod and quickly look down and reach for the next serving spoon to scoop mashed potatoes on my plate. After I feel the coast may be clear, I look back and she is making eye contact with Nate, the other one of us that she saw staring back at her from the floor of the holding room.

I monitor their interaction for a few seconds, and then I look to the right at Thomas who is second in line behind Dave. Josh is in between us. Thomas is also watching Nate and Katie closely, as I am sure he watched me when I was in the hot seat a few seconds ago. Thomas notices me looking at him, and he returns me a concerned look, eyebrows furrowed. I look back at Nate, and he has already moved on, reaching for the spoon resting in the mashed potatoes. Katie looks away from Nate and focuses her attention on Julia. Nate quickly scoops a very small portion of mashed potatoes onto his plate. He hates mashed potatoes, but I understand why he did what he did.

Julia and Katie have a nice conversation that spans about twenty seconds, and then Julia moves on. None of the other kitchen workers are talking to us, which seems kind of odd that Katie is so talkative. Mindy and Ted pass by fairly quickly, each with a nod and a thank you. Could it be that Katie has no recollection of seeing us all yesterday lying on the floor, or could it be that she is not yet putting two and two together? That seems far-fetched to me, but if anyone can cause someone to look but not see it is the Lord. She gave me the same smile today that she gave me yesterday when she caught me looking at her. She has to know. Maybe she is somehow on Thomas's side, and therefore on our side. But Thomas said she was eventually brainwashed by Jared and can't be trusted.

My bigger worry is that she hasn't figured it out yet, but that she will put two and two together sometime soon. Then we are as good as dead, and Thomas will be in big trouble, too. I have reached the end of the food line. I need to focus on carrying my tray of food without dropping it, and I need to act normal and get my drink at the drink station. I'll say it again; whatever comfort level I was feeling from Thomas's rescue is all but gone. I am panicking on the inside. I can't wait to set my tray down at the drink station for fear of shaking my plate right off of the tray. Thomas is filling up his cup with ice. "What

111

do we do?" I whisper. Josh is right next to us and leans in. Dave has already gone to our table and sat down. Thomas quickly leans in and whispers, "Play it cool. Everything's cool." He finishes filling his cup with ice so that Josh can start. We get our drinks and go to the table. No one eats until everyone has sat down. Nate and I purposely sit with our backs to the kitchen workers. It sounds to me like they have all gone back to their business since I hear sounds of banging and clanking dishes, and the sound of the kitchen door swinging open and closed.

I picture Katie staring at the back of my head, piercing it with her eyes and figuring out who I am. I am really panicking right now. I have no appetite for this wonderful plate of hot food in front of me. I decide I have to gather the strength to turn around and take a quick glance to see if she is still there watching our every move. I do, and I am very relieved to see that she has gone back into the kitchen. I can see her moving across the opening in the wall. A sense of relief falls over me, and I can feel my racing heartbeat begin to significantly slow down. I turn back around. Thomas is sitting directly across from me. He says, "That was close. Way too close. I'm not sure how she hasn't recognized you guys both times now." She must not have had as good of a look at you as you thought, Matt." I respond, "She got as good of a look at me yesterday as she did a minute ago. I can't imagine it, either." I then wonder if we were looking disheveled enough yesterday after our long trip that we were unrecognizable compared with how we look today. Before I can think any further, Dave says, "Everything is cool. God is watching out for us. Let's eat." That is the best prayer I've ever heard.

As I take a few bites of food my appetite picks up. Over the course of lunch, Thomas explains to us that he saw a flyer on the bulletin board that a special youth meeting is scheduled for tonight from eight PM until ten PM. I remember our conversation with Jared last night after our recon mission into the Leader's office. We are expected to be there, along with Thomas. I remember from last night's conversation that I worked my way into attending the meeting with the kids. Thomas says quietly to Josh, Nate, and Dave, "Don't worry; Jared won't have any time for private one-on-one sessions to try to brainwash you. I know it wouldn't work anyways, but I'm surprised he found the time to have the meeting tonight. He must really want me back in the youth group, and is taking time away from his preparation for the Leader's visit tomorrow."

My appetite just took a turn for the worse with that one. I didn't want to hear that we are less than a day away from the Leader arriving at the facility. And what a day Thursday will be, the day after he arrives and the day everything is supposed to go down (hopefully literally). Thomas then says, "Just to be safe, at tonight's meeting, let's try to keep Katie away from Matt and Nate as much as possible. We'll try to get there right at eight PM, and I'll try to steer us to a place to sit, hopefully behind Katie, so she doesn't have two hours to try to piece things together in her mind." We all agree. Julia says, "Why do we have to attend the meeting? I don't want my kids at that meeting." Thomas explains to Julia our rendezvous with Jared outside of the room last night. By the end of the story she's scowling at me, like it's my fault. "Don't worry," I say, "I worked my way in so that I can be there with the kids." Julia answers, "But I want to be there with the kids, too!" Mindy quiets Julia as she is getting loud enough to draw attention, even though we are still the only ones in the room besides the occasional kitchen worker behind us. Thomas interjects, "Don't worry. I won't let anything happen to them. We'll go to the meeting, we'll get out quick, and then we'll head straight back to the room. After that, Ted, Matt, and I will go on our late-night mission. Mindy starts to ask what the mission is, but then she remembers our plans to "adjust" the smashing machine once Tom and Barry are done for the night.

Thomas then says, "Our next priority is to finish lunch and then get downstairs to clean up the kitchen and the porridge eating area. We will be busy for the next several hours getting things in tip-top shape for the Leader's tour." While the idea of cleaning something for the Leader doesn't appeal to me very much, it does motivate me to finish my lunch along with everyone else so that we can complete the next item on our task list and keep things moving. Hopefully the best way to minimize worrying about how things will turn out is to keep extremely busy with hard work that will wear us out enough to sleep at night. The next few days can't be over fast enough.

None of us feel like seconds, so we clean up and walk downstairs. We move as a group down the stairs, and the first wave of lunch-seekers is heading past us up the stairs. Little do they know that we have already eaten some of the delicious food they are about to enjoy. Thomas nods and greets the people that we pass, and I try to follow suit if they glance at me on the way by. We continue through the porridge room, and into the downstairs kitchen.

We collect as a group, with Thomas in front. "All right guys, it's our job to make this room shine. After that, we need to make the Saint's eating area look spotless." Thomas motions to the double doors that lead to the room where the Saints eat the porridge. He continues. "That will be the hard part. In the state the Saints are in at the time, they tend to be messy eaters. Mom usually lets that room go a little bit until the Leader comes to visit. The trouble is, when he is set to arrive she expects us to get all of the gray porridge stains out of the carpet, and to clean up any drips of porridge off of the chair legs and the tables. Even after a few weeks, the stuff is still pretty potent and you can't get it on your skin. We'll all need to be really careful not to let any of it touch our skin, not even the water in the carpet shampooer."

Mindy asks a good question. "Whose idea was it to carpet the room, anyways?" Thomas smiles and answers, "Everything was built and furnished according to the Leader's specifications. Wait until you check out the carpet; it's like something out of a 1950's hotel lobby." Mindy rolls her eyes. "Delightful," she says.

Before we start cleaning the kitchen, we all make sure we are outfitted with plastic sleeves and gloves. I make sure everyone slides the plastic sleeves under their shirt sleeves, and then I have them tuck their gloves in under the plastic sleeves. I'm sure as soon as our arms start to get sweaty it's going to feel very uncomfortable wearing the sleeves, but we need to be careful. Thomas also puts on the plastic sleeves, especially since his uniform shirt is short-sleeved.

We go to work cleaning up the countertops and floors in the kitchen. I take mop duty with Josh and Nate, and I'm pleasantly surprised with how clean the mops and buckets are as Thomas wheels them out of the supply closet. Beth and I may be the only two people on earth who would not only clean with a mop and bucket, but also make spotless the mop and the bucket after use. At this moment I decide that maybe I'd better back off a little bit when it comes to cleaning.

Julia, Ted, and Mindy fill up pails with water and bleach to wipe down the counters. Thomas gives them a ratio of two capfuls of bleach to one bucket of water. He provides them with cleaning rags, and they go to work filling their pails with warm water at the sinks at the far end of the kitchen. Nate, Josh, and I fill up our mop buckets with the hose in the porridge room and pour our capfuls of bleach into the warm water. I notice for the first time that the hose has a fancy temperature control valve at the spigot in the wall.

We return to the kitchen and each pick an aisle to mop. Nate picks the outside aisle nearest to the porridge room exit. Josh picks the other outside aisle nearest to the double doors that lead to the Saints' eating area. There is a break in this counter to allow a small walkway to pass through from the double doors into the middle aisle between the two counters. I default to the aisle that runs in between the two counters. The only tricky part will be to not get too far ahead of the crew wiping the counters, or else they will step onto our wet floors and leave marks from the dirt on their shoes. We decide instead to start at the end of the kitchen closest to the supply closet and the porridge room, opposite from where Julia, Ted, and Mindy are starting to wipe down the counters. We hope that we can mop halfway up the aisles and then circle back behind the counter crew to give the floors enough time to dry before they make it more than halfway down the aisles. The plan seems to work, as their shoes don't leave marks on the floor once they reach the places that we already mopped.

We circle around and follow them until they are done. At this point I realize that Thomas and Dave have been gone for quite a while, but soon after they reemerge from the supply closet with a carpet shampooer. I can see from my position about halfway across the kitchen that he has filled the shampooer with water. He takes a few steps onto the floor, and then stops. He puts his arm out to stop Dave and asks, "Is it OK for us to walk on the floor yet?" I answer, "Yes, that part should be dry by now." Thomas responds, "Good work, guys," and continues on into the Saints' eating room with Dave.

After we follow the counter crew to the end of the aisles to touch up any marks that they make on the clean floor, we all head to the porridge room to dump out our buckets and clean out the mops and rags. At that point Thomas walks in and asks us to make our way into the Saints' eating room. He says, "I'll be in there in about five minutes. I'm going to rinse the floor in here and clean out the mops and mop buckets. Actually, we'll need to refill the other buckets with water to clean the tables in the room. We can't use bleach this time, or it will drip on the carpet and make a stain. Let's make sure we give the buckets and the rags an extra good rinse before we go in there."

Once the buckets are refilled with just water, and after several more buckets and rags are found in the supply closet for me, Dave, Nate, and Josh, we all walk gingerly across the clean kitchen floor and enter into the Saints' eating room. I immediately notice the smell, a rather musty version of the porridge poison smell, and then I notice the décor. The carpet is a dark red, with elaborate designs that are light tan in color. Darkly stained round tables with eight chairs per table fill the room. The room is large, with a two story ceiling for much of the room. As I look to the left from where we came in, large columns support a portion of the second floor that juts out into this large dining room about three quarters of the way down the room. I surmise that the second floor room that juts out is the upstairs kitchen. I could be wrong, but it makes sense based on the layout upstairs. Large tapestries and antique-looking light fixtures decorate the walls on all four sides of the room. The tapestries are mostly dark red, and some have designs in brown, tan, and yellow colors that blend fairly well with each other and the carpet. The wall fixtures are an ivory color, and large half-sphere lights hang down from the ceiling and give the room a warm yellow glow.

I'm not sure what ambiance the Leader is trying to create, but this room is very strange and out of place when compared to the rest of the rooms I've seen. The décor of his office is the closest thing to what I see in here, but this room takes the cake for being both agedly tacky and elegant.

We all stand around staring at the room, slowly walking in between the tables until Thomas walks in. That didn't just seem like five minutes, but I guess it was. We all turn and look at him, as if coming out of a trance. "How do you like this room?" Thomas asks, smirking. Mindy speaks up first. "This is the ugliest room I've ever seen!" she exclaims. "Ditto!" Julia adds. Ted says, "Come on, it's not so bad." I begin to say something, but then I suddenly find myself drifting away from the room and into another place.

This time I land back in Cincinnati. I'm going to lunch with two of my coworkers. I remember this, at least the part where we get out of my car and walk into the restaurant. Chipotle is one of our favorites, and that is where we are headed. I like to call it Chipotle's for some reason. It just rolls off of the tongue better.

We walk into the restaurant, and then I see her. It's the strange, flamboyantly-dressed woman from the other vision in the bookstore. She doesn't look the same, though. She is dressed in ragged black clothes, and she has a really unpleasant look to her. Her eyes have dark bags under them, and she does not look to be in good health. She looks at me, and then she looks away. I stop walking when she momentarily looks at us. I freak out on the inside, and I tell my friends, "This is bad.

Really, really bad." They both notice the woman, too, and one of them asks, "Do you know her?" I answer, "No, and I'd rather not start now." The other one asks, "Should we leave, because I am definitely okay with us leaving right now." I answer with a shaky voice, "No, as much as I want to leave, let's play it cool and see how this plays out. This was evidently meant to happen." The second friend says, "But I really don't want to stay. Something is definitely wrong here with that woman." I respond with a prayer and say, "Jesus, help make it right," and I start walking toward the line, knees shaking and all.

We get into the line, which is not very long. The woman turns her head, but stops before her eyes get to us. She stares out the window. She has no food at the table where she sits. Sometimes people sit at that table while they are waiting on their carryout order since it is close to the register. I sat there once while waiting for them to cook more chicken for my burrito. We wait for what seems like an eternity for the people in front of us to order. Then it's our turn. My friends elect me to go first. Usually we're fighting for the front spot in line to make sure that we get our order secured before they run out of chicken, but not this time. Even though I'm not hungry anymore I place my order, and my voice is still shaky. "Salad bowl, please." The server asks, "Would you like some dressing with that?" I answer, "No thanks, but I will take extra fajita and double chicken." He obliges and continues to fill my bowl with salad. Even though I have my back to the woman, I can feel her turn around and look at me. I look over to my friend in line beside me, and he gives me a grimacing look of, "Yeah, she's looking at you." I freeze. The next server who applies the toppings asks me, "What kind of salsa would you like?" I can't answer. I can't even speak. "Jesus help, me!" I think to myself. "Give me strength!"

Just then the woman speaks. "Child of God, what are you doing?" she asks me in a sinister tone. I can't even move. Somehow, while still paralyzed and looking at the server, I say to the woman, "What do you mean?" She answers, "You are writing about the end and you need to stop. If you don't stop writing, it's going to happen and it's going to be *all your fault.*" She puts extra emphasis on the word "fault," and it pierces me right to the core. She tries to continue, but she begins to make this seething sound, as if she is having trouble breathing. At that moment, something strange happens to me. I lose my fear. The Lord has answered my prayer.

I turn around and look into her hideous eyes, and then I force a warm smile. I say, "Ma'am, you're not telling the truth. I have nothing to do with it. You are wrong." She stands up. I look directly into her eyes and can see the evil waiting to jump out at me. In my peripheral vision I can see everyone in the place take a step back when she stands up. This would not be good if Jesus weren't here. She speaks. "I asked you to stop!" she screams at the top of her lungs while stomping her left foot. She says it again, as loud as she can. "I asked you to STOP!" She repeats it several more times, as if she's building strength with each statement. After the fourth or fifth time, I quietly respond with, "In Jesus name, get out of her." She pauses for a minute, and then she gives me a most sinister smile. She repeats her statement, but in a more civil tone. I repeat my statement, but in a louder and more forceful tone. She repeats, again growing in loudness. I repeat, also growing in loudness. Ten times I say it, and then she lunges at me. Then it happens.

She convulses several times mid-lunge, and then it's done. She never makes it to me, but bumps into a chair and falls to the ground. She lands on her left side, her elbow and hip primarily breaking her fall. I remember saying to myself, "It happened, it really happened!" as I bend down to look after the woman to see if she is OK. As I bend down, I begin to be propelled back into reality and back into the Saints' eating room.

That was the most vivid vision yet. This drug is really doing numbers on my brain as it slowly works its way out of my system. Is what I'm seeing real memories of the past, or is my brain just making up these things?

When I come to, while still standing, I notice that everyone has started cleaning but me. I wonder if anyone notices when I check out mentally for these short periods of time. No one is paying attention to me, so I decide I should get to work, too. As I bend down to start cleaning the table nearest to me, I'm startled by a loud noise. I straighten up and turn to my left toward the noise. It's Thomas, and he has turned on the carpet shampooer. I shake it off and return to the task at hand. Over the next hour or so, we scrub off countless dried-up drips of porridge from the tables and chairs with our rags. I leave the room and change out my bucketful of water several times, as does everyone else. Each time I change my water, I also remove the current gloves and sleeves. I wash my hands and arms, and then put on new sleeves and gloves. I recommend to everyone that they do the same. At one point Thomas stops the shampooer and inspects our work. He shows Dave several spots he missed at the table he was working on prior to his current table. Everyone takes note just how exact we must be to obtain good marks on Beth's pre-tour checklist. Thomas then leaves the room for a few minutes to empty the dirty water from the spent water container and to refill the other container with clean water and more cleaning solution.

Thomas is about halfway complete with the carpet. I estimate that we would be more than halfway done with wiping down the tables and chairs if it weren't for the fact that we are going to have to reinspect what has been cleaned already. Thomas returns and reinserts the cleaning solution container back into the carpet shampooer. This time I'm prepared for him to start the shampooer. I return to cleaning my current chair, which is especially dirty. I start to wonder who the last person was to sit in this chair. I make up a person in my mind, an older gentleman. I picture him before being abducted, living a happy and normal life with children and grandchildren. I can see him smiling and standing in front of his house, with his arms around several of his family members. Then I picture the imaginary man sitting in this chair, slurping porridge at the gentle prodding of Beth. He is unable to talk, unable to give anything more than a blank stare as he slowly brings a spoon filled with death up to his lips.

I picture his hand shaking slightly as he brings the spoon to his mouth. His mouth opens slowly, and in goes the porridge. I see him take the next bite with the same slow motions. The next time he misses his mouth, and the porridge runs down the side of his right cheek and drips onto the edge of the chair. It oozes down to the under portion of the chair, and then drips one drop of porridge onto the carpet.

I continue to clean as I think of what comes next for the man. At the end of the meal, the innocent old man is asked to stand up, along with everyone else in the room. The camp counselors move about the room, coaxing the invalids to their feet. They start to form lines, which feed into the main line headed by Beth. Once the lines come together, Beth leads the crew through a door at the other end of the room, which I hadn't even noticed yet. My made-up gentleman is one of the last ones in the line. He slowly plods across the room as the line allows. He stares at his feet. Periodically a camp counselor guides him by the arm to keep him moving. At last he leaves the room.

I don't want my imagination to take this any further. I renew my focus on getting this chair clean, but I can't help but notice the tears coming from my eyes. I cannot believe that a place like this exists in today's world. I can't believe that the people who work in this place think they are doing a good thing. With the exception of the leadership team, the rest of the camp workers probably consider themselves to be good people. They've been brainwashed into the cult, and based on that they justify themselves as being in the right. I wonder if Beth even knows what really happens to these people once they reach the top of the Stairway to Heaven. She has to, doesn't she? Thomas knows, but he's learned the real story through spying. How can he be the only one in here, other than our group, who can see what's really going on here?

I continue to agonize over the horrors of this place until we finally reach the end of our cleaning. I must have emptied and refilled my bucket and changed my gloves and sleeves more than thirty times. I finish up on the other side of the room from where I started. We've all checked each other's work extensively, and are all satisfied that this room is the cleanest it's been since the place first opened. At one point I look up, and I see the exit doors to the room. Even though it's the first time I've physically seen them, they look exactly how I imagined them in my sad story about the older gentlemen. The door handles are even the same.

Thomas finishes with the carpet shampooer, and shuts it off for the last time today. Hopefully it's the last time forever. Thomas asks us, "Which did you like better – making porridge or cleaning this room?" In near unison, we all answer, "Neither!" Thomas laughs, but after the mental anguish that I put myself through the last several hours I am in no mood to laugh. I'm sure my face is still flushed from crying periodically, and probably more so from trying to choke back the tears. I want out of this place, and I want out now. "Get us out of here, Jesus," I pray in my mind.

Then Thomas says, "All right. You are free to go back to the room and get cleaned up for supper. I recommend that everyone showers and puts on a clean set of clothes. I'll stop by your room in about an hour, and then we'll get some supper. After that the kids, Matt and I will go to the youth meeting." Julia sighs heavily. Ted asks, "Can I go, too?" Thomas answers, "Let's give it a try, since Jared met you last night as well." Julia then says, "I want to go, too!" Ted quickly responds, "No, you'll get too emotional. Matt and I will go, and we'll make sure everything is just fine." Julia can't disagree with her Dad's point and begrudgingly approves. She looks at the kids and says, "Don't say a word. Just get in, sit there and listen, and get out." The kids nod in agreement, and then we all dismiss to walk back to the room. We leave Thomas to finish winding up the cord to the carpet shampooer, and we head toward the kitchen to clean out our buckets and rags.

We start to leave the dirty buckets in the sink at the back of the kitchen, but Thomas comes over and instructs us to put them in the nearby dishwasher. He opens it up, and I can see that it is a heavy-duty commercial model. It has a few other dishes in it, and Thomas closes it and starts the cleaning cycle after we place all of the buckets inside. "Don't you need to add the detergent?" I ask. "There is an automatic dispenser that holds enough soap for lots of washes," Thomas answers. "Cool," I say. Thomas then directs us to a laundry hamper near a door at the very back of the kitchen to the right of the sink. We all drop our rags into the hamper.

We follow Thomas to the other end of the kitchen, and then he veers off into the porridge room to finish cleaning the carpet shampooer. "I'll see you in about an hour," he says. After discarding our gloves and sleeves we walk through the supply closet and into the main hallway toward our room. We pass several people along the way who I have seen before in the cafeteria. I smile and nod as we pass them. Once we get back into the room, I feel a lot better. It seems like a burden is lifted from my shoulders when it's just us, and we don't have to pretend anymore. I don't like pretending to be affiliated with this place, but I know we need to keep up the charade a little while longer.

I want nothing more than to lie in the bed, but I know I can't. The kids decide in what order they will shower, and Ted and I defer to Mindy and Julia to decide who will go first. I start to sit on my bed, but then I decide I'd rather not let my porridge-laced clothes touch where I will be sleeping. I pull out my phone. I am surprised to see it is six PM already. I think back on all we've accomplished today. We made porridge, we cleaned the kitchen, and then we made spotless the Saints' eating area. No wonder I'm tired.

It takes us a full hour and twenty minutes to get everyone showered and changed. Luckily, Thomas is thirty minutes late. We all lie on our beds and rest while we wait for him to arrive. When he does arrive, he apologizes for being late. Then he says, "I got tied up with Jared on the way over. He wanted me to know that the youth meeting has been delayed until eight thirty PM, and it will only be one hour. He said he's behind on getting things done for the visit tomorrow, and that's all the time he said he has. Then he talked my ear off for twenty more minutes instead of moving on to get the work done he's so far behind on. At least now we have a full hour to eat before the meeting starts."

We walk with Thomas to the upstairs kitchen. The line is somewhat long, but it does not reach the stairs. We make it through the line in about ten minutes. The cafeteria has enough people in it that we can't find a table all to ourselves. We find one with enough chairs to accommodate our group and sit down. This part of the routine is starting to get old. I would love to bow my head and say a prayer of thanks for my meal, as loud as I can, just to spite everyone else in the room. I abstain, and once again I quietly thank God in my mind.

We all go back for seconds this time. The main course tonight is Lasagna, with garlic bread and mixed vegetables. It is another delicious meal. It's too bad Beth's talents are being wasted on this place. Once we are finished with our second helping, we waste no time cleaning up and leaving the room. Thomas wants us to stop back at the room before heading to the youth meeting. I pull out my phone to look at the time. I'm greeted with a low battery warning as I enter my pass code. It is eight twenty-three PM as we reach the bottom of the stairs. I go back into the text message screen, just to see if my text ever sent. I am greeted with a "Message not sent" notification. I press OK and put my phone away. "Thomas," I say, "I'll need you to charge my phone again tonight." Thomas answers, "Sure. Let's stop at my room first so I can connect it to the charger."

CHAPTER 12 – IN A TIGHT SPOT

Exodus 33:22 (NIV), "When my glory passes by, I will put you in a cleft in the rock and cover you with my hand until I have passed by."

Thomas's room looks about as bland as ours. Bare concrete walls and a concrete floor surround a standard issue bed, dresser, and night stand. The room could hold many more people, but Thomas evidently has it to himself. An equally drab lamp sits on the nightstand. Thomas notices me looking at the lamp and says, "You, know, I never used that thing until I found a good book to read a while back." He pulls a phone charging cord off of the floor next to the night stand. It is evidently plugged into the same outlet as the lamp behind the night stand. He plugs my phone in, and it gives a quiet vibration to indicate that it is charging.

Thomas asks, "Did your distress call ever go out?" I answer, "No, it never sent." Thomas says, "Too bad. That would have made things more interesting." Nate chimes in and says, "It never would have worked in a million years. No chance!" I give him a look and he quiets down. Thomas then says, "Sometimes these meetings can get kind of weird." I look at Julia, who immediately tears up. Thomas continues. "Jared will either be 'in the zone,' where he can give a very convincing sales pitch, or he can make no sense at all. We'll know within the first five minutes whether or not he's on tonight. Regardless, it's all a bunch of BS anyways, whether the delivery is good or bad. It's silly sometimes how much he gushes about the Leader; it's almost sickening."

Ted points to his arm as if he had a watch on. "We'd better go," he says. With that the kids hug Julia, and then she pulls herself together to leave Thomas's room. We drop Julia and Mindy off at our room, and they lock and latch the door behind them. We continue down the hall, walking farther away from the kitchen. As we approach the door to the outside, Thomas turns left into a room with the door open. We walk into a somewhat large room full of teenagers. Everyone looks at us as we file in. Thomas leads us to the back of the dimly-lit room, where we find a pile of beanbag chairs. He starts handing them out to us. We wait for him to make the next move. He doesn't walk very far forward, as the only place on the floor with enough room to hold all six of us is near the beanbag pile. We claim our spot and ease into our beanbags. I notice mine smells funny as I push the air through the fabric when I sit down.

Once seated, I quickly spot Katie. She is not looking at us, but she is talking to a girl next to her. I quickly recognize the other girl as the one working with Katie to wake up the Saints yesterday. Hopefully she doesn't recognize us, either. Suddenly Jared hastily enters the room. He stops in the middle of the front of the room and clasps his hands together in front of his midsection while leaning forward. "Good evening, everyone. Sorry I'm late," he says. Katie says, "You're not late, you're right on time." Everyone except our group laughs, including Jared.

Jared begins to talk. In less than thirty seconds, I can already tell that Jared is not going to be on top of his game tonight. What he is saying makes no sense to me. The kids take turns looking back at me with quizzical looks. Ted raises his eyebrows several times. Everyone in the room seems to be a little bit uncomfortable, including Jared. He repeats the phrase "In the Leader's name" about one-hundred times over the next thirty minutes. I try to listen because I want to learn more about this strange cult, but I just can't put the time and effort into trying to understand his near-gibberish. My beanbag chair, even though it smells, is really comfortable. Several times I feel my head starting to roll backward. It jerks forward each time as I return to full consciousness.

I decide to observe Thomas, who is sitting in front of me to my left, so that I can have something to focus on to help remain awake. Thomas looks as disinterested as me. His chin is resting on his right hand, with his right arm being supported by the beanbag. He is at least half-asleep. He is probably very tired, too, after our long day. For a split second I get the idea to text Julia to let her know there's nothing for her to be worrying about, but I remember that my phone is in Thomas's room and that texting won't work. I decide that it's a good thing we are getting a chance to rest.

I hear a loud clap. I look up. Jared has clasped his hands in front of him again. He concludes his speech that I didn't listen to and says, "That's all the time we have for today. Let's get to our rooms, get some sleep, and prepare ourselves physically, mentally, and spiritually for the Leader's visit tomorrow. Thank you all."

Everyone starts to climb out of their beanbag chairs. "That was it?" I ask myself. Before I make it all the way up, Jared says, "Oh, I almost forgot. We have some new youth group members. I won't put them on the spot tonight, but please say hello and get to know them over the coming days and weeks." As soon as Jared finishes the sentence, he walks quickly through the crowd of teenagers to the far back corner of the room. For the first time I notice Beth standing at the back of the room. They begin talking, but I can't make out what they are saying. There is too much background noise from the beanbag chairs being picked up and carried toward the pile. I realize that we are directly in the way of the pile, so I help the kids and Thomas with putting their beanbag chairs back into the pile so we can get out of the way. I don't want everyone getting a good look at us on the way out, especially Katie and her friend.

The only place to move to get out of everyone's way is closer to Beth and Jared. At one point I hear him say, "I just didn't feel it tonight. I just couldn't connect spiritually like normal. Something was in the air that just didn't work for me." I'll give him three guesses to figure out what it was. Answer: The Holy Spirit of God was in the house tonight.

Surprisingly, despite Jared's request that everyone get to know us, none of the teenagers give Josh, Nate, Dave, or Thomas any acknowledgement as they return their beanbags. After a couple of minutes of standing out of the way, the room clears enough for Thomas to lead our group to the exit. We walk into the hallway, and then a teenage boy starts talking to Thomas. They're making small talk, and Thomas introduces Josh, Nate, and Dave under their alias names. My focus quickly drifts from their conversation to a room to the left of the meeting room we were just in. The room has no door, just a doorway. While the boys talk, I take a few steps toward the doorway and look inside.

I have found the security room, the one that Thomas says has sat vacant since the security guard left many months ago. Most of the monitors are on with the cameras positioned at various points inside and outside the building. A single desk sits about ten feet into the room, against the back wall. The monitors, all flat screens, fill the wall above the desk. I study the monitors for several minutes before Thomas walks up beside me. Evidently the kids' conversation is over. "Security room," he says. I nod affirmatively, still looking at the monitors. Thomas continues, "If you stare at them long enough, you get a pretty good idea where you can and can't be seen on the premises." I nod again.

Josh says, "Dad, let's get back to the room." I agree, and we make the short walk back to the room. Three other lodging rooms separate ours from the meeting room. We get back to the room and knock on the door. Julia opens the door, sees us, and then releases the chain at the top of the door. We come in, and she hugs the kids. I can tell she continued to cry while we were gone. "How did it go?" she asks. "It was really boring," Dave says. We all agree. Mindy says, "See, I told you there was nothing to worry about!" Julia then asks, "Did you get to know any of the other kids?" Dave answers, "Just one; nobody else even acted like we existed."

Julia feels the need to hug each kid once more, even amidst their apparent annoyance. Thomas says, "OK guys," looking at me and Ted, "it's time for our next mission." Ted gives him an un-approving look. Thomas ignores him and says, "I need to get the bug netting from my room, and then we'll be ready to go." That doesn't sound good. "Bug netting?" I ask. "Yes, bug netting," Thomas says. "We'll get eaten alive if we don't take it with us up to the roof. Tom and Barry should finish their maintenance on the smashing machine in about an hour, and the quicker we sneak in and sneak out after them, the better off we'll be."

I'm imagining the size of the mosquitoes they have in the jungle. The netting must have a pretty narrow mesh to keep mosquitoes from biting us. I ask, "Can you give us ten or fifteen minutes to see everyone else to bed before we go?" Thomas answers, "Sure!" and heads out the door. I turn to the group, expecting looks of fear from everyone as Ted and I once again have to go on a harrowing assignment, risking life and limb to accomplish our self-inflicted mission. Instead, the kids are already lying down in their beds. Julia is sitting in Mindy's bed next to her. I think everyone is too exhausted to be exceedingly fearful.

Julia stands up and gives us each a hug, and then she prompts the kids to get back up and brush their teeth. I urge her to say a prayer with the kids before they go to sleep, and she promises she will. Ted hugs Mindy and kisses her good night, and then the two of us head out the door. We walk down the hall toward Thomas's room, and he is just opening the door as we arrive. "Wow, that was quick," he says. I answer, "Everyone was too tired to be clingy, so we capitalized on it and left quickly." Thomas says, "It's probably for the best to let them get their rest." Ted responds, "I wish I could get some rest." Thomas gives him a look as we head down the hallway toward the kitchen.

I am not sure where we are going, and then I realize that we shouldn't let anyone see us. I expect that the bug netting will arouse suspicion if anyone sees us. We get close to the supply closet that leads to the downstairs kitchen, but instead of veering left and going into the supply closet Thomas turns to the right and opens the mystery door that I noticed several times earlier. Inside is a narrow hallway that spans about ten feet and feeds into an equally narrow staircase. We go up the first flight of stairs, and then reach a landing that turns us around to another flight of stairs. Once at the top of the second flight of stairs, we go through a door on the left and find ourselves in a room with no windows, about ten feet by ten feet. Toward the middle of the wall to our left, a metal ladder extends from the carpeted floor to the ceiling. The ladder is painted red, and it leads to a roof access point.

Caution signs and labels are positioned to confront anyone who tries to climb the ladder. From the looks of it, they will soon confront the three of us. Thomas says, "I'll go first. If you hold the netting until I get most of the way up, I'll reach down and grab it from you." I answer, "No problem," and I grab the netting. He has brought quite a bit with him, but it is not very heavy. It is a very fine mesh, almost a fabric.

Thomas climbs to the point where he needs to open the roof hatch. He unlocks it, and pushes it until it opens. The hinges then open the hatch the rest of the way on their own. He then reaches down and motions for me to hand him the bug netting. He has to motion twice before I am able to get the netting to his hand. It must be the exhaustion.

Thomas pulls the netting with him the rest of the way onto the roof. Then it's my turn to go up the ladder. "You're next," Ted says. "Thanks a lot," I answer, and I begin the climb. I go very slowly and deliberately to ensure I don't fall. Once I get to the top, I pause for a second to determine the best way to get myself past the opening and onto the roof. Thomas points to some handles that extend above the hatch opening. "Grab onto these and pull yourself up," he says. I do as instructed and find myself on the roof. Ted soon follows.

The roof is covered in gravel. I can see several air handler units spread out across the roof given both the pale moonlight and the light escaping from the hatch opening. Thomas quickly shuts the hatch behind us. "I don't want them to see the light coming from over here," he says. I can't see the smashing machine from where we are standing. Thomas begins to walk toward the front edge of the roof facing the smashing machine. As we approach the edge of the roof, I notice light shining slightly to the right from center. Once we get closer, the smashing machine comes into view. I see two men standing in front of the machine; presumably Tom and Barry.

Thomas hands each of us a bug net. "Lie down," he whispers, "and put these over you. We have about one minute or less before the mosquitoes find us. Once they do, we're in trouble if we don't have these on." I try to position myself so that I can see what the guys are doing at the machine, but my view is reduced once I lie down. Thomas quietly asks us to move back about four feet so that there is no chance that Tom and Barry can see any part of us. Moving back pretty much ensures that we can't see any part of them or what they are doing.

Once we are settled, Thomas whispers, "Now we wait." I ask, whispering, "How will we know when they are done?" Thomas gives me the obvious answer, "We'll know it's our turn when they turn the lights off." Then I ask, still whispering, "How will we get down there?" Thomas responds, "Don't worry, I'll show you when it's time. It's no more difficult than climbing the ladder to the roof." With that we are all silent for a while. After a few minutes, Ted lets out a yawn. Thomas whispers, "Feel free to take a nap. I'll wake you when it's time." Ted answers, also whispering, "What if you fall asleep, too, and we don't wake up until morning?" Thomas responds, "Don't worry, I'm not going to fall asleep. This is our only chance." I agree with Thomas and assure him and Ted that I will not be falling asleep at such a critical time. Then we all get quiet for quite a while.

I come to at some point and realize I did what I said I wasn't going to do. I can hear Ted breathing heavily, almost snoring. I jolt myself back into full consciousness. I whisper to Thomas, "You awake?" He looks over at me and whispers back, "Go ahead, go back to sleep. I'll wake you up when it's time." This time I decide that sleep is not an option. I sit up, rearranging by bug net to protect me from the hungry mosquitoes. Thomas sits up, too. I still can't see anything but the very top of the machine. The light is still shining brightly.

"How long was I out?" I whisper. "Not long," Thomas responds. "You guys should be really tired after everything you've been through. Especially with that drug still in your system, I can't imagine how you guys are going as strong as you are. Up late last night, up early this morning, and now up late again. You need some rest. "No more than you," I answer. "You've been dealing with this mess for over a year, and you've had no way to escape." Thomas answers, "It was pretty hopeless until you guys got here. Once I realized that I had some help, I knew things were going to change." I pause for a minute. "Why us? Why are we so important?" I ask. Thomas answers, "God must have been speaking to me even before I trusted or even really believed in him. One night about a month ago I was snooping in the Leaders' office. As I went through the records of the groups to arrive at the facility during his next visit, I saw your pictures and your bio's in the V.I.S. folder. I knew at that moment you could help. What I didn't know at the time was whether or not you could escape on your own. When I saw you guys turn and run back down the stairs I was standing in this very spot. I literally jumped for joy because I knew it was you guys, and I knew that God was going to make it happen."

Now I'm getting confused again. I want to get into the details of how Thomas knew that we would be able to help him. Does he know us from the past somehow? And why are we in the V.I.S. category? What makes us so special? Before I can ask any more questions, though, Thomas changes the subject. He asks, "Do you know how hard it's been for me with my mother? And I'm not talking since we got here, or since she got involved with this group, but since my Dad died. I always thought my mom had some mental issues, but my dad was always able to keep her in check. He would be able to calm her down when she would work herself into one of her fits. After he was gone, there was no one left to help her. I tried to do it, but I don't have the touch like he had. It almost made her, not almost – it *did* make her even angrier when I tried to act like him. There was no consoling her at that point. It wasn't until she became a member of this group that she got her episodes under control again, but she definitely went about it the wrong way."

I've temporarily forgotten my other questions. I want to learn more about Thomas's life. "So how long ago did your Dad pass away?" I ask.

Thomas answers, "A little over two years ago. Mom was actually better in the beginning, when it first happened." Then I ask, "What happened? Was he sick?" Thomas replies, "We didn't know he was sick until a few weeks before he died. He had been complaining for a few weeks about a pain in the back of his head that was steadily getting worse. The first time he told us about it we learned that he had been feeling a dull pain in that spot for several months. Mom made him go to the doctor, and they found an inoperable brain tumor. A few weeks later, he was gone."

"How sad," I say, forgetting to whisper this time. Thomas continues. "It wasn't until a few months after he died that Mom starting having real problems coping. She would get angry at the silliest things, which she always did, but she just couldn't let it go. She got so mad at me the one time when I didn't clear my dishes from the dinner table that she started throwing silverware at me. I ran up to my room and locked the door until morning. She apologized the next morning, and everything seemed cool until the next episode. Someone called her on the phone, to this day I don't know who it was, and they made her mad. I was sitting on the couch in the other room, listening to her scream at them. I'm not sure when they hung up, but she continued screaming for quite a while. Her screams changed at some point into this terrible, unspeakable noise. It really freaked me out. She came out of the kitchen with a look in her eyes of pure evil. I ran upstairs and hid, locking the door again until morning. I listened to her scream for hours and hours, banging and smashing things. The house was a mess the next morning."

I really feel bad for this kid. "Thomas, this is terrible. I wish you could have escaped then and gotten some help." Thomas answers, "In hindsight, I should have, but she always went back to normal the next day. She would always apologize, and then she would be the good mom again for a while. After her fifth or sixth episode, she said she was going to get help. She met Jared somehow through her work, and the rest is history unfortunately."

Ted comes to, and rolls over to look at us. He thinks for a moment and then whispers, "What are you guys doing?" I whisper back, "Just passing the time." Ted sits up and rearranges his bug net. Then he says, "I guess I'll join you," and lets out a quiet chuckle. We have our backs to the edge of the roof, but I can still see that the light behind us turns off. "About five minutes until go time," Thomas says. I start to get up, but Thomas motions for me to stay put. I quickly realize that we need to give the two guys time to go back into the building.

We sit motionless for at least ten minutes. I hear the faint sound of a door closing. Then Thomas stands up. Ted and I follow suit. I'm not sure how we're going to pull this off, but I really hope that we do. Thomas keeps his bug net around him until he gets to the edge of the roof. We follow him to the roof's edge, keeping our bug nets over us as well. Once we get to the edge we remove our coverings. For the first time I notice we're only about seven or eight feet above the top of the Stairway to Heaven walkway that we traveled across yesterday. Thomas motions for the three of us to lean in together. He whispers, "There's a window directly below us. We'll hold on to the edge of the roof and lower ourselves until our feet touch the top of the window trim. Then we can place our other foot on the windowsill at the bottom and climb down the rest of the way." Thomas goes first to lead the way.

Ted and I watch how he climbs down. It's not the first time he's done this. I go next, leaving Ted alone on the roof. Once I make it down, Ted follows suit. He makes it down without issue. Thomas leans in to give us the next instruction. "We'll need to work in the dark, but we should have enough moonlight. My only hope is that they left the toolbox unlocked." Thomas then begins the walk toward the smashing machine. I can't help but remember our walk on the same path yesterday. I was so afraid until I realized what the loud boom was, and then I was beyond terrified. This machine has destroyed so many lives; I can't wait to destroy it.

We reach the machine. We all stop and look at it. The only thing I hear is our breathing and the sound of crickets and/or tree frogs. It is just as

I remember it, only without as much color. Ted slowly makes his way to the large piston arm at the far back of the machine. He stops and studies it for several minutes. He reaches out and touches various nuts and bolts. Thomas and I make our way over to the piston arm, too. After what seems like an eternity, Ted whispers, "I think if we can get one of these side support arms to go cockeyed, and if we loosen the other one, it will help the thing pull to the left when they push the button. If we can get the thing to engage and catch against this left edge of the box, it should make it go catawampus enough to break it."

Thomas leaves us momentarily and walks around the piston arm behind the machine. I can see him as he rounds the machine. He stops at the toolbox that I now notice behind the piston arm. He opens the lid at the top. Bingo; we're in. He pulls open the first drawer. He pulls open the second drawer. It looks like we have full access. Thomas comes back around and asks Ted, "What do you need?" Ted answers, "I don't know yet. Let me see what they have first."

Ted rounds the machine and quietly looks through the toolbox. He opens each drawer slowly, looks in each one for a time, and then shuts the drawer and moves onto the next one. After what seems like forever, he makes it through all of the drawers. He comes back around to our side of the machine, and studies the pusher arm some more. After a few minutes of study, he returns to the other side of the machine, presumably to get some tools. Prior to the toolbox, however, he stops and looks at the other side of the pusher arm.

The pusher arm is a large piston-driven device. A very large motor and gearbox combination are at the back base of the pusher arm, which is connected at its base to the platform that holds the smashing machine. At either side of the pusher arm are support arms that extend from the smaller pistons at each side of the pusher arm and connect to the top sides of the holding container where the Saints are loaded. The side support arms look surprisingly thin, but I guess they do the job. They are probably there more for adjusting the position of the main pusher

135

arm to make sure it is centered to travel down the middle of the holding container without crashing into the sides.

Ted is examining the support arm on the other side. He studies how it is connected to the main arm, and then he walks over to where it connects to the side of the container. While he studies that side, I take a look at the connections on this side of the machine. If Ted wants to loosen these connections, then we'll have a tough time reaching the connection at the top of the container. After studying the setup for several minutes, I'm not sure if there is enough adjustment available at the connections to send the pusher arm far enough off of its course to get the job done.

Ted walks back over to the toolbox. He opens a few drawers until he finds what he is looking for. He pulls out a ratchet set. Then he walks back over to me and Thomas. He whispers, "I'm not sure if this is going to work." I whisper back, "Me, too." Thomas chimes in, "We need to try something." Ted grimaces, and then he kneels down to the ground and opens the box containing the ratchet set. Thomas and I kneel down as well. Ted whispers, "The first thing we need to do to try to adjust this thing is to loosen this doo-hickey (pointing to one of the support arms) where it connects to the piston. After that, we'll try to slide the piston over as far to the left as it will let us, and then we'll tighten it back into place. We'll probably have to loosen the other side first to give us some play. The thing I don't know is how heavy all of this stuff is going to be to try to scoot over a few inches."

Thomas and I nod in approval, and Ted stands up with the socket wrench and a few sizes of sockets he thinks will fit onto the bolts that connect the support arms to the side pistons. He tests a few of the sockets and finds the one he needs. He loosens the first bolt, and we are on our way to destroying the machine. He gets the last bolt loosened, and then he begins to walk toward the other side. I whisper, "Don't we need to loosen the other end?" pointing to where the support arm connects to the container. Ted answers, "Not right now. We may not need to."

Thomas and I follow Ted to the other side. He loosens the bolts on the other side. During the loosening of the last bolt, some kind of animal makes a howling noise in the distance. The noise startles us all, given that we are already on edge. Since we have spent so much time in the building, I keep forgetting we are in a jungle. And then I realize we don't seem to be getting bitten by mosquitoes. I ask Thomas, "Where are all of the mosquitoes?" He answers, "Tom and Barry spray some mosquito fog up here before they begin working. Other than what it's doing to our lungs right now, we should be OK for a little bit before it completely dissipates."

Ted finishes loosening the second support arm, and he leads us back around to the left side of the main pusher arm. Ted whispers, "And now it's time to loosen this doo-hickey, pointing to the left side piston arm with the ratchet. I ask the question, "Why didn't they design this thing to have the main pusher arm be the only piston?" Ted answers, "It looks like it was originally. But my guess is that it wasn't strong enough to do the job, and they had to add the additional, smaller pusher arms after the fact." We both look at Thomas. He whispers, "I'm not sure, that would have been before I started snooping around. For as long as I've seen the machine, the side pieces have been in place." Then Ted says, "I noticed different dates on the drawing next to the side pusher arms compared to the date at the bottom of the blueprint. The dates were later."

Over the next fifteen minutes, Ted loosens bolts on the left side pusher arm. Each time he yanks on it, trying to get it to move. He doesn't have any luck until Thomas points to a bolt on the piece that connects the side piston to the main arm and to the support that runs from the side pusher arm to the ground. The bolt is a different size, much smaller, and Ted returns to the ratchet set to get the correct socket. He gets it in one guess, which is impressive since it is pretty dark. After he turns the bolt a few times, it looks like the side piston is moving slightly toward the main piston arm. I say, just as Ted is figuring it out, "Turn it the other way," and he nods and reverses its course. The side arm returns to its original position, and then it starts to move away from the main piston arm. Very quickly the bolt gets hard to turn. Ted thinks for a second, and then moves to the ground and loosens the bolts that secure the support piece from the side piston arm to the platform base. When he returns to loosening the adjustment bolt, it turns much easier. I notice a line that marked the side piston arm's original position.

Ted cranks the bolt, which is not coming out at all, until he can't turn it anymore with a medium amount of force. Then Ted says, still whispering, "Now we need to do the same thing to the other side. I ask, "Do we need to tighten this back down first so it doesn't move around?" Ted answers, "Not yet. I actually want to move that side as far as we can and tighten it down first, and then see if we can get any more play on this side. I also want to see if there is any adjustment like this on the main arm. Even if we can scoot it over an inch or two, we'll have a much better chance of wrecking this thing come Thursday morning."

Thomas and I follow Ted back to the other side. Ted makes quick work of loosening the necessary bolts on this side. He loosens the bolts that connect the side piston support to the platform before he turns the bolt that adjusts the position of the side piston. I study the point at which the side piston connects back into the main pusher arm. The side piston arm reconnects to the main piston arm via a weld. The weld is about one foot past an outer metal sheath out of which the main pusher arm extends. Given that the connection is a weld, there won't be much adjustment at this end of the side pusher arm. I then follow the small support arm from where it connects to the side piston arm all the way to the point where it connects to the holding container. As I stare at the connection, my attention drifts to the nearly full moon above it in the clear sky. More stars than I have ever seen in my life, combined, are in a vast array above me. I'm sure the bright light from the moon is blocking some of the stars from being visible, but it is still a brilliant display. As I look toward the horizon, I can see a break in the trees slightly to the right of where I am standing. I see the moonlight shimmering off of a body of water. The Atlantic Ocean or the Gulf of

Mexico I wonder. It could just be a river or a lake, because I can't see very much of it from where I am standing.

I hear Ted and Thomas walk up beside me. Ted asks, "Do you think we need to loosen those connections?" pointing to where the support arms connect to the holding container. I answer, "You tell me. It probably wouldn't hurt if there's enough play to slide them to the left a little bit. I can't tell if there will be, though." Ted studies it for a minute. Then he says, "You'll have to give me a boost if I'm going to reach it. I look over at the toolbox. If the top section of the toolbox sits on top of the larger base without being connected, then we could use it as a stepstool. I motion for Thomas to follow me. I get on one side of the toolbox, and he seems to get the drift of what I am trying to do. We lift up on the top part of the toolbox by the handles on each side, and it lifts off with no issue. The thing is heavy, so I'm glad there are two of us. We carefully set it down right next to the container so we don't make any noise. Ted steps up onto the toolbox and reaches for the first bolt with the socket wrench. It needs a different size, of course.

Thomas retrieves a few smaller sizes for Ted, and he finds the right one on the first try again. He still has to reach quite a bit over his head to loosen the bolts, but he is able to get the three bolts loose that connect the support arm to the container. Once he gets down, he is able to turn a few more cranks on the adjustment bolt to the side piston arm. "Good," I whisper, "Now can we tighten everything back up?" Ted answers, "Not yet. Remember, I want to see if we can move the main arm over a little bit." I nod in agreement and let Ted crawl under the main pusher arm to study its connections to the platform. After several minutes, Thomas, who is crouching next to Ted, smacks the back of Ted's neck. "Mosquito!" Thomas whisper-yells, before Ted can let out a yelp. Ted grimaces and says, "Thanks," and then goes back to his work. Thomas says, "We have about ten or twenty more minutes before we get eaten alive. We need to finish up quick."

Ted gives him an un-approving look. After another few minutes of study, Ted sits up. "I don't think we'll have the strength to move this thing very far; it's going to be too heavy. I can try to loosen these main bolts that connect the base to the platform, but it might not do us any good since this main arm is also connected at the back where the large motor sits." I say, "We've come this far; it's worth a try." Ted answers, "But we won't get done before the mosquitoes attack." I respond, "We probably won't anyways, so let's hurry and give it a try." This time I get the look of non-approval. Ted quickly finds the correct socket and begins to loosen the bolts at the base of the main pusher arm. Twelve bolts in all connect the pusher arm base to the platform. Eleven of the bolts come out fairly easy, but the twelfth one is a real pain. After a couple of minutes of struggling, I ask Ted to wait. The bolt that is causing the trouble is at the front left of the base. If we can swivel the main pusher arm to the left with the bolt still in place, it may be just enough.

I explain the plan to Ted and to Thomas. The next challenge is to find someplace to push against on the main pusher arm. We find a place past where the side pusher arms connect at an angle to the main pusher arm at the weld point. We count to three and push with all of our might. It feels like we are pushing against a rock wall. This thing is not budging. We make a few more vain attempts, and then Ted walks up to where the shaft of the main pusher arm goes into the holding container. "See, he says, "it goes into the container through this connection that probably has some bearings that keep it in place. Pushing isn't going to do it. Our only hope is that when we tighten everything down aimed to the left, it's enough to knock it off of center as it goes through this opening."

This time Thomas smacks me in the back of the head. "Sorry," he says with a grin on his face as I turn to look at him. I turn back around and remind Ted about the connection of the other support arm to this side of the container. We still need to loosen it. And of course the toolbox is still on the other side of the machine. Thomas and I hurry over to retrieve the toolbox top. We accidentally bang it on one of the side rails of the platform. Ted gives us both a look as we round the machine. We get the toolbox in place, and he hands the socket wrench to me. "Your turn," he says. I take the wrench and try to loosen the first bolt. It's the wrong size again. I hand Ted the larger socket he used to loosen the bolts at the base of the main pusher arm, and he quickly hands me the socket I need. I loosen the three bolts. Ted says, "Excuse me," and climbs up onto the toolbox with me. There is barely enough room for both of us. He pushes on the support arm, and it moves to the left. "Tighten quickly," he says. I go to tighten the left-most bolt, but then I realize I forgot to change the direction of the socket wrench. Once I flip the switch on the socket wrench I tighten the bolt as hard as I can. Ted says, "That's good," and then I tighten down the other two bolts.

We hop down, gently, off of the toolbox. Ted takes the socket wrench and changes it out to the one he needs to work the adjustment bolt on this side's pusher arm. He's able to get several more turns to move the side piston arm to the left of center a few more millimeters. Hopefully it is enough. It will have to be, because Ted then changes out his socket once more and begins to tighten all of the bolts. Each time he pulls on whatever he can to make sure the side pusher arm is aimed as far to the left as possible. He waits until last to tighten the bolts that hold the side pusher arm support to the platform, also pulling on the support as hard as he can. We then move to the side piston on the other side of the machine.

Thomas takes a turn working the wrench, and Ted takes over mosquito watch. I help Thomas push or pull on whatever it is he is tightening. At one point a mosquito lands on Thomas's shoulder, and I give it a whack. "Thanks," he says, after being startled for just a moment. The mosquitoes are becoming more troublesome now. We get done tightening the bolts that connect the support piece for this side pusher arm to the platform, and then Thomas and I stand up. I see Ted looking at where the support arm connects to the container. I realize that we still need to tighten down the bolts, and the toolbox is again on the wrong side. Thomas and I hurry to get the toolbox, but this time we are careful not to bang it on anything. We set it down, and I climb up onto the toolbox to begin tightening. Ted climbs up next to me, and pushes the side support arm to the left as far as his leverage allows. I tighten the first bolt, and he climbs down. I tighten the other two as I hear Ted and Thomas repeatedly smacking mosquitoes off of themselves or each other. We are out of time.

I get down off of the toolbox, and I see several mosquitoes on my clothes. I ask, "Where is the bug netting?" Thomas runs over to get the bug netting where we left it at the entrance to the smashing machine platform. Ted and I pick up the toolbox top and carry it over to the main toolbox. I try to line it up like it was when we got it, but I can feel a mosquito biting my neck. We set it down and I smack the back of my neck. Thomas returns with the bug netting, and we brush ourselves off as much as possible. The only bolts left to tighten are the ones that connect the base of the main pusher arm to the platform. Hopefully we didn't miss any important bolts along the way.

Ted grabs the ratchet set and all three of us sit down on the platform next to the base of the main pusher arm. We cover ourselves with one of the bug nets. It is darker under the bug net, but enough of the moonlight is still present that Ted finds the large socket that he will need to tighten the eleven bolts. He puts the first one back into the hole and begins to tighten. The trouble is there is nothing to tighten into. Ted stops and looks at the bolt for about thirty seconds, and then he whispers, "There must have been nuts on the underside of the platform. When I loosened these bolts and pulled them out the nuts must have fallen all the way down to the ground." He looks at Thomas, who shrugs his shoulders. "Oh well," Ted says, and he begins placing the remaining ten bolts with washers back into their places around the base of the main pusher arm. He gets to the twelfth bolt, the one that would not come out, and he tries to tighten it back down. "This doesn't make sense," he says, "Because I would need to hold the nut with a wrench on the underside to be able to loosen or tighten." Ted is able to make a few turns before the bolt locks up. It is raised about a quarter of an inch off of the platform. I try to tighten it further, but it won't budge.

142

Thomas gives it a try with no success. "Oh well," I say, "Hopefully Tom and Barry won't notice." Thomas answers, "They probably will short of some divine intervention, so let's just hope for the best." Hopefully keeping the main pusher arm loose will only help to knock it off of its course.

The next step is to figure out how to get the ratchet set back into the toolbox without letting too many mosquitoes under the bug netting. Ted packs up all of the sockets that he has in his pocket back into the ratchet set box along with the ratchet. We all stand up on the count of three and proceed to the toolbox. Ted quickly flips his right arm out from under the bug net and places the ratchet set onto the top of the toolbox base. He quickly returns his hand into the bug net and then reaches for the ratchet set from under the bug net. He grabs the ratchet set, and then realizes that he needs to open the drawer that it came from. Thomas and I inch closer to give him enough slack in the bug net. Ted opens the drawer, gently sets the ratchet set into the drawer, and then closes the drawer. We begin to walk away as a group, but then the drawer opens back up. The bug net was caught in the drawer. Ted closes the drawer, making sure we are not caught again. Thomas has the other two bug nets in his hands. Thomas and I cover ourselves with our bug nets from under Ted's. We then quickly move out and leave him to his own. Ours are folded in half, but his is fully extended and is leaving a long trail behind him as he walks in front of us back toward the roof.

We get to the window, and Thomas says, "We'll need to take these off for a minute to climb back up. You guys go first, and then I'll throw the nets up to you once you are up." I think for a second, and then I ask, "Thomas, can you go first to show us the way to do it?" He agrees and takes off his bug net. He places his left foot on the windowsill, which is about waist-high, and then as he straightens his left leg he grabs onto the window trim at the top of the window. His right foot follows his left and rests on the windowsill. The good news is that the roof does not hang over at all. Thomas keeps his right hand on the top of the window and places his left hand on the roof. He then starts pulling himself up, bringing his left foot to the top of the window. All in one motion, he brings his right hand to the roof and his right foot to the top of the window. He collects himself momentarily, and then he jumps from his toes and lands on the roof. Ted and I, who look, feel, and are, much older, share concerned glances.

I motion for Ted to go next from under my bug net, but he waves me off. I quickly remove my bug net and climb up onto the windowsill. My hands are holding onto the window trim at the top. I'm not sure how I'm going to do this, as gravity is pulling me back with great force. I reach for the roof with my right hand, only to find that there is enough of a lip that I will have a much better grip than expected. I make my move, and bring my left leg up to the window sill, opposite of how Thomas did it. As my left leg comes up, I bring my left hand to the roof and my right foot follows my left up to the top of the window trim. My momentum causes me to continue forward onto the roof and I lose my grip on the edge of the roof. I narrowly avoid a face-plant, and as I come to rest on my stomach my feet dangle over the edge of the roof. I made it, at least.

It takes Ted a couple of tries to get his feet onto the top of the window trim, but he soon meets us on the roof. We all quickly cover ourselves with our bug nets. I turn and take one last look at the smashing machine. I pray, "Lord, may you bless our work so that this machine destroys itself Thursday morning without anyone else dying for your name's sake. In Jesus' name, Amen." I turn back around, and Ted and Thomas are nearly back to the roof hatch. I walk quickly to catch up, trying not to trip over my bug net.

We get to the hatch. Thomas kneels down and takes his hand out of his bug net. Then he gets the idea to drape the bug net over the hatch. He lifts it up about an inch, but then he stops. He freezes. I'm about to ask him what the problem is, but I'm glad I don't get a chance. I hear voices coming from the room below. This is not good.

We all remain absolutely still. Two men are conversing, but I cannot make out the specifics. Thomas, with the gentlest of touches, lowers the hatch back to its resting position. Hopefully the two men don't notice the movement. Then even more fear grips me. What if they saw us go up the stairs and followed us? What if they're waiting for us to come back down to take us into their custody? What if Katie finally figured us out and turned us in? What if they have already taken Julia, Mindy, and the kids and they are waiting for us? This is really not good.

I notice my breathing becoming heavier. I have not moved from my crouched position for a few minutes, and I am already noticing a burning sensation in my leg muscles. I try to calm myself down. I hear one of the men laugh. They seem to be having a pleasant conversation. I hear the word "Leader" very distinctly, but that is all I can understand. Thomas makes the slightest of movements and sits down. Over the next several minutes, Ted and I carefully follow suit. At least my legs feel much better, but my heart is still racing.

Thomas, Ted, and I sit perfectly still for at least a half hour. The two men are very talkative, but I can only catch a few words here and there. It does not seem like they have any idea that we are sitting just above them, but I still have no idea why they are in a room with seemingly no purpose but to provide access to the roof. Thomas very slowly and quietly changes position. The trouble with the roof is that it is covered with large gravel, which makes it both very uncomfortable and very loud to move around on.

The three of us continue to sit. Every hideous possibility of what is going to happen crosses my mind. But nothing bad actually happens. Thomas, Ted, and I slowly work ourselves into more comfortable positions until we are eventually lying down. The two men continue with non-stop talking back and forth. At one point, I remember to pray. I ask God to calm us down, to protect, Julia, Mindy, and the kids, and to deliver us from this situation. I pray the same words over and over again. I lie there for what seems like an eternity. And then suddenly a bright light startles me.

Chapter 13 – The Escape

Acts 12: 5-11 (NIV), "So Peter was kept in prison, but the church was earnestly praying to God for him."

"The night before Herod was to bring him to trial, Peter was sleeping between two soldiers, bound with two chains, and sentries stood guard at the entrance. Suddenly an angel of the Lord appeared and a light shone in the cell. He struck Peter on the side and woke him up. 'Quick, get up!' he said, and the chains fell off Peter's wrists."

"Then the angel said to him, 'Put on your clothes and sandals.' And Peter did so. 'Wrap your cloak around you and follow me,' the angel told him. Peter followed him out of the prison, but he had no idea that what the angel was doing was really happening; he thought he was seeing a vision. They passed the first and second guards and came to the iron gate leading to the city. It opened for them by itself, and they went through it. When they had walked the length of one street, suddenly the angel left him."

"Then Peter came to himself and said, 'Now I know without a doubt that the Lord has sent his angel and rescued me from Herod's clutches and from everything the Jewish people were hoping would happen.'"

I wake up. Something is wrong. As I come to my senses, I lift up my head and look down at my body. I'm covered from head to toe in some kind of blanket. My whole body aches. I remove the blanket, and then I remember that it is my bug net. The roof looks totally different in the morning light. Most of the roof is still covered in shade, but the sun is just coming up over the trees behind us. I am facing the west based on where the sun is rising, the same general direction where I looked to see the body of water last night. I can no longer see it from my current vantage point. Thomas begins to stir. I shake Ted gently to wake him up. Over the next several minutes Thomas and Ted wake up, remove their bug nets, and stand up. As we stretch, we all groan from our aching muscles. Sleeping on a bed of rocks is not my idea of a good night's sleep. Thomas whispers, "I'm not sure who that was last night, but let's get back to the room before the music starts." It takes me a minute to remember what he is talking about. I reach for my phone to see what time it is, but it is not in my pocket. I remember that it is still charging in Thomas's room.

Thomas opens the hatch and starts down the ladder. When he gets about half way down, he reaches up so that I can hand him the bug nets. He climbs the rest of the way down. I reach down to grab the top handles of the ladder, and Thomas gives me a look from the floor below. His eyes are as big as watermelons. He moves his index finger over his mouth. I'm not sure what the issue is, but at least I understand that I need to be quiet. I climb down very deliberately and slowly to make sure I'm quiet. When I reach the bottom, I see the reason why Thomas became so concerned. Two men, both lying on the floor with their backs propped up against opposite walls of the room, are asleep on the floor. One has a booklet spread across his stomach. It has a picture of an air handling unit on the cover. The other guy has several manuals and schematics littered around him. I look up to Ted. I give him the same signal to be absolutely quiet on his way down. I look over to Thomas, who is giving him the same signal.

Ted climbs down very slowly. Once on the ground, he turns and looks at Thomas. Thomas points to the exit. The door is closed. I lead the way to the door. When I get there, I reach for the handle. My hand bumps it gently, making a dull banging noise. Feelings of pain grip my chest. I turn and look, but the two men remain motionless. I try again, this time making quiet contact with the door knob. I turn it, and the door opens quietly. We quickly leave the room, and I quietly close the door behind us. I breathe a quiet, yet satisfying sigh of relief as we head back down the stairs. Thomas looks back at me momentarily as we walk down the narrow staircase. He mouths the words, "Tom and Barry."

We get to the bottom of the stairway and quickly cross the short hallway to the door that will lead us to the main hallway. Thomas moves to the front and opens the door. The door opens in, so he is able to peer out of the doorway and look in both directions. He looks to the left and to the right. He takes a few steps out into the hallway, and then motions for Ted and I to follow. We waste no time falling in behind Thomas as he leads us back to our room. I can only imagine that Julia, Mindy, and the kids have waited up all night agonizing over what may have happened to us. I can't wait to come into the room and calm their fears.

We get to the door. I look back to see if anyone is in the hallway. The coast is still clear. Thomas knocks on the door, quietly. No answer. After about thirty seconds, he knocks again. Still no answer comes from anyone in the room. I am starting to get worried. What if one of my many pessimistic scenarios came true, where Katie turned us in and the rest of the group has been taken to some holding cell awaiting our capture as well? Thomas begins to knock more loudly and more often. After what seems like several more minutes of agonizing, the door begins to open. A very tired-looking Julia opens the door.

Once she sees it is us, she releases the chain and lets us in. I give her a hug, and say, "I was getting worried that you guys weren't in here." Julia answers, "We were asleep. We knew you guys would be a while, so we said a prayer and laid down to rest. It evidently didn't take long for us to fall asleep. God answered our prayer really well." Then Julia asks, "So how did it go? Did you break the machine? I can't believe it took you all night. You guys must be exhausted." Ted answers, "No, we got some sleep. Once we got done breaking the machine, we tried to climb back down from the roof, but some people were in our way. We had to spend the night on the roof so we didn't get caught." Thomas says, "That was Tom and Barry. Evidently they were trying to read up on the maintenance work they have to do today. I'm not sure why they picked that room to spend the night. That was really weird."

Julia asks, "So you broke the machine? I hope nobody notices between now and then." Ted answers, "What we did might break it, and it might not. We won't know until tomorrow." Julia's look of hope turns to disappointment. I add, "We'll make sure we're there tomorrow for the first cycle of the machine in case it doesn't break immediately. Then we'll have to go to Plan B." At that, all three kids jump up out of bed, almost simultaneously, and almost run where we are standing. "What do you mean?" Josh asks. I say, "We'll need to be in the front of the line tomorrow when they run the test cycle of the machine in case it doesn't break. If it makes it through the first cycle, several of us will have to tackle Tom and Barry, and several more will have to help Ted make some impromptu adjustments to the machine to try to get it to break."

Josh says, "Wait a minute. We have to go back up to that machine, *and* we have to be in the front of the line? I don't want to go anywhere near that thing ever again. I want to get up first thing tomorrow morning and escape through the hole in the fence. I'd be OK with doing that today to be honest with you. I want to get out of here." I try to respond, but Josh continues. "What happens if Tom and Barry force us into the machine if it still works, and they smash us all to bits?" I answer, "Well then at least we tried to save everyone who will die after us. Everything we are doing is to try to make sure no one else dies in this place ever again. Tomorrow will be the scariest day of our lives, but we have to see it through to the end. No matter what, we need to do everything we can to destroy this place."

Josh walks back to his bed and sits down in a heap. Dave asks, "Dad, isn't there another way?" To my surprise, Nate answers, "No, we have to do it this way. The machine will break, but we need to be there to either knock out Tom and Barry or to trap them inside the broken machine. If we don't stop those two, they'll be the first ones to know something is going on. If they call for help, we'll be doomed for sure. If we can stop them and lock them up, then we have a chance to get back down the stairs and out of here." I'm thankful that Nate explained the plan better than I could have. Julia asks, "Thomas, you said that there is an airstrip somewhere nearby. Do you know how to get to it?" Thomas answers, "Yes, but it's been a while. We'll follow the roads and head east until we reach it. We'll find some way to sneak on one of the cargo planes and get away from here. I'm not sure where we'll land, or what we'll do when we get there, but at least we'll have escaped.

Mindy asks, "So what did you guys do to the machine?" Thomas looks at me and Ted and smiles. Ted answers, "The thing may pull to the left a little now." Thomas adds, "If that thing still runs after the first cycle I'll be really surprised. Julia walks to Thomas's side. "Look at your neck," she says, "It's covered in bug bites." Thomas answers, "Mosquitoes, lots of mosquitoes. I feel the back of my neck with my hand and feel several itchy bumps are present. I also feel my forehead itching. I rub my hand on my forehead, and Nate notices. He says, "Yeah, one bit you right between the eyes."

Just as I'm about to thank Nate for stating the obvious, the wake-up music starts to play. Thomas says, "We are so lucky that we woke up before the music started, which would have woken up Tom and Barry. We would have been dead meat if we were trapped on the roof. There would have been no explaining our way out of that one." Ted answers, "No, but if we were awake we could have jumped back down to the walkway and gone down the stairs." Thomas says, "Yeah, but the door at the bottom is always locked, and there is no handle." I respond, "That's true, but if it doesn't shut completely, you can still get it open. I wish I would have thought of that last night!" Thomas smiles, as I presumably put another piece of the puzzle together for him how we got back into the building the first time. Ted mentions, "Yeah, we probably could have taken the stairs to the second floor and found a way back into the building, too." Thomas responds, "Yes but we would have run into locked doors trying to go back inside the building from the second floor."

Then Thomas says, "I'm going to head back to my room and get cleaned up. How about you guys meet me at my room when you're ready and we'll go to breakfast." We all agree. Risking death at the smashing machine has made me hungry. As Thomas turns to leave, I stop him and say, "Thomas, before you go, let's say a prayer." He nods and walks over to where Josh is sitting on the bed and sits next to him. I get down on one knee in front of the bed, and we all joins hand in a circle, either sitting, standing, or kneeling.

"Dear Lord," I begin, "Thank you for helping us to accomplish Phase Two of our mission. Thank you for protecting us last night. Thank you for helping Thomas, Ted, and me to try to break the smashing machine. In Your Name, I ask that the machine never kills anyone again. I also ask, in Your Name, that you continue to protect us and see us through to the end of this terrible situation. Give us the power of your Holy Spirit to be brave and to do the things that we need to do to help destroy this place. Nothing we do will be successful without you. May your Spirit go ahead of us and prepare this place for destruction. Make us a blessing in the midst of this terrible place, and please continue to disguise us to all of the people here. Thank you for helping us to sneak past Tom and Barry this morning as they were sleeping on the floor. That was a miracle in itself. Now I know how Peter must have felt when he was led out of the jail by the angel and past the prison guards. Thank you, Jesus, for being with us today, tomorrow, and to the end. In your name we pray, Amen."

We stand up. Thomas pats the kids on the shoulders on the way out. We spend the next twenty minutes or so getting cleaned up for breakfast. I'd like to take a shower, but I am sure this morning's work will make me sweat a lot, so I should wait until later. I go into the bathroom and change my clothes, brush my teeth, and wash my face. When everyone's ready, we regroup in the middle of the room. We proceed to the door and make our way to Thomas's room. When we arrive, Ted knocks on the door. Thomas opens the door and shuts it behind him. As we start toward the kitchen, Thomas reaches into his pocket. He hands me my phone. "Thanks," I say.

Breakfast goes smoothly for us. The crowd seems less than the past few mornings. Maybe the crowd is simply more spaced out. Everyone who comes into the cafeteria is very quiet. Not much conversation occurs. People come in, eat, and leave fairly quickly. We take our time eating, and most of us go back for seconds. We, too, are quiet, since there is no conversation noise in the room to mask any conversations we would like to have.

I'm eager to find out what is next for us. There is still likely plenty of work to do to prepare for the Leader's arrival this afternoon. After my second plate of food, I look around at everyone to see if anyone else is still eating. Thomas is the only one still eating, but he is taking his last bites. Once he finishes, we all make a quick exit from the cafeteria.

As we start down the stairs, Julia asks, "What's on the agenda for this morning?" Thomas pauses until he reaches the bottom of the stairs. He turns and looks at Julia and says, "I'm not exactly sure yet. There are always some last minute chores to do before he arrives. I figure we'll go check with Mom to see what she needs help with." Once we all reach the bottom of the stairs, Thomas continues to lead the group. We walk through the porridge room and into the downstairs kitchen. Beth is not in the kitchen. Thomas proceeds through the doors into the Saints' eating area, and we follow.

Beth is sitting at one of the tables in the strangely decorated room. She has paperwork all around her, and she is filling out something as we enter. She looks up at us. I divert my eyes from hers. I assume they'll be especially crazy-looking today. As I look at the wall behind her, Beth says, "Good morning! What a blessed day." I don't share her enthusiasm. She continues, "I wanted to let you guys know what an excellent job you did cleaning up this room. It was as messy as it had been in a while, and I couldn't find anything that you missed. Good job!" Thomas answers, "Thanks, Mom!" I look at Thomas momentarily, and then I look back in Beth's general direction. I don't see her looking at us, so I look directly at her. Her head is back down and she is looking at her paperwork. After a few more seconds of waiting, Thomas asks, "What else can we help with this morning?"

Beth thinks for a short time and then says, "I think we are in pretty good shape inside the building. The only thing left to do will be to do one final cleanup of the upstairs kitchen after lunch. The kitchen crew should have it covered, but I'll let you know if we get short on time. It all depends on when we get the call that he is on the ground and on his way to the building." I assume Beth is talking about the Leader. She thinks for a few more seconds and then says, "Thomas, why don't you guys go outside and help the grounds crew clean up the property until lunch. There are always plenty of things to do out in the yard." Thomas responds, "Sure thing, Mom!"

I try to hide my excitement. It has nothing to do with my love for yard work and being outdoors. This might be our chance to sneak down to the reservoir and deactivate the valves that will otherwise be opened tomorrow to release its vile contents. Thomas looks at me momentarily as I look at him, and then he looks back at his mom. "We're on our way," he says, and he leads us out of the room. "Thanks," Beth says as she continues with her paperwork. As we walk out, Beth says, "Don't forget to come in for lunch. Everything will be shut down by one o'clock sharp at the latest." Thomas doesn't look back, but he nods affirmatively and says, "Got it." We continue out of the room and walk back through the kitchen. Thomas leads us through the supply closet and into the hallway.

I wonder if Thomas will have us go back to the room to discuss plans before going outside, but we walk right past our room. We pass the room where the youth meeting was held. We walk past the security room, which is the last room before the door to the outside. Thomas opens the door and walks outside. He holds the door for the rest of us while we file out of the building. As I walk out into the morning air, I can feel the warmth hit my skin. The sun is shining brightly now. A small overhang shades where most of us are standing, but I have moved into the sunlight. Once everyone makes it through the door, Thomas lets it shut behind us. It feels good to be outside of the building. I feel less confined, less trapped.

Thomas begins to walk along the sidewalk that spans the length of the building front to back. We are heading to the right of the door where we exited the building. I don't see anyone working in the yard on this side of the building. The lawn looks very nice and extends about thirty feet to a wooded area. The wooded area looks more like a jungle and is very overgrown. I see a few flowering bushes and trees blooming in the sunlight along the edge of the jungle. As we near the back edge of the building, a noise startles us. I soon realize the sound is that of a lawn mower being started. After a few more seconds, we round the corner of the building. In front of us, about thirty feet away, is the Stairway to Heaven and the smashing machine. The stairway extends up the three stories of the building, and is encased in netting. As we get closer, I see that the netting is attached to the ground by some metal rings that must have been placed into the concrete just before or after it was poured.

Thomas leads us into the grass. It is still very wet with dew. We walk around the stairway and the platform that holds the smashing machine. I look to the left, and I can see that the lawn extends further on this side of the building. He walks us around the metal support beams that hold up the smashing machine. The support structure looks similar to what one would see on an electrical tower. I look up and can see the underside of the platform that Ted, Thomas, and I were working from late last night. I can see some spring-like arms that are most likely involved in tipping the container during or after its smashing cycle. There are also several pipes that extend out of the bottom of the platform. The largest pipe hangs down from the left end of the platform and extends further to the left around fifteen feet. It appears to be open at the end. Several more, smaller pipes extend from the right end of the platform past the large pipe and then on into the woods at the side of the property. In my mind I deduce that the large pipe is for the solids and the smaller pipes transport the liquids to the reservoir. That's as far as I want to take my analysis.

As we round the platform, I look out toward the edge of the lawn where the jungle begins. The lawn slopes down somewhat as it extends away from the building, and there is also a slope down from right to left. At the far edge of the lawn, starting at about halfway across the lawn from our vantage point and extending to the right, is a steep hill that extends at least ten to fifteen feet above the ground. The hill looks covered with the same well-manicured grass as the lawn. I assume that this is the edge of the reservoir. The trees on the outside edge of the jungle look somewhat farther back behind the hill. It was evidently too dark to see the reservoir from atop the smashing machine platform last night.

Once we pass the smashing machine, we don't have far to walk to reach the edge of this side of the building. We walk into the shadow cast on us by the smashing machine. I look over at the building and can see the walkway on the second floor where we escaped from the holding room after we woke up. It is from there we were forced onto the Stairway to Heaven by the approaching camp counselors. What an experience that was, and unfortunately one that we will have to relive tomorrow. I hope this crazy plan somehow works. We turn the corner at the back of the building. The lawn mower sound has been growing louder, and becomes even louder as we reach the point where we can see it. The riding lawn mower is sitting idle as it runs. It is one of those fancy rider units that have the lever handles and at least four or five blades underneath. Several camp workers in the camp counselor outfits (short sleeve versions) are standing near the mower. Another worker emerges from a room with double doors that are fully open. He is pushing a smaller, but still sizable, walk-behind mower. One of the workers in the group notices us and walks up to the riding mower that is running. He slows down the motor, which makes it considerably quieter. He walks up to our group, who is standing about ten feet behind the mower.

"Good morning, Thomas," the man says. He looks at the rest of us and says, "Good morning, folks." We all return the good morning, and then

Thomas says, "Morning Jim. We've been sent out to help. You got anything for us this morning?" Jim looks at Thomas and rolls his eyes. "Need some busy work, eh buddy?" Jim asks. "If you have anything," Thomas replies. Jim turns and looks back at his group, and then he turns back toward us. "Sure!" he exclaims. Jim seems to be a really upbeat kind of guy. He continues. "How about we get you some gloves, shovels, and trash bags, and you guys can comb the back lawn for anything that might give us trouble while we're mowing. These guys will take care of the front and sides before they mow." Jim points to the workers behind him. The sound of another mower being started comes from the room with the double doors as Jim points to his crew.

I say, "Trash duty, I'm good at that," trying to be funny. Thomas says, "We won't find much litter on the grounds to be picked up." Jim nods in agreement and says, "Yeah, it's not like you'll find any hamburger wrappers or newspaper ads blowing around here. What you'll be on the lookout for is more organic in nature." Thomas adds, "I call them presents, from the resident animals." The excitement I had about this opportunity to be outside and to get near the reservoir valves just vanished. Jim continues. "Be on the lookout for any piles left behind by the animals, or any dead critters, whole or partial, that need scooped up so we don't run one of the mowers over them. The Leader likes the lawn to be perfect; that's why he puts his best people on the grounds crew." Jim looks back at his crew again. Several members of his crew look back at us, bewildered by the sudden attention. He looks back at us and rolls his eyes.

The second riding mower pulls out of the lawn equipment room. It is equally as fancy-looking as the first one and equally as clean. The increased noise will make it hard to hear. Jim yells, "Wait here; I'll be right back." We nod as he turns and walks into the equipment room. He motions for one of his workers to follow him. They both disappear into the building. Thomas calls us in for the huddle. He says, as quietly as he can, "This is our chance to get to the reservoir valves. I'm not sure what we can do, but at least we can take a look at the setup. We'll spread out over the lawn and collect 'trash' for about ten or fifteen minutes, and when I give a whistle we'll make our way toward the reservoir. I'll lead the way, but follow me by meandering more than walking directly over."

Josh asks, "What if any mowers come out to where we are before we get there?" Thomas answers, "Good question. We'll have to abort the mission if they make it to the backyard before we get done. Even though the mowers are running right now, for whatever reason the crew lets the mowers run for about thirty minutes before they actually start mowing. It seems like a waste of gas to me. The guys over there will do the same thing that we're doing in the front and side yards. Once they get it cleaned up, then they'll mow up there before they come back here. We'll play it by ear and see what happens."

I look back at the remaining workers, who are still standing together talking. There are three of them; two who were standing there as we walked up, and the other one who came out of the building with the walk-behind mower. The other worker who brought out the second riding mower is now bringing several weed eaters out of the equipment room. After a few seconds of me looking at them, one of the workers notices me looking at him. He looks away and motions for the other two guys to go into the equipment room with him.

We wait another five minutes or so, and then Jim returns with our supplies. After a few seconds his helper follows with more supplies. Jim first hands out pairs of work gloves, all larges. Next he hands each of us a pick shovel. After that we all get our large, dark green trash bags. As he finishes handing out the trash bags, I see the other workers coming out of the equipment room with similar supplies. I'm kind of worried about how wild this wildlife is around here leaving all of these presents for us. Jim says, "You guys are all set. Good luck, and thanks for the help!" He pauses for a second, and then he says, "Oh yeah, keep your eye out for the snakes." He receives a collective gasp from the group. He smiles and says, "They shouldn't bother you. If you see one, just keep your distance and give him time to slither away. Don't worry; you can't miss 'em!" I'm not amused. Jim continues and says, "And make sure any critters you pick up are dead before you scoop them into the bag. Poke 'em first, and if they move, whack 'em until they stop." I look over at Julia and Mindy who have horrified expressions on their faces. Ted, who also knew to look over at them, says, "Just call one of us if you need any help." He chuckles and looks back at Jim who nods approvingly.

With that, Jim turns and starts to walk back to the building. His helper follows. Thomas turns and motions for us to follow. Nobody moves. He stops after a few steps and says, "Come on guys; it's not so bad. I've done this many times and I've never seen a snake. Just be careful, and if you find something just call me over. Thomas starts walking again. This time we follow him, and after we get further into the lawn he says, "Spread out guys." We begin to fan out, but we all keep our backs to the building and our aim at eventually reaching the reservoir. Very quickly Josh calls Thomas over. He must have found something. I walk over to see what he found, since I am close by. When I arrive, Thomas has already directed Josh to scoop up his discovery. It is the bony remains of some creature. A few pieces of fur are stuck to the bones, most likely from the predator as opposed to the prey. Whatever the predator was he didn't leave much meat behind.

I return to my search. I do more looking around at my surroundings than looking for animal remains or excrement, but I do a thorough scan for snakes about every thirty seconds. I love yard work, when it's my lawn, but I don't feel very obliged to do a good job cleaning up the Leader's lawn. I monitor the group to ensure we continue to meander in the general direction of the reservoir. At one point Nate starts to wander back in the direction of the building. I walk over close to him, and call out, "Nate, this way." He turns and looks at me and says, "OK, I thought I saw something over here, but I guess not." He walks back toward me. I say, "Maybe you did see something, but it scurried away." He looks back and me and says, "That's not helping." I respond with a smile. Nate and I stick together as we continue searching. I see a patch of cool-looking mushrooms growing in one spot, so I scoop them up and put them into my bag for good measure. I notice a sprinkler head right near where I am digging. This Leader guy is serious about his lawn.

Thomas lets out his whistle. He gives the signal sooner than I expected. We follow him to the left edge of the reservoir. We start up the hill, and I can quickly see that we are going over a small hill that extends out from the left front edge of the reservoir. Once we get near the top I can see that behind this part of the hill is a small ravine with some mechanical equipment. I look to my right, toward the reservoir, and then I see it in full view. "The blood!" I exclaim loudly. I'm sure everyone looks at me, but I don't care. My stomach, which has already been made queasy by our job assignment this morning, is immediately turned in knots. The reservoir, this most vile of things, is filled to within a few feet of the upper edge. Some kind of black lining extends up out of the terrible mixture on the edges of the reservoir, and it is tucked in at the top by grass growing over the edge.

We stare in horror for what seems like forever, even though it probably doesn't last for more than thirty seconds before Thomas calls to us from the bottom of the hill's backside. "Guys, we don't have much time! I can already hear the mowers starting to go back and forth in the front. I forgot that since we're doing the cleanup in back that they had the whole crew to clean up the front and the sides. Those guys don't mess around. I need someone to stay high enough on this side of the hill to keep watch for when they get to one of the side yards, and then we need to head back." Julia and Mindy volunteer to keep watch, and the rest of us join Thomas at a concrete slab with two large pumps. Piping enters and exits the pumps. Actuated valves are positioned prior to and after the pumps. One valve appears behind each pump, and two valves are positioned after each pump.

Thomas says, "Sorry guys; I know that must have been tough for you to see for the first time. I can't believe there is someone in this world with so much hate for a group of people that he would do something like that. And then to collect part of their remains just to do whatever he needs to do with them when he gets here; it's just plain criminal." I look at the kids and they are all choking back tears. I am, too, as I think of how many people had to die to fill up that reservoir. Ted pulls us back into the situation at hand. "So what we need to do is deactivate these valves." He pauses for a few seconds, and then says, "But I'm not sure if we want to do it right now." I ask, "Why not?" Ted continues to look at and touch one of the valves as he says, "If I remember what I've learned about valves and PLC's, these valves are constantly sending information to and receiving information from the main PLC about their status and whether anything is going wrong. If we try to disconnect these valves now, it's going to send a signal to the main PLC that something is wrong. And if Tom and Barry are as good at being maintenance technicians as I think they are, they'll have some bells and whistles go off if anything is going wrong with something that the Leader wants to have working during his visit. The more I think about it, the more sure I am that we can't do this right now."

Ted gives a pretty convincing argument. God makes it apparent that Ted is right when Julia calls down to us to warn us that she sees a mower coming into view. We all make a quick run back up the small hill to meet Julia and Mindy. As we come down the hill, I can see that the guy working the mower has seen us retreating from the reservoir. Thomas looks directly at him as he looks at us. Then Thomas says, still looking at him, "Everyone play it cool. I'll come up with something. Everyone get back to looking for stuff in the grass, and spread back out." Now I'm worried, as I'm sure everyone else is. We have been caught being somewhere we shouldn't have been.

The guy on the mower makes his way toward us. We all go back to looking for things in the grass. I notice that he has raised the blades on the mower so he doesn't cut a crooked line through the back yard. When he gets to Thomas, he puts the mower in neutral and slows down the engine. "Tom, is everything OK?" he asks. Thomas answers, "Yeah, everything's OK now. One of the kids ran into a pretty big one, so I coaxed it over the hill. He was already headed that way, but I used the technique Jim showed us to persuade it to keep moving. It worked pretty well. Everyone followed me over the hill at a safe distance to make sure I was OK."

Thomas's story seems to placate the worker. He says, "You guys be careful; those things can swallow you whole!" The worker then cranks the mower back up near full throttle and puts in into gear. He makes a quick turn and aims for the right side of the building. "Good job!" Ted says to Thomas once the worker leaves us. "Thanks," Thomas says. I ask, "What do we do now?" Thomas answers, "We'll spend a few more minutes looking for stuff out back. Once the mowers start to get close to us we'll head back to the building and dump our stuff. After that I think we'll have a chance to sneak into the woods for a few minutes to check out the hole in the fence that I told you about. I want to make sure I can get the whole group through the woods and to the escape point if we get the chance." The way he worded that doesn't sit too well. "I hope we get the chance," Dave says.

We continue to search for any imperfections in the lawn for at least ten more minutes before the mowers make their way to the top of the back lawn. The sick feeling in my stomach hasn't gone away from seeing the contents of the reservoir. I hope the Lord enacts vengeance on these people for what they have done, and I hope it happens while we are here so I can see it. What a waste of life; so many innocent people killed, as it seems, for what they believe in. I need to try to find out more about what the general camp workers think is going on. I make my way over to Thomas, who is scooping something into his bag. "Thomas," I ask, "what does the typical camp worker think he or she is doing to the Saints who are brought here?" Thomas continues to scoop the animal droppings into his bag. Without looking up at me he says, "What I've been told, what we've been told since I got here is that the people brought here are Saints who have lost their way. The Leader is bringing them to this place to save them, and the purification meal prepares them for Heaven where the Leader will show them the truth about him. The Leader, supposedly, exists in Heaven and on Earth, and he has come down to Earth to save the Saints, both those who are in his cult and those who have supposedly lost their way. The camp counselors are supposed to be rewarded, eventually, with their own trip to Heaven, but not until his work is complete."

I want to ask how people could be so stupid to believe such a hokey story of a man posing to be the Savior, but I don't want to say anything bad about Beth and make Thomas feel worse than he already does. Thomas continues. "It took me a while to piece it all together, and I pretty much had it figured out even before I started snooping around. Once I saw the smashing machine in action for the first time, it all made sense. No one except Tom and Barry are allowed on top of the platform, so no one is supposed to know where the Saints go once they reach the top of the staircase. I don't think any of the other camp counselors have ever seen it, except at a distance from ground level if they are walking out in the yard. Most of the camp workers don't come outside very much for fear of the wildlife." Thomas looks up at me and asks, "If you hadn't been up there to see the machine, would you have known what you were looking at when we walked under the platform earlier?" I answer, "No," and Thomas continues to talk. "I asked Mom once when we first got here where the Saints go once they reach the top of the Stairway to Heaven, and her answer was they are taken straight to Heaven to be with the Leader. I never believed her, but little did I know at the time that the people were simply being murdered. Only now do I have a little comfort knowing that the Saints who have died have gone to the real Heaven to be with God." I add, "The real Savior."

I notice one of the mowers is getting close as the noise is becoming significantly louder. The worker with the walk-behind mower is cutting a swath around the edge of the property. He is coming down the gentle slope about twenty feet to our right, and he is smartly aiming the discharge chute into the woods. Thomas yells out to the group, "This should be good!" No one else seems to be in the middle of picking up anything, so hopefully we did a good enough job. My bag is almost empty and only contains the mushrooms that I found. We head back up the lawn to the building. Jim is there to greet us, weed-eater in hand. He powers off the weed-eater and sets it down as we make it to the sidewalk.

"Good job, guys," Jim says, even though our large bags are mostly empty. "I heard you guys saw Stretch!" he exclaims. Our quizzical looks prompt him to say more. "Our pet snake, Stretch, of course," he says. We all smile and nod approvingly. Thomas says, "Your technique worked like a charm. I told them not to worry, but they all had to follow me to the edge of the lawn to make sure I didn't get pulled into the woods and eaten, I guess." Jim laughs, and then he says, "I think we're in pretty good shape now. Thanks again for your help. You can drop your trash bags in the dumpster inside the room there, and just leave the shovels out here so I can give them a quick rinse later. The gloves can go back on the shelf in there where you see the other gloves. Just pile them up wherever you can."

We set our shovels down on the other side of the left double door of the equipment room. We all walk in and toss our mostly empty garbage bags into a plastic dumpster just inside the room. As we remove our gloves and place them on the shelves, Jim walks in and grabs the handle of the dumpster, which is on wheels. He says, "I'd better get this thing out of here or the room is really going to smell." He wheels it out of the room and out of sight. Once everyone is de-gloved, we follow Thomas out of the room. I expect him to turn left so we can go back the way we came, but he instead turns right. Jim is just turning the corner at the front of the building, still pulling the dumpster. Thomas stops once Jim turns the corner. He says, "I'm going to pretend to take you on a walking tour of the front of the building. If the opportunity presents itself, we'll sneak into the woods at the side of the building and see how difficult it is going to be for us to get to the hole in the fence." Without giving anyone a chance to respond, Thomas turns back around and leads us down the sidewalk toward the front of the building. I look up, and I surmise that we are walking directly under the door of the holding room where we woke up on Monday morning. I look to the left to study the foliage that I first saw when we exited the holding room. This side yard is more narrow; maybe only fifteen or twenty feet to the woods. I hear something scurrying in the brush. I'm not very excited about venturing into the jungle, even if it is behind the electric fence.

Thomas gives us a nice tour of the front grounds while Jim loads more trash bags into the dumpster at the edge of the building. He walks us down the main driveway to the edge of the property. A gate extends across the driveway to keep unwanted intruders off of the premises. Dave asks how the gate opens. Thomas points to a guard shack just outside the gate and says, "The guard opens and shuts the gate electronically. It usually only opens for deliveries in and for the garbage trucks that go in and out. Two guards rotate in twelve hour shifts every day of the week. They never get a break, which seems kind of silly." If we do escape, I hope we don't have to run past the guard shack while out in the open. I'm certain that the guard is heavily armed.

I look back at the building after studying the guard shack. Jim rounds the corner of the building with the dumpster and walks back toward the equipment room. The white building, a large three story rectangle, looks unassuming and somewhat normal. Walkways span the second and third floors, with the sidewalk running across the length of the ground level under the second floor walkway. The driveway turns and makes a large oval in front of the building. It connects to the sidewalk right in front of the main double doors to the building. This must be where the Saints get unloaded when they arrive, but I do not understand how they are brought to the second floor. The double doors are at ground level, with no stairs required to reach them. More nicely manicured lawn is contained within the oval-shaped drive. No trees, shrubs, or flowers accent the inner oval; I guess the Leader just likes his grass.

We walk back up the driveway and around the front of the building. As we near the front entrance, I notice the fancy woodwork on the front doors. The doors are painted white, and they each have symmetrical floral patterns encased in a trim border about six inches short of the edges of the door. Thomas stops our group in front of the doors. We are still in the driveway, about twenty feet from the doors. He points to the gate entrance and says quietly, "When the first Saints delivery gets here in the morning there will be an all-hands call to empty the trucks. There will be about three truckloads' worth of unconscious people that will need to be unloaded onto stretchers and wheeled up to the holding room in shifts tomorrow. This is grueling work trying to lift the dead weight of unconscious people onto stretchers. You'll have a partner to help you load your Saints onto the stretchers. Then the two of you will be responsible for wheeling your Saints up the ramp to the second floor holding room and unloading them onto the floor. You'll take at least fifteen people up to the room, depending on how quick you and your partner are. Once the first group is transferred to the room, then the resuscitation team goes in to wake them up. Once the folks in the first group start to wake up, then the call is made for the second group to be delivered."

Thomas continues. "Three groups are coming tomorrow, but hopefully we gum things up enough that the second group doesn't make it past the holding room. We'll make sure we're helping feed the first group their porridge to avoid getting stuck carting in the second group. As the first group is led out to the Stairway to Heaven, we'll sneak out and put on our robes. We'll get to the stairs ahead of the group so we are in the front of the line." I cut in and say, "At that point, everything else that happens is in God's hands." I look over at the kids, who are standing next to each other. They look scared, just like I probably do. I say, "Guys, this will be the hardest thing that any of us has ever done in our lives. I'm not sure how we're going to have the courage to do it, but I know that if we trust in Jesus he will help us through it. I'm so sorry to have to ask you guys to risk your lives to try to save others, especially with a plan that may not work." I start to cry. "I'm sorry," I say.

Surprisingly, the kids remain strong. They come over to me and give me a group hug. Josh says, "Don't worry, Dad. We're ready to see what

Jesus can do." I smile and try to collect myself. I have the best kids in the world, which makes it all the harder to subject them to this horrible situation. Thomas says, "Let's keep moving." He leads us the rest of the way across the front of the building. We turn the corner to the side of the building from where we first emerged. I see the door back to the hallway where our room is located.

Thomas leads us to the edge of the lawn. He pauses for several minutes and looks all around to see if anyone is else is in the area. As we all stand by the edge of the woods, I notice that the mowers have been turned off. The lawn work must be finished. I ask Thomas, very quietly, "Will the lawn crew keep on working now that the lawn is cut, or will they go back inside?" Thomas answers, "They'll spend at least a half hour cleaning up the equipment and putting it back into the room. They'll stay on the other side of the building for a while. Now's our chance; let's go."

Thomas walks about ten more feet toward the back yard, and then he ducks into the woods. He holds back the branch of a large fern so that we can all enter into the jungle. I try to tell myself that it's not the real jungle since we are still inside the electrified border fence, but it sure looks like the real jungle. Once we are all in, we try to position ourselves in open spots where we can stand while we wait on Thomas. He continues to look back toward the building to make sure we were not seen. He slowly returns the large fern leaf to its original position. I look over at Dave, who is standing next to Nate and pointing to something above where they are standing. I see a large spider web with, by far, the biggest spider I've seen in the wild. As we all stare in awe at the spider, Thomas walks past us and says, "Guys, let's keep moving." We shift our attention to our current mission and follow Thomas deeper into the jungle. We can't go in too deep, or we'll get zapped by the fence at the edge of the property.

After much stepping over and ducking under branches, we arrive at the fence. I don't see any holes at this point. We continue to follow Thomas. I spend as much time looking for spiders and snakes as I do looking where I am going. Luckily the rest of the group is not trying to go any faster, Thomas included. After about ten more minutes of hiking through the narrow strip of jungle that separates the front lawn from the electric fence, we arrive at the hole in the fence. Along the way I wonder if the hole would be somehow repaired when we arrived, negating our plan to escape. But there it is, plenty wide enough and lifted off of the ground enough for each of us to easily crawl under. We could even dig out some of the dirt underneath it to ensure we don't accidentally make contact with the bottom of the fence. It's more of a fence bend and displacement than a hole, given that the fence is still fully intact. I'm not sure what kind of large animal or piece of equipment could have caused the opening, but I thank the Lord it's still here.

As we continue to stand as a group in front of the hole the thought crosses my mind that we could simply try to escape now. Ted vocalizes my thought. "Well, what are we waiting for?" he says, chuckling. It is very tempting. Thoughts justifying the escape continue to pass through my mind. We've de-poisoned the porridge. We've hopefully adjusted the smashing machine enough that it will destroy itself during its test cycle in the morning. Now's our chance; I have to think about the kids. I can't risk their lives any more if I have a chance to get them out of here. What kind of father would I be to not get my kids out of here while we have the chance? Tomorrow we will likely die if we stay. There's no guarantee that all of the Saints who are brought in tomorrow won't die as well. Once we're killed the place will most likely continue to run as normal. No one in the outside world will ever know what we tried to do.

I've just about convinced myself to suggest we get out while we can when I hear Josh call from behind me. "Guys!" he says, "Let's go. We need to get back to the building and get cleaned up before lunch." I turn and look at him. Thomas is standing next to Josh a few feet behind the rest of us. Josh repeats, "Guys, let's go!" Josh is right. We need to get back to the building and finish what we started. The hole will still be here tomorrow, whether or not we are able make our way back to it. My children know the Lord, and even if we all die tomorrow we'll be reunited in Heaven with Jesus. What an opportunity they have, we all have, to lay down our lives in Jesus' name.

I take one last look at the hole in the fence, and then I turn to follow Thomas and Josh back out of the jungle. Julia is walking right beside me. I put my arm around her until we get to the next obstacle to clear. I look her in the eyes. She has been crying, too. She was probably thinking the same things that I was. No mom loves her kids more than she does, and this must be breaking her heart to have to see them live through this ordeal. I whisper, "It will be OK, it will be OK." She nods, and then we separate to duck under and around branches. I let her go ahead of me the rest of the way. I look back at one point and see Ted helping Mindy maneuver around a bush. Nate and Dave are bringing up the rear, helping each other through the brush.

It seems to take us longer to get back out of the jungle, but we eventually get there. I know that we are doing the right thing, but the thoughts keep trying to creep back into my mind that we just passed up a perfectly good opportunity to escape. We stared right at freedom, and we passed it up. I decide as we reach our entrance / exit point to give it over to Jesus. I pray in my mind, "Jesus, we are doing this for you. I give this whole situation over to you. May your Holy Spirit go ahead of us and prepare this place for destruction. We are laying down our lives for you. In your name I pray, Amen."

Thomas reaches the edge of the jungle and stops. He peers out at the building and the lawn for several minutes. Finally he seems satisfied that we can reemerge from the jungle unnoticed. "Let me go first," he says. "I'll wave you guys out once I'm sure everything is OK." Thomas quickly steps back into the lawn, letting the large fern leaf fly back in our direction. Josh pulls the branch back so we can see Thomas. He very quickly starts to wave his hand to motion us to come out. Josh leads the rest of us out, and within thirty seconds, we are all back onto the lawn. Thomas doesn't waste any time leading us back to the building. We make it to the door, and it doesn't seem like anyone is around to see us. As he opens the door for us Thomas says, "Well, was that the nickel tour or the dime tour?" Ted responds, "That was more like the silver dollar tour. I'm tired and sweaty." Thomas says, "Good, then we'll get cleaned up for lunch." Thomas closes the door behind us once we are all back inside the building.

I reach into my pocket to check the time on my phone. Somehow the battery is already low. Thomas beats me to the punch. He says, "It's just after eleven o'clock now. Let's get showered up and you guys plan to meet me at my room at noon. We'll grab some lunch before lockdown." Thomas starts walking down the hall toward our rooms. As I walk past the security room, I stop as I notice one of the monitors showing where we just were outside of the building. The camera then swivels to the left. I realize that Thomas must have been watching the camera position as we entered and exited the jungle. Since no one monitors the security cameras it probably didn't matter, but it probably didn't hurt to be extra careful in case someone was watching.

I wait until last as everyone files into the room. I hand Thomas my phone and ask him to charge it yet again. He obliges and walks toward the door to his room. I shut the door to our room, and we start the cleanup process. I wait for Julia and Mindy to get showered, and then it's my turn. While I'm showering, I think about how this could be the last shower I take in this place, or anywhere. I spend most of the shower praying to ward off the thoughts of fear and of dying. I pray for peace and for wisdom, as well as for deliverance. I pray for the strength to stand tomorrow in the face of death. I pray for help. I pray for God's love to transcend everything that happens from now on and for us to feel his love in a real and powerful way. I pray for the Holy Spirit to be pouring out of all of us as we try to turn this place upside-down tomorrow. And then I remember that Ted still needs to shower after me, so I hurry and finish.

Chapter 14 – The Good Times

Micah 7:7 (NIV), "But as for me, I watch in hope for the Lord, I wait for God my Savior; my God will hear me."

I emerge from the bathroom, clean and dressed. I slip on my shoes and see Ted walk into the restroom behind me. The kids are all done showering and are sitting on one of the beds. They are praying together. Julia and Mindy are in front of the mirror in the kids' bathroom. I walk toward the kids. Dave is shaking his fist as he prays. I stop short and look at them, and for the first time since we got here I realize that the kids look quite a bit older than I remember them being. What a strange feeling. I continue to struggle with the effects of the drugs. My memories of them stop in the six-to-eight age range as of this moment. I shake it off as I continue my walk toward the kids.

I kneel down on the floor next to the bed. I put my hand on Nate's hands folded on his lap. I startle all three of them for a second, but then Dave continues with his prayer. "Jesus help us, Jesus help us," he says over and over again. He stops, and then Josh says, "Give us strength Lord, give us strength." Nate chimes in and says, "We need you Jesus, we need you here to help us." I join in. "Save us Jesus from this place. Save us now." We continue praying for several minutes, each taking turns to speak from our hearts to our God. Then we are interrupted by a knock on the door. I get up and urge the kids to continue. I assume it is Thomas because we are probably taking too long to get ready for lunch.

I arrive at the door and I open it. It is Thomas. He comes into the room and says, "We're going to run out of time if we don't hurry. Is everyone ready?" The kids join us near the door. "We're ready," Dave says. He says it like he is referring to more than just lunch. Julia and Mindy emerge from the kids' bathroom and line up next to us. Thomas looks at us and laughs gently. "You guys look rough," he says, "and I don't blame you." He gets us to laugh, too. Ted then emerges from the bathroom. "Are we ready?" he asks. Thomas answers, "We're ready when you are." Ted grabs his shoes and sits on the nearest bed. He puts on his shoes while Thomas opens the door. When Ted stands up we walk through the doorway to make yet another trip to the upstairs kitchen. I don't feel hungry at all due to my nerves, but I plan on eating a reasonable amount to keep up my strength.

I am surprised by how many people are in the hallway. Even though the total number is probably under fifteen people, it's still more than I've seen except for at the youth meeting last night. Most are walking toward us, presumably back to their rooms. The rest are standing outside a few of the rooms talking to each other. I overhear two women talking by their doors as we walk by. The one on the left says, "Something just feels different this time. I hope it means this visit will be the most special one yet." The one on the right nods and says, "I hope so, too." I hope that the different feeling is the Holy Spirit filling this place in preparation for its destruction by God Almighty. But I keep my opinion to myself as I walk by.

The rest of the walk is uneventful. Thomas hands me my phone at one point during the walk and says, "Quick charge." I expect that since we are late that the line for food will be very long. When we get to the top of the stairs, we are able to walk most of the way across the eating area before the line starts. "Not as bad as I thought," I say to Dave who is directly in front of me. "Thank goodness," Dave says, still with a determined look on his face. "I wasn't sure if I was going to be hungry, but then I decided that I was," he says. That's my boy. After about ten minutes, we reach the trays. We fill them up with sandwiches and pizza slices and salads across the eight of us. We grab our drinks and find a seat. Our usual table is open this time, the one near the restroom.

At Thomas's urging we filled our trays with food since there won't be enough time for seconds today. I eat my first turkey wrap and part of the second, and I finish my salad. For not feeling hungry I did pretty well. Everyone else is finishing up when a binging sound fills the room. It sounds like the fasten seat belt chime inside a passenger jet. We all

171

look at Thomas. "That's the signal that the Leader is on his way to the facility. We have about thirty minutes to get back to the room for lockdown. I ask Thomas, "Do you need to stay in your room, or are you allowed to stay in ours during the lockdown?" Thomas says, "I was hoping that you would invite me over to your room. I'd rather not be alone right now." I respond, "We would love to have you," as if I'm inviting him to Sunday brunch. Thomas says, "Thanks," and we all stand up to leave. Dave puts his last bite of sandwich into his mouth and chews while he walks his tray toward the trash can.

The path back to the room is not as crowded as it was on the way up. We make it back to the room fairly quickly and lock ourselves inside. Once in the room, we all take a seat on a bed. We look at each other like, "What do we do now?" This is going to be pure torture to have to sit and wait the rest of the day and night to get to our likely demise in the morning. I decide that I can't let that happen. We need to escape, at least mentally, from this place. We need to try, as much as possible, to forget where we are and have a good time enjoying each other's company. I can't figure out how I'm going to break the ice, so I give it to God.

"Can we pray for a minute?" I ask the group. Everyone agrees, so I try to voice my feelings in my prayer to the Lord. "Jesus," I begin, "we have a long time to sit here and wait before we can go anywhere else. Without your help, this will be a long afternoon, evening, and night as we wait for the morning to get here. Somehow, in some way, please calm our fears. Please fill us with the peace that comes from your Holy Spirit, the peace that surpasses all understanding. Instead of worrying about tomorrow, please help us instead to have a fun afternoon and evening together, somehow, and please help us to have a restful night. I'm asking for yet another miracle, but so far you've come through every time. Thank you, Jesus, for being here with us now. Thank you for being our God. Thank you for being you. In your name. Amen."

Josh is the first one to speak after my prayer. "Thomas," he says, "I think it's time you learn more about our family." Thomas asks, "What do you mean, Josh?" Josh answers, "It's time for you to hear some stories. Let's start with Dad." A smile begins to form on my face. My prayer is already starting to be answered. For about the next hour, Josh, Nate, Dave, and Julia all tell rather hilarious stories about various predicaments I've gotten myself into, and about various dumb things that I've done. Julia tells the story about me almost driving us off a cliff one night in Pittsburgh (in my defense I was doing exactly what the GPS said to do). Josh tells the story of how I was slimed by trying to pick up a newborn baby deer in the middle of the road to move him out of harm's way (he was a slippery little bugger). Nate and Dave co-tell the story of when all three of us fell down the basement stairs at the same time when they were only three years old. Nate was halfway down the stairs when Dave tripped on the second stair (luckily they were carpeted). I had started down the stairs behind Dave, and when he slipped I tried to reach out to stop him from falling, but then I lost my balance. Nate got caught in the avalanche and we all hit the bottom pretty hard. Nate and Dave burst out in tears for about three seconds until they saw that I was hurt, and then they burst out laughing in the middle of crying.

Josh follows that story with a time I was catching for him in the back yard. He was in his first year of kid-pitch baseball, and he was practicing his pitching. He was pitching with the hard baseball since that is the kind they were using in the games. Nate was batting while I caught. Dave was either in the field or swinging on the swing set. None of us could remember for sure which one he was doing. Josh pitched a few out of the strike zone, so he came back with one down the middle. The ball broke more than I expected and skipped under my glove. It bounced off the ground and hit me in a very unfortunate area. The way Josh tells the story I was screaming like a girl, but the only thing I remember is all three of my children laughing uncontrollably as I lie on the ground writhing in pain. It took a good five minutes for me to be able to stand up after that one. I never missed another pitch again.

The kids tell a few more recent stories that I don't remember, but they are still pretty funny. I think it makes it even funnier for me since I can't remember them happening. It's like I'm hearing the stories for the first time. Nate goes back to a story that I can remember, the time he got sick all over my new SUV on the way to Sunday school. I bought the car used, but it still smelled new. And it had a black leather interior. The worst part was that he threw up on the seat belt (along with everything else around him), and when I unbuckled him once we returned home the vomit rolled up into where the seat belt retracts. I spent hours taking apart the car trying to get the vomit out of every possible orifice it could have gone into. Then I got the bright idea to take my bottle of cologne and spray it at least one hundred times over everything on which the vomit had made contact (with the exception of the leather seats, of course). The car never did smell like vomit again, but I could hardly breathe in it for several days due to the overpowering cologne smell, even with the windows open.

After the first hour, I get in on the act of telling stories. I tell the story of the time that it took me three diapers to get baby Dave changed. Each time I removed one dirty diaper, I had to move quick to replace it with the clean one before he soiled the floor. I told the story of the time Nate got stuck in the tree just as we were getting ready to leave to go to my birthday dinner. I had just pulled in the driveway coming home from work, and Julia climbed up in the tree after him but couldn't get high enough to help him. After a lot of coaxing, he eventually overcame his fear and climbed down on his own. We eventually made it to dinner and had a nice time, but I was really unhappy with him on the way to supper. Then Julia tells the story of when two-year-old Josh and his cousin decided to make up a new game. They opened the refrigerator in the basement and started pulling out small bottles of yogurt smoothie, the ones with the foil film tops. They started shooting the yogurt drinks at the mini basketball hoop. Each time one of the bottles hit either the hoop or the floor, it exploded. Yogurt drink covered the carpeted floor before she caught up with them.

The time passes very quickly. Hours go by as we share story after story. Ted and Mindy recall some stories from their college days, and then they tell even more stories about Julia and her siblings as they were growing up. Mindy tells about the time Julia's older sister coated her face and hair with diaper rash cream. Ted tells Thomas about the time I pretended to need help with my car so that I could show him the engagement ring I had bought for Julia. When I showed him the ring and asked for his blessing, he responded by saying, "If you want her, you can have her!" Mention of the car reminds Julia of the time in the snow when I spun the car down the hill leading down to our first house. The car came to rest right next to our mailbox. That story reminds her of the time, before kids, we ate breakfast at that same house and then left in our cars for work. I was in my car and Julia was behind me in hers. When I got close to the street, I started to feel like I was going to be sick. I opened the car door and vomited on the driveway. I sat there for a minute afterward and decided that I felt fine. I closed the car door and went to work. Julia was grossed out as she had to drive around my vomit. When we got home that night, I discovered before dinner that the loaf of bread had mold on one side of it. I guess I didn't notice when I made my morning toast. It seems like a lot of our funny family stories involve falling, getting hurt, or vomiting.

Thomas gets in on the act. He tells many funny stories about him and his Dad. Beth was even involved in a lot of the silliness. The more he talks, the more they seemed like a normal family, at least while his Dad was alive. He doesn't have any recent stories, but the ones he tells from when he was younger are plenty funny. After a long round of stories from him, Ted and I take turns telling funny stories from our childhoods.

After Thomas has his turn, the floor goes back to Josh who started the whole thing. He tells another story I don't remember. At the end, everyone looks at me expecting me to explain my side of it. Mid-laugh I say, "What makes it so funny is that I can't even remember this story." Everyone cracks up even more. Then I say, "I'm serious, I can't remember at least the last five years of my life." I almost can't get the line out I'm laughing so hard. Dave is having trouble breathing he is laughing so hard, and he doesn't even have any breathing issues. "Thank you Jesus," I say in my mind, "for answering my prayer." When the laughing finally subsides, a clicking sound fills the room. It takes me only a second to realize it is the PA system. At first I think it's going to be the Leader's address, but then I remember that his speech is scheduled for the morning. "Good evening everyone," says a voice that sounds like Beth. "The kitchen will be opening in about thirty minutes. Everyone have a most blessed rest of the day."

Even though we are brought back into reality, I'm not ready to let go of the good feeling I now have in my heart. I look at the time on my phone and I'm amazed how much time has passed. For the last four hours or so we had our lives back. We had fun. We got to know Thomas a lot better, and he got to know us a lot better as well. I'm glad he got the chance to hear about all of the silly things that have happened in our lives. I'm also glad to hear that most of his life has been good until the last couple of years. Hopefully someday soon, somehow, his life can get better again.

Thomas remembers a few more funny stories from his childhood and tells them during the next half hour. When he gets halfway through the last one, where his Dad has the family van stuck in the mud after trying to drive through a field, we hear the chime noise again. Thomas finishes his story, with his uncle pulling the van out of the mud with his truck after Thomas and his Dad cover themselves in mud from head to toe trying to get the van out by themselves. Once Thomas is done, Ted asks, "Does that sound mean we're free to roam about the building again?" referring to the chime noise. Thomas says, "Yes, we can go eat now. Mom and crew usually cook something really good when the Leader arrives. They fix some special plates for the Leader and for his executive team, as he calls them. A few of the team members come up to the kitchen and take the plates of food back to the Leader's office where they eat. During their last meeting, when I was spying, that was the only time I heard the Leader talk about anything other than the business of running this place. He said the highlight of his visit is getting to eat the excellent food that Mom prepares. Of course I couldn't tell her that I heard him say that, but she knows she's a good cook."

I go to stand up. I realize that I have been sitting on the bed for hours. My muscles are very sore, probably from all of the hard work we have been doing over the last several days. I slowly rise from the bed, and I grimace as I straighten my back. I stretch my muscles while everyone else stands up. Then we all follow Thomas out the door so he can once again lead us to the upstairs kitchen.

CHAPTER 15 – CHRIST ALONE, CORNERSTONE

"My hope is built on nothing less,
Than Jesus' blood and righteousness,
I dare not trust the sweetest frame,
But wholly trust in Jesus' name." – Edward Mote

Dinner looks excellent. Thomas didn't adequately describe the amount and variety of delicious foods that greet us once we arrive at the food stations. There is so much to choose from. I start with a plate of turkey, mashed potatoes, and gravy. I add some corn and steamed broccoli to my plate. Ham, roast beef, chicken, and several other kinds of meat sit alongside the turkey. We fill our plates as full as we can and grab our drinks. Once again we find that our usual table near the back exit has enough chairs for us to sit.

I say a silent prayer of thanks in my mind and then I begin to eat. This kitchen crew has outdone themselves this time. Everyone agrees that the food is extra awesome as we take our first bites. An enjoyable meal ensues. Seconds are obtained and devoured by everyone in our group. The cafeteria is very full, the fullest I've seen, and it remains that way for several hours. It's also louder than I've heard it before. We continue to swap funny stories with Thomas after we finish our second platefuls. After time passes, one of the cooks announces dessert. I have absolutely no room for dessert, but I'm going to eat something anyways.

Several more cooks bring out carts full of cake slices, pie slices, and other delicious-looking delicacies. An ice-cream machine on wheels is also brought out. Beth thinks of everything. The carts are lined up across the middle of the room where everyone usually walks from the top of the stairs over to the food stations. The ice cream machine is placed at the end closest to the kitchen, with an extension cord extending back into the kitchen. One of the cooks pulls out a roll of duct tape and tapes down the cord in a few places.

Once everything is in place, people start to get up to get their desserts. We wait a few minutes to see how the operation works before trying it ourselves. Thomas waits with us until the crowd lessens. I notice as a tray of desserts is emptied, another one is rolled out of the kitchen to take its place. Beth and her crew must have worked all day to get this meal ready. I am really glad they did.

I watch several people as they pick up a bowl from a stack on a cart next to the ice cream machine. Each one dispenses a bowlful of ice cream from the machine, and then proceeds to a topping bar on a cart that was placed next to the machine after I had stopped paying attention to what the kitchen crew was doing. When I look back over at our table, I notice everyone is getting up. I follow suit.

After my double chocolate cake and vanilla ice cream, we sit and talk for what seems like several more hours. Very few people leave the cafeteria, and many come back for second desserts. Josh, Nate, and Dave all go back for seconds. Ted does as well. I'm so full I can't bring myself to eat another bite. At one point I pull out my phone to look at the time. It's eight-thirty already! This day has flown by. I remember back to how it started, waking up on a roof covered with a bug net. I still can't believe we snuck past a sleeping Tom and Barry undetected. The Lord our God is really watching out for us. It must be because he has something really important for us to do tomorrow. Tomorrow. Tomorrow is almost here. The good feelings of the afternoon and evening just vanished. The fear hits me like a ton of bricks. I don't want tomorrow to ever get here.

I hide my sudden discomfort well as everyone continues to talk. Everyone else still appears to be enjoying themselves, and I don't want to ruin it any sooner than it needs to happen for everyone else. I begin to calm myself down again by praying to God. I then realize that soon we will have to go back to the room for the night, and we will be faced with trying to go to sleep on what could be our last night on earth. Whatever calmness I obtained from my prayer goes away with that thought.

I look at my phone again. Nine thirteen PM is the time. I stare at my phone wondering for the first time how my phone knows the local time even though it's not connected to a network. Perhaps it learned the time during the short period when I was connected to the wireless network and was trying to send the text to my Dad. I wonder what he could have done if the text had gone through. How could they trace a GPS signal that would soon vanish, anyways?

When I look up, Thomas is looking at me. He says, "They'll be closing the kitchen soon. I can already see the kitchen crew lining up to start cleaning." I look back. Several kitchen workers are milling around behind the food stations. Several others are starting to clean up the dinner food. I notice Katie is not in the group. She must still be in the kitchen. Thomas stands up, sighs, and says, "It's time for us to go." The way he says it wipes the smiles off all of the faces in our group. I had wiped off my own smile about a half-hour ago.

We follow Thomas back to the room. As soon as we get into the room, he asks us if he can stay in our room tonight. Julia says, "As long as your Mom won't miss you or go looking for you." Thomas answers, "She will be up all night tonight preparing for tomorrow. She never seems to sleep when the Leader is here." That answer satisfies Julia, and so it is settled. Thomas will sleep in one of the many spare beds in our room tonight. It probably works out for the better so that we can finalize our plans for tomorrow well into the night tonight.

Everyone takes turns in the restrooms, and then we all sit down on the beds, mostly in the same places we sat this afternoon. The mood isn't nearly as light as it was earlier, with good reason. We are about twelve hours away from being found out that we are trying to stop the evil planned for tomorrow. I'm not sure how to even begin talking about how to get ready for tomorrow. My heart is racing. My left hand is visibly shaking as I try to rest it on my left knee while sitting on the bed. Everyone knows that the inevitable is nearly upon us, and we can't put it off much longer.

No one speaks. Thomas is the last one out of the restroom, the one that the kids use. I am facing the door to the restroom as he comes out. He looks at me as I look at him. He returns as serious of a look as I give him. I wish I could continue to see the joyful expressions on Thomas's face that I saw earlier. But now is not the time. Now is the time to get ready for tomorrow morning.

Thomas sits down on a bed directly across from me. We are all sitting in somewhat of an oval as dictated by the layout of the beds. Starting with me, Ted is next to me on my left. He is lying in his bed, eyes open. Mindy is sitting at the end of his bed. Nate sits at the top end of the bed that is next to Mindy. Thomas and Dave are sitting on the bed directly across from me. Josh is sitting at the top of the bed to their left and my right. Julia sits next to me on the same bed as me. No one speaks. We all sit staring at each other. I really hope that Thomas will break the ice and start talking about what we need to do tomorrow, but he doesn't say a word. After about thirty seconds I become impatient. I don't know what to say, so just like earlier in the day I use a prayer to end the silence.

"Lord Jesus," I begin, "we ask that you be here with us now." I look around momentarily before I bow my head and close my eyes. Everyone else moves closer together and joins hands. I grab Ted's hand and Julia's hand and then I shut my eyes. Never before have I wanted to concentrate so much on a prayer to the Lord. I continue by saying, "Jesus, we need you now. We need your strength. I don't know what's going to happen tomorrow. I'm not sure if anything we are trying to do is going to work. Without you it won't work, but with you all things are possible. Please hear my prayer, Jesus, and please know that we love you with all of our hearts. In this time where it seems like we have no hope, be our hope Jesus. Fill us with hope in you and only you. Not in our lives, not in our well-being, not in the plans we have already put into motion, but help us to hope in you. Be with us now, because we are very afraid, terrified even. I pray that your Holy Spirit may go ahead of us in this place and prepare it to be destroyed. I pray that your Spirit may roam the halls tonight and foil any plans of evil that are scheduled for tomorrow. Our plans only go far enough to try to stop the Leader and this group of people from killing anyone tomorrow. Our plans fail to rescue everyone, even if we are able to stop them from dying in the machine. We need something more to rescue everyone else, not to mention us. We need you."

By this time in the prayer I'm choking back tears. I can hear that most everyone else is crying as well, but it's not because of my prayer. I continue to pray. "Lord God Almighty, our Savior and Friend, give us the strength to know that whatever happens tomorrow is your will. When I saw that machine kill all of those people the other day, I knew it had to be stopped. I knew these people had to be stopped. You have brought us to this place. You have made miracles happen the whole time we have been here. You made it so that we could come to our senses before we should have. You helped us to escape and avoid eating the poison that would have destroyed our insides. You again helped us escape undetected when we ran back down the stairs away from certain death in the smashing machine. You gave us the closest thing to an angel this side of Heaven, Thomas, to rescue us from being caught while trying to escape. You have allowed us to persist in this place, and to live quite comfortably since Thomas rescued us a few days ago. You worked another miracle by helping us to make gallon after gallon of porridge that won't kill anyone. You gave Thomas, Ted, and me safe passage into and out of the Leader's office. You also helped us to modify the setup of the smashing machine in the hopes that it will smash itself tomorrow morning. I pray in Your Name that it does. I pray it in your name."

I feel more confident as I continue to pray. I don't feel the terror anymore. I say, "Jesus, you worked another miracle as you led us past the sleeping men who almost found us on the roof this morning. How we snuck down off the roof and past them I'll never know. It's only by your grace and goodness that we made it. All of these miracles are from you. Every good thing comes from you. Thank you, Jesus."

"Now, Lord, I ask that you continue to provide us with miracles and blessings. The first is that I ask that you give us sharp minds and strong hearts to finalize our plans for tomorrow. Help us to be able to get some rest tonight after our plans align with your will. Help us to remember that you will be with us. You will be right next to us as we go up those stairs again tomorrow. You will lead the way as we make sure the smashing machine won't kill anyone else. You will lead us back down the stairs and out to the reservoir to destroy the valves. I don't want the Leader to make another one of his sacrifices. I want to give some dignity to those who died and shed their blood for the Leader's evil plans. I want him stopped. I want you to give us victory over this place tomorrow. I want you to have victory over this place tomorrow. Lead us wherever you would have us to go and to do whatever you would have us to do tonight, tomorrow and forever."

"We love you Jesus. You are our Savior and our God, our dearest friend. Even though we are in the worst of situations, please help us to remember how fortunate we are to be in a situation where we feel helpless. We are helpless to do anything else beyond our feeble plans that may not work. We are completely and entirely dependent upon you. We have no other hope but you. Thank you, Jesus, for being our hope. In Jesus name we pray, Amen."

I forget to open my eyes and look up for at least ten seconds after I'm done. I don't want the prayer to be over. Every moment that passes brings us closer to the next unknown. Once I realize that everyone is probably looking at me I open my eyes and look around. Everyone else still has their eyes closed and heads bowed. One by one they lift up their heads and open their eyes. Perhaps each one was praying their own prayer silently, not even listening to mine. I'll often do that in church when the pastor is praying. Julia looks at me first. Then Josh opens his eyes. Ted and Mindy look over almost simultaneously. Nate is next, and then Dave. Thomas is last. After about ten more seconds he lifts up his head and says, "I know that our plans will work tomorrow. I know that God will not let us down. Jesus will be with us, and he will make everything work out for the best. Don't worry. God is with us."

That boost of confidence certainly helps me, and it seems to help the rest of the group. Then Thomas says, "Let's get down to business. We'll get moving right away tomorrow. We'll make sure to go up for breakfast in the morning. Mom will be looking for me then. She always feels guilty about not spending any time with me when the Leader visits, so she always makes sure to eat breakfast with me the morning that the Saints start to arrive." I don't like the idea of trying to keep my cool in the morning during breakfast with Beth, but we'll have to do it to avoid raising suspicions. Thomas continues. "After that, we'll go back to the room to listen to the Leader's PA address. Then we'll head to the front of the building. I'll show you where the robes are before the Saints arrive. We'll each take one and stash them in the downstairs kitchen closet so we'll have them later. Then we'll head back to the front of the building and help with the unloading of the first group of sleeping Saints."

Thomas looks at Mindy. Then he looks over at Julia and says, "You two make sure you're paired up with at least one of these strapping young boys. Trying to lift a sleeping adult onto a stretcher is not an easy thing to do. Once you get the person onto the stretcher, then it's a matter of raising it back up and wheeling them up the ramp and into the holding room. We'll make many more trips than our bodies want us to, and we'll be sweating profusely before we're even close to being done. Once we get the first group into the holding room, we'll probably have a little downtime again before we head to the kitchen for porridge duty. I'll make sure we stay in the kitchen so that we can make our escape at the right time. Once the first group is fed and is being led toward the stairs, we'll sneak away into the supply closet and put on our robes. Then we'll go out the back door and wait for the group to start up the stairs. The Saints will actually be led around to the stairs on a floor above where we will be, so we'll have to keep an eye on the camp counselors who lead them to the stairs. The camp counselors don't lead them up the stairs unless there is a problem. We'll have to find a way to sneak into the group as soon as we can and then work our way to the front of the line once we are past the counselors."

Josh interrupts. "Thomas, don't forget we need to bring something to cut the netting at the bottom of the stairs before we go up to join the group." Thomas replies, "Yes, good thinking. We'll need that escape point once we get back down the stairs. The netting is thick, so I think we will need a sharp knife as opposed to scissors. We'll find something that will work in the kitchen while we're preparing the porridge."

Thomas looks over at me and says, "Next thing we know we'll be at the smashing machine. Then things are going to get interesting." Josh says, "I don't know if I can go back up those stairs." Nate adds, "Me either!" Ted says, "We'll be right there with you. The safest place you can be at that point is with everyone else." Josh answers, "I know, but that's not going to help me force myself up those stairs. My legs are going to want to take me in the other direction."

Then I remember something. I say, "Years ago I heard this saying. At least I think I heard it. Either I heard it or I made it up. When you're walking up those stairs tomorrow, think these words or say them quietly to yourself. Then repeat them over and over again. Christ behind me. Christ in front of me. Christ beside me. Christ inside of me." I repeat the words. "Christ behind me. Christ in front of me. Christ beside me. Christ inside of me." I look around and see some quizzical looks. Then I say, "When I get up early in the mornings to run outside at 5 AM, sometimes thoughts go through my mind of what would happen if someone tried to sneak up and attack me or something. These kinds of thoughts crept into my mind a lot for a while after the time I had to chase away the person snooping around our front porch when I got back from my run one morning. It took quite a while to feel comfortable going for a run in the dark after that one. One thing that I found helped me was to say those words any time that I felt afraid during my run. I would time the cadence with my steps, and I would often find that it helped pick up my pace in addition to calming my fears. Christ behind me, because Jesus always has my back. Christ in front of me, because Jesus is always leading the way. Christ beside me because he is my friend and brother.   Christ inside of me because he is my Savior and my God."

Dave says, "Now I get it. I like that. Why didn't you ever tell us that story before, about the guy on our porch?" I answer, "You were very young when it happened. Your Mom and I weren't about to worry you guys with anything like that. It never happened again. At first I thought it was a deer walking through the yard. But as I ran closer I saw it was a person, and he was heading for the front door. Instinct took over and I sprinted as fast as I could toward the house. When I got to the neighbor's yard, I yelled in the loudest voice I could muster, 'What are you doing in my yard?' My voice echoed up and down the quiet street. The poor guy must have jumped five feet in the air as he took off running. Hopefully it scared him enough to never try anything like that again."

Josh says, "What are the odds that you would come down the street right as he was walking into our yard?" Then I say, "What are the odds that we are here right now getting ready to try to stop any more bad things from happening in this place? The strange thing was on that day, for whatever reason, I woke up earlier than normal and went for my run before I normally would. It was for that reason that I finished my run earlier than normal, to meet him in our yard. I'm not sure exactly what he planned to do, but he was definitely up to no good."

Thomas speaks up. "Let's focus guys. When we get to the top of the stairway, we'll stay at the front of the line. You guys need to keep me hidden behind you since Tom and Barry will recognize me. Once we get to the platform, they will run the test cycle for the machine. If everything goes right, the machine will crash. We'll be able to sneak back down the stairs while they are occupied with the machine, and then we can head to the reservoir."

Mindy asks, "What if it doesn't work? I mean, what if our plans don't work and the machine does work?" Ted answers, "If the machine does work, then it probably won't sound right to those guys. We made some pretty big adjustments to it, so it should at least go off course a little bit." Then Thomas says, "If the machine cycles OK, or even kind of OK, then the only way to make sure no one gets smashed is for us to lock Tom and Barry inside the machine. They are both pretty good-sized guys. Tom claims that he used to be an MMA fighter before his 'conversion,' so it's not going to be easy to overpower him. Even if the machine does crash, it will probably be a good idea to find a way to lock them into the machine to buy us more time to escape. If they are stuck in the machine, they can't call down for help. No one will know that there is a problem for a while."

Nate then asks, "But what about the camp counselors at the entrance to the stairs? What happens when they see us running back down the stairs? Even if we do manage to lock Tom and Barry into the smashing machine, the camp counselors will see us and will know that there is a problem." To that Thomas answers, "We'll have to make it a game-time decision. They may have already left by then, or there still may be enough Saints on the stairs that they won't notice. At that point we'll have to see how it plays out."

Julia asks, "And then what?" Thomas answers, "And then we get to the ground level and sneak out through the hole in the netting. Another game-time decision will be whether or not we run to the valves." I interject, "We need to destroy those valves." Ted responds, "I know you want to destroy those valves. I do, too. But if the opportunity presents itself to escape at that point, we will need to skip the valves and make our way to the hole in the fence. If it works out that we can get to the valves in time and still escape, then that's what we will do." I say, "Agreed." I look over at Josh. He gives me a determined look.

Thomas continues. "Once we get to the hole in the fence, we'll have quite a hike to get to the air strip. It was like a twenty minute bus ride to get to the building once we left the landing strip. I have no idea what people or animals we may encounter along the way. One thing that I'm sure of, though, is that we'll have to find a way to avoid being seen by the guard at the front gate. We may have to travel in the wrong direction through the brush until we are out of sight. Then we can cross the road and work our way through the brush on the other side until we are far enough past him going in the right direction. Hopefully after that we can walk on the side of the road the rest of the way." Dave says, "If we get to that point."

At this point I feel we have our plans as set as we can get them. I still can't get over the thought of not destroying the valves. It is so important to me that we make a statement to the Leader and completely ruin his day. I try to let it go. The group continues to converse back and forth about the details of tomorrow's possible events. I stay mostly quiet as Thomas gets hit with at least one hundred more questions about what-if scenarios that could happen. By the end of it I feel completely worn out. Ted, who had sat up for quite a while, is lying down again. I pull out my phone and check the time. Eleven-fifteen. "Wow," I think to myself, "this day won't slow down for anything."

I stand up. Josh and Thomas are talking about what would happen if someone discovers the robes we have hidden in the supply closet. Josh stops mid-sentence when he sees me stand up. "Guys," I say, "Enough is enough. There's no way we can think of every possible thing that can happen tomorrow. A very wise man named MacGyver once said something like, 'If you plan too much, you close your mind to other possibilities.' Let's call it a night."

Julia, still sitting on the bed, looks up at me and says, "You can't possibly think anyone's going to be able to sleep tonight, do you?" I answer, "No, but let's get cleaned up and then try to have some quiet time. Let's all lay down on our beds for a little bit. If no one can fall asleep after an hour or so, then we'll figure out something else to do. If our tired bodies and minds get the best of us, then we'll be that much more alert and ready for tomorrow when it comes. At this point there's nothing we can do but give it to God. He's the only one who can help us now."

I must have sounded convincing enough, because everyone seems to follow my instructions. Within about twenty minutes we are all ready to lie down in our beds. Julia and I give each kid a hug. She starts with Nate, who is closest to her, and I start with Dave, who is closest to me. Mindy and Ted both hug Josh. We make our rounds with the hugs and more than a few tears flow. At first we forget about Thomas, but we quickly rectify the situation. If everyone else is like me, we all want to express our fears to each person that we hug. But we all avoid bringing up anything negative. "I love you," is exchanged with all parties, and eventually we somehow all end up in a group hug. Ted hits the nail on the head and says, "Be with us, Jesus," and soon after the group hug dissolves. I walk over to my bed thinking we have a zero percent chance of getting any sleep. Everyone lies down except Ted, who walks over to the kids' bathroom. He turns on the light and pulls the door mostly closed. Then he walks over to the main light switch for the room and turns it off. A sliver of light emerges from the bathroom. I look up and notice that someone has already shut the curtains.

During the first few minutes after lying down, I hear lots of sighs, a few coughs, and some beds squeaking from everyone trying to get comfortable. I start to think that I should say another prayer to help calm everyone down. Instead of saying anything out loud, though, I first think about what I would say. It all sounds very nice. If I say these words that I am thinking of, I'm sure they will calm everyone down. Just thinking the words are calming me down. At one point I think that I am saying the words out loud to everyone, but then I realize that it's still just a thought. The words, "Help us to sleep, Jesus," keep repeating in my mind in my own voice. And then I realize that he is answering my prayer.

Chapter 16 – D-Day

1 Samuel 14: 1-14 (NIV), "One day Jonathan son of Saul said to his young armor-bearer, 'Come, let's go over to the Philistine outpost on the other side.' But he did not tell his father."

"Saul was staying on the outskirts of Gibeah under a pomegranate tree in Migron. With him were about six hundred men, among whom was Ahijah, who was wearing an ephod. He was a son of Ichabod's brother Ahitub son of Phinehas, the son of Eli, the Lord's priest in Shiloh. No one was aware that Jonathan had left."

"On each side of the pass that Jonathan intended to cross to reach the Philistine outpost was a cliff; one was called Bozez and the other Seneh. One cliff stood to the north toward Mikmash, the other to the south toward Geba."

"Jonathan said to his young armor-bearer, 'Come, let's go over to the outpost of those uncircumcised men. Perhaps the Lord will act in our behalf. Nothing can hinder the Lord from saving, whether by many or by few.'"

"'Do all that you have in mind,' his armor-bearer said. 'Go ahead; I am with you heart and soul.'"

"Jonathan said, 'Come on, then; we will cross over toward them and let them see us. If they say to us, 'Wait there until we come to you,' we will stay where we are and not go up to them. But if they say, 'Come up to us,' we will climb up, because that will be our sign that the Lord has given them into our hands.'"

"So both of them showed themselves to the Philistine outpost. 'Look!' said the Philistines. 'The Hebrews are crawling out of the holes they were hiding in.' The men of the outpost shouted to Jonathan and his armor-bearer, 'Come up to us and we'll teach you a lesson.'"

"So Jonathan said to his armor-bearer, 'Climb up after me; the Lord has given them into the hand of Israel.'"

"Jonathan climbed up, using his hands and feet, with his armor-bearer right behind him. The Philistines fell before Jonathan, and his armor-bearer followed and killed behind him. In that first attack Jonathan and his armor-bearer killed some twenty men in an area of about half an acre."

I wake up. Something is wrong. As I come to my senses, I lift up my head and look down at my body. Everything appears to be in order as I study my limbs in the very dimly lit room, but I am lying on a twin-sized bed in a room with many other twin beds. And then I remember where I am. I remember what day it is – Thursday. It's D-Day, but I hope the "D" stands for deliverance from evil in this case.

I sit up in the bed. I look around and see everyone else sleeping peacefully. I reach for my phone on the night stand next to my twin bed. I look at the time and it says six-fifty six in the morning. I woke up before the annoying music one last time. I also notice that my phone battery is almost dead. That was poor planning on my part. I should have asked Thomas to charge it in his room before we got back to our room. I also could have remembered to turn it off before I lay down in the bed to save some battery.

I am amazed that we were able to sleep last night. I slept for at least six or seven straight hours even despite knowing that there is a pretty good chance that we will all die today. I hope that everyone else fell asleep quickly, too, and did not have to worry about what today will bring. I feel like sitting in the quiet and connecting with the Lord to ask for his help today, but then I realize that I really need to use the bathroom. By the time I get back, the music is going off and everyone is beginning to stir. Once everyone is fully awake, I'm sure we'll be doing plenty of praying to Jesus before we start the day.

Everyone wakes quickly, even Thomas. I feel completely and totally recharged from one of the best night's sleep I have ever had. "Thank you, Jesus," I pray in my mind. Once everyone is up and has had a chance to use the bathroom, we reconvene in the center of the room. We stand in a circle, knowing that the next step in our day is to pray. We join hands, bow our heads, and close our eyes. The music stops, and the room is completely quiet except for the sounds of our breathing. No one says anything out loud for about thirty seconds, but I am sure everyone is praying silently like me. I begin to feel the need to pray out loud, but Thomas beats me to it.

"Jesus," Thomas starts, "Today is the day. Today is the day we see what you can do. Today is the day that we will stand in awe of your amazing power. Today is the day that you will rescue us and all of the Saints from this place. Today is the day I believe you can, and I believe you will." I'm standing next to Josh on my left and Julia on my right. The circle starts with me, then Josh, Ted, Mindy, Nate, Thomas, Dave, and Julia. Julia squeezes my hand several times as Thomas speaks. Then she says, while fighting tears, "Jesus, we love you. Be here with us now. Give us your strength to make it through the day. Keep us safe in the face of danger." The tears then get the best of her. Mindy speaks next. "Lord God Almighty, help us now. Get us out of here." Then Dave says, "Jesus, we know you can. We know you can do it." More loudly, he says it again, "You can do it! You can save us!" After a few moments of silence, I say, "Your will be done, Lord, may your will be done this day. Turn this day into a blessing, somehow. I don't know how, but in your Name turn it into a blessing." Then Nate says, "O Lord, you are my God, and I will ever praise you." Everyone repeats the verse from the Psalm several times.

I can feel the power building in the room. The only one who hasn't yet spoken, Josh, says, "Christ behind me, Christ in front of me, Christ beside me, Christ inside of me." We all repeat the words, in unison. "Christ behind me, Christ in front of me, Christ beside me, Christ inside of me," we all say over and over and over again. Each time we say it a little bit louder. Each time we feel a little bit stronger. The last time we repeat the cadence we all look up at each other. It's almost like we say it so loud that we startle each other. The ground feels like it moves a little bit beneath my feet, but it could just be my legs shaking. After that I finish the prayer with an, "In Jesus' Name," and everyone else chimes in by saying, "Amen." I feel ready to face this fateful day, and I am confident that everyone else is ready, too. Whatever happens today, it will be of the Lord.

Thomas brings us back to the reality of this place. "Shall we get ready for breakfast?" he asks. I am not at all hungry and say, "I don't think I'll be able to eat anything." Thomas answers, "This will be the only meal we'll have time for today. On Saints days you get breakfast and that's it until the late evening, if at all. I recommend we force ourselves to eat something to keep up our strength. We have a lot of hard work to do unloading and transporting the first group of Saints to the holding room. After that, we may have a long hike from here to the air strip."

Thomas makes a very valid point, so I will at least try to eat. Hopefully I can keep it down given the butterflies in my stomach. I say another silent prayer for strength as Thomas opens the door to the room. "I'll be back in thirty minutes," he says, "so get ready quick." Before he shuts the door I run over to him. I hand him my phone. "Quick charge," I say. "Quick charge," Thomas repeats back to me, and then he shuts the door. "All-right," Ted says, "let's make it quick." We all nod and get to work.

Amazingly, we are all ready by the time Thomas gets back. None of us said a word as we efficiently showered and changed. The only time I paused to think was while I was brushing my teeth. I thought about how it might be the last time I get to brush my teeth for at least several days, if not forever.

Thomas enters the room and says, "I gave you an extra ten minutes, but I'm still impressed that you guys got ready so fast." Ted says, "We aim to please." With that, Thomas leads us out of the room. One more time we follow him to the upstairs kitchen. I take in everything more carefully this time. No one is in the hallway at this moment. We walk past the hallway on the left that leads to the bottom of the Stairway to Heaven. I see the door to the supply closet through which we snuck into the Leader's office the other night. Then I look to my right and see the door that leads to the roof access room.

We enter the kitchen supply closet. I quickly look around for a place to stash the robes that we will bring back after breakfast. I think the best place will be underneath where the aprons hang on the back wall of the supply closet. Many folded aprons are on the floor underneath the ones hanging, which will provide a good cover for the robes if we hide them at the bottoms of the piles. We momentarily walk into the downstairs kitchen and then enter the porridge room. The air in the room still smells faintly of the poison. Down the hallway and up the stairs we go. The food line is very long. We have to stop on the top steps and wait until the line advances. While we wait, Thomas hands me my phone. "Quick charge," he says. I put the phone in my pocket after I check the time. Seven minutes after eight.

Twenty minutes pass before we pick up our trays. Everyone in the line and in the cafeteria is very quiet. For as light as the mood was last night it has now turned to dead serious this morning. Once we finally take a seat with our food and drinks, I find myself sitting directly across from Thomas. We are at our usual table. It was the only table that I saw with enough chairs for our group. It's like we have been here long enough now that everyone else knows where we like to sit.

I look at Thomas and mouth the word, "Quiet." Thomas leans in very close and whispers, "No one is looking forward to how much work they have to do today." He leans back in his chair and places his paper napkin on his lap. I follow suit and begin forcing food into my mouth. In the middle of my first bite, I remember to thank God for our meal. Surprisingly my appetite kicks in. As I eat I reason with myself. Everything is still OK right now. No one suspects a thing. Everyone else is focused on the jobs they have to do today. No one will pay attention to anything that we are doing as long as we act like we are just doing our jobs. Everything will be OK. If we play our cards right, and if we can get Tom and Barry locked inside the smashing machine, no one will notice that we are gone until we are a long ways down the road. As long as we can keep up a good pace, we'll be to the air strip in no time. God will help us to hitch a ride without being caught, and we will be back in a civilized country before we know it. Considering the circumstances, everything has worked out for the best so far, so why would anything change now?

A voice startles me out of my internal dialogue. "Good morning, Thomas!" Beth says. I forgot about Beth. There is one empty chair next to Thomas at the end of the table. Beth places her tray of food next to Thomas and sits down in the empty chair. I realize that I will have to look at Beth and her crazy eyes for the rest of the meal. I lose my appetite again.

Beth unfolds her napkin and places it on her lap. Then she says, "Thomas, I'm sorry I almost missed breakfast with you this morning. We outdid ourselves with last night's dinner, and it took a really long time to clean up. I actually caught a two hour catnap last night, but it set me behind this morning. We barely got breakfast ready in time. I love it when the Leader comes to visit, but I'll be glad when this day is over and I can get a good night's sleep."

Beth looks at me. My eyes lock onto her crazy eyes. Her eyes look tired but not so crazy this morning. She asks me, "Anyways, how are you doing this morning?" I answer, "Good, thank you." I quickly look down at my food and take another bite. I hope that she loses interest in me before I look back up again. Even though I'm not hungry I immediately refill my fork with more food without looking up. Then Beth says, "Thomas, have you explained to these folks what they will be helping us with today?" I look up again now that her attention is no longer on me. Thomas nods affirmatively while chewing a mouthful of food. She says, "Good; I knew that you would. We all get to be a part of something very special on days like these. We get to help people who are not able to help themselves. And it's all thanks to the Leader."

I really want to say something to refute her statement, but I keep quiet. Nothing I can say will help with what we are trying to accomplish. I try to keep a good poker face as she glances at all of us. I look to my left and across the table where Julia is sitting. It looks like she is holding back tears. I may look the same as far as I know.

The rest of the meal is pretty uneventful and very quiet. Once Beth starts eating, she finishes very quickly and does not say another word. Once she is finished, she stands up and scoots in her chair. She reaches down and gives Thomas a hug and kisses him on top of the head. She says, "Goodbye, Thomas." Thomas looks up at her and says, "Goodbye, Mom." Beth picks up her tray and takes it back into the kitchen with her. I set down my fork, as I no longer need to pretend that I want to be eating. At least I forced some more food into me. I look over at Thomas. Now it looks like he is trying to hold back tears. The emotions of the day have probably got the best of him given the encounter with his mm. If our plan works, even partially, Thomas will have a hand in going against everything his mom has helped to build since she arrived. What's worse, if we get caught, it will likely be uncovered that Thomas was working with us to foil the plans of the Leader. One thing is for sure; the Leader won't be very happy with us.

I look away from Thomas and survey the rest of the group. No one else is eating anymore, and everyone's plates still have food on them. I say, quietly, "Are we ready?" Everyone stands up, almost simultaneously. I follow suit and we leave the cafeteria for what is probably the last time. This room has been the highlight of our trip for sure. Once again I think what a shame it is that these peoples' cooking talents have been wasted on this place. As we head down the stairs, I hear the chime noise again. Without anyone asking, Thomas says, "That's the ten minute warning before the Leader's address. Everyone is supposed to go back to their room during the address. Mom and her crew are the only ones beside the executive team who are allowed to be out of their rooms for the address. They will stop what they are doing, of course, to listen to what he has to say."

We make it back to the room without issue. We lock ourselves inside for what is hopefully the last time. After everyone takes turns using the bathroom, we gather in the center of the room. I sit on one of the beds, hands folded. Nate sits down next to me. I put my arm around his shoulders. Everyone else finds a place to sit. We wait silently for the Leader's address to begin. We wait for several minutes without saying a word. I start to wonder if he's running late. I also wonder how long his speech will last. After several more minutes of waiting, a clicking noise comes from the PA system. It's show time as the Leader's address begins.

CHAPTER 17 – THE ADDRESS

Habakkuk 1:2-5 (NIV)

Habakkuk's Complaint

"How long, Lord, must I call for help,
*   but you do not listen?*
Or cry out to you, 'Violence!'
*   but you do not save?*
Why do you make me look at injustice?
*   Why do you tolerate wrongdoing?*
Destruction and violence are before me;
*   there is strife, and conflict abounds.*
Therefore the law is paralyzed,
*   and justice never prevails.*
The wicked hem in the righteous,
*   so that justice is perverted."*

The Lord's Answer

"Look at the nations and watch—
*   and be utterly amazed.*
For I am going to do something in your days
*   that you would not believe,*
*   even if you were told."*

"Good morning. I want to thank you all for all of your continued hard work and dedication to making my dream a reality. I once dreamed of a way to help others, others who could not help themselves, to find their way to me. I am the only one who can help them, but without me they will die. As you have willingly decided to follow me here, and as others who are not here have decided to follow me, you all will have a place with me forever. There are those in this world, however, who are blinded from the way to me through their own disbelief and disobedience. I wanted to help them, just as I have helped you to find your way to me. That's why I made this place, that's why I brought you here, to help these people who cannot help themselves. The ones I bring here I have chosen because I know that they will turn to me in the end. They will see me as they ascend and will believe in me. Then they will be mine forever."

"Today marks the four-hundredth day of operation for our gateway to Heaven. I am so glad that each one of you has given yourselves to service in this place. You have helped so many through your hard work and dedication to our cause. Do not be discouraged that there are so many more who need helped in this world; look at each new day as a new opportunity to help others with their eternity. Only I can help them, and by helping them you help me. Someday soon, you too will ascend to be with me forever. Be patient, remain strong, and you will be rewarded in the end for your service to me. I also understand that some additional members have come here to help us. I have already heard what great work they have done in their first week to help our cause. I hope that they are enjoying themselves in their new home and are looking forward to helping these groups of people today, people who have lost their way but who will turn to me in the end. It is good that they have come to reenergize and revitalize the group at this time."

"Today is going to be a great day; I can already tell. We have a lot of work to do, but it the end we will have helped hundreds find their way. The first group is already on its way; they will be here ahead of schedule. Because of this I will keep it brief this morning. One thing I wanted to address is a concern brought to me by the leadership council. I have heard that someone was saying one of the names that are banned in this place. I want to make it very clear; I want no mention of that name or any other name in this place. You know who you are, and your guilt is upon you. I will spare no one who knowingly disobeys me. I am the only one who can help you. I am the only one who can help anyone. I am the only way and no one else can take my place."

"Enough of that for now. Let's return to the good news about today. What's that? Oh, that is good news. Everyone, the first group of the day is about five minutes away. Let's take our positions to graciously receive them and send them on their way to a new beginning, to a new forever. Thank you, everyone, and my blessings are upon you."

CHAPTER 18 – SHOWTIME

Psalm 36 (NIV)

"For the director of music. Of David the servant of the Lord."

"I have a message from God in my heart
  concerning the sinfulness of the wicked:
There is no fear of God
  before their eyes."

"In their own eyes they flatter themselves
  too much to detect or hate their sin.
The words of their mouths are wicked and deceitful;
  they fail to act wisely or do good.
Even on their beds they plot evil;
  they commit themselves to a sinful course
  and do not reject what is wrong."

"Your love, Lord, reaches to the heavens,
  your faithfulness to the skies.
Your righteousness is like the highest mountains,
  your justice like the great deep.
  You, Lord, preserve both people and animals.
How priceless is your unfailing love, O God!
  People take refuge in the shadow of your wings.
They feast on the abundance of your house;
  you give them drink from your river of delights.
For with you is the fountain of life;
  in your light we see light."

"Continue your love to those who know you,
  your righteousness to the upright in heart.
May the foot of the proud not come against me,
  nor the hand of the wicked drive me away.

See how the evildoers lie fallen—
   thrown down, not able to rise!"

The Leader's address abruptly comes to an end. We all have been looking at each other with looks of contempt on our faces. The Leader gave a rather lackluster speech; it was not at all what I was expecting. I'm glad he had to cut it short due to the first group coming in ahead of schedule. I assume that the names that are banned in this place are God, Jesus, and the Holy Spirit. Well guess what, Leader, I'm going to be audibly calling on those names a lot today when the time comes, and you'll have to kill me to stop me.

Thomas quickly stands up. He says, "Guys, we don't have much time. Let's get to the front of the building so we can get our robes. We'll have to move quickly since we probably won't make it to the supply closet and back before the first group arrives." And with that, we all leave the room. Thomas leads us through the kitchen supply closet and through the porridge room. We go up the stairs and into the cafeteria. Several of the kitchen workers are cleaning up breakfast. We quickly pass "our table" and walk through the exit at the back of the cafeteria. The bathroom is at our left as we pass through the exit, but we turn right and proceed down a hallway that is taking us toward the front of the building. Once we reach the end of the hallway, we turn right again. There is a dead-end about ten feet ahead of us, and there is a door to our right as we continue to walk. Thomas opens the door and we walk down a set of stairs. Once he reaches the bottom of the stairs, Thomas opens the door that allows us to exit the stairwell. We all move into another hallway. If I have my bearings right, the wall to the right is likely separating us from the room where the Saints eat the porridge. The hallway stretches ahead of us about thirty feet, presumably to the front of the building. The hallway also juts around the stairwell and continues behind us. If I have pieced it together correctly in my mind, the double-doors in the Saints eating room should be on the other side of the stairwell and should open into the hallway that extends behind us.

As we walk down the hallway, I notice that there are no windows on the wall to the left. I presume that this would be the far edge of the building, but maybe not. Then I remember that the lawn equipment room is somewhere on this side of the building, probably behind us and on the other side of the wall to our left. We reach the end of the hallway, and I can see natural light shining on the floor as I look to the right. We turn right and continue to walk down another hallway toward the main entrance to the building. To our left is a ramp with a rail. The ramp descends and reaches the floor about twenty feet from the front doors. I look back up the ramp and see that it turns left toward the back of the building. A large window on the right allows the sunlight to flood the landing of the ramp before it continues left and up to the second floor.

We continue to be the only ones in the various hallways throughout our walk. We reach the front doors. I see that someone has opened the doors, but no one is around except for us. I look out the doors expecting to see a truck delivering the first group of Saints, but nothing is there. We have a narrow window of time to grab the robes and return to the kitchen supply closet. I look over at Thomas who is standing next to a large metal cage on wheels. The cart stands about six feet high and is about six feet long by four feet wide. The cart is packed full of neatly folded robes. He opens a hinged door about four feet up the side of the cart to access the robes. The hinged door swings down when he releases a latch on the side. While I stand there watching Thomas, I can feel the warm sun shining on my legs through my camp counselor pants as the sunlight passes through the doorway. It reminds me of Jesus, the light of my life. It won't be long until I am standing in the light of his presence, and the things of this world will be no more for me.

Thomas quickly passes robes to each of us. As soon as we all have one, he closes the door on the cart. He immediately leads us back the way we came. We turn the corner; no one is there. I am wondering if I should try to hide the folded robe under my shirt, but Thomas keeps his in plain view. We make it back to the stairwell and go inside. Back up the stairs we go and down the hallway toward the cafeteria. Once we are halfway through the cafeteria, I see the first of the camp workers coming up the stairs. They are presumably making their way to the front of the building for the first delivery of the Saints. How silly this seems. How can these people be so ignorant of what they are doing? Are they so brainwashed that they can't understand that they aren't helping anyone but simply aiding in murder? How can someone lead so many astray? How can the Leader have fooled them like this? Or do they know exactly what they are doing?

As we pass the first group of camp workers, one man looks quizzically at Thomas and says, "Wrong way?" Thomas quickly answers, "We need to take care of something real quick; we'll be right back over there." The answer seems to suffice, and the camp workers continue on their way. No further questions are asked about the folded robes that we all are carrying. We get similar questions about ten more times as we pass other camp workers on their way to the front of the building. Each time Thomas gives the same answer. No one seems to have the time to make any further inquiries, which means they aren't really that concerned about what we might be doing. We finally make it to the kitchen supply closet. When we get there a group of camp workers is just passing through. No one from this group seems to care what we are doing, and they all walk past us without giving us the time of day.

Once this group leaves the supply closet, Thomas peers around the corner to see if anyone else is coming. He turns back and begins to survey the supply closet for the best place to hide the robes. I remember from earlier that I thought under where the aprons hang would be a good hiding place. I point to the floor under the aprons and say, "Here." Without any further justification, Thomas bends down and begins to move the pile of aprons on the floor underneath the ones hanging on the pegs in the wall. The pile is a mixture of folded and unfolded aprons; it has to be the messiest thing in this place. Hopefully the Leader saw it and got mad at it. As soon as I think of him, my mind returns me to the picture of the Leader hanging in his office. As I view the image of the picture hanging above his couch, a placard appears in the frame at the bottom of the picture. I do not remember the placard being on the actual frame in his office, but I might have missed it. It's kind of like I'm standing in his office, and I walk closer to read the word contained on the placard. Even though I don't move much closer I see the word. Antichrist is the word.

Thomas jolts me back into reality as he tugs at my robe. After a few tugs I release it. "Are you OK?" he whispers to me. I answer, "Yes, just fine," as he places my robe on the floor behind the pile of aprons. My robe is the last one to go in the pile. Thomas then moves the pile of aprons on top of our neatly folded robes. I hear voices from outside the supply closet. Thomas pops back up without doing any more placing of the aprons. The robes are hidden, so we should be OK. Two women walk into the supply closet. They are moving rapidly. One looks back after they pass us and says, "Come on guys, we're going to be late."

We fall in line behind the two women for our return trip. No one is the wiser so far. As we walk into the kitchen, I can't help but think more about the placard that I saw under the Leader's picture. Then I think back to the earlier vision that I had when we were making porridge where I saw the Leader on TV and freaked Julia out by yelling, "Antichrist!" over and over again. I'm not sure what to make of it all, but I don't have a good feeling about what or who we are going up against today. Thomas, who is leading us behind the two women, suddenly reaches both arms out sideways and stops, as if to hold us back. The two women do not notice and continue into the porridge room. Thomas turns around and whispers, "Knife." He walks to one of the kitchen counters and opens several drawers until he finds a large knife. The knife is in a plastic sheath, and he tucks it in the waist of his pants on his left side. He lowers his shirt so that the knife cannot be seen.

I quickly realize that the knife is for cutting the netting at the bottom of the Stairway to Heaven. Thomas leads us back through the supply closet. No one is in the hallway that leads back toward our room. Thomas, now jogging, turns right and leads us down the hallway toward the door to the bottom of the Stairway to Heaven. We all jog in place behind him. It is a slow jog, so everyone is able to keep up. Thomas reaches the door first and opens it. He whispers, "Don't let it close behind us." Nate responds, whispering, "Dad knows how to get it back open." Thomas continues through the door. Ted, Julia, and I follow him out. Nate holds the door with Josh and Dave standing in the doorway. Mindy stands right behind them. Thomas pulls out the knife and removes it from its sheath. He grabs hold of a portion of the net. It is pulled rather tightly, so hopefully it will be an easy cut.

Thomas has to saw the knife back and forth for about ten seconds at each piece of netting to make the cut. He starts about three feet above the ground. After about half way, Ted gives him a break. He cuts the rest of the netting down to ground level. Thomas hands him the sheath for the knife and this time Ted hides it under his shirt. Our escape port is ready, if we are fortunate enough to use it. We hastily reenter the building. The door shuts loudly behind us. Thomas leads us in a slow jog back down the hall. He slows down to a walk once we reach the end and turn left toward the kitchen supply closet. When we reenter the kitchen Thomas returns the knife to the drawer after getting it back from Ted. Now we are ready to join the group who by now are probably starting to unload the Saints.

Our return trip to the front of the building is even faster than our first trip. Once again we see no one along the way, at least until we round the corner that leads to the front doors. The area immediately around the front doors is filled with camp workers. As we walk toward the crowd, the sea of people parts in the middle. Two camp workers emerge from the crowd on each side of a stretcher with wheels, and they are quickly pulling it toward us. A presumably unconscious person, the first Saint off the truck, lies on the stretcher. We move out of the way to allow the two workers to pass with the stretcher. I turn and follow them up the ramp with my eyes. They turn left at the landing and soon disappear from sight. The sunlight still shines through the window at the landing. Several more groups of two pass with stretchers. I look at the face of each robed Saint who passes by. It makes my heart hurt to see these innocent people in such a state. I hope we can find a way to help them all, at least long enough for the Lord to rescue them and hopefully us as well.

I notice that I am still breathing heavily from our recent trips across the building. I begin to regulate my breathing, and I wipe the sweat from my forehead. My heart is racing now that we are fully immersed in our plan to bring this place to its knees. I only hope that Jesus will help us and save us. The best thing for me, for all of us, will be to move on to the next phase of the plan. Unfortunately, it is going to take us a while to work our way out the front door given that we are at the back of the line. About ten more stretchers pass us carrying Saints. Then I notice Thomas making a move through an opening toward the doorway. Julia motions for the kids to follow as they are closest to Thomas. The kids squeeze through the opening. Julia, Ted, Mindy, and I follow. No one seems to want to stop us from cutting in line. Thomas continues to the back of the large tractor trailer parked out front. The trailer itself is very long; it looks to be a fifty-three footer. The doors to the trailer, which open out, are locked in place at the sides of the trailer. The trailer is equipped with a ramp that has been lowered to the ground. The ramp is at least fifteen feet long. It looks like the ramp folds in the middle and likely has controls to extend it and to retract it automatically.

This was not what I was expecting. The tractor and trailer both look very new and are very clean. Both are painted black and shine in the bright sunlight. The tractor trailer is facing left as one comes out of the building and its front is aimed at the guard shack at the edge of the property. Thomas, in a fairly loud voice, says, "Split up into groups of two like I told you." I remember Thomas telling Julia and Mindy to pick strong partners. Thomas pairs himself with Mindy. I start to pair up with Julia, but then I realize that each group should have one adult with one kid. I quietly ask Dave to help Julia. I pair up with Nate, and Josh pairs up with Ted. Thomas leads Mindy up the far left side of the ramp as a group exits the trailer. I watch as the camp workers carefully guide the stretcher down the ramp. The ramp is shallow enough that it does not look like there is much risk of the stretchers tipping over. There are also little speed bumps all along the ramp that seem to help keep the stretcher from gaining much speed. If the Saints were awake, then it would certainly feel like a bumpy ride for them.

Nate and I are the next group to venture into the trailer. As warm as it is outside, the trailer is oppressive. The air has a definite stench to it. Sleeping people are lined up on the floor from about fifteen feet inside the trailer to the back of the (I'm guessing) fifty-three foot trailer. I notice that everyone in the truck is already wearing a robe. On the right wall of the trailer are shelves. The shelves are high enough that a person can be laid underneath them. The shelves hold the stretchers, which answers my question of where the stretchers were coming from. The stretchers are held in place with straps. It looks like as people are emptied from the trailer, the next set of stretchers becomes reachable to un-strap and use. One question is how they got to the first set of stretchers without stepping on someone. I also wonder how everyone got robed so quickly. Hopefully I'll never find out the answers to either question.

Thomas has free access to one of the stretchers on the shelf before the rows of people start. He grabs the end of the stretcher furthest into the trailer, and Mindy grabs the other end. They lift the stretcher down to the floor and set it on its wheels. The stretcher is folded down, so it sits just a few inches off of the floor. Thomas wheels it next to one of the sleeping people in the first partial row. It is a young girl, not more than fifteen or sixteen years of age. My anger again burns against the Leader for what he is doing. Thomas says, "This is an easy one," and gently reaches under her shoulders. Mindy grabs her legs and the two of them quickly lift her onto the stretcher. Josh and Ted as well as Julia and

Dave have entered the trailer and are standing next to us. Thomas points to a red button on the right side of the stretcher. He then pushes the button and the stretcher automatically extends up very slowly. After about ten seconds the stretcher makes a clicking noise. Thomas grabs the side of the stretcher and pulls up. It makes a louder clicking sound. I notice that he positioned his foot on one of the bottom rails of the stretcher as he pulled up.

Thomas looks at us and says, "For the big ones, don't be afraid to roll them onto the stretcher. They can lay on their side or their stomach as long as they're stable." We all nod in agreement. Thomas turns and starts to ask Mindy to grab the other side of the stretcher, but she already has a hold of it. The two begin their walk out of the trailer, into the building, up the ramp, and to the holding room. I begin to wonder how we get to the holding room from the ramp. As Thomas and Mindy are exiting the trailer, Thomas turns his head and says, "We'll wait for you on the ramp inside." With that they start down the ramp leading out of the trailer.

It's now up to me and Nate to load the next person. I wish Thomas could have supervised us the first time, but I understand the tight schedule we are under. Nate and I take a stretcher down from the shelf and set it on the floor. I purposely take the back position so that I can lift the top half of the next person. I turn around half-hoping to see another small person. No such luck as the next person in line, a man, is at least a healthy two hundred and fifty pounds. Nate and I position the stretcher as close to the man as possible. We begin to lift him up with little initial success. We gently set him down and try again. This time I'm able to get his shoulder on the stretcher. Ted comes over and places his foot on the stretcher to keep it from moving. Josh grabs the man's left arm and helps to scoot him onto the stretcher. "Careful!" I whisper to Josh.

Once we position the man comfortably on the stretcher I look for the red button on the right side. I find the button and push it. The stretcher slowly extends to the upright position. It clicks twice before I implement Thomas's technique of locking it into place. It doesn't make the louder click the first time I try it, so I pull harder a second time and it clicks into place. Instead of leaving, Nate and I push the stretcher far enough to get it out of the way. We then return to help Josh and Ted, and then Dave and Julia, to get their people onto the stretchers. Once the three Saints are loaded, we leave the trailer as a caravan. The next group of camp workers enters the trailer as we walk down the ramp. It feels good to be out of the hot, smelly trailer.

Once we reach the bottom of the truck ramp, we have to backtrack a few feet to make our way through the doorway into the building. What's nice is there is no lip for us to push the stretchers over as we go through the doorway. The concrete walkway to the doors is flush with the concrete floor inside the building. We make the easy transition into the building and everyone gives us room to turn right toward the ramp. We venture onto and up the ramp. When we reach the landing I take a brief look out the window. I see the tractor trailer shining in the sunlight. We make the left-hand turn at the landing and continue up the ramp. At the top of the ramp is another landing and a door. Thomas and Mindy are standing at the door. Thomas has the door propped open with the stretcher halfway through the door. When we get close Thomas pulls the stretcher the rest of the way through the door and Mindy holds the door open for us. Once Nate and I are through the door, I can see it is going to be a short trip to the holding room. I recognize where we are now from that fateful first day we were here. We are on the second floor walkway that spans the perimeter of the building starting from here and going around the back and around the other side of the building.

Thomas and Mindy proceed toward the door to the holding room, the one from which we escaped several days ago. I wait with the stretcher outside of the door as Nate holds the door open. As Thomas and Mindy approach the door, two camp workers emerge from the room carting an empty stretcher. I start to scoot our stretcher over to give them room, but one of them, a middle-aged man I've seen before in the cafeteria, says, "No, no. You first." He speaks with a British accent. Nate joins me on the other side of the stretcher as Julia and Dave are pulling their stretcher through the door. Nate and I guide the stretcher past the camp workers toward the holding room. I say, "Thank you," as we pass the camp workers. The man who spoke before says, "Welcome." Nate and I enter the room. An eerie feeling comes over me as I enter the room where this nightmare started. What an unimaginable feeling it was to wake up in such a strange place and in such a strange way.

It helps that the lights are on, which makes it seem a little different than the other day. Nate and I make our way over to where Thomas and Mindy are unloading the girl on their stretcher. They have lowered the stretcher back to floor level. Thomas comes over to us and presses the red button on the stretcher. This time he holds it for about five seconds until it clicks. Our stretcher begins to lower. Soon Julia, Dave, Josh, and Ted are all in the room with us. Once the first set of Saints is unloaded we pause momentarily and look around the room. We then exchange glances. I mouth the word, "Freaky!" to Julia who nods in agreement. After what seems like only a few seconds, two more camp workers and a Saint on a stretcher enter the room. Our time to reminisce is over so we exit the room.

Back and forth we go at least seven more times. I may have miscounted by one. Nate and I always draw a very heavy person. My clothes are drenched with sweat halfway through the ordeal. The loading and unloading goes without issue. By the fifth time I enter the holding room it doesn't bother me as much as it did before. I notice that the Saints in the room are already being given their injections to be woken up, even before the truck is completely unloaded. This is evidently different from our experience the other day as the room was completely filled and dark when I woke up. As we go back and forth, especially during the last few trips, I see groups of camp workers leaning against walls and resting. Some of them are drinking from bottles of water that I would be willing to buy for a substantial amount of money by the fourth trip. I don't blame them for resting; this is hard work. I hope they at least feel somewhat guilty when they watch us pass by them while continuing to work hard.

Finally we return to the truck and it is empty. A group of about ten camp workers is collecting the stretchers and loading them onto the shelves of the truck. We hand in our stretchers and retreat into the somewhat cooler building. I feel like lying down on the floor and not moving for quite a while, but I know I can't do it. There is no time to rest. As we walk down the hallway that runs adjacent to the ramp I'm about to ask Thomas where we can get some water. Before I can ask, Thomas says, "We're going back through the upstairs kitchen on our way to get the porridge ready in the downstairs kitchen. We can stop at the restrooms up there and get something to drink before we head back downstairs." That is music to my ears, which I notice are ringing pretty noticeably at the moment.

Chapter 19 – The Discovery

Isaiah 35: 3-5 (NIV),

"Strengthen the feeble hands,
steady the knees that give way;
say to those with fearful hearts,
'Be strong, do not fear;
your God will come,
he will come with vengeance;
with divine retribution
he will come to save you.'"

"Then will the eyes of the blind be opened
and the ears of the deaf unstopped."

After our restroom and drink break, Thomas leads us downstairs through the porridge room and into the kitchen. As we walk through the porridge room I notice that the box filled with poison packets has been pulled out from under the counter. The flaps have been opened from the box. It seems strange to me that someone would need to take additional packets out of the box, especially since the person would think that we added the poison to the porridge during production.

I try not to think about it too much as we enter the downstairs kitchen. As we enter the room Thomas turns and looks at us. He says, "Wait here," as he continues into the kitchen supply closet. There are quite a few people already in the kitchen preparing for the Saints' meal, but not as many people as we saw the other day during the actual service. I'm sure the others are on their way from unloading the Saints just as we are. Thomas emerges from the kitchen supply closet with an armful of aprons. At first glance the aprons look like the robes that we will be putting on in a little bit. Needless to say my heart momentarily tries to jump out of my chest when I mistake the aprons for the robes. Once I settle down a bit, I take an apron from Thomas and put it on.

Thomas then leads us to the left counter where we will set up shop. We walk part of the way down the aisle in between the two counters. He stops us next to another group who is getting their workstation ready. Thomas gives them a polite, "Hello," but they only reciprocate with nods as they work. The mood in the room is very serious. It causes me to be almost certain that these people know what they are doing. They know that they are about to murder more people. How can they not know what they are doing?

The first thing Thomas has us do is put on some plastic sleeves and latex gloves. While I am applying my protective equipment I notice several workers placing stacks of empty bowls at the workstations. They have just started at the far ends of the counters. They have the supplies of bowls stacked on wheeled carts that they are bringing down the aisles. We should have our bowls fairly soon. Thomas sends Josh, Nate, Dave, and I to the refrigerators to bring over pails of porridge. We each return with one pail. While we were gone, the rest of our crew set several trays on the counter as well as piles of soup spoons. The workers delivering the bowls are almost to us. I ask Thomas, "Do we need more pails to start?" Thomas answers, "No, this should be plenty. We will likely need to go back for some more later, but we don't want to get our work area too cluttered."

Then I think of something that worries me. The other day when we were making porridge, I remember the kids taking the first pails of completed porridge out to the refrigerators. What I am not sure of is whether there were some leftover pails from a previous batch in any of the refrigerators. It's possible that there could be some pails with the poison in them, which would not be good if somehow we are able to destroy the smashing machine only to have some people still die from the poison. I quietly ask Thomas, "How do we know that there aren't some pails from a previous batch still in the refrigerators?" He gives me a brief smile and says, "Don't worry, we aren't allowed to keep the porridge for more than forty-eight hours because it starts to break down. At the end of the day, whatever porridge is left will be dumped down the drain. There have been some days when we had to give smaller portions to the last group to make sure we had enough, even though the bowls are supposed to be pretty full to ensure the full effect."

I feel somewhat better now, but I am still nervous beyond belief. Each time I think of another potential problem or failure in our plan, my heart feels like it is going to explode. I pray for peace from the Lord, because that is the only thing that is going to calm me down now. The workers then arrive with our bowl supply. We help them set the stacks of bowls on the counter. Mindy has the counter organized to maximize efficiency, and she instructs those of us setting the stacks of bowls on the counter where to place them. Right now each one of us is running on instinct, too scared to think straight. We have to rely on our past experiences and practices to continue to function in the present. Mindy is a person who always looks for ways to maximize efficiency in whatever job she has to do, and she is applying those same principles even now, in the face of death.

Mindy leaves us enough room to place fourteen stacks of bowls at the back of the counter behind the three trays she has set out. Three piles of spoons destined for the bowls sit on the left of each of the three trays. The workers thank us for the help and move on to the next station. Several groups have taken the workstations to our left. The room is beginning to fill up with workers. There is not much chatter, but there are plenty of dishes clattering, refrigerator doors opening, and people walking around the room. As I look around the room I see Thomas's friend Katie walk in from the porridge room. She must have finished cleaning up breakfast upstairs and is ready to move on to the next job. I realize that I never saw her during the unloading of the Saints, which makes sense given that she is part of the upstairs kitchen crew.

She stops at the entrance to the room and begins to scan the room with her eyes. When she spots our group, she stops her scan. Her eyes lock onto mine. She has a different look today. She looks troubled. On the inside I freak out when she realizes that I was looking at her. I quickly look away and pretend to get back to work. I see Mindy beginning to set bowls onto the trays, so I join in. "Eight bowls per tray," she says. I look over at Thomas, who nods in agreement. I look back over to where Katie was standing. She is no longer there. I look back at Thomas, who is separated from me by Mindy and Ted. I mouth the word, "Katie," and Thomas quickly looks around for her. He spots her, and she is still looking at us. She returns a wave and what looks like a contrived smile. Something doesn't seem right. I'm worried that she has figured things out. I hope she can somehow go a little longer without saying something if she has figured out that she saw us in the holding room the other day. Thomas turns back around and looks down at the counter. He has a troubled look on his face. That doesn't help me at the present moment.

There's no hope of calming down my racing heart or my nerves at this point. I decide to focus on the work in front of us. The three trays are filled with eight bowls each. The bowls are a little larger than what I would consider a standard size. The next step is to fill the bowls with porridge, so I reach down and pick up one of the porridge pails sitting at our feet. I lift it to the counter, but I realize that I have no place to set it. The trays extend almost to the edge of the counter. I am standing in front of the third tray, the farthest one to the right of our workstation. The edge of the counter is rounded, and there is not quite enough room for me to rest the pail without it trying to slide down the rounded edge. While I have the pail lifted in the air, Mindy and Julia move quickly to slide the remaining stacks of bowls over to the left far enough that I can scoot the third tray back using the bottom of the pail. I am able to scoot it back just far enough to let the pail rest on the counter. I continue to hold onto the pail to ensure it doesn't fall off.

Thomas walks behind Ted, Mindy, and Julia and approaches me and the pail. He grabs the edge of the pail lid, and begins to bend it to pry it off of the pail. As he loosens the pail lid, he looks back at Josh, Nate, and Dave, who are standing behind us. He says to them, "How about you guys start getting some more pails out of the refrigerators and deliver them to the other groups if they need them." With that the three set out toward the refrigerators. I help Thomas pry the lid off of the pail with my one free hand. "The first one is always the toughest," he says. I manage to crack a nervous smile.

With the lid off, I change my grip to hold the pail in a good position to begin pouring its contents into the bowls on the tray in front of me. Thomas says, "Carefully," and I immediately go against his wishes as I try to fill the first bowl. I spill quite a bit onto the tray and into the bowls beside and behind the intended bowl. A little bit of porridge spills on the edge of the counter and drips onto the floor. I go to set the pail down to find some towels to clean up my mess, but Thomas reaches for it and says, "Here." I hand him the pail and he says, "We'll clean it up in a minute. I've spilled a lot more porridge in my life than this, so don't worry about it." Next he says, "This is how it looks after you've done it thousands of times." Within about twenty seconds, Thomas has all eight bowls filled on my tray. "Wow," Ted says.

Thomas moves to the next tray over. Julia and Mindy swoop in with towels to wipe up my mess. Julia hands me one and I wipe the edge of the counter and the floor as they stand on either side of me to clean up the tray. About halfway through the second tray, Thomas runs out of porridge in the first pail. Ted lets out a grunt as he picks up a second pail. He and Thomas rearrange bowls and trays so that the pail can rest on the counter in front of the middle tray. They work off the lid more quickly than the first. I notice that Mindy has placed a spoon on the left side of each of the eight bowls on the first tray.

I stand up from wiping the floor. I notice some of the porridge splashed on my apron. I wipe it with the towel as best as I can. It leaves a slightly crimson but mostly gray stain on my apron. Thomas goes back to filling bowls with porridge from the second pail. He almost finishes the third tray before running out of porridge again. At this point Josh, Nate, and Dave return from delivering pails to the other workstations. I lift our third pail onto the counter and Ted and I remove the lid from the pail. Thomas gives Josh, Nate, and Dave instructions to take the empty pails and stack them over near the sinks at the back of the kitchen. He also asks that they do the same for other groups with empty pails.

Suddenly I hear a noise from behind us. Someone has opened the double doors that lead into the Saints' eating room. I turn and look to see Beth standing in the doorway. As she holds the left door open she says, "Everyone, the first group of Saints is being led into the room for their meal. Let's start bringing out the food for them." As soon as she finishes her sentence, she turns and goes back into the Saints' eating room. The door swings shut behind her.

Ted and I hand Thomas the third pail of porridge. He fills the last bowls on the third tray. He spills a tiny amount onto the tray. He looks at me and says, "See, no one's perfect." I grab my towel from the pocket of my apron and wipe up the tiny spill on the tray. I return the towel to the pocket of my apron. As I look around, I notice several people carrying trays toward the door to the Saints' eating room. Josh, Nate, and Dave are walking toward us as well. Josh quietly says, "Everyone's caught up on pails and empties for now." Thomas says, "Good, now we'll need some runners to carry the trays into the room."

I volunteer by picking up one of the trays. I am curious to see if I recognize any of the Saints that I wheeled off of the truck and into the holding room. Thomas picks up a tray. At first I think he is going with me into the room, but instead he hands it to Josh. The trays are pretty heavy when full. He asks Nate and Dave to stay in the room to continue to shuttle full and empty pails to and from the workstations. Julia picks up the third tray. Ted asks her if he can take it, but she says she wants to carry it in. Thomas says, "Ted, I could use your help with the pails. Mindy, if you could replace the trays and bowls on the counter with new ones that would be great." Mindy says, "I'm already on it," as she reaches down to get more trays from under the counter.

With me in the lead, Julia, Josh, and I walk toward the double doors through the walkway that cuts through the counter nearest to the double doors. I feel the weight of the tray pulling on my arms. It's difficult to keep it steady given my nerves, but I am able to make it to the door with no issue. Someone goes through the doors ahead of me, but he doesn't bother to hold the door open and lets the door swing back at me. I anticipate the lack of courtesy and stop short of the door hitting my tray on its return trip. I wait until the door swings back the other way and I proceed through the door. I catch the door with my right elbow and I turn to the right to allow Julia and Josh to walk through the open door. Both Julia and Josh enter the room. I look back to make sure no one else is waiting to come through the door before I let it go.

Inside the room most of the tables are filled with seated Saints. I am impressed with how quickly the Saints are brought from sleep to supper. Beth and a few other camp counselors, including Katie, are managing the room. At the far left corner of the room, the last of the Saints are being helped to their seats. Normally in a room this full of people there would considerable noise. The room is almost completely quiet. The only noises I hear are the porridge bowls being set on the tables, the shuffling of the Saints who are sitting down at the tables, and a few gentle words from the camp counselors who are helping the Saints to their seats. Beth is standing to the right of the double doors near the wall. She is smiling, almost beaming with joy. When she sees me look at her, she points to one of the tables and quietly says, "Over there." I carry my tray over to the table and balance it on my right side to free my left hand to begin setting the bowls and spoons on the table.

Josh and Julia start handing out bowls to the Saints at the tables next to mine. I soon realize that there is some logic to the trays being sized to fit eight bowls as there are eight seats to a table. Once I hand out my bowls, I look around the table to see if I recognize anyone from earlier. I do not, but I am saddened by the vacant expressions of the people sitting around the table. All of them look like they've just woken up after a rough night.

Next I realize two things. One, I am standing at the table that I was cleaning yesterday when I pictured the older gentleman eating the porridge. Secondly, I see an older gentleman sitting in that very seat! He doesn't look the same as I imagined, but it still freaks me out even more than I already am. I hear Beth say, "Everyone, it is time for you to eat. Once you receive your food, please start eating. We have a lot more to do today, so you need to start eating as soon as you get your food." She says it in such a nice way, but it doesn't sufficiently cover the evil intentions. I am not sure if I should return to the kitchen right away, or if I should help my table to get started. I choose, instead, to just stand and observe for the moment. Julia and Josh are done handing out their bowls and are doing the same.

I look back at the older gentleman at my table. He sits, motionless, as if he didn't hear anything. I start to walk toward him with the intent to help him get started. Beth comes over to the table before I reach him. She stands over the gentleman and then bends down. She gently grasps his left hand, which is down by his side. She lifts his hand to the table, and she uses her other hand to place the spoon into his hand. He grabs a hold of the spoon, and then he lowers it on his own into the bowl. I look around the table and others are taking hold of their spoons. There is suddenly more life to the group than before as they slowly begin to work the spoons into the bowls and up to their mouths. The older gentleman lifts his spoon out of the bowl and to his mouth. His hand shakes slightly as he brings the spoon to his mouth. His mouth opens slowly, and in goes the porridge. I see him take the next bite, with the same slow motions. The next time he misses his mouth, and the porridge runs down the side of his right cheek and drips onto the edge of the chair. It oozes down to the under portion of the chair, and then drips one drop of porridge onto the carpet.

Beth looks at me and smiles. She says, "You can head back to the kitchen for more. We've got things under control in here." I nod and then look back at Julia and Josh. The three of us make our way back to the double doors. As I get close, one of the kitchen workers places her empty tray on a cart near where Beth was standing. I do the same. Josh and Julia follow suit. We reenter the kitchen and return to our workstation. The kitchen is quite busy with people moving in all directions. Nate and Dave are each carrying another full pail to our station. Thomas, Ted, and Mindy have the next three trays ready to go. Ted picks up one of the trays and says to Julia, "My turn this time." Josh and I pick up the other two trays. Julia agrees to stay back and help Mindy.

I lead the way into the Saints' eating room a second time. Once in the room, Ted, Josh and I each pick tables further into the room that have not yet been served. Ted observes us momentarily to learn what to do. Once we place our eight bowls and eight spoons on the tables, we quickly start our return trip to the kitchen. On the way back I notice that Beth is helping someone else at the same table as before. Before we have a chance to go through the double doors, a woman blasts both of them open into the room. The three of us stop in our tracks to allow the woman to pass by us. She mutters a "Sorry," and continues walking very quickly into the room.

Josh and I catch the doors on the backswing and allow Ted to pass first. Once we see that the coast is clear, we reenter the kitchen. The process is repeated once again. Josh, Ted, and I make the third trip into the room with trays full of porridge. When we go in the third time, Beth has a bowl half filled with porridge in her gloved hands. She is looking intently at the porridge as she stirs it with the spoon. She lifts the spoon out of the porridge and drops it back in several times. I observe her as I walk to one of the tables toward the back right of the room. It is difficult to find a table that has not already been served. I find one and quickly pass out my eight bowls and eight spoons. At this table I think that I recognize one of the Saints as a man that Nate and I brought in off of the truck.

Josh had to go to the back left corner of the room to find a table. Ted found his relatively close to mine. Ted and I begin to slowly make our way toward the double doors once we see that Josh is done serving his table. As we get close to Beth again, I can hear her say, "Something is not right." Ted and I are behind her walking toward the double doors. Josh is walking across the room and is now a little bit ahead of us and in front of Beth. Almost as if she senses me and Ted behind her, she turns and looks at us. She shakes her head and says, "Something is wrong." Ted gives her a grunt akin to, "I don't know," and we continue to walk past her.

We meet up with Josh. He looks back at Beth, who is most assuredly following us out of the room. Even though my nervous meter is at a new lifetime high I almost, in a strange way, feel good that she has noticed our handiwork. We continue into the kitchen and back to our workstation. Just before we arrive, Beth lets out a "Thomas!" in a very loud voice. Thomas, Mindy, and Julia, who were not paying attention to us, quickly look up. Ted, Josh, and I instinctively stop in our tracks at the shrill call. Everyone else in the kitchen takes notice as well. Beth pushes her way, rather forcefully, between me and Ted. "Thomas," she says, "What did you do?" Thomas answers, "What do you mean, Mom?" in a very calm, yet concerned tone.

"This food, something isn't right. The consistency is off. Did you follow the procedures? Did you forget something?" Thomas answers, "Yes Mom. I've made this stuff hundreds of times. I know just what to do. What's wrong with it?" Beth answers, "The color is off, the consistency is off, and the smell is off. It's like it's got food coloring in it or something. I can see different colors swirled in it." Thomas says, "I don't know what you're talking about." That was the wrong response. Beth straightens up and looks even angrier. Thomas continues defiantly and says, "I made it just like I always do."

222

Beth takes two more steps closer to Thomas. She leans in and invades his personal space. She half-whispers, "No you didn't, or it would be right! Why today of all days did you do this? This day had to be perfect and you may have ruined it! The Leader said everything had to go perfect this time! If this day gets messed up because of you, I'm going to strangle you!"

Whoa, wait a minute. That's not the way a mother should talk to her son. It wasn't like she was letting off some steam; she meant what she just said. I start to straighten up at her comment, as do the other adults in our group. I get ready to say something, I'm not sure what, but then Beth storms away. When she reaches the far end of the counter, she slams the bowl of porridge onto the counter. The porridge sloshes out of the bowl and the spoon flips out and hits the floor after bouncing off of the counter. The room is otherwise silent until she doubles back and barrels through the double doors and back into the Saints' eating room. The eyes of everyone in the room are fixed on us. Things seem to have taken a turn for the worse in a hurry.

After about thirty seconds, the activity in the room returns to normal. Our group continues to stand, as if we are protecting Thomas who is standing in the middle of us. Mindy places her hand on Thomas's shoulder. After another thirty seconds, Thomas looks up and smiles. A tear streams down his right cheek. He says, "At least that makes my decision a lot easier." Ted pats him on the back. Then Thomas says, "It's time for us to go. Someone else can clean up the mess this time."

As we walk out of the room, I sense that all eyes are on us. Thomas leads the way and we follow. Once he enters the supply closet, Thomas turns and walks backwards. Once we are all in the supply closet, Thomas stops just before the other exit where the aprons hang. He and Ted scoop piles of aprons out of the way to reveal the robes that we have hidden. What is so very strange to me is that everyone in the kitchen who can see us is likely watching our every move. They have no idea what we are doing. I was one of the last ones in the supply closet as I was guarding the rear of our procession. I turn and look back into the kitchen from the supply closet. I am surprised to see only one or two glances in our direction by the kitchen workers that I can see. No one seems to care that much about what we are doing.

I am handed a robe by Josh. He is handed another robe by Nate. Nate gets his from Dave. Dave's robe comes from a crying Julia, who gets hers from a crying Mindy. Ted and Thomas are already robed. I realize we need to act quickly and get out the door to the Stairway to Heaven. But is it time yet? Don't we need to time it with the Saints going up the stairs?

I put on my robe. I look back again, but no one is looking at us. It boggles my mind that no one is taking further interest in us. Then the double doors open. Beth pokes her head out of the door. She doesn't look our way, but she looks across the room. I look over and I see an older woman back by the wall. It's the same one from the other day who made the phone call telling whomever that the Saints were finished eating and on their way to the Stairway to Heaven. I hear Beth quietly say, "They're ready," and the woman picks up the phone. I look back at Thomas. He may have heard the same thing I did, but I still say, "It's go time."

Thomas leads us out of the room. No one is in the hallway. We turn right and go down the hallway that dead-ends at the door to the Stairway to Heaven. My legs are shaking quite a bit. I am still at the rear of the group. I am amazed that the kids are able to stand strong as they walk ahead of me. Julia and Mindy are holding hands. Ted is second in line behind Thomas. We pass the door to the small supply closet nearly at the end of the hall. I envision the Leader and his team sitting at the conference room table just on the other side of the wall. The thought doesn't help me in any way at the moment.

Everything is happening so fast. There is no time for me to think. What if there is something we haven't thought about? What if Beth noticed we left our workstation? What if Beth and Katie start to talk and they figure out that they had better have someone chase us down? What if our feeble, half-baked plan doesn't work? How can we expect to save any one of these Saints, let alone ourselves with this silly plan of ours? There are so many unknowns, so many variables that we probably haven't thought about. I look back, half expecting to see a posse coming around the corner to apprehend us. But there is no one. I look forward again, only to see Thomas standing next to me. We have made it to the door to the outside. Ted is holding the door for everyone. For the first time on this trip, and for as long as I have known him, I see him crying.

Thomas puts his right hand on my left shoulder. He reaches his left hand under his robe. He continues to search for something with his left hand. He finds it and pulls his hand out from under his robe. He has a gun! Thomas says, "Matt, this is for you." He hands me the small gun. This is the second time in my life I've held a gun. The first time was when I was a kid and my grandfather was teaching how to shoot a BB gun at his farm. Why is Thomas handing me a gun? I don't even know how to use it.

Thomas looks me in the eye. He says, "There's one bullet in it." I interrupt. "But Thomas," I say, "I don't know how to use this thing. What am I supposed to do with one bullet and a gun I don't know how to use?" He answers, "You'll know when the time is right. Trust in the Lord." His words pierce my heart. Ted calls us out the door. I quickly tuck the gun under my robe and into my pants pocket, barrel down. I figure if the thing accidentally goes off, I would rather shoot myself in the foot than in the head.

Thomas and I walk through the door. Ted shuts it behind us. We are all standing at the bottom of the Stairway to Heaven. The slit in the netting calls to us to escape right now. We ignore its call. Instead, we join hands, all shaking, and bow our heads. The tears are dripping from my closed eyes as my head is bowed. I say, "Lord, give us strength." I pause to the sounds of sobbing from everyone, myself included. I continue by saying, "Lord, if there was ever a time we needed you it is now. Right now, in Jesus name, Name above all names, give us the

225

power of your Holy Spirit. May your will be done Lord. Not ours but yours. May your will be done." With that, I can't hold back my own sobbing any more. That's the extent of my prayer. I pause and wait for anyone else to speak. No one does. I lift up my head. Everyone else lifts theirs just after me. Thomas, amidst tears, says, "It's time. In Jesus' name, let's go."

CHAPTER 20 – THE REBELLION

Daniel 3: 13-18 (NIV), "Furious with rage, Nebuchadnezzar summoned Shadrach, Meshach and Abednego. So these men were brought before the king, and Nebuchadnezzar said to them, 'Is it true, Shadrach, Meshach and Abednego, that you do not serve my gods or worship the image of gold I have set up? Now when you hear the sound of the horn, flute, zither, lyre, harp, pipe and all kinds of music, if you are ready to fall down and worship the image I made, very good. But if you do not worship it, you will be thrown immediately into a blazing furnace. Then what god will be able to rescue you from my hand?'"

"Shadrach, Meshach and Abednego replied to him, 'King Nebuchadnezzar, we do not need to defend ourselves before you in this matter. If we are thrown into the blazing furnace, the God we serve is able to deliver us from it, and he will deliver us from Your Majesty's hand. But even if he does not, we want you to know, Your Majesty, that we will not serve your gods or worship the image of gold you have set up.'"

Thomas starts to lead us up the first flight of stairs. After a few stairs he stops. He turns around and says, "You guys should probably go first in case there is someone along the way who will recognize me. I need to remain anonymous until it goes down at the top. I need to stay toward the back with the guys." He is talking about Josh, Nate and Dave. We quickly decide that Ted and I should go first. Then Josh, Nate, Dave and Thomas will follow behind us. Mindy and Julia will bring up the rear. We all fall in line and continue to move up the stairs. I'm not sure how we are going to merge with the group of Saints and get to the front of the line undetected. When we get to the second floor, there is no one in sight. Evidently the group has not yet arrived.

Ted and I both turn and look at Thomas. He says, "This should work. Let's go partway up the stairway in between the second and third floors.

We'll make sure no one can see us from down here. As long as the camp counselors stay at the entrance to the stairway, we'll be able to let the group catch up to us without us being seen by anyone down here." It sounds like as good a plan as is available right now. Ted and I lead the group up this flight of stairs to the landing. The next flight of stairs continues to go up in the other direction. We can plainly see that we will still be visible to any camp counselors on the landing, so we continue up the next flight of stairs. Another landing awaits us before the stairs turn one more time, this time at a ninety degree angle, to lead us to the third floor walkway that runs just below the roof where Thomas, Ted, and I spent the night. We crowd into the landing area. We are in the one spot where we will not be seen by the camp counselors below or by Tom and Barry above.

In my impatience I walk back down a few stairs. I get down on my hands and knees and peer down to the second floor walkway. Julia whispers, "What are you doing?" I answer, "Watching for the group to come." She quietly says, "Don't let them see you!" I don't have time to answer her before I see someone come around the corner. I wait just long enough to make sure it is more than just one or two people. Two camp counselors, both men, are leading the group of Saints along the walkway. Neither one was looking at me. I quickly spring back up and onto the landing. Now we wait to be joined by the Saints.

We can hear when the front of the group reaches the second floor entrance to the Stairway to Heaven. The sound of mass shuffling feet stops. One of the camp counselors says, "Now you just go up the stairs and keep walking until you see two nice men. They will help you get to where you need to go, OK?" He repeats the same line again. I immediately start to worry that he will have to lead the group up the stairs. Then what do we do? Soon after, though, I hear him say, "That's it. Yes, just keep going until you see the two nice men. They will help you." I start to hear shuffling up the stairs. The leaders of the group reach the landing, and they are all wearing white robes. One of the men leading the group looks up at us, but he only gazes with a blank stare.

When he is only a few stairs away, I take a deep breath. I take my position at the front of the group with Ted. We begin to walk up the last flight of stairs.

I'm still nervous, scared, and terrified beyond belief, but in a strange way this feels right. I'm where I need to be. In this moment, somehow, I find peace in the Lord. As we reach the top of the last flight of stairs, I hear voices from behind me. It is the kids. They are saying, in quiet unison, "Christ behind me. Christ in front of me. Christ beside me. Christ inside of me." My heart wells with a strange feeling of sheer exuberance. They repeat the cadence. "Christ behind me. Christ in front of me. Christ beside me. Christ inside of me." They say it again, a little louder this time. "Christ behind me. Christ in front of me. Christ beside me. Christ inside of me." I can hear Thomas's voice this time. Next time I join in. "Christ behind me. Christ in front of me. Christ beside me. Christ inside of me." Ted joins in the next one as well. "Christ behind me. Christ in front of me. Christ beside me. Christ inside of me," we say again.

We continue down the walkway. My courage builds with each repetition of our battle cry. I can tell by everyone else's voices that their courage is building as well. The Holy Spirit of God is with us and in us as we walk. By the time we get to the small flight of stairs down to the platform, we are reciting our battle cry very audibly. "Christ behind me! Christ in front of me! Christ beside me! Christ inside of me!" I see Tom and Barry, but they are paying no attention to us at the moment. They are both at the control panel looking at something. I immediately wonder if they have detected a problem given the work that Ted, Thomas, and I did the other night. Then my head starts to hurt. Everything around me starts spinning. Not now. What is happening?

In an inexplicable rush, all of my memories seem to slam back into my mind. Every memory that I had lost since we arrived here, everything that was being blocked by the drugs we had been given at our capture, all appear in chronological order before my very eyes. I have never

229

experienced anything like this before in my life. I'm not sure how long my episode lasts, but when I come to I am holding onto the rails on either side of me. Ted has a hold of me under my right arm, and I look to my left and see Thomas holding me up on the other side. Ted asks, "Are you all right?" I answer, "I am now." As the stars continue to clear, I look over at Tom and Barry. We have their attention now. I'm glad that we do, because I remember everything. I know what we need to do now.

■■

I steady myself and walk down the stairs. The nervousness is gone. One of the two, I'll call him Tom since I have a fifty-fifty shot, keeps a close eye on me as we approach the platform. Barry returns to his work at the control panel. Ted and I stand shoulder to shoulder to block Tom's view of Thomas. We reach the platform. Tom takes a few steps forward and extends his arm out to stop our progress. "Just a minute," he says, "We're almost ready." He continues to hold his arm out. I look over at Barry. He looks back at Tom and says, "Clear." Tom replies, "Clear." With that Barry pushes a button on the control panel. The pusher arm activates. It seems to start without issue. I brace myself for the extremely loud crashing noise I heard the other day. BOOM! The impact shakes the platform and the insides of everyone nearby. As the pusher arm slowly retracts, I hear a sound that is music to my ears. It is the sound of metal scraping against metal. Barry and Tom share puzzled looks. The pusher arm is able to make it back to its original position even though I can see the metal side of the container bending all along its trip back. Tom walks over to where Barry is standing at the control panel. Ted turns into the group and says, "It's not enough. We need to go to Plan B, now!" Even with my memory being returned, I can't presently remember what Plan B is supposed to be. Regardless, I take the lead and start toward Tom and Barry. Thomas somehow gets ahead of me and runs right up next to the control panel. I stop momentarily, with Ted at my right. I am about three steps away from the control panel.

"Thomas, what are you doing up here?" Tom asks. Barry asks the same question right after Tom. "Plan B!" Thomas shouts in response. He lands a quick uppercut right under Barry's jaw that sends him reeling back toward the smashing machine. I run over and grab the back of Tom's shirt. I pull him away from Thomas with everything I've got and more. I somehow manage to hurl Tom, who has at least one hundred pounds on me, away from the control panel. He lands several feet to my left. Nate, Josh, and Dave immediately pounce on him, before he has a chance to get up. I turn and run toward the pusher arm. As I run past Barry he has just gathered himself and is starting to lunge at Thomas. I give him a hefty push and knock him into the wall of the container. When I get to the pusher arm I look back. The kids are beating the daylights out of Tom, and Thomas has Barry pinned to the ground. I yell over to Ted, who has moved over to help Thomas. "Ted," I yell, "push the button!" I look back at the main pusher arm. I grab the smaller side pusher arm with both hands. I lift my legs up and push my feet against the main pusher arm, just under the side pusher arm. I look back as far as I can and yell, "Push the button!"

I see Julia standing next to me. She yells, "You're going to kill yourself!" I answer, "I don't care! Push the button!" I pull back on the side pusher arm with all of my might. I can feel my core muscles extending way beyond their comfort zone. My head is leaned back so far that I can see Ted standing at the control panel. I see Julia back up away from me. Then Barry knocks Thomas off of him and stands up. Ted sees him, and then reaches out and pushes the button. WHOOM! The force of the pusher arm throws me off of the machine and onto the ground. I hit the ground hard. I hear metal screeching very loudly during the first half of the pusher arm's cycle. Before I can decide how hurt I am, Julia helps me up to my feet. I see Barry, who is now only about three feet away from me, looking at the side of the container as it bulges out just before the door.

The pusher arm can't move forward any farther. It contracts back slightly, tearing a small slit in the side of the container just before the door. And then it comes to rest. Tom and the kids have also paused to watch the destruction of the smashing machine. Barry looks at Ted and says, "You broke it! You broke it!" Thomas runs at him and tries to tackle him at the waist. I rush over to help Thomas, and as I do I see Tom throw Nate off of him and start to stand up. Mindy is standing next to the kids, trying to find a way to help them. She is standing behind Tom, and she hits him in the back with both fists clenched as hard as she can. It causes him to roar in a most inhuman way. While all this is happening, I launch myself into Barry's upper body and end up landing on his head as we both hit the ground. I pop back up almost immediately and yell, "Mindy, get the door!" She turns and runs toward the door to the container as I rush over to help the kids with Tom. As I approach Tom and the kids, Julia passes me on the right to go help Mindy with the door. Luckily Tom is still fixated on Mindy who just hit him in the back. I give her props for giving this monstrous, demon-inhabited man such a painful blow.

The element of surprise is just what I need. As I leap into the air, I connect my left fist to his right temple. I kind of miss most of his body, but I manage to crash into him enough to knock him off balance. My left hand doesn't seem to be able to function immediately after I hit him, so it must have been a good one. I land right behind Tom. The kids pounce on top of him. Josh bludgeons his face with repeated blows. I stand up and tell Nate and Dave to grab his arms. Nate is nearest to me and grabs onto Tom's right arm. Dave grabs his left. I yell, "Pull him through the door!" Josh jumps off and grabs Tom's left arm with Dave. I help Nate with the right arm. The four of us start pulling at the same time. Tom doesn't put up a fight until we get near the door. He pulls the four of us forward with his arms and tries to walk himself up with his legs. Suddenly Thomas and Ted appear in front of us. Ted has Barry in a headlock, and he and Thomas are pulling him toward the door. They manage to push Barry up against Tom's legs. Tom pushes us down to pull himself the rest of the way up. The four of us let go of Tom's arms. Ted releases Barry out of the headlock. The six of us collectively push Barry into Tom, who loses his balance. He tries to grab the edges of the doorway, but his right hand slips. He falls back into the container with Barry falling on top of him. Since Tom is still holding on with his other hand, his body turns to the right as they fall into the container. The force of Barry on top of him causes Tom to lose his grip with his other hand, and the two roll back into the container. The six of us men/boys jump back out of the way, and the two women slam the door shut. Mindy turns the handle, and then Julia drops the bar that will keep the two men locked inside the container. The small slit that was cut in the side of the container is not nearly wide enough for the men to escape. We did it. We took the smashing machine out of commission and trapped its operators inside. Praise the Lord God Almighty!

■■■

We take about thirty seconds to breathe in some much needed air. After that one or both of the guys locked in the container starts banging on the door. Thomas says, "We need to keep moving." I find a way to remove my elbows from my knees and stand up. Thomas takes off running toward the stairs that lead back up to the walkway. When he gets to the stairs he stops and says, "You guys go ahead. I need to get something out of the toolbox." We fall in line in the same order as before, except for Thomas. When Ted and I get to the top of the landing stairs, I stop and look back at the kids. I say, "I want you guys to continue our battle cry back down the stairs. Adults, our job is to wake up the Saints. The Lord is in this place and he can wake them up! As we go back across the walkway and down the stairs, say to all the people, in Jesus' name, wake up!"

I turn back around. Ted nods and we begin to work our way through the crowd of Saints on the walkway. The kids, with a joyous cadence, yell out, "Christ behind me! Christ in front of me! Christ beside me! Christ inside of me!" Over and over again the strength of the Almighty fills my soul as they repeat the words. In a voice quieter than the kids, but in no way less confident, I repeat the words, "In Jesus' name, wake

233

up," as I walk past the Saints. We are moving slowly enough that I try to make eye contact with each dazed face as we walk back through the line. I can hear Ted, Julia, and Mindy repeating the same words in between the cheers from the kids.

We make it to the end of the third floor walkway. Thomas catches up to us. He takes his place in line behind me and Ted. He is holding a large hammer in his hand. We continue down the stairs. The line of Saints ends between the second and third floors. Once we get past the crowd, we quickly run down the rest of the stairway with no camp counselors in sight. We reach the bottom of the Stairway to Heaven. We have a choice. We can either run to our escape point at the fence, or we can continue to fight for the Lord and run to the reservoir.

I grab one side of the netting where we cut the slit, and Ted holds the other. In a way I am deferring the choice of where we go next to the rest of the group. The group makes the choice quickly. Josh darts out through the netting first. Nate, Dave, and Thomas follow closely behind. Julia and Mindy go next. Ted and I bring up the rear. Everyone is running straight across the lawn, toward the reservoir.

The adults have no chance of matching the speed of the kids. They are sprinting at full speed. Thomas raises the hammer into the air as if he is holding a spear and charging into battle. The kids make it to the lip of the reservoir before us adults are halfway across the lawn. Soon after the kids disappear down the other side of the small hill that leads to the valves. We soon arrive at the reservoir to the sound of shattering glass and plastic. I reach the top of the small hill and see Thomas wailing on one of the valves with the hammer. I run down to the manual valves that are downstream of the automated valves before the pipes dive into the ground. I change the position of one of the manual valves from the open to closed position. Ted closes the other manual valve on the second pipe that runs alongside the first one.

We walk back over to Thomas. All of the automated valves are sufficiently damaged. Thomas hurls the hammer into the woods and runs back up the hill. We all join him at the top of the hill where he has stopped. Ted looks at me and says, "We did it! We accomplished our plan. Now what?" Before I can answer, I look over at the far left side of the building where Thomas is looking. A figure emerges from around the side of the building. It is a man, and he is running very quickly toward us. Thomas and I run down the hill and back onto the lawn, right next to the reservoir. The rest of the group follows. Thomas is at my immediate right. I look over and see Josh, Nate and Dave next to Thomas, in that order. To my immediate left is Julia. Ted and Mindy are standing right behind the two of us.

The man gains speed with every step. He looks like some kind of ungraceful gazelle as he runs. When he gets close to us, he slows down. I can see his face. It is the Leader.

CHAPTER 21 – THE MIRACLE

Ephesians 6:10-17 (NIV), "Finally, be strong in the Lord and in his mighty power. Put on the full armor of God, so that you can take your stand against the devil's schemes. For our struggle is not against flesh and blood, but against the rulers, against the authorities, against the powers of this dark world and against the spiritual forces of evil in the heavenly realms. Therefore put on the full armor of God, so that when the day of evil comes, you may be able to stand your ground, and after you have done everything, to stand. Stand firm then, with the belt of truth buckled around your waist, with the breastplate of righteousness in place, and with your feet fitted with the readiness that comes from the gospel of peace. In addition to all this, take up the shield of faith, with which you can extinguish all the flaming arrows of the evil one. Take the helmet of salvation and the sword of the Spirit, which is the word of God."

He stops about eight feet away from us. A look of horror is on his face. He says, in a strange but mild accent, "Who are you, and what did you do?" We remain silent. He scans the group. "Thomas, is that you? Are you a part of all of this?" Thomas answers, emphatically, "Yes I am!" The Leader starts to seethe. It makes me happy. He continues to address us, now screaming. "You have destroyed everything that I have worked for Thomas, everything that I have built here. Who *are* you people? Why did you do this to me? This was not supposed to happen! You will pay for this!" At this moment the Leader starts to breathe very heavily. His eyes turn to pure evil. I don't back down, and I don't look away. My right hand disappears under my robe, and then it reappears with the gun. I aim it at the Leader's head. I pull back the safety with my thumb. Then I say, "Remember me (I so badly want to call him a bad word at this moment, but I decide not to stoop to his level), I wrote 'The End.'" His look of pure evil turns to pure shock. I pull the trigger and the gun fires. A hole appears just above his eyes in the middle of his forehead.

He stares at me momentarily before he falls to his knees. Soon after he falls forward and face first into the ground. The Leader is dead. What is left standing in his place is the abomination of desolation. I never understood what the term meant until now. The presence of pure evil is directly in front of us. Staring at pure hopelessness, or, more accurately, a complete lack or absence of hope, is enough to bring anyone to their knees. We stand strong, however, even as the presence begins to move toward us. Before I can get the words, "Lord; help us!" completely out of my mouth, a brilliant light flashes before our eyes. With a force stronger than I have ever felt before, the evil presence is whooshed away in an instant. The Leader's body is gone, too. It feels like I should have fallen to the ground, or that I should have been destroyed by the force that I felt when I saw the flash of light, but somehow that same force instead helps me to stand. I turn and look to my right at the kids. They all appear to be OK. Looks of frightened amazement are on their faces. I'm sure my face looks the same way. I look to my left. I drop the gun with my right hand and I reach my left arm out and put it around Julia. Then I can faintly hear what sounds like singing. It very quickly grows louder. We both turn and look back behind Ted and Mindy, from where the sound is coming. Then I see the most amazing thing.

Behind us is a stairway, gleaming white, which extends from the ground behind us up into the sky over the trees! Who I surmise to be angels fill the stairway. They are walking down the stairs, and when one reaches the ground, they take off at an amazing speed to our left as we are facing the stairway. I try to follow one as he takes off, but he is much too fast to be able to turn my head to see where he goes. The angels are singing the following chorus:

> "Holy, holy is our God!
> His love endures forever!"

The melody that they are singing is absolutely the sweetest sound I have ever heard. There is no way I will ever be able to repeat something so beautiful, at least here on earth. The song continues to be sung, and the angels continue to take off at the bottom of the stairs. I turn away from the staircase, the real Stairway to Heaven, even though I really don't want to. I look back at the building. I see Saints still standing at the top of the walkway behind the "smashed" smashing machine. If we didn't wake them up before, they are awake now. They have the best view of all from where they are standing.

I can see the angels running up to the building. I notice that camp counselors are now running outside of the building to see what is going on. Unfortunately for them, the angels are meeting them as they come outside. I quickly see that a spiritual battle is underway. The evil spirits that have possessed the camp counselors and the executive team are under attack. Needless to say if their Leader couldn't withstand the forces of the Lord, neither will they. I see Jared emerge from around the corner of the building. Even from this far away I can recognize him. He runs out into the lawn, surveys the situation, and then puts on the brakes. He tries to turn around and run back the way he came, but it is too late for him. He is engaged by one of the angels, the whirlwinds of light, and he is no match. Next I see an angel run through the slit that we cut in the netting around the stairwell. He blasts through the door and into the building. Many more angels soon follow.

I begin to hear and feel a faint thumping noise. It grows louder, but it does not grow loud enough to cover the angels' hymn to the Lord. Suddenly a helicopter appears over the building. A second one quickly emerges from over the tree line. The helicopters are black, and they look futuristic to me. It surprises me how small the propellers are on the two helicopters. They both advance to the back of the building and then pause in midair. After a few seconds, they advance again, closer to above where we are standing. They hover above us for about a minute, and then one of the two helicopters begins to descend. The one on the left remains at its position in the air.

The helicopter lands very quickly about twenty feet away from us. I brace for the wind that I expect to feel from the propellers, but I feel very little during the short landing. After about thirty more seconds, a door opens on the left side of the helicopter facing us. An army officer steps out of the helicopter. He looks to be high ranking based on his attire. When the officer reaches the bottom of the stairs, a second person emerges from the helicopter. "Dad!" I cry out. He did get the text after all! He looks at us momentarily, and then he looks down at his phone in his hand. He touches the screen as if he is typing a note, and then he puts it in his coat pocket. He probably sent a text to Mom that he found us and that we are all OK.

We all begin to walk toward the helicopter as Dad and the military officer walk toward us. As I get closer, Dad extends his arms. I extend mine expecting a hug, but instead he hugs Josh, Nate, and Dave, who run into his arms. Now I know who he was really worried about. After the group hug with the kids, he gives me and Julia hugs. He hugs Ted and Mindy next. Then Ted says, "It's about time you showed up!" I shake hands with the officer, as does Julia. He introduces himself as General Sharp. I notice the General is paying close attention to the real Stairway to Heaven. I look over at Dad, who has his eyes fixed on it, too. I walk over to Dad, put my arm around his shoulders, and say, "Surprised?" He doesn't answer as he continues to stare in amazement at the miracle he is witnessing. There aren't too many people in the world who have ever seen this, and we are beyond blessed to have the opportunity.

My attention turns to the reservoir. Amidst all of the joy and relief of these events, my heart sinks as I remember all of the Saints who gave their lives before this day. I walk up the hill far enough that I can see the blood. What a terrible sight. I kneel down on the hill and I pray. "Lord God," I ask, "I pray that you may avenge the blood of the Saints that was spilled in this place. In Jesus' name I pray, Amen."

When I stand back up, I look back toward the building. I still see the Saints on the walkway. Several angels appear to be attending to them.

The camp counselors, for the most part, are by themselves now. Some are in groups, and some are sitting or standing by themselves watching what is going on. The angels seem to have left the camp counselors, at least the ones who are outside of the building. And then something else peculiar happens. The camp counselors who are standing all fall to the ground, almost in unison. The ones who are sitting are persuaded by an invisible force into a lying position. In unison each one is pulled by the invisible force, feet first, toward us. I notice a few of the camp counselors are being pulled at a faster rate than the others. As they get closer, I can see that Jared is one of the ones being pulled faster. Tom and Barry were evidently freed from the container by the angels who gave them their spiritual beat-down, and they are being pulled very rapidly by their feet toward us as well.

And then I see her. Beth is being pulled the fastest of all. She emerges from the building through the door at the base of the fake Stairway to Heaven, but I am just now recognizing that it is her. She is facedown, and she is clawing at the ground trying to stop the progress of the invisible force. She is tearing up a path through the Leader's yard that will make him turn over in his grave as she tries to resist the force. Her movement begins to slow as she reaches us. She is screaming at the top of her lungs. I quickly walk over to Thomas and try to put my arm around him, but Julia has already beaten me to it. I can see tears streaming from his face. I look back over at Beth. The force pulls Beth up the hill and into the reservoir. The General runs up the far edge of the hill. Most of us follow, but Julia and Thomas stay back.

When I arrive at the top of the hill, all I see is a withered, bony hand extending from the pool of blood. The skin on the hand looks bone white as it descends into this most hideous of graves. One by one the camp counselors are brought to eternal justice for their crimes against humanity. I can't take the sight, even though I asked for it, so I jog back down the hill to further console Thomas.

I look at Thomas and say, "I'm so sorry you had to see that." Before I can go any further, Thomas, says, "It's OK. It's sad but OK. She got what she deserved, just like everyone else in this place. Besides, you of all people should know I've had a few weeks to prepare for this moment."

Now that I have my memory back, it all makes sense to me now. The book that I saw on the Leader's desk when we broke into his office a few days ago was the book that I wrote many years ago titled, "The End, Volume 1". It's the same copy of the book that I signed for the Leader in the bookstore recently. Thomas broke into the Leader's office a few weeks before we arrived, noticed the book, and started to read it. Once he somehow realized that we were earmarked for abduction, he started to believe that the book would come true. On that fateful day when we arrived and he watched us escape death from his position on the roof, it was his sign that the rest of the book would come true. No wonder he was so eager to ask Jesus into his heart once we arrived; he had already read about doing it!

Very soon the rest of the camp counselors are gone. The angels are now returning to the real Stairway to Heaven as quickly as they departed from it during the battle. Our group consists of me, Julia, Josh, Nate, Dave, Ted, Mindy, Thomas, Dad, the General, and a few other military officers who are carrying large automatic weapons. The second helicopter continues to hover quietly over us. We start to tell the General the full story of what happened. Partway through we are interrupted by an angel. He appears in our midst, standing next to the General, and says, "Hello friends. Thanks be to God Most High that he has rescued you from this place! May His love and mercy endure forever! You will have until the third day from now to leave this place. You have the rest of today, the rest of tomorrow, and until sunset of the next day to get everyone off of this island. You may take pictures of whatever you want in this place as evidence of the crimes committed. But you must not take anything out of this place except for the clothes you are wearing and anything else that you came with. Everything else in this place is devoted to the Lord and will be destroyed, along with this whole island. At sunset of the third day a consuming fire from the

Sovereign Lord will come down from Heaven and destroy this entire island and anything and everything that is on it."

The angel continues. "Also, no one may watch as the island is being destroyed, or they will certainly die. No one may watch it at a distance or through video or they will certainly die. Listen to my instructions, and it will go well with you all. Again, thank you all for what you did here. Praise be to our Lord Jesus Christ, Son of the Most High God!"

As quickly as the angel appeared, he disappears from our midst. I turn and look back where the Stairway to Heaven was, and it is gone. At least it is no longer visible. I turn back to the group and let out a big sigh of relief. Ted reciprocates in kind. What a relief. It happened, we survived, and Jesus saved us. Thanks be to God!

CHAPTER 22 – THE AFTERMATH

John 15:9-17 (NIV), "As the Father has loved me, so have I loved you. Now remain in my love. If you keep my commands, you will remain in my love, just as I have kept my Father's commands and remain in his love. I have told you this so that my joy may be in you and that your joy may be complete. My command is this: Love each other as I have loved you. Greater love has no one than this: to lay down one's life for one's friends. You are my friends if you do what I command. I no longer call you servants, because a servant does not know his master's business. Instead, I have called you friends, for everything that I learned from my Father I have made known to you. You did not choose me, but I chose you and appointed you so that you might go and bear fruit—fruit that will last—and so that whatever you ask in my name the Father will give you. This is my command: Love each other."

As if the last four days haven't been enough of a whirlwind, things seem to move in fast-forward over the next several hours. The General gets word over his phone that the airstrip and the harbor have been secured by American forces. Zero casualties for the American troops, and everyone so far who was stationed at the airstrip and at the harbor was found dead at the scene. The General gives orders to prepare for a mass evacuation of the island. The second helicopter quietly lands. About ten troops emerge from the second helicopter; only four troops were in the first helicopter with Dad and the General. The General barks instructions to determine the total number of abductees in preparation for the evacuation. He sends a group of soldiers to help the Saints down from the stairway. Many of them have already made their way to the ground level.

Thomas says to the General, "Sir! A normal load of Saints, I mean abductees, is between one hundred and fifty and two hundred. We unloaded one group this morning; one more was probably in route or is pulled in at the front door." One of the troops tells the General, "Sir,

243

that must be the big truck parked at the front of the building." The General says, "Take some of your men with you and investigate." The soldier responds with a, "Yes Sir!" Without him asking four men fall in line behind him and they quickly jog up the yard and around the left side of the building. I lose sight of them as Thomas says to the General, "There is one more group that will be found at the outpost at the edge of the island. The first truck that we unloaded was on its way back to the outpost to transport the third group for the day."

The General contacts one of his men at the outpost via his phone and has him search for the third group of Saints. Thomas tells him that the other two groups are likely still unconscious from the drugs given to them prior to transport. The General shakes his head in disgust. "What kind of monster...," he starts to say. Then the General receives another call on his phone. The soldiers who ran to the front of the building have opened the trailer and found a large group of unconscious people lying two wide from back to front in the trailer. The General asks, "How do we wake them up?" Thomas answers, "Normally a drug is used to wake them up, but it won't be good for them. They will wake up on their own soon enough." The General receives another call, this time from the outpost. The third group of Saints has been found unconscious and loaded onto a trailer. It's probably the same trailer that we unloaded this morning.

Julia says, "I'm going to go help our group of Saints figure out what's going on. I'm sure they're very scared right now." We all agree to help and make our way up to the group. Thomas and Dad stay back with the General. The stairway to the smashing machine is empty now, and it is empty for the last time. The troops are conversing with several groups of the people. I thank God that the Saints are normal people again, and not heavily drugged shells of people about to die. I look down and realize that I am still in my robe. I instruct our group to take off of our robes so that everyone else can tell that we are not part of the group who has no idea what is going on.

We ask the people to form groups around us so we can explain to them what happened. My group contains the older gentleman whom Beth was helping feed the porridge. I feel kind of strange explaining such an unbelievable story to a group of people who have no reason to believe it other than the fact that they are standing here in a strange place thousands of miles from home. I tell them that I was abducted along with my family and arrived at the island a few days before them. I explain what I saw and felt and how we narrowly escaped death. I tell them of our adventures and how the Lord delivered us all from certain death. I also tell them that there were thousands who died before us, and that the blood of some of them remains in the reservoir at the edge of the property. Several say that they saw the reddish-brown reservoir as they stood at the top of the stairway after coming back to their senses. One girl says, "I woke up, standing up, and I saw some people running past me. I couldn't go anywhere, so I stood next to Dad and watched." I say, "That was us running past you once we destroyed the machine that was going to smash us all to bits." She continues and says, "Then all kinds of crazy stuff started to happen. I guess that was you guys who ran out into the yard, and then that guy came after you. I heard the gunshot, which scared me, and right after that the sky opened up and the angels started coming down the stairs behind you guys." I say, "Yeah, I didn't even see them at first." Then she says, "The freakiest part was when all of those people got pulled into the red lake." I say, "Those were the camp workers who were helping to kill the thousands of Christians like us that they were bringing into this place." Another man says, "They got what they deserved then."

We continue to spread the word and calm fears for quite a while. There is crying and praying and rejoicing all at the same time. Eventually the General comes over and calls everyone together. He addresses the group with instructions on how we will leave the island. Several transport trucks with seating in the back have already arrived to take the first groups back to the airstrip. The abductees will be transported by air back to the US on a direct flight. Several large military planes have already arrived ready to transport this group immediately.

Everyone cheers and praises the Lord, including me. A feeling of joy wells up in me like no other. Knowing what I now know, only in my wildest dreams could a plan as crazy as this have worked.

Then I remember something. I make my way to the General. I say, "General Sharp, the one thing no one's thought about is these people have been unconscious for several days. Pretty soon they're going to realize how hungry they are and how badly they need to go to the bathroom. Can we take them all inside, let them use the bathroom, and let them grab some food from the kitchen and possibly a clean set of clothes before they leave?" The General looks skeptical for a split second, but then he agrees with me. He gives the orders and puts our group in charge of helping everyone get what they need inside. After a little thought, we split everyone into groups of twenty by counting them off as they enter the building. A member of our group leads each group of twenty into the building. We each get a uniformed escort with a large weapon just in case there would be any trouble inside.

The rest of the time with the Saints is uneventful. Everyone gets to use the restroom, and everyone gets to raid the kitchen for some food. The microwaves in the kitchen get some major use. We go into the kitchen one group at a time to make sure it does not get too crowded. There is plenty of food so that everyone can find something to eat. My group is not one of the first ones into the kitchen, so I sit them down in the eating area and tell them I'll be right back. Thomas has his group right next to mine, and I ask him to come with me to get a change of clothes for everyone in our groups. We move quickly down the stairs and through the porridge room. We dump out the contents of two large boxes in the kitchen supply closet to use to carry the clothes. Then we jog down the hall into the room we stayed in. We empty out the contents of the dressers into the boxes. Both boxes are half full, so we go into another room and empty more clothes into our boxes. Our boxes are overflowing at this point and have become pretty heavy. In light of recent events, we're not fazed by the weight of the boxes. We carry them back up to the second floor and set them on the tables in front of our groups. Some people want to change, but others do not. We make quite a mess emptying the clothes onto the tables trying to find the correct sizes for the people who do want to change.

Groups continue to shuffle in and out of the kitchen with food. Julia, Mindy, and Dave stay in the kitchen and prepare the food. Their groups were the first ones through the kitchen and are eating at the tables. Thomas sends Josh and Nate down to another couple of rooms to get more clothes. At one point the General and Dad come into the room, and they arrive through the entrance near the restrooms. They must have entered at the front of the building. I send my group into the kitchen, but I stay behind to talk to Dad and the General. Ted and Thomas walk over to the General as well.

The General talks to us about needing some help gathering the evidence of the crimes committed in this place. Thomas is a given to stay, but Ted and I agree to stay back and help as well. There is nothing I would like more than to get out of here, but I know I need to stay. Dad asks if he can stay and help, and the General agrees. Josh and Nate have returned and are standing behind us, listening. "Can we stay?" Josh asks. I say, "No, you guys need to return with Mom and Grandma to make sure they get home safe. We'll be home in a few days. Besides, Grandma Holson needs to see you guys to make sure you're OK."

Dad says, "I texted her to let her know that I found you guys and that you are OK, and I called her just a little while ago. She is so relieved. But she will need to see her grandkids as soon as possible to really be OK." At this point Julia joins us from the kitchen. Then Josh says, looking at me, "I knew you weren't going to let us stay, but I thought I'd ask anyways." Dad says, "If you don't get home to see your Grandma, she's going to come down here looking for someone to put the hurt on for taking her grandkids from her. She'll come down here with her wooden spoon looking for someone to beat on." Everyone laughs as if it were the end of a Scooby-Doo episode.

Then I ask, "Josh, what did you mean when you said that you knew I wouldn't let you stay behind?" Josh answers, "I read the book Dad. Don't act so naïve." I look at Julia and say, "I didn't want them reading the book until they got older." She rolls her eyes at me and then looks at Ted. She says, "Dad, your group can go in and get some food now." Ted leaves us and takes his group into the kitchen. Julia follows them back in to help.

Once everyone is fed and has had a chance to freshen up, we lead the groups to the front of the building. There is a mixture of people who have changed into the camp scrubs and those who decided to remain in their original clothes. I imagine the ones who changed realized that their clothes were soiled during the trip. Five large military-style trucks are waiting at the front of the building. The large truck beds are covered with domed canopies, and wooden benches line the sides of the truck beds. While they have plenty of seating in the back, I am not sure how the entire group will make it onto the five trucks. I soon see that everyone finds a seat, including Julia, Mindy, Josh, Nate, and Dave. Hugs, tears, and short prayers of thanksgiving are exchanged prior to them climbing into the back of the last truck. The trucks pull out, starting with the first one in line. One by one they pull out and exit the property at the guard shack. The trucks are turning left as they leave. I wonder if the guard's body still remains in the guard shack, or if he, too, was pulled into the reservoir. I shake off the morbid thought and see that the last truck is pulling away from us. I wave as the rest of my family pulls away. I know that they will be safe. I have trusted in the Lord. He has delivered us with his mighty and outstretched arm, and he will watch over them as they return home.

CHAPTER 23 - THOMAS'S SURPRISE

Philippians 4:4 (NIV), "Rejoice in the Lord always. I will say it again: Rejoice!"

Almost immediately after the last truck exits, two more trucks pull in and park near the entrance. The trucks are the same type as the ones that just left, and they are full of soldiers. Thomas, Ted, Dad, and I stand back as the General talks with the two highest-ranking officers who emerge from the two trucks. The General gives instructions to the men, but we are standing far enough away from them that I can't hear what is being discussed over the sound of the engines.

I am impressed with how many military-type people Dad was able to bring with him. I look at Dad and ask, "Did you ever think in a million years that this could happen?" He looks at me and shakes his head. "No," he says, gently laughing, "never." Ted says, "If I wasn't here to see it, I wouldn't have believed it either." Dad says, "You lived it," looking at Ted, "and I don't know how in the world you guys kept your cool." I answer, "Nothing but the Spirit of the Living God got us through this." Then I say, "It seems like you brought the whole army with you." Dad answers, "Yeah, evidently they've had their eye on this area for a while. When I got your text they were able to trace it to these coordinates. It was the last piece of the puzzle that they needed to get approval to come down here."

The General approaches us. He says, "Are you guys ready to get to work?" Thomas answers, "Yes, let's get this over with and get out of here. The first place we need to go is to the Leader's office." The General says, "Leader?" Ted answers, "He was the head guy who ran the place. He 'expired' just before you arrived." Ted glances over at me. I don't really feel good about what I did, but it had to be done. Dad says, "He sounds like a real piece of work." The General looks at Thomas and says, "Lead the way, Mr. Fields."

One of the two officers accompanies us along with two armed soldiers. We enter the building and turn right. We walk past the ramp that leads to the second floor and turn left. We continue down the next hallway, but this time we pass the stairway that goes up to the second floor kitchen and eating area. The General makes a call on his phone. We continue further and walk past the doors that the Saints walked out of to leave their downstairs eating area on their way back upstairs to the second floor access to the stairway. One of the doors opens and two more soldiers join us from the Saints' eating room. As we walk down the hall, I remember that the lawn equipment room is on the other side of the wall. We reach the end of the hallway. We can't turn left, because a wall is in our way. The only option is to go out a set of double doors to the outside. The wall that blocks our travel to the left contains a single door. Thomas says, "It's probably locked." The General looks at one of the soldiers and says, "We can fix that." Thomas reaches for the door handle to see if the door is locked. To his surprise, the handle turns and the door opens. Thomas leads us into another new area of the building. A dimly lit hallway makes a sharp turn to the left about ten feet ahead of us. The hallway is carpeted with tacky carpet similar to that in the Saints' eating room and in the Leader's office. We reach the turn to the left and continue on. We pass a wooden table with a small lamp on it, providing the light for this section of the hallway. The hallway has several more twists and turns along with a door that Thomas leads us past. We pass several more wooden tables and lamps of the same type as the first. We reach another door. The group stops and looks at Thomas who is in front. With his back to us he says, "Let's give this one a try." He turns the handle. Locked. "Shoot!" he says. "My thoughts exactly," says the General. Everyone backs up. Instead of firing his gun, one of the soldiers smacks the door handle several times with the back of the handle. Then he kicks the door in.

We enter the Leader's office the direct way, as opposed to crawling through a cold air return vent. I immediately look to my right, my eyes expecting to see the painting of the Leader over the couch. The frame is still there, but the painting is gone. I can see nothing but the wall

250

encased in the frame. I see the nails and the wire that hold up the picture. I move closer to the frame and lean into the couch. I see a few singed edges of the painting canvas sticking out from the frame. The canvas burned up, but the wall and the frame weren't burned. I notice that there is no placard at the bottom of the frame.

Everyone makes a lot of noise when we first enter the room. Thomas leads the General and everyone else over to the Leader's desk. I look over at them momentarily before returning to the painting. As the room quiets down, I hear the slightest sound of whimpering. I pause for a moment, and then I hear it a second time. The General comes near to where I am standing. "What was that?" he asks me.

"Thomas," I say. "Yes Matt," he says as he walks over. I say, "You didn't get to read the end of the book, right?" He answers, "Right. You guys showed up before I could finish." Then I say, "Why don't you go over and look behind the file cabinets." He gives me a quizzical look and then complies. When he makes it to the corner he turns and looks in the space between the last file cabinet and the back wall of the room. He steps back, like he sees something he didn't expect, and then he says, "Katie! You're alive!" I say, "Surprise, Thomas!" but he doesn't hear me. Katie jumps out from behind the file cabinet and hugs Thomas. After a few seconds he says, "It's OK now. We're safe. The Leader's dead, God sent angels to help, and the troops are here to get us out of here!" Everyone in the room walks over and shares in their joy, even the ones who don't know them.

Thomas says to Katie, "I thought you were dead. I thought that Jared finally got to you and turned you to the dark side." Katie answers, "No, I just pretended so I could finally get him off of my back. He wouldn't leave me alone, and my Dad wouldn't help me to get him to leave me alone. So then I realized the only way he'd lose interest is if I pretended to go along with his stupidity. I wanted to tell you, but I had to pretend to not be your friend anymore to make sure he bought my act. I was going to tell you one night when I saw you sneaking around. I followed you without you seeing me and I saw you go into the closet. At that point I was going to come in and tell you what I was up to, but then you weren't in there. Once I saw the vent cover on the floor, I bent down and saw you walking around in here. I didn't know it was his office yet, and I was freaked out about what you were doing. I left and went back to my room. I cried the rest of the night because I was afraid you were doing something that would get you in trouble."

Thomas says, "I'm glad you didn't tell anyone. I would have been a goner for sure." Katie continues. "After a few weeks of avoiding you and everyone else around here, I snuck back into the closet using my Dad's key. I crawled through the vent and realized where I was. I was so scared, but I forced myself to snoop around. That picture on the wall was so freaky. Once I found the book on his desk I would sit and read it right next to the vent until I was too scared to stay any longer." Thomas exclaims, "You read the book, too?" Katie answers, "Well, part of it. The one on his desk. You read it, too?" Thomas answers, "Yes, and that's the guy who wrote it!" He points at me. For the first time Katie realizes that there are other people in the room. She gives me a quizzical look, and then she looks like she recognizes me from the last few days, and then she gives me an even more quizzical look. She evidently didn't make it far enough through the story to understand.

I wave, sheepishly, and then she returns her focus to Thomas. She continues her story. "I snuck in three or four times. I was going to sneak back in the other night to read some more of the story, but then I saw you and two other guys coming out of the closet." She looks over at us. Ted and I raise our hands. "I freaked out and ran back to my room. I hoped that you didn't see me." Thomas says, "We didn't, thank goodness, or it would have freaked us out." I was really mad because I wanted to read more of the story about this place, a story that I was in. I assumed the Leader wrote it as some kind of a twisted journal or something."

Thomas and Katie continue to catch up. The General soon loses interest and makes his way over to the file cabinets. He begins to open drawers and hand the contents to his men to set out on the conference table.

Ted, Dad, and I each take a handful of hanging file folders filled with documents over to the table. We make several trips back and forth until the cabinets are empty. Thomas joins in to help us begin dissecting the data. Katie follows him closely. The General says, "I want pictures of every document. We can't take anything with us, so I want every detail captured; even if you have to take one hundred pictures of one piece of paper!" His men get to work. Ted, Dad, Thomas, Katie, and I watch over their shoulders at first. Soon, though, we fall in line helping to return documents to folders and to pull new documents out of folders, ourselves scanning them as we assist. Once a set of hanging file folders is completed it is returned to one of the file cabinets.

After several hours, we decide to take a break. The General has been in and out of the room, periodically returning to ask Thomas questions about the facility. The General has special interest in the security room once it is found, and Thomas tells him the story about its lack of use for quite a while. He returns to the room and surprises us during our break. He doesn't get angry with his men. Instead he asks about the porridge machine, and Thomas gives him the whole story. The General's heartfelt anger grows with each story that reveals the atrocities of this place. The soldier's shake their heads in disgust. How could this happen in today's world? How is it even possible that something like this could fool everyone for this long?

The General directs us to work for another hour. He asks for Thomas's help to accompany him to the kitchen to see if enough food remains to sustain everyone over the next several days. The General tells us not to worry as he has enough MRE's to get us through. From what I've heard about MRE's, however, I hope Thomas finds enough food in the kitchen for all of us. Thomas and Katie leave with the General, and we continue preparing the documents for the soldiers to capture electronically. I am amazed at the level of detail and organization with which the Leader maintained his records. Virtually every imaginable document regarding the construction and operation of the facility and its assets are in these folders. I see several documents dating back to the year 2011. The

Leader has spent many years building this place, and I am so happy that it will be completely destroyed in less than three days.

Before we know it, an hour and a half goes by. We stop where we are and see that there are many more documents to review before we leave. Ted walks over to the Leader's desk. Dad and I follow. He looks at the book sitting on the Leader's desk and says, "He had the key to foiling our plans right on his desk. Based on where the bookmark is, he evidently didn't get very far. If he would have read it all the way through, he could have stopped us before our memories came back and we never would have been the wiser." Thomas, who has just come into the room and walked up behind us, says, "The Leader was a busy guy. He evidently forgot to take the book with him after his last visit and didn't get a chance to finish it. Each time I put it back on his desk after reading it, I would make sure the bookmark was in the exact same spot and that the book sat in the same place."

I pick up the book. The bookmark is almost at the beginning. I open it to the page where the bookmark rests: Page 9. It's a good thing he didn't make it much farther. I turn back to the inside cover. It has my signature. For a moment I expect it to say, "God bless, Matt Hall," as I wrote in most people's books that I signed. Instead, it only has my name as I remember having signed it that way. I look back at Thomas. He says, "It's a really good thing that the Leader was such a busy guy."

I return the book to the top of the desk. We leave the Leader's office and go upstairs to eat. We work for many hours after supper until we can take no more. The soldiers continue to work after we leave. We all crash in the same room that we stayed in before, but it is different now. The pressure is off. Now it's just a room. I fall asleep saying prayers of thanks to Jesus in my mind.

■■■

I wake up. Something is wrong. My eyes don't want to open because I feel so tired. My mind quickly puts everything together and I open my eyes. It is the day after the most exciting, miraculous day of my life. It is a new day. It is a good day. The Lord is with us. Even though my body does not want to get up, I force myself out of bed. It is Friday morning, and we have a long day of data gathering ahead of us.

Luckily for us, there is enough food for breakfast. Thomas estimates that there will be more than enough food to get us through tomorrow afternoon, when we are targeting to leave. We spend from late morning until evening taking pictures of the rest of the documents in the Leader's office. The general's crew is there when we arrive after breakfast. Our efficiency is slowed by studying the documents, and at times by going back and looking a second time at documents already captured electronically.

Thomas spends more time away from us on Friday than with us. The General takes him up in one of the helicopters so that Thomas can help identify and capture key photographs from the air. When Thomas returns, he tells us what he saw. He says that over five thousand pictures were taken from the air. Evidently the building we are in is on the southwest side of the island. The airstrip and boat harbor, both small and well-disguised, are northeast of our position. The rest of the island is covered with thick vegetation, except for the building, the airstrip, and the single road, which remains fairly narrow except right in front of the building.

It seems odd that the Leader didn't build his compound right next to the airstrip and the harbor. On several of the documents we find that the Leader wanted time for the people to react in case of an "invasion" of the island. If the invaders arrived by air or by boat, there would be time for the camp crew to prepare for attack or to escape after being notified by personnel at the harbor. On a document that we find in the evening, we learn of a secret escape port very near to where the reservoir dumps into the ocean. Several small motorized boats, the document explains, are hidden in a small covered building. The document also vaguely

255

describes a situation called "self-destruct mode," but we can't tell from the documents exactly what that means. At least the Leader decided to run after us instead of pressing a self-destruct button.

By about seven o'clock in the evening we have just about finished with the documents in the Leader's office. Thomas, who has been back with us for several hours, recruits me, Ted, Dad, and Katie to help prepare dinner for us and for the military personnel who have been stuck in the Leader's office all day. When Thomas was gone Katie stayed behind to help with the documents. Among other things I learned that she was a junior in high school in Lincoln, Nebraska, before her Dad pulled her out of school to come to the island. Her Dad was Barry from the Tom and Barry duo.

After we eat we are invited to a staff meeting with the General. He has set up his command center in the Saints' eating room. We arrive at around eight thirty at night. I am surprised at how many military personnel are in the room. More reinforcements must have arrived today while we were stuck in the Leader's office. The General clears most of the room when we arrive except for his direct reports. About twelve total people remain in the room, and several of them I have not seen before. Long story short, tomorrow's activities will involve detailed surveys of the building and premises. Everything must be captured via photo or video.

One of the officers updates the General on the status of the data gathering in the Leader's office, even though he was not there with us for more than a few minutes over the last day and a part. He gives an accurate update, however, and shares that over fifteen thousand pictures were taken. The officer then hands us some fancy-looking cameras for use in tomorrow's surveys. The General again urges us to capture everything that we can. We'll be on a team of about thirty people, and we will be split up into zones in the morning. We are assured by the General that part of the day will involve being outside. Except for the thought of the bugs and the snakes, I am excited to see more of the island. The General concludes with a direct order that all activities must cease by sixteen hundred hours tomorrow. All remaining crews must be to the airstrip by seventeen hundred hours. Everyone must be off of the island by no later than eighteen hundred hours to give enough time before sunset. It sounds like the General took the angel very seriously.

Then the General says, "On a lighter note, you guys will be happy to hear that your family made it back safe and sound to the States. They should arrive back home sometime tomorrow." I instinctively pull out my phone to see if I missed any texts from Julia, since I now have it connected to the Wi-Fi provided by the military, but I find that I let it run out of battery. I had checked it once in the morning, but there were no updates. I was too busy the rest of the day to remember to check it again. After I put my phone back in my pocket, our group is dismissed. We exchange "good nights" with the General and his officers and leave the room. We take a calm, leisurely walk back to the room. Thomas stops in his "old" room to bring his phone charger to our room. Once there our group makes quick work of getting ready for bed given that we are all extremely exhausted. Within an hour we are all in our beds with the lights out. At first I have some trouble falling asleep. I can't help but think about everything my family and I have been through. I'm glad they are home. I hope that the media hasn't caught wind of the event yet for their sake. I'm not looking forward to the attention that will come from this, but I know that it will be my job to use this experience to spread the gospel. What an amazing story I have to tell.

After worrying about the things to come for about an hour, I decide to give it to Jesus. He got me this far, and it's not like he is going to abandon me now. I ask for his peace and for the strength of his Spirit in the coming days. I thank him again for this miracle, and for the miracles to come. One thing is for sure; souls will be saved as a result of telling this story. If even one person, as a result of hearing this story, decides to seek out Jesus and gives his or her life to Him, then it all will be worth it.

Chapter 24 –The Last Flight Out

Matthew 11:28 (NIV), "Come to me, all you who are weary and burdened, and I will give you rest."

I wake up. Even though the room is dark, I waste no time coming to my senses. Something still feels wrong, but at least it is almost over. I lay in the bed for a few minutes as I chart out the day in my mind. We must be off of the island before sundown. While I am somewhat excited to explore more of the island, I am much more excited to get away from it.

I get up, and soon everyone else begins to stir. We get cleaned up, eat, and report to the General for duty. Thankfully, Thomas or someone else has figured out how to turn off the morning music. We enter the Saints' eating room. We are assigned to an officer who immediately leads us back out of the room and tells us we are going to work from the top down. Thomas leads us to the roof via the same route he, Ted, and I took the other night. We take pictures of the roof, the equipment on the roof, and the views of the area surrounding the building. It seems like there are too many of us at first, but the officer lets us know that he doesn't mind if we take some redundant pictures.

From there, we take pictures of every intricate detail of every room in the building. Based on what the General said we assumed that there would be other teams taking pictures, but we do not cross paths with any other groups. We get more efficient as we go, splitting into groups of two per room. By late morning we have covered all three floors of building. We enter many rooms that I had not seen before, especially at the front of the building past the main entrance. We find the large laundry room on the first floor, more living quarters on all three floors, and many more rooms that appear to have been unused. We find several rooms filled with tools and equipment. The first floor lawn equipment room does have access from the inside, and Tom and Barry had a tool crib in a room right next to it. We find a smaller satellite tool crib on the second floor.

Before we go outside, we decide to eat again. The officer tells us that we have a lot of work ahead of us outside, and this will likely be our last chance to eat before getting off of the island. At that point our only option until we get back to the U.S. is MRE's, which the officer says may cause permanent damage. We heed his words and make our way to the kitchen. We realize this is the one room that we haven't captured yet on our cameras, so Ted and Dad take the pictures while the rest of us prepare lunch. The food supplies are starting to get low, but we find enough to make a good meal. Thomas gives us some snacks to put in our pockets for later.

The afternoon is hot and grueling, but I don't mind it too much. I'm too excited that I can count down the hours until we leave. We cover a lot of ground around the building. It seems like we take pictures of every angle of the building, every landmark, every tree, bush, shrub, leaf, and blade of grass. We capture the front of the building, the sides, and the back, including the smashing machine from its base to the very top. We take pictures of the inside of the container, even though no one seems to get a bright enough picture. We make our way to the reservoir and capture every square foot of the surrounding area. I am impressed with the memory on my camera as there is plenty of room to spare even though I have taken over one thousand pictures and several short videos. I take pictures of the gun that I left lay next to the reservoir. The officer goes to pick it up, but I remind him that everything must be left behind. Thomas lets him know that he got the gun from the top drawer of the Leader's desk, and that the only bullet in it was spent. The officer complies and leaves it on the ground. After the reservoir and a short walk down a small hill toward the river, we find the small building on the western edge of the fenced area and of the island where the escape boats are stored. There we find several surprises.

The small building's back wall butts up against the edge of the small hill. When we go inside, there is a door on the back wall. It is locked, as several others were inside the main building, but the officer persuades it open. Inside the door is a hallway carved out of rock with emergency lighting. We follow it from one end to the other. At the end of the long hallway we find a ladder that leads up to a hatch. We aren't able to get the hatch open, even with persuasion, but we surmise that it opens up into the Leader's office. We return to the boat shack and take some more pictures. Then we make another discovery.

On the outside of the building, a ladder allows roof access. Right next to the boat shack is a very large tree. The tree has boards nailed into it on the side facing the sea, starting just above roof level. I go first and climb about fifteen feet up to a treehouse-like perch. It is the Leader's perch, which is too small to fit all of us at one time. The rest of the group, except for Katie, takes turns going up to see it and to take pictures. It has a single plastic chair on the small wooden floor. The control button rests on the short stretch of railing at the front of the perch, facing the sea.

We finish up taking pictures of the area. The officer receives a call from the General to report back to the command center in fifteen minutes. I look at my phone, which is already showing low battery. I took quite a few pictures on my phone during the day as well. It's already four o'clock; we are running late. We quickly walk back to the building and walk through the torn netting and into the building via the door next to the stairway to the smashing machine. The air conditioning feels really nice as we walk inside. I quickly realize that we never took a picture of the supply closet. I find the door unlocked as I turn the handle. I snap some pictures of the closet and of the cold air return access to the Leader's office. I emerge from the closet to find that the group has waited for me, except for the officer. Thomas says, "He went back to the Leader's office to verify that the access hatch we found is on the floor under a rug somewhere. He asked us to report back to the command center and update the General."

We proceed to the Saints' eating room and Thomas gives the General an update. We turn in our cameras to another officer. After a few minutes of waiting, the officer who accompanied us for the day enters the room. He reports back to us and to the General that he found the access hatch inside a small closet in the Leader's office. It had a large steel bar across it to prevent opening the hatch from underneath. After several more minutes of discussing our day, the General gets word that our ride is here. No mention is made of what the ride is, but everyone expects a truck will pick us up and take us back to the harbor. Instead, when we arrive at the front of the building, three large helicopters are waiting for us. They look cool, but not as cool as the smaller, sleeker helicopters from the other day. The helicopters are running, but the two sets of propellers on each one are not moving. I suggest a quick restroom break before climbing into the helicopters and everyone agrees.

After we return we wait thirty minutes while the General ensures all military personnel are out of the building. Our group all loads into one helicopter. We wait at least another fifteen minutes before it sounds like the helicopter powers up. The General and two officers climb in. One of the officers shuts the door behind him. The General immediately proceeds to the cockpit, where two pilots sit. Within fifteen more minutes the helicopter lifts off of the ground. There are benches that run along the walls of the helicopter. I am sitting on the bench against the left wall of the helicopter along with Dad and Ted. One of the officers takes a seat to my left. Thomas and Katie are sitting on the bench across from us, to the left of the door from my vantage point. The other officer sits on a small bench to the right of the door. As we rise into the air, I briefly see the building through the windows in front of me. There are no windows on the wall behind me.

Soon we are away from the island. We are heading north – northwest, and there is nothing but blue sky and blue sea as we peer out the windows facing east. What an amazing feeling to leave the island. What an amazing experience and what a story. At first we are all talking excitedly. Thomas leads us in a prayer of thanksgiving that we made it off of the island. We pray for the families of all those who lost their lives, and that God can make good come from the evil actions of the

Leader and his followers. One thing is for sure, the whole world is going to be shocked when they find out who the Leader was.

The sun has nearly set. It seems to set earlier than I would expect. Everyone starts to get quiet. We are all exhausted from the trip. I pull out one of the fruit and nut bars that Thomas gave me at lunch. Even that doesn't give me enough of a burst of energy to keep me awake. I lean my head back, letting it rest against the top back of the seat. Within seconds I am drifting into a wonderful, peaceful sleep. My head is swimming in the pure joy of the moment, and then a thought comes into my mind to ruin it.

My head jolts forward and I immediately come to my senses. I look around and everyone else is asleep, including the two officers. How could I have forgotten? I stand up and walk into the cockpit. I look at the General and say, "The angel said that we couldn't videotape the destruction of the island. Why did you allow your men to set up cameras? This is not for us to see." The General, who is sitting in a chair to the right of me and behind the pilots, looks away as I speak. I continue. "One of your men has already died because you didn't listen. Call to the other people near the room to stay away or they will die, too!"

The General quickly reaches for his phone. He immediately begins calling the name of the soldier running the video control room at the military base back in the U.S. There is no answer from his man. He watched the beginning of the destruction and immediately died. The General starts yelling for someone else. Another voice answers, but it is too late. He fixes his eyes on the television screen and dies. The General gets a hold of the commanding officer of these men and orders the power cut to the video room. He yells at the commanding officer to keep everyone away from the room until morning. The commanding officer naturally doesn't understand the orders, but he complies.

I leave the General, who is crying now, in disgust. His men talked him into it, but he should not have let them set up the cameras. One of the other two helicopters that left with us remained behind to capture footage from the air; it is lost, too. What a disaster. How could I have forgotten? I sit back in my seat. I pray to the Lord. I must be making too much noise for Ted, as he has stirred. I explain to him what happened. Even though he is concerned, he continues to rest his eyes. Next, I go back to talk to the General. By the end of our talk, which is basically a pep talk to urge him to continue living, he gives his life to the Lord.

I talk for some time with the pilots and the General. The main pilot and his co-pilot both profess their faith in Jesus and share their stories with the General. The pilots ask me to tell the full story of what happened to us on the island. We talk for what seems like several hours. I want to ask how much longer it will be until we land, but I decide not to ask. Eventually the General urges me to get some rest, so I leave them and return to my seat. It doesn't take me long to fall asleep, but I wake up periodically throughout the rest of the trip home.

■■

When we arrive back in the US, I tell the others that my return home will be delayed by a day or two. I must go with the General to oversee the destruction of the equipment in the video room that captured the destruction of the island. Reluctantly they agree. We determine that Thomas and Katie will go back home with Ted until everything is sorted out with them. The General agrees that it is a good idea. After a good meal and after everyone gets a shower and a change of clothes, I part ways with the rest of the group. Ted, Thomas, Katie, and Dad aim for Ohio, and the General and I get on a military plane headed for Utah.

We arrive at the military base in Utah. It is in the middle of nowhere, in a dry and desolate wasteland. I get a tour of the facility, which ends at a small room with no power. The two men who died have long since been removed. The General gives the base commander strict orders to do whatever I say. I tell him to remove everything out of the room, even the desks, chairs, and trash cans, and load them into a truck to be carried off site and burned. I make the commander promise me that no one has removed anything from the room, and that the video feed of the event was not transferred to any other computer or device. The three of us inventory the items in the room to ensure every item listed is present at the burn site.

Within hours the room is gutted, which I then inspect to ensure everything short of the drywall, trim, and outlet covers has been removed. The commander leads me to the truck filled with the contents of the room. I attempt to check the contents with the inventory list, but it is too difficult while it is piled up in the back of the truck. The truck is pretty good size. The commander and I climb into the truck. The commander orders the driver to a place off of the base. Next, we drive to the edge of the military base and then through the security gate. We drive down the road for a few hundred yards and then veer to the right. After about ten minutes of driving through the desolate wasteland, I say to the driver, "Stop here."

We get out of the truck. I look around and can see nothing but flat, barren terrain in all directions. Realizing that we are the only three people out here, we quickly begin to unload the truck in the blazing heat. I wish I would have remembered to ask for sunscreen before we left. It's a dry heat – a really hot dry heat. After about fifteen minutes the truck is unloaded. We do a mental inventory as we pile the PC's, video monitors, chairs, desk pieces, and other equipment into a pile. When the truck is mostly empty, the commander hands me the clipboard with the hand-written inventory log. I check off everything as present and then I ask, "So how are we going to make this pile burn?" The driver says, "It should catch fire on its own in about ten minutes!" As hot and sunny as it is, it probably wouldn't take much more than a magnifying glass to get it going.

The driver climbs into the back of the truck. He hands the commander a large gasoline container. Then he straps a flame thrower on his back. I say, "You guys don't mess around!" The driver replies, pointing to the gas can, "That's my special blend to make sure there's nothing left but ashes by the time I'm done." The commander douses the pile with the special blend. He leaves the container about one third full and hands it to the driver. The driver empties the rest of the contents onto the middle of the pile, where the wooden desktop is sticking out above the pile. The commander and I take about twenty steps back. Once we get there we realize that judging the wind direction would be a good idea. The driver takes about ten steps back in the direction of the truck. He looks at us and yells, "You're OK!" as he lowers his goggles. He fires up his flame thrower and launches instant destruction onto the pile. The initial blast causes him to recoil back into a crouching position. The end of the flame thrower falls to the ground, still spitting out small bursts of flame and smoke.

The heat from the burning pile makes the hot day even more oppressive, which is surprising given the wind direction and given how far back we are standing. The driver collects himself and stands up. He looks back at us to make sure we are OK. The pile burns. It burns for some time. As I watch, I begin to drift into a vision, slowly at first. The burning pile takes the shape of a black throne. It appears to me as if it is hovering just off of the ground. The black throne rises to about ten feet off of the ground. The fire vanishes, and the throne hovers. For a split second I feel afraid, but then the fear is replaced with anger. I really don't like the black throne. As my anger grows, the ground begins to crack in front of the throne. It's almost as if my anger made the ground crack, but I am not sure. Out of the dry, cracked ground, in which nothing could grow, a single rose grows out of the ground. It does not grow as normal, but the flower emerges from the ground fully bloomed and shines brilliantly red in opposition to the darkness of the throne.

Quickly, though, the flower begins to wither and droop in front of the black throne. My heart goes out to the flower. For some reason I feel the need to help the flower, to keep it from drooping, or bowing, before the dark throne. The dark throne has no real power over the flower,

265

but the flower does not realize it. I try to think of a way to help the flower. I focus on the flower, trying to hold it up with my mind. I concentrate so hard on the flower that the ground starts to crack immediately behind it. Then, out of the crack in the ground behind the rose comes a second rose! The second rose is larger than the first one, but as it emerges from the ground I can see that it does not look as brilliant as the first rose. The second rose is a pale red, and the edges of the petals are just starting to brown. The second rose looks like one whose petals are a few hours away from starting to drop to the ground at the urging of the wind.

The second, older rose grows up and forward to cover the young rose with its leaves. A large leaf reaches from the old rose to the young rose to lift it from drooping. The next thing that I hope to see is the old rose and the new rose teaming up to destroy the black throne, but I am immediately returned to the reality of the burning pile. The commander has his hand on my shoulder. "Are you OK?" he asks. "Sure," I answer, hoping my facial expressions weren't too weird during the strange vision.

At the urging of the commander, we return to the air conditioned truck. The driver turns the truck around so that we can watch the fire through the windshield. Within an hour, the pile is nothing but ash. The driver pulls a long, metal rod out of the back of the truck as we go to inspect the ashes. He pokes at the pile to make sure nothing remains. "You were right," the commander says to his soldier. "I told you, sir, that's good stuff," he says. The pile continues to smoke and burn as we drive away. I am able to watch it in the side mirror until it dips below the horizon. We turn a little bit, which takes the small wisp of smoke coming from the pile out of the view of the mirror.

We return to the base. The General introduces me to several high-ranking military and government officials who want to hear the story. I spend the rest of the day telling the story, but I just want to go home. I don't even have time to think about trying to call home. By the time the storytelling is over, it is very late. I stay the night at the military base, but I don't sleep well enough to call it a night's sleep. I need to get home so that I can rest.

CHAPTER 25 – THE RETURN HOME

Matthew 16: 24-27 (NIV), "Then Jesus said to his disciples, 'Whoever wants to be my disciple must deny themselves and take up their cross and follow me. For whoever wants to save their life will lose it, but whoever loses their life for me will find it. What good will it be for someone to gain the whole world, yet forfeit their soul? Or what can anyone give in exchange for their soul? For the Son of Man is going to come in his Father's glory with his angels, and then he will reward each person according to what they have done.'"

The next morning I'm rushed onto a military plane back to Ohio. Before that I have just enough time to eat breakfast and then thank the General for getting me on my way home. He thanks me for telling him about Jesus. I sleep for a couple of hours on the plane. We land at a military base less than two hours from Cincinnati. At first I wonder how I am going to find a car to drive home, but a ride is already arranged for me. The driver and I leave the base in a non-military vehicle. I am so very hungry, but I can't bear to complain or to ask if we can stop for food. Given what I've been through over the last week, I've eaten really, really well. That most likely explains why I am so hungry right now. I decide to strike up a conversation with the driver to divert my attention. He is in the military, but he doesn't give any details about his rank or position. He has no interest in asking me about what happened, even though when I ask him he says he heard the story. The majority of the car ride is quiet, since it is clear that the driver doesn't want to talk to me.

When we get within ten miles or so from home, I start to get really excited. I think about how I felt on the island before my memory returned, about how I had resolved that I would never see home again. I was fine with it then, because I knew, no matter what, I would make it to my heavenly home with Jesus. What a blessing, though, that I can go back to my house and sleep in my own bed tonight.

As I look out the window I see all of the usual landmarks. They look a little different to me now, but still very familiar. The last few minutes of the trip seem like an eternity. I try to speed it up by diverting my focus. I say a prayer of thanks to Jesus in my mind. Finally we pull into the neighborhood, and then into the driveway. I instinctively let out a big sigh of relief. Home. Done. Made it. I thank the driver for the ride and try to think of something thoughtful to say as I get out of the car. He already has the car in reverse and is starting to inch back, so I push the door closed and wave. I turn toward the house. It doesn't look like anyone is home. The garage door is shut, so I walk over to the keypad. I freeze in front of the key pad because I can't remember the code. Given everything that my mind has gone through over the last week, I cut myself a break. I relax momentarily and it comes to me. The door opens and both cars are inside the garage. Maybe Julia and the kids are inside the house.

I open the door into the kitchen. I expect to hear the chirping of the security system, but it is not set. I stand on the rug inside the kitchen door. I listen for a few seconds before I call out to Julia and the kids. No one is home. I have no idea whether they should be at home or not. My phone died before we got off the helicopter, and I haven't had a chance to charge it since. I know they are doing fine, and I'm sure they will return home soon. As I survey the kitchen and the family room, my eyes rejoice at the familiar sight. I am glad to be home.

I stand on the rug by the kitchen door for another few seconds, I take a deep breath, and then I start to walk into the house. It's time to submit Volume Two for publishing.

Epilogue

Habakkuk 2: 14 (EST), "For the earth will be filled with the knowledge of the glory of the Lord as the waters cover the sea."

I wake up. Everything is good. As I come to my senses, I lift up my head and look down at my body. Everything appears to be in order as I study my limbs in the somewhat dimly lit room. I am in my own bed in my own room. Julia is sleeping next to me. I can hear the kids making noise downstairs. Life is good.

Late one night in early 2013 I woke up with a start. I had just dreamed much of this book, which then was in a distant future. I woke up in a cold sweat. I sat up and looked around. It was the most realistic, detailed, action-packed dream I ever had. I'm not sure at which point I woke up, but I told myself I had to fall back asleep so that I could finish the dream. After a quick potty-break, I returned to the bed. For the next few minutes, I was in a state of half-consciousness. I quickly returned to sleep and dreamed the rest. I woke up the next morning, and even though it was still pretty cool that I had such a detailed, action-packed dream, my mind was troubled and remained so for many weeks following the dream. It had a profound effect on me. Over the next several months, I expected the dream to fade into one or two faint memories like all dreams do over time. Instead, my recollections of the dream grew stronger. The whole story kept repeating over and over in my mind. I couldn't shake it.

The whole dream occurred as if I was looking out of my own eyes. Even now I can see Thomas operating the strange looking porridge machine. I can see Beth staring us down through her large, thick glasses with those wild eyes. I can recall the sheer terror in the moment of getting to the bottom of the so-called Stairway to Heaven after running away from the smashing machine the first time and finding a door with no handle. I can still see my hands trying to pry open the door with my

270

fingertips. I remember the moment that I realized, part way through the dream, that the kids were much older and taller than they were in real life at the time of the dream. Most vividly I remember the look on the Leader's face when he figured out I wrote the very book that he had me sign but didn't bother to read. Contrast that with the look on Dad's face when he emerged from the helicopter and saw we were OK. The image of Beth's hand sinking into the reservoir was especially troubling.

By the time summer rolled around, I was beginning to realize that the only way to get this dream out of my mind was to write it down. I fought the silly notion, especially since I had never written anything more than lab reports, book reports, or e-mails. I'm not a writer, and the thought of writing a book was like the thought of having to pull out my own teeth with a pair of pliers and no anesthesia. I couldn't imagine wasting so much time to record this long, detailed story.

In June of 2013 we took a family trip to Disney. Seven days of fun and relaxing. Disney is a different kind of relaxing, but we had been there before and knew how to maximize the fun while minimizing the craziness. It was on that trip that I decided I would start writing down this dream when we got home. One June 24th, 2013, I typed my first words. Soon I was several chapters in. It was very difficult to find time on nights and weekends to write. My full time job of fifty plus hours a week, fall baseball practice and games for the kids, my six-days-per-week P90X and P90X2 workout schedule, homework time with the kids, fun time with the kids, the holidays, time with Julia's family and with my parents who just recently moved into town, and many, many other things didn't leave much time to write this book. I was somewhat sure I would give up at some point during the exercise, or that the memories would finally start to fade. They didn't fade, and somehow I was able to find bits of time, sometimes even as short as thirty minutes, to continue on. Over time I found I needed several hours of dedicated time to get into a writing groove, so there were many weekend nights where I was up way past my bedtime knocking out big chunks of the book.

Many times during the writing of the book I reminded myself of the last verses in Revelation. It freaked me out that I was writing about an apocalyptic-type dream. I wanted to make sure that no one ever tried to mistake this book, this dream, as an attempt to add anything to or subtract anything from the Word of the Living God. I prayed to the Lord asking him to stop me from writing this if it was not his will. I asked him to take away my memories of the dream, to erase the file from the computer. I did not want to write this down, especially if it was against the will of my Savior.

About fifteen chapters in, I realized that there was no turning back. I had changed my prayer to ask God to use this book as a way to introduce people to Him, to give them insight into one (strange) person's spiritual life with the hope that the seed would be planted for them to seek the Lord. If one lost person reads these pages and then eventually gives his or her life to Christ through the reading and understanding of the Truth in God's Word, the Bible, then it was worth it.

At the start of 2014, I learned a new way to pray. Instead of just asking the Lord for help with the book, I thanked him for its future success. I continued to pray this way. From this point forward it was in his hands; I trusted that he would not let the 110,000 words in this book to go to waste.

By early January, the end of the book was in sight. Finally, one Saturday in early February 2014, Nate and Dave were invited to a friend's house for the afternoon. Josh had one of his friends over after feeling snubbed that he wasn't invited along with Nate and Dave. My window of opportunity opened to write the last chapter and the Epilogue. Finally, on that February day, The End, Volume One, was finished. May the name of my Lord and my God, Jesus Christ, be praised forever. In His name I pray, Amen.

www.ingramcontent.com/pod-product-compliance
Lightning Source LLC
Chambersburg PA
CBHW050017180626
46810CB00002B/452